THE BIG SMOKE

JASON NAHRUNG

CLAN DESTINE PRESS

First published in Australia 2015
by Clan Destine Press

PO Box 121 Bittern
Victoria 3918 Australia

National Library of Australia Cataloguing-in-Publication entry

Nahrung, Jason.

The Big Smoke

Vampires in the Sunburnt Country 2

ISBN   (pbk) 978-0-9942619-4-6

          (eBook) 978-0-9942619-5-3

Cover Design: Motivating Marketing

Design & Typesetting: Clan Destine Press

Printed and bound in Australia: Lightning Source

www.clandestinepress.com.au

To the Harper clan:
sometimes you do get to choose your family

PROLOGUE

Kevin could still smell his mother's corpse on the back seat of the car. A month since, but the reek remained. It'd lain there only a day, under a blanket, in a garage; but a day in the Queensland outback, at the height of summer. By the time he'd returned, there'd been bloat and leakage and that unmistakable smell of rot. He'd taken her down into the ground, his body against hers, cloth to cloth, skin to skin; he still smelled her on him, at odd times, when sleep wouldn't come. He saw the cruel rips in her chest, her arms, her throat. He heard the flies. He imagined their eggs in the torn flesh and the worms chewing at the corruption. But she was gone. Except for the smell. And for the memories – the life taken from her veins, ingested and preserved in the unnatural veins of another.

His maker, Taipan, had told him that taking something and keeping it were two different things. He'd been talking about von Schiller's goons impounding the Monaro, but the thought still tormented him. His father was well and truly gone, but his mother lingered inside Mira, the Strigoi; Maximilian von Schiller's daughter.

Kevin still felt Mira's presence at the edge of memory. He had a little of the bloodhag's extraordinary blood in him, fused into his DNA when he'd been in the change from human to vampire. They were linked, he and she; she was seared into his molecules: the sound of her, the feel, the scent. Possibly he even possessed a little of her ability to use blood and the life experiences it contained in almost magical ways. It helped to make him a quick learner, but it also meant he could never get Mira out of his system. He relived Mira fucking him, blood smearing her chest, cruel delight twisting her lips. He couldn't think of her without his cock growing hard, even as the bile rose in his throat. And he thought of her often.

He thought of his mother, trapped inside Mira, and was revolted.

Mira knew his mother better than he did.

But that would change when he killed her. Killing her would set them all free.

Kevin drove.

ONE

He missed his mp3 player desperately. It was long gone, lost in the battle at Jasmine Turner's. Destroyed or stolen, it didn't matter. The coupe's passenger seat was empty, and despite the roar of the Monaro's engine, the thrum of wheels on bitumen, the shake and shiver from passing trucks, that emptiness was deafening.

Kala and Danica had refused to join him, had tried to talk him out of leaving. Having escaped Mira's net, they were content to swelter in the tropical isolation of Cairns. They'd recruited red-eyes who were happy to feed and guard them in return for the benefits that came from drinking vampire blood: accelerated healing, faster reflexes, greater strength, slower aging.

At least Kala had given him the Monaro. 'It's hot,' she warned, 'they'll be looking for it.' But he didn't care: the V8 coupe was a classic, an Australian icon of the late sixties. This parting gift was all he had.

It took three nights to drive down the coast to Brisbane, almost 2000 km of cane fields, brown paddocks and towns the highway hadn't bypassed yet, all-night roadhouses smelling of diesel and dust, grease left too long in the hot box. Days were spent parked under whatever shade he could find as far off the road as he could nurse the Monaro. Farm tracks, forestry access roads, gravel pits. Lying on the seat under a tarp, too scared of discovery to sleep, but unwilling to leave the car for fear of finding it gone, this last link to his recent past, his one *good* thing.

And the entire way, he was stuck with radio, having to constantly retune as he passed town and city in the night, condemned to playlists of classics and current flavour, interrupted by inane chatter and irrelevant news. What matter to him the latest war, a new casino, the price of the dollar?

Close to Brisbane, he turned off the radio, the better to concentrate as the lanes grew from one to two to four. As the lights brightened, the stars dimmed. He squinted at road signs, clenched the wheel and peered at the cars closing in on him.

What if he couldn't find his way? What if Maximilian and his stormtroopers knew he was coming? What if one man – he used the term liberally, clung to it, in fact – wasn't enough to stop them?

He followed the barest threads of memory, grasped them like a swimmer to rope in an oil-slick sea, and like a float was pulled along in their wake into the city's reach. Through the sprawl of shopping centres, car yards, neon beacons for motel pay TV and air-conditioned rooms; a confusion of signs pointing to places he didn't know, hadn't even heard of. The cloying petroleum stench invaded the cabin; the stars faded behind the bright wash of the streetlights and the city's sickly amber glow.

It was close to midnight and few vehicles other than buses, taxis and police cars cruised the lanes. Signs told him where he couldn't go, where he didn't want to go, where it would cost him to go. He stop-started through the traffic lights, working his way toward the centre, following the bare clues in his blood, an uncertain second-hand familiarity stale with time and too-little exposure.

And yet he found it, like a bee to a hive: Maximilian's towering base, Thorn.

He drove slowly past the dark monolith, feeling small and obvious, bathed in light in the middle of the night. A gate of iron bars in a surrounding wall revealed a wide fan of stairs leading to glass doors. Guards in green uniforms stood at the top. The building loomed, a black marble tombstone carved from a mountain.

Mira was in there somewhere. She might even be hidden behind the glass, watching him drive past. Kevin clamped down on the vestiges of Mira within him, the elements of her that had hooked into him during the change. Danica had made a *putsi* for him with blood magic, the amulet warm on his chest even through the leather pouch from which it hung around his neck. He trusted the combination of it and Danica's mystical training would keep him from Mira's sight. If she knew he was here, his mission would be over before it even began.

He pulled into a cross-street and tried to work out if he could park there. Would he be ticketed, clamped, towed? Would he return to find a ring of Maximilian's soldiers circling the Monaro? Would he turn the key to have the car explode while a cheery assassin wiped their hands for a job well done?

From beyond the horizon he felt the pull of the plains, calling him home. But home was gone. He saw again his mother, still and pale on the sofa at Jasmine Turner's property; felt again the earth parting around them as he sank in the graveyard soil, bearing her down to final rest. Heard again Mira's taunt:

She tastes like sunshine

He forced himself to get out; a snail without a shell, feeling the threat of voracious magpies perched in the shadows.

Kala and Danica had told him not to come. To stay. To find a new life. But they couldn't tell him how.

How to forget the murder of his family.

How to forget the fact that his mother had been consumed, probably lingered still, an album of experience kept alive inside her killer's bloodstream.

How to turn his back while this place, these people – these *creatures* – remained.

Pale-barked trees shaded the pavement. He took comfort in the many darknesses where street lights and glowing shop fronts didn't reach. Hands in pockets, hood up, shoulders slumped, he hunched in a doorway; a metal grille sealed the door but left enough space in the entrance to shield him from the light.

On the other side of the street, towered Thorn – all dark concrete and black glass. A red warning light blinked atop a spire. The tower had been named for a fortress of old. That memory too nestled deep, an aside, but he clung to it as an omen; the Teutonic fortress *had* fallen. He regarded the tower, hoping for history to repeat. He was struck by the memory of a movie, of people with guns, lots of guns, kicking open doors and battling their way to the upmost floors, of righting wrongs, of saving the world.

Thorn had a wall, a forecourt, armed guards and many, many floors. There would be no kicking down of doors. He would need to be cleverer than that.

Kevin returned to the car and found it untouched, unguarded. So far, so good. He turned the ignition, felt the instant comfort of the motor's rumble, the chassis' vibration; the suppressed power under the bonnet.

Now to find the one they called the Needle.

The city was bigger than he remembered. He had been here once, his own memories less useful than the memories of the others residing within him. Brisbane was quite the haystack. But he had time.

As long as no one knew he was here, he had all the time he needed. All the time his hunger would allow.

TWO

'I hope this won't take long, Reece. I go on duty at nine.'

Felicity's voice followed him up the stairwell, echoing with their footsteps. The air tasted stale; the warehouse had been shut up for a long time, and Reece's occasional visits had done little to freshen the place.

'You still on the soup van?' he asked.

'It could be worse.'

'Ticket collector.'

'You haven't fallen that far. Yet.' Half humour, half warning. Fair enough. He hadn't told her why he'd called her here. It wasn't just the heat that'd made her take her jacket off. Basic training made a point of warning them how hard it was to pull a Staker from a shoulder sling; it was either that, though, or stick out like dog's balls in a trench coat if one was to conceal the metal tube.

He was in civvies today. Jeans, button-up shirt, leather jacket and Broncos cap. Sword in scabbard held in one sweaty hand.

She drew level with him. 'You're still hunting Matheson? Is that what this is about?'

'Kind of. I figure he's up north. Far north. Fuel thefts, some clothing, a couple of sightings of the Monaro.'

'You and that damn car.'

'It'll turn up. Whether he'll be with it is the thing.'

He paused at a landing, catching his breath. He was too old for this. And getting older by the day.

She waited beside him, her freckles glowing with exertion, her hair pulled back in a tight, short ponytail. She carried her jacket over one arm, exposing the double shoulder holsters for sidearm and Staker, her tightly stretched blouse he had to remind his eyes not to linger on. They'd been partners, after all; of sorts. Still were; of sorts.

Felicity had proven capable in the outback, when they'd been tracking Taipan's gang of outlaw vampires. So capable, Mira had taken a shine to the plucky Hunter.

That relationship linked them now in this conspiracy: save Mira, save themselves.

'So what is this about?' Felicity asked.

'All in good time. Have you heard anything about Mira?'

'She's still under wraps, still borderline bedlam. Though I think the doc's sugar coating it, for the Old Man's sake.'

The Old Man. That was an understatement. Maximilian von Schiller was centuries old, a product of his time. By all accounts, he was struggling to keep up with modern developments, and concepts such as democracy and women's lib. He relied on his vampiric daughter to help him cope, using her blood magic in his service. The power had come from her mother, Danica: Danica the betrayer, who had, tired of death and politics, fled Maximilian's organisation. The disastrous attempt to recapture her at Jasmine Turner's outback property had forced them to this risky course of action.

Reece had been there when Mira had fallen, one of the most horrible sights he'd ever seen. And after decades in her service, that was saying something.

Mira, injured and craving blood, had killed one of her own and taken his life into herself. It was the straw that broke the camel's back. Unable to navigate the storm of the lives she'd absorbed, she'd lapsed into the coma-like state, a prisoner in her own overcrowded mind.

Reece shrugged away the memory and resumed clomping, until they emerged on the roof. He blinked, the sun staring at him from the west where it hung low over the mountains, swollen and dirty red as it glowered through a haze of pollution.

Felicity reached for her sunglasses, then almost dropped them as she saw the figure tied to a rusting air-conditioning unit.

'Jesus, Reece, you've had him up here all day?' She stared around at the surrounding buildings. 'Over-exposed, aren't you?'

'There's no one around.' The building, one of the highest in this part of South Brisbane, was empty; one of many waiting for the urban renewal creeping out from the city like a slow wave of chrome, glass and lattes.

'Batcatcher? Aerial?'

'No reason for the foxes to be this far south. And the chances of airpol taking their cameras off the highways long enough to notice is remote. No money in it.'

She walked to the prisoner.

Bhagwan's groans were barely audible. Bone showed through the blistered flesh; he looked like a log that had rolled off a fire, black and grey and veined with soot. And there was the smell.

'Is this how you did it, back when you were a real copper?'

Ouch. 'We were more subtle back then. And the crims were more ordinary.'

She looked at him, biting her lip in that endearing manner. 'Was it worth it?'

'He gave me a name.'

'Do you believe him?'

'No reason not to.'

'And I'm here because?'

'To witness. You found him, after all.'

She looked around again. The city's lights were coming on, warning lights flashing, a slick Legoland of dark and light burnished by the sunset. Buildings reflected blood.

'If anyone saw–'

'We'd know it. I only called you in so you could know it was over.'

'Noble of you.'

'Despite the popular misconception, chivalry is not quite dead.'

Felicity had found Bhagwan staked out in a hidey hole in the wreckage of Jasmine Turner's place, one of few survivors of the clusterfuck referred to around Thorn as "The Debacle". She'd smuggled him away, desperate to find some advantage in the disaster that had befallen them.

Reece drew the standard-issue broadsword, a cheap replacement for his Hunter's blade – a personal gift from Mira – that was probably rusting away somewhere out west.

'It's time for Bhaggy to go back to being dead,' he said.

Felicity nodded, her arms folded across her chest.

The blade cut through the throat as though it were dry grass and clanged against the metal of the air conditioning unit. The head plopped on the ground. Bhagwan had had a few years on him. The decay accelerated, the body shrivelling in on itself, until the ropes fell slack and the corpse crumbled. By the time the sun had sunk to touch the mountains, there was nothing left but a pile of dust. It eddied in the faint breeze coming in off the river, a dry wind carrying the smell of brine and petrochemicals. Reece sheathed the sword, then rolled and lit a cigarette.

Felicity held a hand up against the sunset. Her mirrored shades reflected the out-of-kilter world, an out-of-kilter Reece.

'So what was the name he gave you?'

'Are you sure you want to know?'

'We're both in it, Reece. Unless Mira recovers and reinstates us, we're in the doghouse for the rest of our days.' She rubbed her throat, an instinctual act of longing or loss; the skin there was unmarked. She was no one's favourite now. 'And that might not be that long.'

'Bhagwan said the Needle told him about Jasmine.'

'Why would he do that?'

'More to the point, how did the Needle know? He's not part of the firm.'

'We've got a leak.'

'And I'm going to plug it. See if I can't get us back in the good books.'

'Nice of you to care, old man. You going looking for the Needle then?'

'In the proverbial.' He gestured to the city, lights sparkling in the descending dusk. He imagined he could see Thorn amid the towers clustered in the city centre.

'I can check the rota, see when he's due to tithe,' she said.

'Not for two weeks. No, I'll have to find him sooner than that. Which means finding a snitch of my own. What you can do is start tracing from the other end. Draw up a list of anyone and everyone who might've known about Jasmine's expansion into the bovine business.'

'Should be a reasonably small list. It was meant to be hush-hush.'

He gripped her arm. 'Do it quietly. We don't know if the leak was intentional or just careless. Either way, they'll be keen to keep it quiet.'

She pulled on her jacket. An object fell from the pocket and bounced off her shoe. She retrieved the MP3 player, rotating it in her hand as though she was reassuring herself it was the one she'd dropped. Something red flashed as she turned it. She rubbed a thumb over the piece of tape, smiled grimly, the player bringing back a bad memory perhaps.

'Is that new?' Reece asked.

'Souvenir.' She tucked the player away, adjusted her holsters. 'Don't worry, Reece. I've got your back. We might not be able to save the Strigoi, but we just might be able to save ourselves.'

To hear her say it, there with the sunset reflecting bloody on her shades, the set of her mouth, her hand squeezing his arm, he could almost believe it.

THREE

Fortitude Valley. It sounded all right – fortitude was just what he needed – but as Kevin stared at the crumpled map he'd bought at a servo, he found little comfort in the maze of meaningless names and streets, his forehead aching as the lines and titles morphed into a mess of doodles. He rubbed his eyes, tried to ignore the dryness in his mouth, a sensation in his gut that was empty and tight at the same time.

He needed to rest. A cheap motel? Maybe one of those boarding houses with the peeling paint and rusted roofs he'd driven past? No, the idea of sharing space with other people didn't appeal. It wasn't safe. For anyone.

Of one thing he was certain – he wasn't leaving the Monaro. Fuck that. He'd given up too much as it was. He wasn't letting the car go. Not until he had to.

He threw the wrinkled map on the passenger seat and fired up the car. The burble of the engine, the feeling of control as he steered out into the traffic, helped settle his nerves. A little. He had until dawn.

Driving slowly, letting the streetscape sink in, he noted the haphazard mix of rundown housing, new apartments, shops and offices. A mall opened, threatening with the flash of lights, clumps of shadowed figures, cops patrolling in gangs of four. There was an obviously Asian sector that, according to his map and the various signposts, was Chinatown. Hard to mistake the big wooden gate with the lion statues. Or were they dragons?

Didn't matter, there could be no shelter for him there.

So where could he hole up while he searched for the Needle? Afraid to park on the street, he'd spent the day under cover at the airport, just one of many in the long-term section. He'd slept in the boot. It had cost a fortune and he was low on cash. Hours passed as he drove around and around the Valley. Seedy and busy, it was a place close to Thorn where he could blend in, he hoped.

Like a meter for this confidence, the petrol gauge arrowed toward empty. The hollow space in his gut expanded, the pressure causing his temples to throb as dawn crept closer. His vision clouded, the iris of black contracting until all he could see was dead ends.

Kevin almost missed the shop and had to reverse to check it out.

It was on a quiet back street a few blocks from the Brunswick Street Mall, surrounded by tin sheds and sagging, decrepit houses. Boards covered the windows, spray-painted warnings of *No Trespassing* discernible under the tags and graffiti.

Hope flared. His vision cleared; the weight on his chest lifted. He could just read the faded *Merle's Coffee* sign fixed to the stained bricks of the front wall. At the rear, he found a lane and loading dock that suited perfectly. He used the tyre iron to break the chain. The metal door slid up with a rusty screech. Cobwebbed crates and bits of esoteric machinery cluttered the bay, but he had room to park the Monaro.

Bugs scuttled in the headlights. The smell of coffee lingered in a musty mix of dust and mildew that made his nose itch. This could be it – sanctuary.

A quick look around revealed a large, empty space backing on to the dock, and an office and reception at the front.

He crept up creaky wooden stairs. His eyes adjusted until he could see the webs and vermin shit.

Dirty water flowed from the tap in the kitchen, gradually running clear. The initial shriek of the pipes made him wince. He hadn't been aware of his ramped-up hearing scanning for any hint of danger, but he felt it retreat from the piercing noise, filtering back to a less painful level. He was ready for the scream and rattle when he tested the taps in the bathroom with its crusty shower-head, brown-stained bath and toilet. He could smell rotten wood; if he concentrated, he could hear the drip-drip-drip of the hidden leak, the scuttling of cockroaches and rats behind the walls, the munching of termites.

There was no hot water, no bulbs for him to test the lights. He imagined the power had long been cut off. But this place would do. Hell, yes, anything to get out of sight and out of the sun.

He returned to the car and nestled into the driver's seat. The night was almost spent. His energy drained away; finally, he could stop running, take stock, rest.

He checked his map once more. He'd made a list of tattoo parlours from a search at an internet café, leaving the coffee untouched but filling several pages of a notebook with addresses. It was a massive task, with more than fifty parlours just in the central city area. He'd marked the locations as accurately as he could on the map. One of them, he hoped, would lead him to the Needle; and the Needle would lead him to Mira. Hungry and impatient, he folded the map and fumbled with the tuner until he locked on to the strongest FM signal he could find. Talking Heads were singing about running away from a psycho killer. He laughed, the sound brittle and humourless. He settled back, closed his eyes, tried not to think of the odds against him succeeding.

He could understand Danica not wanting him to kill Mira: Dee was her biological mother, after all. But Kala?

Her words came back to him, the two of them arguing as he packed his duffel bag. 'Don't pretend this is about me,' she'd said. And he saw her again, fingering her ear lobe, the flesh smooth now, no sign of the hole left by Mira's savage removal of the silver earring.

It wasn't about Kala, or the things that had been done to her.

'Don't go,' Danica had told him, even though she admitted there was nothing more for her to teach him. 'Killing Mira will resolve nothing.'

Fresh is best. Straight from the vein

Taipan, as though he was saying it for the first time.

So much for a dish best served cold.

He was Taipan's child. That was true. And an orphan twice over. Taipan had also died. And maybe he had found the peace that eluded him in preternatural life. But both Mira and her right-hand man, Hunter – Kevin always thought of the man by his rank, not his name – had survived.

While Kala, Danica and he had escaped – skulking at the arse end of the country, living like leeches in the mud and tropical heat – it did not feel like victory. Not while Mira was free.

Kevin turned off the radio and covered himself with a coat as he laid his seat down, lacking even the strength to crawl into the back.

Dawn came, thin lances of sunlight glowing in the dust. The hunt would begin at sundown.

FOUR

Blood.

Ink. Sweat.

Fainter: bourbon. Fainter still: marijuana.

Overriding it all, though, there was blood. Kevin's vision blurred as the smell triggered his hunger. His gut ached to be filled.

'Yeah?'

Kevin blinked, focused. Night three, tattoo parlour number eight on his list.

He was leaning on a glass counter; the cabinet was filled with trinkets covered in silver skulls and marijuana leaf motifs. A book of flashes lay open: pegasi and tigers, rainbows and skulls. From behind a curtained doorway, a tattoo gun buzzed. In plastic chairs along one wall sat two lads no older than him, short hair and thick necks, tattoos dripping down biceps.

And behind the counter, the girl, slightly younger – late teens, perhaps – pierced through eyebrows and nose and lip, dreadlocked hair, her nipples misshapen with rings where they pushed against her tight singlet.

'Hello?' she said, waving her hand in front of his face.

She stared with red-rimmed eyes from under pencilled brows. Pale skin highlighted the montages on her upper arms, the Asian script on her forearms, the purple veins pulsing under skin and ink.

'I'm lookin' for the Needle,' he told her, his voice low and rasping, his throat dust dry with thirst. He'd drunk nothing but water for a week.

'We got lotsa needles.'

'A person. A tattooist. Called the Needle. Does silver tatts. Know him?'

'Silver tatts?' A blink, a flinch. He smelled – felt – her rush of adrenaline. Veins pulsed in her throat. She stood back, crossed her arms. Physically, she reminded him of Kala. Flat, bare belly, framed by hip bones; a dangling chain sparkling with gems at her navel. Jeans so low her pubis bulged above the clip.

The flesh there would be soft. There, and inside her arms, on her throat.

His gums throbbed. His fangs ached in their sheaths to tear into that skin, to free the sustenance his body craved.

She backed up against the wall, her eyes never leaving Kevin, and rapped on the thin sheeting beside the doorway.

'Flash?' she called.

The lads looked up, more curious than threatening. Kevin was in blue jeans and an AC/DC shirt. They wore black and ink. Not that different to the eye. They avoided his gaze, huddled over a piece of paper and continued to talk about colours.

The tattoo gun stopped.

A bearded face emerged from behind the curtain.

'What's up, Jen?'

Kevin didn't give her a chance to answer. 'I'm lookin' for a bloke goin' by the name of Needle.'

'Who's askin'?'

Kevin licked his chafed lips, his tongue like sandpaper. 'A

friend recommended him. Silver tattoos. Egyptian.' The man's veins stood out under his throat, in his upper chest. There was a smudge of blood on his white surgical glove.

How long had it been since Kevin had eaten? Really eaten?

'I can ask around,' the tattooist said. 'Where can I reach you if I find this fella?'

'You know him?'

'Silver tatts, that'll stand out. You sure he's in Brissie?'

'Pretty sure.'

He jerked a thumb at the girl. 'Give Jen your number.'

'I'll come back.'

'We open at noon.'

'After dark.'

'We close at seven, unless you want a job done.'

'I'll be here at sundown.'

'Suit yourself.'

Kevin stepped out and leaned against the nearest wall as he willed his body back under control. Hunger uncoiled inside him, a balled python in his guts reaching up and up, making his throat clench.

He had tried normal tucker and succeeded only in making the hunger worse. He could eat regular food – should eat, in fact – but he needed blood. Maybe the Needle could provide some baggies or decant.

A moment surged through his weakness; Taipan feeding him:

Fresh is best, fella: remember that

He forced the phantom back, behind the doors in his mind that Danica had taught him to use. A way of controlling the lives he'd absorbed, the experiences he'd been gifted by his maker. To prevent him from being overwhelmed.

Kevin pushed off from the wall and headed for base.

The city knotted around him like lantana vines, thick and barbed. Traffic, the rhythmic bass of night clubs, the constant burble of voices and hyena laughter, the scents of booze and colognes and the melange of foods, stale water, rotting trash. Bodies flashing hot – arms and legs, chests and bellies – naked and glistening in the humid February night. And underneath it all, the drumbeat of hearts, the pulsing of blood, the warmth within that thin, vulnerable skin.

He had to get off the streets. The last thing he wanted was to hurt any more innocent people, and with his hunger running rampant, he doubted he could stop at just a sip. As bad as the cravings were, he had to hold on one more night. Always, just one more night.

FIVE

They'd got lucky with the room: third floor, and a viable angle onto the tattoo parlour on the opposite side of the street, and no awnings blocking their view. But then, empty offices in this part of the Valley weren't hard to find.

Reece stared out the Venetian blind, absently wiped his dusty fingers on his trousers. The street lights had recently come on, glowing jaundiced in the dusk, dotting the footpaths with light and shade. His red-eye vision rendered the scene in hues of grey, but pulled fine details from the gloom. Litter in the gutter; a prostitute hugging a doorway, her face illuminated by the flare of her cigarette; two youths in baggy pants and backward caps sauntering toward Wickham Street as though they owned the place. *Kings of the jungle. Huh.*

Behind him, Felicity, sitting on a plastic milk crate, sipped coffee from a travel mug, then asked, yet again, 'How reliable is your snitch?'

'As much as any junkie I pay for information.'

'Wow, that much.'

She was on edge, understandably, since he'd convinced her to keep Bhagwan under wraps. At the time, he'd thought it might offer them a valuable secret, but with Mira in bedlam and tensions running high inside Thorn as recriminations flew over The Debacle, it'd become necessary to dust the bloodsucker.

Everyone thought he'd died back at Jasmine Turner's; explaining why he wasn't dead would have got them in hot water. Having finally extracted the information he'd needed – Bhaggy had held out for the best part of a month, the tight-lipped bastard – Reece had simply been fulfilling everyone's expectations. And Felicity had admitted it'd been the only course of action. If they were to get back into favour with the firm, they had to produce something very valuable indeed.

Now, only days after Bhagwan's demise, he'd got the break he needed.

'You saw the picture Jen lifted from the shop's camera last night. Matheson's here, asking about the Needle. It can't be coincidence.'

'We should've brought back-up,' Felicity said. 'The grease monkey's tough. More than that: he's lucky.'

'We can't trust anyone, Flick. Finding the leak would've been a good start; giving them Matheson, and maybe Danica, that's a game changer.'

'Reece,' she said, sounding weary with the repetition, 'don't call me that. And what makes you so sure Matheson even knows where Dee is?'

'If he doesn't, he can find out. He was with her at the gorge.'

The gorge, where the kid had got the better of him, left him for dead, damn near killed Mira too. Long-healed wounds throbbed with the memory.

'He'd better show,' Felicity said. 'I had to pull favours to get off shift tonight.'

'Voi–fucking–la.'

Kevin Matheson looked little different to the last time Reece had seen him. Jeans and a T-shirt, clearly nervous, not knowing where to look. The turn of the tables wasn't lost on Reece;

he'd have been lying if he said he wasn't enjoying having the upper hand for once.

He raised the camera and fired off a couple of shots. Maybe it should've been a rifle. Drop the kid right there on the street, publicity be damned.

Felicity hurried to the window and pried open the blinds.

He'd seen her like this before, out west, the adrenaline colouring her face, lighting her eyes, making her chest pump. A Hunter, like him, hot on the trail.

His own heart was beating faster, his mouth dry. That old familiar buzz.

He fingered the Staker on his belt. His hand shook. This was a young person's game and he was old.

'When do we take him?' she asked.

'Wait for him to go inside. Then we make our move.'

'Will they protect him?'

'Lethal force is authorised. But we need him, Flick.'

She gave a grim smile. After a month in the doghouse, they were both ready to break some heads.

Movement in the tattoo parlour window: a sheet of paper being tacked to the glass. A picture of something snake-like.

'And there's the signal,' Reece said. 'Looks like we might have company. The Needle perhaps.'

Suddenly, back-up sounded like a good idea. With surprise on their side, the two of them could take Matheson. But a second vampire? That could get awkward.

Felicity grabbed his arm.

'What?'

'There.'

'One of the Needle's people?' He snapped the new arrival's photo.

'I think so, yes. I've seen her hanging around at the soup van.'

'She must be the contact. Red-eye?'

'Just a wannabe, I think. Fairly sure she's not on the roster.'

'That's a relief.'

'Take her as well?'

'Sure, but Matheson's the bigger prize. The firm can sort out the Needle.' Reece drew his pistol. 'Let's get this party started.'

'Wait,' Felicity pointed. 'There – crossing the street. That's Johnny Slick, isn't it?'

'Fuck. What's that streeter doing on this side of the river? This isn't Viscounts territory.'

'Getting a tattoo?'

'This early? Nah, we've been sideswiped.' He ran his hand through his hair, considering options. 'I don't know what Slick's doing here, but we can't take the risk. We have to have Matheson alive. Call back-up. Let's move in.'

'The rest of Slick's gang won't be far behind.'

'Tell back-up to hurry.'

Reece took a last picture of the Viscounts' leader entering the parlour, then gestured that it was time to leave.

Felicity looked at him as she phoned, her eyes glossed red in the uncertain light. 'This feels like déjà vu, Reece. Like we're about to be fucked over again. Because of that grease monkey.'

'Imagine how the kid must feel, walking into not just one trap, but at least two.'

That was when he heard the shot.

SIX

Kevin unbuttoned his overcoat, bought from an op shop to replace the hoodie that didn't hang low enough to cover his weaponry. He felt ridiculous, as light as the material was; the heat of day still simmered on the footpath. He'd seen plenty of white collars in suit jackets, a few swampies in trench coats, but he couldn't shrug off the feeling he was sticking out like a sore thumb in his long coat on a summer's evening.

He paused, checking himself in the glass of a Chinese travel agency's window, finding his dim reflection amid the posters for holidays and phone cards. Where would he like to go? Who would he like to call? He checked the heavy belt at his waist: the long tube of the Staker, the holster with the automatic, the pouches of extra mags – all stolen from Hunter.

Who the fuck was he; the wild colonial boy?

The tattoo shop was two doors away. He studied the street, the sky, the buildings. Something niggled at him. Some sense of familiarity. A prickling of the nape, an itch between the shoulder blades.

Traffic on the main street made a constant growl,

interspersed by the roars of accelerating trucks and bikes and occasional honking horns. A few people strolled the footpaths, but none paid him any attention.

Kevin approached the tattoo shop, one hand on the pistol. A buzzer sounded as he opened the door. As it closed, he heard the drone of a tattoo gun at work.

A trendy couple flicked through designs where the young bucks had sat last night.

Jen, the assistant, stood behind the counter, fingers flicking nervously at a tattoo magazine, chewing gum like a cow in a hurry.

'Is he here?' he asked.

Jen shook her head and told him to take a seat. He stayed standing as she came out from behind the counter and stuck a piece of paper – a dragon, maybe – to the front window.

'Won't be long,' she said, and went out the back.

He heard Jen talk to someone; a name, Flash, carrying clear enough – and then she returned to the counter, teasing her hair, inspecting her nails, chewing ruthlessly. Ignoring him completely.

A shadow hunched in a hoodie appeared at the window, peering in.

Kevin's grip tightened on the pistol.

The door buzzed open. The hoodie entered, revealed to be a hooded army jacket with bulging pockets. A suspicious gaze stared out from under the peak; she checked him out, made eye contact with Jen and checked him out again before walking to within mumbling distance.

'You the bumpkin lookin' for the Needle, are ya?' The voice was gravelled, but it was definitely a girl under that shapeless outfit of lumpy cloth and baggy pants thrust into lace-up purple-red boots.

'Maybe. Who are you?'

'Greaser. We need to go. Out the back.'

Jen made a small O with her lips as the door opened.

The buzzer sounded one long note. A twenty-something chap stood in the entrance, reeking of Brylcreem and cigarettes, in tight jeans and pointy shoes and a bowling shirt with a dancing skeleton on the chest, slicked back hair, sunglasses.

He stepped forward, silencing the door buzzer, and pulled a mighty big pistol from behind his back.

'You shouldn't be this side of the river, Slick,' Greaser said, voice quavering.

'I just need the mechanic,' he said. 'I'm guessing that's you.' He pointed the handgun at Kevin.

Jen hunched against the wall, eyes wide. The two kids in the chair shrank down, arms around each other.

'No one needs to get hurt,' Slick said.

A man's voice from the back of the room: 'What the fuck's this?'

Slick's gun moved toward the interruption and Kevin drew, his action masked by Greaser. He pulled the girl to one side as he raised his automatic and just beat Slick to the trigger. The gun bucked, just the once. Slick went down, a splash of lumpy blood spraying the door. The trendy girl screamed, knees up, hands in front of her face. Her boyfriend stared, face flecked with gore, as he cowered, shouting, 'Don't shoot, don't shoot'.

Kevin pointed the gun at Greaser. 'You set me up?'

'No, not me. I just gotta take you to the Needle.'

'Hey,' said the tattooist again; pointing a shotgun at Kevin.

Ears ringing, nose filled with gunpowder and blood scent, muscles quivering, Kevin waited to see what the man would do.

'Fuck off, the both of you.'

'Out the back,' Greaser said.

The tattooist opened the counter so they could flee. He grabbed Greaser's arm, whirling her to face him. 'The Needle better make this right.'

'Sure – sure, Flash.'

The door buzzed as the young couple ran out.

The tattooist released Greaser and pulled a mobile phone from his pocket.

'Well, fuck off, then!'

Kevin followed Greaser into an alley at the rear of the shop. No one was around. He holstered the pistol and draped his coat across it. 'Which way?' and Greaser pointed, 'Down the end, then back into the Valley.'

'Lead the way, mate.'

They were maybe halfway down the alley when a vintage Caddy pulled into the far end, headlights on high beam. It charged toward them.

Kevin pulled Greaser behind a clutter of bins and boxes. 'Friends of yours?'

'Viscounts,' she said. 'Johnny Slick's mates. He was the fanger you just iced. They won't be happy.'

'Tell me quick: where do I find the Needle?'

'You don't. He finds you.'

Damn, but he had no choice. He pushed Greaser against the wall, reefed her collar aside and bit into her throat. She howled and kicked and punched.

'Get off, get off!' And then, 'Stop! Stop! God, please stop.'

Her blood poured into him, gout after gout as he sucked it down. Her life gushed through him, so hot, so fast: the Needle, elusive flashes, but Kevin couldn't focus, couldn't filter. His hunger was paramount, greed vanquishing all else. He had to stop.

Had.

To.

Stop.

'Hey,' someone shouted. Three rockabillies were pointing handguns at him.

'Sorry,' he told Greaser as she slumped, hands to the wound. 'I had no choice.' *Keep telling yourself that*, he thought. He eased her against the wall and slipped his sneakers off.

'You're comin' with us,' a rockabilly said, all Brylcreem and big lapels.

Kevin jumped to the wall. Fingers and toes found purchase in the cracks. He clung there for a heartbeat, like a frog, and then he scrambled jerkily up the bricks.

No one reacted until he was almost at the top, when a ganger shouted, 'Bring him down, you bloody morons,' and started firing.

Kevin hauled himself over the lip of the roof, bullets sparking around him. He lay there for a moment, checking that he hadn't been hit, his body sizzling with Greaser's blood.

'Where'd he go?' he heard the ganger ask.

'Where's Johnny?' another said, and the third told them not to worry about Johnny, 'the others are sorting it'.

A man shouted, 'Freeze! Freeze, the whole fucking lot of you. VS Security!'

Shouts followed, then running footsteps. Shots rang out. Doors slammed. Glass shattered. The Cadillac sped away.

The man swore, and this time, Kevin recognised the voice; Hunter. He didn't risk a look though.

Hunter said, 'Did you see which way the Snipe went?' and a woman said no, she hadn't. There were more shots and Hunter said, 'Now we're screwed.'

SEVEN

Kevin ran across the rooftops. There were sirens, but there had been sirens since he'd arrived in Brisbane. He didn't know if these were for him; he kept running. A lane separated the roofs, the gap a little more than a car-width wide. He jumped it easily enough, despite a moment's hesitation. The roofs ran out at the end of the block, a main road bustling with traffic, pedestrians oblivious as they waited at the lights or strolled along.

Kevin stopped, huddled behind a parapet, and vomited a sticky drool.

On the run with Taipan outside Rockhampton, he had killed a girl. Her name was Nicola. Taipan had fed her to him and he'd swallowed every drop. Her life – her experiences, her feelings – haunted him still. Before he left Cairns, he'd promised himself he'd never again take without asking. He'd never risk stealing another person's life. But tonight he'd done just that.

Greaser's memories swirled through him, a kaleidoscope of impressions mixed with his own visceral memory of having just shot a man through the head. But he'd seen the tell-tale flash of green in the gunman's eyes; there was little doubt that the vampire had been intent on harming Kevin, and that he would recover. It was little consolation. Taipan's words, having sunk like fishhooks into him, jagged at his conscience:

See, fella. You ain't that different

And here, on this first test, he had proven his maker to be correct.

And it had all been for nothing.

Greaser's blood provided only teasing information about the Needle, master tattooist to the vampire underworld and, Kevin gathered, a kind of saint to Brisbane's street kids. The man with the finger on the pulse of the city's nefarious operations and a spare bed for the dispossessed. Just the man Kevin needed to find if he was going to commit murder.

'Yeah,' he muttered to Taipan's memory as he rubbed at the stains on his lips and chin, 'I'm just like you.'

Kevin climbed down the rear wall of the building and walked barefoot, hunched inside his coat, taking care to conceal the weapons belt.

He kept to the quieter streets, a mishmash of flat-packed businesses and flats, and rundown houses waiting to be made into businesses and flats. There were few people on the streets: young, mostly; goths and hippies and suits, gabbing on their way to somewhere, or like him, huddled solo against the night.

He sifted the bloodmemories from the girl. The connection to the Needle was obvious. There was affection there, fatherly, but aloof. He got the impression of a Winnebago-type vehicle, covered in graffiti, but no idea of a location. Damn it.

And now he was hungry – hungrier. The blood, the adrenaline, had whetted his appetite. People moved away from him. Some even crossed the street when they saw him coming.

Maybe Danica had been right; maybe he had been stupid to come here. But what else could he do? Mira had killed his mother; he couldn't let that rest. He simply couldn't.

Finally, he reached the coffee house. All the comfort of home except power, which he barely required. Food was also a secondary concern; what he needed most came hot, direct from the vein. He'd have to eat before he faced Mira.

He climbed up the wall to the window he'd left ajar and levered himself inside, then shut the window behind him. The smell of stale coffee beans and neglect rose up; somewhere, stagnant water lay. He made his way to the office where he'd set up camp and checked his pistol before placing it within easy reach on the desk – one of the few pieces of furniture in the building, its surface scratched and dented beneath the dust. Thank goodness no one knew about this place; he'd never find another hideout this good.

But someone had found out he was in town. Had Hunter seen him? Would the Needle search him out, as Greaser had said? Could Kevin trust him if he did? Regardless, it seemed he'd lost his element of surprise along with his shoes. The shit could only get deeper from here.

Kevin was still trying to work out his next move when the squeak of a floorboard caught his attention. Someone was in the building.

Pistol in hand, painfully aware of having only three mags, he crept to the door and listened.

Someone on the stairs.

He cracked open the door enough to see out. Just in time. A head. Enough light to make out the features. Despair and a horrible sense of anticipation ran through him.

It was Greaser. He tasted her again, had to push through the memories of her life, the father, the mother, the drugs, incidents of life on the street. Hunger stabbed at his guts like a blunt knife.

Somehow, she'd followed him. How? Had Danica's *putsi* lost its power to shield him?

Why had Greaser come in? She had to suspect he was here.

She would've seen the car downstairs. So what the fuck was she doing? She didn't even have a gun!

Greaser crept, hunched, nervous, one careful foot after the other. Alone? He couldn't hear, couldn't smell, anyone else. She reeked of fear.

Go away, he urged her. *Turn back*. Should he run? Leave the Monaro and scarper out the window?

Or he could fight. Could taste her again for information about the Needle. He could *feed*.

The girl was at the door. All she had to do was push.

She sneaked past; still crouched, still nervous. Something yellow flashed in her fist.

He let the door swing open slowly, stepped out behind her, gun levelled.

The hunger howled.

He swallowed it down, and said, 'You shouldn't be here,' and was rewarded with the sight of her jumping and stumbling, ending in some strange, karate-like huddle with her eyes as round as hubcaps. Pointing the yellow object at him.

Movement from behind. A figure – rushing from the stairwell! He turned – too slow! A hand grabbed his chin and reefed him back, held him tight against his attacker. A sharp point dug into his throat under the jaw.

'You shouldn't be here, either, chum.'

Greaser straightened, her chest heaving, body trembling. 'Took your time, Mel. What if he'd shot me?'

'One thrust, this goes into your brain,' the woman, Mel, told Kevin. Her breath blew warm and blood-tainted across his cheek. 'Do you understand?'

'Sure,' he mumbled. The hand on his lips was covered in a lace glove that left the fingers exposed. Her fingers moved down to free his mouth but kept the grip tight. The sharp object pierced his flesh, making him wince.

Greaser took his gun and stood facing him, as though deciding whether to shoot.

'You took from Greaser without asking,' Mel said. 'That's a capital offence.'

'I had to.'

'Why?'

'I'm looking for someone.'

She pushed the weapon into him. 'The Needle, I know. But why?'

'My business.'

'I'm the one with the stiletto.'

'Are you the Needle?'

'Interesting leap of logic there, Sherlock. Incorrect, as it happens. Greaser?'

The girl shook her head and stepped back, behind Mel, keeping the gun poised.

'You gonna behave?' Mel asked.

'Sure.'

'Good. This is bloody uncomfortable.'

Mel was as tall as him and thin. Everything was thin – eyebrows, lips, hair pulled back tight from her long, pale face, dark shadows around eyes that glistened chartreuse. Her arms were pale, her torso sheathed in a kind of purple velvet vest, her wide stance stretching a black skirt that didn't quite reach the knee-high boots, a patch of purple-and-white striped tights filling the gap. A handbag hung at her side, the strap cutting diagonally across her chest. She bent to slide the long, silver blade into her boot.

He could see Greaser more clearly, shorter and chubbier. She wore cargo pants, singlet and hooded army jacket, straggly hair poking like straw from under a beanie, those Doc Marten's of almost clown-like size.

'I'm Melpomene,' the woman said. 'You've *met* Greaser, so you probably know all about her.'

Shame washed over him again. 'Melpo…?'

She rolled her eyes. 'Not my real name. It's all rather tragic.' A smile, but the joke was lost on him. 'Mel is fine.'

'Kevin,' he offered.

'Just Kevin?'

'That's enough, isn't it?'

'For now.'

He rubbed his jaw. 'How did you find me?'

Greaser fetched his shoes from the stairs and handed them across, soles out to show the coffee beans stuck in the rippled soles. He couldn't tell if that was an answer or just an act of politeness.

He stood, awkward, facing the two women, barefoot, his shoes in his hands.

'Invite us in?' Melpomene asked.

'You're already in.'

'Somewhere to sit? A biscuit and a nice cup of tea?' There was a hint of accent. Pommie?

'You can sit, if you don't mind the floor.'

They followed him into his room.

Melpomene took Kevin's pistol from Greaser and sifted the gear on the table: the Staker, the sword and other stuff he'd taken from Hunter during their last encounter out west. 'This is VS issue.'

He shrugged.

'You continue to surprise.'

Greaser leaned against the wall, close to the door. 'What was with the gecko action?'

'Just something I can do.'

'Why do you want to see the Needle?' Mel asked.

'Like I said: it's private.'

'Well, he is a very *private* man. He doesn't see just anyone.'

'I hope he'll see me.'

'You got something to offer?'

'I won't know until I talk to him.'

'You didn't get what you needed from Greaser's blood?'

'No. And I'm sorry. I didn't want – I wouldn't have done it, not if I thought I'd had a choice.'

'He did say sorry,' Greaser conceded, perhaps offering an argument for a quick death rather than a slow one. She rubbed her throat where a hint of a wound still marked the skin.

'That your motor downstairs?' Mel asked.

He nodded.

She scooped his gun and belt, Staker included, into her handbag, making the cloth bulge like a snake that had eaten building blocks. She passed the sword to him. 'Let's go.'

'To see the Needle?'

She shook her head. 'First, you need to see Blake. He vets all of the Needle's appointments. Sorry.'

'Why "sorry"?'

She grimaced. 'It's poetry night.'

EIGHT

'We're going into the city?' Kevin asked, following Mel's directions, Greaser perched in the back seat.

'You can read,' Mel said. 'Excellent.'

'VS is in the city.'

'I'm not taking you there.'

'But it's risky, right?'

'Moderately. Blake won't come to us, so we have to go to him.'

Pollution-stained sandstone buildings held their shadowed ground amid modern towers. Storefronts on the ground level were closed except for the occasional 7-Eleven. There weren't many people on the streets, though once they reached the city centre, things livened up with clots of bodies outside pubs, a taxi rank, waiting to cross the road toward a train station.

'What can you tell me about Thorn?' Kevin asked.

'You don't want to go there.'

'It's heavily guarded,' Greaser offered. 'Green Shirts, Black Shirts, cameras, the works.'

'You carrying a grudge, Kevin?' Mel said.

He didn't answer, and they drove in silence until Mel told him to take a parking spot wherever he could.

They were on a sloping street lined with stone buildings. An intermittent line of straggly trees poked out of the footpath. A shopping centre near the bottom of the hill blazed a neon P, but he was able to find a street park.

'The car,' Kevin said as they got out. 'I can't risk losing it.'

'We won't be long,' Mel said. 'Promise.'

'You want me to watch it?' Greaser asked.

'If the police check it–'

'Didn't think it'd be yours. Thing's worth a buck or two, eh. Give me the keys and I'll see no one takes it.'

He hesitated.

'Dude, you bit me. You're not dead. I think you can trust me not to nick your wheels.'

He handed her the keys.

'Why, thank you.'

Her gleam of delight filled him with doubt again.

Mel grabbed his arm and tugged him away. They entered an arcade, passed clothes shops and cafes with shuttered windows and barred doors. At the top of a narrow flight of stairs was a tattoo parlour – one he hadn't got to in his quest – and a record store proud of its vinyl, both closed, and another clothes shop with a gargoyle perched above the lintel. The windows glowed with candlelight.

Mel led him inside. The air was warmer, thick with sweat and perfumes, with incense and candle wax and liquor. The racks were crowded with black splashed with burgundy and emerald, rare patches of white. Jewellery glittered in display cabinets. Little angels clung to the walls side by side with black-and-white photographs of black-clad people in cemeteries. A large painting of a sad woman lying in a rowboat surrounded by water lilies hung behind the cash register. Candles cast flickering shadows across the group of perhaps twenty swampies spread across two antique-looking sofas and a scattering of cushions in one corner.

There was a polite round of applause as Kevin and Mel

entered, but he quickly realised the two things weren't related. A young fella was just sitting down on a cushion, a book in his hand.

Standing centre stage, like a circus ringmaster, another man was gesturing to the youngster with an open hand, saying 'very nice, very nice'. The MC wore a long black coat with a velvet vest over a lacy white shirt, the ensemble capped off with top hat and cane.

'Blake,' Mel told him.

The ringmaster greeted them with a flourish. 'Ah, my dear Melpomene. So glad you could make it. And you've brought another poetry lover to our little murder; how kind.'

Murder? Kevin baulked, but no one seemed to notice his confusion.

A girl squealed and juggled over, her tits barely restrained by a corset, to smooch Mel on the cheek.

'Hi,' she said to Kevin, looking at him from behind a comb of thick lashes. 'I'm Bella. As in Bella*donna*.' She pouted, as though daring him to take a bite.

Others shouted greetings. Blake struck his cane on the timber floor and the group settled. Kevin leaned on a counter next to Mel. He was aware of kohl-rimmed eyes regarding him. Bella hovered, quivering on knee-high boots with two-inch heels. Her eyes caught the light, reflected red like a dog's in headlights: one of Blake's favourites then; or Mel's. How many more red-eyes were there in the group? The leeches would be hard pressed to match a vampire one on one, but their presence emphasised to Kevin that he was on dangerous ground.

Blake recited some verses about a lost girl. The gathering seemed to be into it, and while Kevin couldn't doubt Blake could tell a story, he couldn't help feeling he was missing something. Maybe it was the old language the poem was written in, or the rhyme, or just that fact that the swampies seemed to hang on every word.

When the applause ended, Blake said to him, 'What about you, young man? Want to give it a shot?'

'I don't write poetry.'

'No? Well, that wasn't one of mine, more's the pity.' A polite chuckle from the audience. 'Where are you from? What *do* you do?'

'I'm from out of town. I am – was – a mechanic.'

'You want a look under my hood?' one asked, a tall, pale lad with a goatee, his clothes all lace and velvet. Looked like he'd snap in a strong breeze.

'I could use an oil change,' said Bella, so much cleavage you could rest a stubby there.

'Give it a rest, Bella,' another said.

Giggles and teases rippled through the audience.

'Share your good things, Mel,' Bella said, her tone more pleading than seductive.

'Give us a poem, just a short one,' said another.

'Now that you're here, go right ahead.' Blake waved magnanimously with his cane. 'Your audience demands it!'

'Sure,' Mel said, and they fell quiet. 'In honour of our new guest. But we can't stay.'

She put a hand on Kevin's chest, right on top of the AC/DC logo on his T-shirt, and began to recite. Bon had never sounded like this. Nor Brian. Without music, with her emphasis and spacing, her non-rock beat, her woman's voice bragging about dirty deeds, offering to be a back door man. Whoa!

'Well, that was different,' Blake said as the applause died away. 'We might as well get down to it. Talk among yourselves while our guest and I have a chat. Melpomene, lead the way.'

They went to a back room where the main feature was a sewing machine. A couple of limbless dressmaking dummies stood in various states of undress. The room was littered with cloth, the walls decorated with pages torn from magazines and pencilled patterns.

'You lose your phone?' Blake asked Mel as he shut the door behind them.

'Greaser needed me. A spot of bother in the Valley.'

'So I gathered. No reason not to call.'

'I'm here now.'

'You taste him yet?'

'We've been busy.'

He raised his eyebrow at that, swept his gaze over Kevin. 'Well, get to it. Let's see what he's got.'

She turned to Kevin. 'Do you mind? I have to taste before you can see the Needle.'

'You didn't mention that.'

'Didn't want to scare you.'

Blake chortled. 'Yeah, she's *so* scary, ain't she? Wait.' He left the room, leaving them staring at each other, Kevin nervous, she seemingly amused, and returned shortly with a silver chalice, which he passed to Mel.

Kevin held out a hand. She pulled the blade from her boot. Blood splattered into the chalice. The wound closed before the cup was full, but she was satisfied.

Mel sipped.

Her pupils dilated to black: 'Fuck me.'

Mel filled her mouth again, then turned to Blake and kissed him, long and tenderly. The poet stumbled back, eyes shut, face turned to the ceiling, a thin trickle of blood running from one corner of his mouth. Mel wiped it with a finger.

Blake moaned. His face was swollen and ruddy, his eyes fevered and bulging, the whites webbed with scarlet veins.

'Dangerous, isn't it – tasting one of us?' Kevin asked. 'Bedlam and all that.'

'You're too young to have that many ghosts,' Mel said. 'Besides, I have an aptitude.'

'Aptitude? I had one of them once.'

She gave him a curious look, as though she should know

what he meant, but didn't. Like hearing a song she'd heard once, but not knowing its name or even where she'd heard it.

'I guess I should thank you for asking,' he said. 'You could've put that spike in my heart and taken what you wanted any time.'

'Between you and me, I prefer the head, if you can afford the risk. Longer recovery time if you don't do any permanent injury.' She winked. 'And don't think I wasn't tempted. Not after that chomp you left in Greaser for me to heal. It was only the extremity of the situation that prevented me, that and your apparent contrition.'

'Oh, yes,' Blake whispered. His lips drew thin and tight, eyebrows almost meeting over the furrow as he stared at Kevin. 'Quite the time you've been having, chum. Making friends in all the wrong places. I think the Needle will definitely want to meet you.'

'How soon?'

'I'll get Greaser to set it up; once we're done.'

'I'll see Kevin gets to him,' Mel said.

'Um, we're *meeting*,' Blake said.

'He's all I've got for you tonight. That should be plenty of grist for the mill.'

'I want you here.'

'Viscounts have already taken a shot at him. VS will be all over it by now.'

'All the more reason to stay.'

'He needs to get to the Needle. You should come too.'

'I'm *meeting*.'

'And I'm not.'

For a long moment, they stood with gazes locked.

Blake blinked. 'Come, come, I have forgotten my hospitality.'

'Blake,' Mel said, but he was ushering Kevin out, his hand hot on Kevin's elbow, his breath gusting with the heavy scent of fresh blood.

Blake pointed at a hooting boy in velvet and said, 'Ambrose, our guest needs a drink. A little something for the road.'

Bella huffed, and the rest went quiet. Kevin could hear the candles flicker; the room was so silent.

'It's short for Ambrosia, don't you know,' Blake said, in a stage whisper that made his fawning gang giggle.

The blushing boy came to him, arms out, wrists up. 'Unless you prefer it somewhere else.'

Kevin shook his head. 'I've eaten.'

Mel touched his arm. 'It wouldn't hurt. You've been running on empty for days; that nip you took from Greaser hasn't even touched the sides. I can tell.'

'He's already had Greaser?' Ambrose said. 'That Snipe?'

'*That Snipe* is my friend,' Mel said.

'Sure, but–'

'The arm is fine.' Kevin pulled his knife.

'A blade? Really?' The kid looked crestfallen.

'The country boy is shy,' Blake said, and was rewarded with another chuckle from his flock. It did little to ease the air of anticipation, however; all gazes meeting on that pale patch of flesh in Kevin's grip.

Kevin cut the kid's arm, was rewarded with a quick intake of breath, from Ambrose and those watching; the wound gave up its liquid, and he lapped. If Blake had expected him to be squeamish about eating in public, well, guess again, wanker. Besides, he needed information, and neither Blake nor Mel was being overly forthcoming.

'Better than goon,' one murmured.

The connection came, a deeper current under the crimson rush. The boy – estranged from his parents on account of his homosexuality, working his way through art school, a living cliché – was one of Blake's three red-eyes, fed on blood passed around in a chalice. They and the rest of the gang called themselves The Romantics; they hung out in cafes and clubs when they weren't at university or working behind counters or dole bludging. They knew the reality of Blake's nature; that was why they'd joined his Murder. Blake needed a big gang of red-eyes and wannabes. There were other vampire gangs out there, gangs like Johnny Slick's Viscounts – hungry for turf, hungry for veins. It was only VS that kept them from tearing each other apart, by restricting the numbers of vampires and red-eyes, and enforcing hunting grounds to keep the factions apart. Certain bars and clubs, certain hospitals at certain nights of the week, made available to certain gangs outside their own little ecosystems of give and take. Making other vampires was strictly verboten unless the Old Man gave the nod for some act of loyalty. Mel was Blake's only vampire offspring. They had arrived together a few years back, on Blake's Grand Tour of the world; he called her his muse. Others called her his slave, his daughter, his second. Ambrose's blood didn't reveal what she called herself.

A part of Kevin – the loneliness, or perhaps merely the ever-present hunger – wanted very much to know. So compelling, the thought of opening her flesh, there on her pale neck, firm yet soft, the taste of her, the life she'd led, the lives she'd consumed, and often he sensed, at Blake's request.

Kevin clung to Ambrose, his heart pounding as the blood and memories sizzled through his veins. The aroma of lust and blood clouded his senses. Hopeful faces peered at him. Bella's fleshy hand was at her throat, as though already feeling his fangs in her.

Hunger urged him to sink again into the boy, but he resisted.

'Another? More? A growing boy needs to eat.' Blake peered at him, face flushed with fervour.

And Kevin saw in Ambrose's lifestream:

Blake, thrashing Ambrose with his cane. The boy, naked crouched, his ribs and back striped and mottled with welts. Melpomene saying, enough, and Bella in the background, staring, with big, wet eyes. And Blake, pushing Mel away, and stabbing. And turning back to Ambrose, a single slash spilling crimson: 'suffer for your art, boy'. And Ambrose thanking him. Thanking him as Bella licks at the blood, and Blake takes her while he sprouts poetry, and Mel slowly heals, rumpled and forgotten

'There's more where that came from,' Blake said.

Kevin forced himself to let Ambrose go. 'I've had enough.'

The kid slumped and someone helped him to a nearby sofa. They watched the cut heal where Kevin had smeared his own blood on it. The boy was a red-eye, suckled on Blake's blood; despite the anti-coagulant in Kevin's spittle he'd have healed quickly enough, but Kevin figured he owed the kid something for the donation.

'In that case, get out.' Bloody sweat beaded Blake's forehead and upper lip. 'Out. All of you. Out!'

Blake scrabbled with shaking hands at a satchel hanging from a coat rack, and took from it a notebook bound in leather, and a long box, which he opened quickly, like an asthmatic digging for a puffer, and pulled free a fountain pen.

He saw Kevin staring and said, 'Nothing like the scratching of the nib upon parchment. So pure!' And then, when no one had moved, 'Out! Out!'

Kevin said, 'What about the Needle?'

'Yes, yes. Melpomene can keep you off the streets until the arrangements have been made. Now, out, the lot of you – out!'

'Blake's a twat,' Mel said as soon as they hit the street.

'What's that?'

'Giving you Ambrose like that. Risking, maybe even hoping, you'd lose it.'

'Why would he do that?'

'To make a point. To me.'

'I don't understand.'

'Don't worry. Just remember that Blake always puts Blake first, and you'll be fine.'

The car was where they'd left it.

'How was his lordship this evening?' Greaser asked.

'His usual charming self,' Mel said.

'So, what now?'

'Let's drive. Give Kevin the Cook's tour of Brissie.'

Kevin held his hand out. Greaser scowled, but gave him the keys.

Once they were rolling, he said, 'Those blokes back at the tatt shop–'

'The Viscounts,' Greaser said.

'Yeah, the *Happy Days* bunch. Why were they there?'

'The bowling alley was shut?'

Mel ignored Greaser's joke. 'They're from the south side. They aren't meant to be this side of the river. They'll get their knuckles rapped.'

'But they were looking for me. How did they know I'd be there?'

'Jack Flash might've been having a bob each way,' Mel said.

'No, he was the Needle's mate,' Greaser said. 'He wouldn't have crossed him. Why even bother to tell us Kev was in town if he was going to shop him?'

'The bint?' Mel suggested.

'You mean the counter girl?' Kevin asked.

'Jen might have connections, I s'pose,' Greaser said. 'I don't know her too well.'

'And why the Viscounts? Why would they care?' Mel wondered.

'A favour? They want West End, but the Vultures won't have a bar of them. And everyone wants the Valley. Maybe they thought the bumpkin, sorry mate, no offence, but maybe they thought Kev would give them a bargaining chip.'

'But why would Jen go to them? Why not go straight to VS?'

'No contacts?'

'What, she couldn't get the number out of the book?

Couldn't drop a note through the letter box? No, there's something going on.' She looked at Kevin, as though he had some secret written on his forehead.

Greaser huffed and sat back in her seat. 'I don't know why we stay here, Mel. Why do we stay here?'

'That's why.' She poked a finger at a queue lined up for cabs or a bus, or maybe to get into some fancy club.

'Nom, nom, nom,' Greaser said, sarcastically.

'Brissie's not the only town in Queensland,' Kevin said.

'It's the biggest. Easy to get lost in. To go unnoticed in.'

'Except for VS watching everyone,' Greaser said. 'Taking tithes.'

Mel looked at Kevin. 'Get rid of VS, and this could be a very nice town indeed.'

'That's not why I'm here.'

'No? I've seen inside your blood.'

'Then you know who I want.'

'What makes you think you can get Mira without going through the rest of them?'

'That's what I need to speak to the Needle about.'

No one spoke for a while and he turned on the radio. Mel turned it down.

'Nice car,' Greaser said.

'Yeah,' he said. 'A friend gave it to me.'

'Subtle,' she said.

'It's a classic.'

'If you die, can I have it?'

Mel scolded her, but Kevin laughed. 'Why not?' And then sobered. 'When do I get to see the Needle?'

'Blake's off in reverie,' Mel said. 'Could be tomorrow night. Maybe the night after.'

'Damn.' His hands tightened on the wheel as he stared at the valleys of concrete and bitumen. Now that Hunter knew he was here, the clock was ticking. He would never see Hunter coming in this crowded, foreign wilderness.

'Are you in such a rush to die?' Mel asked.

'Should I drop you two somewhere?' Kevin asked.

'Why? Where are you going?'

He gestured to the city, a vague somewhere.

'Don't be silly,' Mel said. 'You'll stay with me tonight.'

Greaser shook her head. 'Now who's in a rush to die?'

'You can mind the car,' Mel told her, and Greaser mumbled, 'Well, just remember that I get your flat when you kick the bucket.'

NINE

They'd been told to report immediately on arriving at Thorn, but Reece was taking a detour.

'We'll be late,' Felicity said as they rode the lift.

'Better late than dead on time,' Reece said.

'You think we're for it?' She trembled, and he admired her control as she pulled herself together in a matter of seconds.

'Clock's ticking. I want to see if Mira can buy us some time.'

'She can't even tell the time.'

'We'll see.'

They got out on 11 and stepped through the sliding doors into the ward: off-white walls, rows of beds, tinted windows. A suffocating scent of antiseptic, the stale-breath hint of blood, clouded around them. Hospitaller Dr Tran and esteemed Treasurer Tony Campbell had their heads together at the far end of the room, right outside the restricted area. They looked up like startled emus as Reece and Felicity approached. Campbell jerked his head in their direction, an action akin to throwing a stick for a dog, and Tran strode toward them, his hands in the pockets of his white smock, stethoscope looped around his neck like a snake.

'What are you two doing here?' the doctor demanded to know.

'Wanted to check on the boss,' Reece said.

'No visitors in isolation.'

'Since when?'

'Since now.'

'How is she?' Reece indicated the sealed door at Campbell's back, marked by a No Entry sign and the newly placed scarlet psi symbol marking it as a mental isolation room, dangerous to enter.

'The cacophony has worsened. The Strigoi is deep in bedlam now. Any deeper, she may never surface again.' He shrugged. What was one to do?

'I need to talk to her. It's important. About a case.'

'It is hard enough for her to manage her internal world, without you muddying the waters.'

The door to Mira's room opened and Vee emerged. Reece groaned, and felt rather than saw Felicity's warning glance. Vee smirked at him, minced across in her – his/their – knee-high pumps.

Tran stepped back as Mira's understudy reached them, as though Vee radiated cold.

Vee looked as though he/she/they had come out of a freezer: short hair frosted silver, eyebrows shaved to the skin, eyelashes and lips silvered, a figure-hugging sheath of white PVC. Sexless, no tell-tale bumps anywhere. Bluish fingernails glinted like shards of ice.

Pale malamute eyes regarded Reece, the unblinking gaze settling on his throat, his wrists, his groin. 'Back again, Hunter? Getting thirsty?'

Reece's hand was on his sidearm before he realised it, closely followed by Felicity's restraining hand.

'We're late,' she said.

'In trouble again, are we?' Vee asked, feigning ignorance.

'I'll be back,' Reece said. 'Mira is my bludger, after all.'

'Bludger?'

'Host.' Reece savoured his minor jargon win over Vee.

'*Was* your "bludger", I think you mean,' Vee replied, unabashed. 'The Hospitaller has declared isolation. There are no visiting hours. For anyone.'

Tran added: 'Regardless of who they are; or were. It's for her own good, and that of her visitors. Someone in bedlam cannot be expected to react rationally.'

Campbell sauntered over to eye Reece over the top of his narrow, frameless glasses. He didn't stand too close to Vee, either. 'Don't they want you upstairs?'

Felicity tugged on Reece's arm, mumbled, 'Better not keep the Old Man waiting.'

'Nice seeing you, Hunter Reece.' Vee smiled, a corpse-like grin.

Felicity pulled Reece into the lift and hit the button for 13. Boardroom. His last view was of Tran, Campbell and Vee watching him leave, like Macbeth's three witches, all but rubbing their hands at his impending fall from grace.

Reece breathed out, trying to relax the tension in his muscles. 'I hate that fucking mutant.'

'Your prejudice is showing, old man. I think Vee's the most honest person in the building.'

'How's that?'

'Vee's all vampire. Not male, not female. Just vee.'

'Well, I still don't trust he/she/vee; whatever.'

'With Mira out of commission, Vee is Strigoi.'

'That freak's no Strigoi.'

'Someone's got to do the mojo.'

The door chimed open. 'Bend over, here it comes,' Reece said, and she slapped his arm; then she straightened her jacket as they walked side by side into the reception.

'Go in,' the red-eye Familiare behind the desk said. His

uniform patches showed him to be one of Maximilian's, loyalty all but guaranteed by shared blood. All the board members had such lackeys, although younger members such as Treasurer Tony Campbell preferred to call them personal assistants – a sign of the gulf between the bright young things and their ancient leader. Reece imagined it must be frustrating for the up-and-comers; what *was* the retirement age for a vampire warlord?

The boardroom was utilitarian: a long table, a blank wall with a retractable projection screen, a side door to a kitchen area, another to the toilets. Another wall was taken up with a framed tapestry of knights butchering pagans in a dark forest under the banner of a black cross. Wide windows looked across the river to the mountains in the west; traffic pulsed over the bridges and along the riverside expressway. On South Bank, the sightseeing wheel rotated in a slow blur of colour. If only the wheels turning inside Thorn were so brightly illuminated.

Hochmeister Maximilian von Schiller stood statue-still, arms clasped behind his back as he took in the view. He was five-foot-six, as solid as a brick shithouse, with no neck to speak of. His jumper hung to his mid thigh; combined with his bowl haircut, it gave him a certain monkish air, but the man's demeanour always reminded Reece of a member of the Inquisition. He could imagine Maximilian extracting confessions with hot pokers and cages of rats. It made his own Special Branch interrogation techniques seem incredibly amateurish. The man's eyes were reflected green dots in the window and Reece could feel them shift their focus to regard the two of them.

Maximilian's second-in-command stepped from a patch of darkness between two downlights. Preceptor Heinrich had a reputation for blending with the shadows, despite being a full head and shoulders taller than Maximilian and even wider in the chest. He wore a shiny jacket open to reveal a tight shirt, his narrow waist sporting sword and sidearm.

'This had better be good,' Heinrich said.

What irked him more – the mess at the tattoo shop or the fact they were late – was impossible to know. Reece didn't bother apologising for either, just gave his report as succinctly as possible. A rumour of Kevin Matheson in town, provided by a snitch, now dead, along with her tattooist boss; Reece thinking to follow the grease monkey to see who his connections were, the Viscounts wrecking the plan.

He didn't mention the Needle or the girl the gang leader had sent to meet Matheson. Dangerous to withhold information, but worth the risk.

Maximilian turned, his intense eyes sweeping across them like a searchlight's beam from his long, thin face.

'Definitely this "grease monkey" from the outback?'

Reece slid a hard copy of one of the photos he'd taken across the table. 'It's him, all right.'

'And no sign of Danica?' Maximilian stretched her name out, Daneetza, as though tasting some exotic honey, a complicated flavour of love and hurt, confusion even.

'Just Matheson.'

Maximilian touched the image, one finger pressing it into the timber as though he could draw information from the ink itself.

Heinrich asked, 'Who killed the tattooist?'

'The Viscounts, presumably. Johnny Slick was down from a headshot when we arrived, but he was gone when we returned. Flash had turned off his security cameras, but it's a good bet the gang cleaned house while we were trading pleasantries out the back.'

'"Presumably". And what are you presuming now?'

'That someone tipped off the Viscounts, and they saw a chance to get a leg up.'

'The tattooist?'

'Unlikely.'

'Why was Matheson there?'

'We're looking into that.'

Heinrich snorted. 'Unfinished business, Lieutenant Reece?'

'It's not something I'd rule out.'

'Unfinished business,' Maximilian said, studying the photograph again before turning his attention to Reece. 'With you? With my daughter?'

'It's an avenue of investigation we're considering.'

'Do that. And the killing of the tattooist and your informant; tracks are being covered?'

'So it would appear.'

'The way forward?'

'Johnny Slick. Find out who pointed him in Matheson's direction.'

Heinrich nodded his approval, his meaty lips pressed tight as though still tasting the plan for hidden flavours.

Maximilian's hand closed slowly, nails scraping on the table as he scrunched the photograph. He loomed huge, those eyes filling Reece's vision, like staring into a landslide.

'And now, the thing you're not telling us. The reason you didn't mount a full operation to secure the mechanic.' He held up the ball of paper. 'Even though you knew it was he.'

Felicity licked her lips and said, 'We may have a leak, my lord Hochmeister.'

'A leak?' Heinrich said, as though they had just shat on his shoe. 'You'd better have bloody good evidence before accusing anyone in this operation of treachery.'

Felicity swallowed, then continued: 'We think someone, accidentally, or on purpose, told the Needle about Jasmine Turner setting up her farm; and the Needle told Bhagwan. Bhagwan didn't want to compete against Turner – he was afraid of losing his special privileges as a supplier of cattle blood to us – so he told Taipan, who hated Jasmine Turner. Taipan obligingly went Rambo on Turner's operation before it was up and running.'

Reece added, 'Of course, it didn't work out quite as Bhagwan hoped. His farm was destroyed and Jasmine took his head.'

Maximilian stared at the scrunched photo in his palm. 'Quite the debacle, wouldn't you say, Hunters? Turner is dust and our bovine supply chain shattered; Danica is still at large; Mira is in bedlam. And now the agent of this destruction is here, in my demesne.' His eyes flicked up, settled on Reece. 'What do you make of that, Hunter?'

'With all due respect, I'm not a Hunter anymore, my lord.'

'And yet, you still hunt. Not well, as it happens. You failed my daughter, and now you let this boy escape again.' He brandished his fist. 'This boy who has a link not only to my former consort, but to my daughter as well.'

Maximilian thrust the photo into his pocket. 'How do you know about this chain of communication?'

'Something Bhagwan said. Before Jasmine dusted him.' Reece ignored Felicity's sudden tensing, trusted to his forty-odd years of bullshitting to vampires and humans alike to gloss over his lie. 'A hunch, my lord. I'm still looking for the proof.'

'Then keep looking, Hunter. Find Slick. Find the traitor who betrayed my daughter.' He turned back to the window, meeting dismissed.

'My lord?' Reece asked.

Maximilian regarded him over one shoulder.

'Matheson. He could lead us to Danica. Danica could cure Mira.'

'Which is the real reason you went after him alone, is it not? The favourite, attempting to protect his mistress.' Maximilian turned away once more. 'Loyalty is admirable, but results speak louder.'

Heinrich showed them to the door. 'Who have you told about this supposed leak, Lieutenant Reece?'

'No one, my lord Preceptor.'

'Keep it that way. Now, do what the Hochmeister has ordered. Both of you. Find this leak. And most importantly: find Matheson. The Strigoi's life – *your* lives – depend on it.'

Felicity looked paler than usual as they waited for the lift. 'Did he mean it?'

'About offing us? We're red-eyes. Parasites. Tools. We don't have a lot of longevity.'

She leaned against a wall, arms crossed.

'You're young,' Reece said. 'You've got time to recover from this.'

'Yeah, right. Any thoughts about where to find Slick? Surely he'll be so far underground–'

'Come back to my room for a minute.'

'Reece–'

'Business, Flick.'

She rolled her eyes, but accompanied him down to 3. He wondered how long it would take Human Resources to shift him, now that he was no longer under Mira's protection. She had secured him this private room, as close to hers on 2 as she could get. And while GS officers, as he now was, were allocated a room to themselves on this floor, there were higher ranks that would kill for his balcony. The view wasn't great, but you could smoke out there without fear of setting off an alarm.

'You have any joy working out who was in on the Jasmine Turner plan?' he asked once they were inside his quarters with the door shut.

'It was Jensen's op; he's head of logistics, so that makes sense. But all the board knew about it, which means their Familiares and staff.'

'Just them, huh.'

'Yeah, you wanna bring them in for questioning?'

He frowned, as though considering it, and she shook her head to show he wasn't fooling anyone.

'So which of them had something to gain by throwing a spanner in the works?'

'Who didn't?'

'Dead end, then.'

'Unless you can lean on a Familiare and keep their bludger from knowing about it long enough to prosecute.'

He smiled at her use of his old police slang for a pimp – as good a term for a vampire running red-eyes as any other; dealer, maybe? The small satisfaction that he was rubbing off on her couldn't overcome the frustration of trying to investigate people who were untouchable. 'So we're back to Johnny Slick.'

While his laptop booted, he poured generous shots of Bundy, hers on the rocks, the ice cubes about the only thing in the bar fridge.

She turned away from his small collection of pulp fiction paperbacks and a row of CDs that were his music to drink by, as he handed her the glass. They clinked once and he took the chair in front of the computer.

'You're going to google Slick?' She stood behind him; close enough to feel her heat against his shoulder.

She put down her drink and shed her jacket. 'Warm,' she said. Ice cubes rattled as she retrieved her rum. The hard drive whirred. 'You need an upgrade.'

'Tell me about it.'

His back felt cold where she'd moved away. Her subtly floral fragrance lingered. He took a big sip, and then punched the keys in his two-fingered style. She was right; it was hot in here. He loosened his tie while the screen filled with the results of his search.

'This one.' He looked at her over his shoulder, quietly triumphant, just a little desperate. 'I guarantee you Johnny Slick will be here.'

'Roller derby?'

'Not only do the Viscounts play the half-time show, but Johnny Slick's moll is a star player. No way will he not turn up.'

'I heard his band play, once. Technically, not bad.'

'But no soul?'

Typical vampire problem: good at replication, not so good at innovation. Except in scheming. Of animal cunning, they had no shortage.

Felicity kneeled down, one arm across the back of his chair, breast pushing against him, her scent wrapping around him. She pointed at the screen with her glass. 'This next match, it's tomorrow night.'

She pushed on his chair to rotate him toward her, put her glass down, then stepped back and slipped out of her shoulder holster. 'How about we take the rest of the night off?'

TEN

It didn't take long to get to Mel's apartment building in New Farm. The suburb was tucked inside one of the river's meander bends, and the dilapidated concrete monolith was set back from the water, surrounded by a mosaic of fenced-off development sites and exhausted homes waiting for the right offer to end their misery.

Crumpled beer cans glimmered among the sparse stalks that passed for lawn. Graffiti made camouflage patterns on the stairs and walls. Timber doors opened on to a foyer, heavy with mustiness and cat piss. Corridors stretched off but Mel led him to an ancient lift. A yellowed sheet of paper said the outer doors had to be shut for the lift to work.

'Where's Greaser taking the Monaro?' he asked.

'There are a couple of empty garages. It'll be safe.'

He kept his silence as the lift wheezed to a halt. A dim bulb showed initials cut into the wood, graf swirls, chewing gum like zits. She hit the top floor: 7.

'Lucky number,' she said, 'if you believe in such things.'

He grunted, not knowing what he believed in any more. A

chip packet lay on the floor. Cigarette butts. A sign said *No Smoking*.

'It takes its time,' she said, 'but it's much nicer than the stairs. Besides, it's not like we're in a rush, is it?'

Vampire time. He hadn't got used to it, found it maddening. Those weeks in Cairns, learning what he could from Danica, trying to be patient, to not think about the years – the decades, the centuries – ahead. Trying not to wonder how a man filled those days without dropping dead from boredom. Assuming he could drop dead, of course. What was the vampire equivalent? They'd not got to that in his month of Undead for Beginners.

And Kala, she'd become so distant so quickly. He'd expected their relationship to grow stronger, him being her maker and all. Maker. Everyone had a different word for it, but he still hadn't found one that suited him. Violator, maybe. Whatever you called it, it hadn't brought them closer. Sure, he'd saved her life by bringing her across. But all she'd done with immortality was shack up with a couple of human leeches, doing to them what Taipan had done to her, trading their blood for hers. The ultimate recycling program; but, as in the mundane world, the number of cycles was limited. Human flesh could take only so much. Reality could only be held at bay for so long. Death would have its way.

'We're here,' Mel said.

Kevin jerked himself out of his thoughts; he'd been deep in the bloodwalk, the moments of his recent past so well defined in his memory it was almost as though they were happening again. He silently cursed his lapse – it was dangerous, to be distracted in the presence of strangers – and followed her out; hearing the lift door shut, the floorboards creak, televisions behind doors, voices, a baby gurgling. Hallway lights, more out than on, made a hopscotch of light and shade on the worn carpet.

'I know you're afraid of bedlam,' she said as they walked,

'but delirium is also a risk. The vacuum of your own life will suck you down as surely as the cacophony of others.'

'Just got distracted,' he said.

'You need fresh input – fresh dreams. Meals, not snacks.'

'Between Greaser and Ambrose, I've had enough to keep me going.'

'This is me.' She took a key from her purse; a deadlock thunked.

In the small entrance, she balanced like a stork as she pulled off her boots and threw them against the wall. He followed her down a hallway. Newspapers covered a small dining table. Crammed in among the furniture was a keyboard – 'easier than bringing a piano up here, as much as I'd love one' – big TV, a stereo and turntable. Books and CDs and DVDs were scattered all over, as though a willy-willy had hit a music store.

'Check out the view.' She opened curtains to reveal a picture window. A strip of red-tiled roofs separated them from the river; the far bank was a cliff lined with mansions lit like a small town. Upstream, the river curved around a well-lit behemoth that Mel told him was a theatre repurposed from a defunct power station.

'There's a handy ferry terminal near the theatre,' she said.

And all the time, his heart jack-hammered as he waited for the other shoe to fall. Greaser had his car, his weapons in the boot.

'Music?' she asked.

He nodded, and regretted it as the stereo pumped hip hop.

'Maybe something softer,' she said, thumbing a remote. A rippling piano tune filled the space.

An iPod, he realised, jealously.

'How do you do all this?' he asked. His life on the run with Taipan had been one of abandoned houses and sheds, of – he shuddered – murdered inhabitants in isolated homesteads: food and shelter.

'There are people who fix such things. One advantage of

being plugged into Maximilian von Schiller's network. Someone to pay the power bills, keep the landlord off your back.'

'Does Blake live here, too?'

'Too quaint for him. He's got a nest in Paddo, kind of an artist's commune with some of the Romantics on tap.'

'You and him–'

'He turned me. A while ago, before he came to seek "inspiration in the Antipodes". An act of undying love, he called it. Quite the stalker, he was.'

When he said nothing, she filled the silence. 'Would you like to see?' She held out a pale, slender wrist.

He shook his head, looked again at the view, the flat; anywhere but at those purple veins.

'You've got a lot of music and stuff.'

'I like to stay up to date,' she said. 'Not always easy. Things change so fast. Would you like a drink?'

'Sure,' he said, not thinking, and then wondering if he could change his mind as she grinned, teasingly, triumphantly. She reached down a wine glass from a display cabinet, studied it against the light with a sniff of "good enough", then pulled a knife from a block.

He opened his mouth to say 'no' but the word drowned in the scent of blood as she opened her wrist and let the blood half fill the glass before the wound closed.

'Bedlam?' he said as she walked to him, glass out. 'Oh, that's right: you've got an aptitude.'

'For giving *and* receiving.'

He took the glass and she stroked his cheek, his chin.

'You aren't like him.'

Did she mean Taipan or Blake, or both? Just how much had she seen in his blood? He kept his eyes on the glass, the liquid sloshing with the trembling of his hand.

'You said you were plugged into Maximilian's organisation.'

She cocked her head, eyes hardening. 'You aren't dead yet, are you?'

He hesitated.

'You can trust me, Kevin.' Her fingers guided the glass to his lips. 'Let me show you.'

He drank. Swayed, as the sound of the sea rose up, a crimson surf dragging him down.

Felt, distantly, her lips on his throat. Her teeth. The sharp, tearing pain, but her grip was strong. Together, they fell.

A long, bright pier; cards on a velvet-covered table, one a picture of a man done up like a medieval prince, another of a tower collapsing; a woman running on a pebbled beach and dragged down into the swash, her blood running out, dark in the froth. Blake: wielding his cane like a cudgel, and then, terrifying, twisting the knob in response to a shout to cease; twisting it clockwise, a click, the whisper of steel leaving its home a counterpoint to Blake's fevered whisper, 'There is no going back'; and Blake ramming the naked blade into Mel's chest, and the syrup gushing from her mouth as she falls in slow motion, and then her coughing fit as the sword is withdrawn to leave her to recover, and him holding her, telling her how much he needs her; her, his muse.

They had something in common, Melpomene and Danica. Other than being very good at keeping secrets.

From what little they had allowed him to see in their blood, it was obvious they were both bloodhags; like Mira, they were able to use blood in almost magical ways that most vampires could not. He suspected Mel's powers were much narrower than Danica's whose, he gathered, were off the scale. And Mel kept that small aptitude a secret, for fear of being recruited into Maximilian's inner sanctum.

Back in the day, both women had made a name as soothsayers. Danica's fame had drawn Maximilian. Mel's had drawn Blake. And both women had ended up being dragged in the slipstream of the men who'd made them. Danica had already rebelled. And Mel?

You aren't like him

He wasn't so sure. He was using Mel to get to Mira; Mira had used him to get to Danica. And Maximilian, he realised, the knowledge suddenly apparent, had used Mira to get to Danica.

Maximilian had come calling, looking for a Strigoi, and when Danica knocked him back, he'd found a more receptive ear in the daughter. Where daughter went, mother followed, two for the price of one, but Mira turned out to be her new father's daughter and Danica had run.

Perhaps that was where the mess had started: some hovel in a European backwater, a mother desperate to keep a daughter already lost to her – a daughter who eventually tried to kill her mother, to consume her.

That was the reason he was here. Mira had already consumed one life too many. If he couldn't *recover* his mother, he could at least make sure no one else had to go through this. Whatever it cost.

He turned to Mel, caressed her cheek, murmured sleepily, 'So, tell me again what you know about Maximilian's tower.'

They were in the bedroom, shielded behind the velvet curtains of a four-poster bed, a border of grey light above the rail like a twilight horizon. He felt heavy and hot with blood, exhausted by the heat of the day. He had seen little of Mel's life. A measured dose, she'd fed him. How much had he shown her? He had no way of knowing. She hadn't killed him in his sleep, which was a good sign.

Not so good was what she knew of Thorn. The entrances were few and thoroughly screened, and access to the upper floors was even more strictly controlled. To sneak inside with a stolen ID was possible; to penetrate to where the vampires lurked, highly unlikely. Not without "considerable bother".

He regarded the sleeping woman beside him, her smooth, pale shoulder naked above the sheet. Would Mel help him? Was that what last night had been about? She was already risking her life by having him in her home. Is that why he was awake so early – guilt?

Or was it because bother had come calling, and he'd been too busy plotting revenge to notice the sound of the door opening?

A footstep. Beside the bed!

His heartbeat tripped.

Greaser reefed aside a curtain. She stared at them with a stony expression.

'Shouldn't you be in school?' he asked, clutching for a sheet as he jack-knifed into a sitting position. Mel sat up, hair mussed, face ruddy, chest unselfconsciously naked.

'It's almost sundown, arsehole,' Greaser said. 'Besides, I haven't been in school for years.'

'Greaser does not play well with others,' Mel said, sounding weary.

'Depends on the others,' she said, blushing, and looked away.

'How's the Monaro?' Kevin asked.

'Comfortable,' she said. 'You aren't dead yet, huh.'

'Not yet,' he said, though his neck throbbed; and his chest, where Mel had bitten him. He closed his eyes, then, glad of the pillow behind him as a moment swirled from his bloodstream, of fucking Kala when she was warm, of the sudden cooling afterward. Mel's blood swam through him like an electric eel. His nostrils flared at the smell of blood, as thick as sex. Greaser stepped back as he eyed her, and let the curtain fall. She'd bathed, smelled of soap and deodorant. Her blood pulsed inside her flesh; her heart thudded like a bass drum causing shockwaves in his senses.

Mel finger-combed her fringe, wiped her face, swung her legs from the bed and reached for a gown draped over a nearby chair. Her absence left him alone and vulnerable. She stood, spine rippling, and slid the silky material on and belted it at her waist. 'News, Greaser?'

'Yeah,' she said. 'Blake rang. The meet's on for tonight. Sandgate.'

'Well, then, bring the car around.' She shot Kevin a sly grin. 'Fortunately, we've already eaten.'

Kevin hauled himself out of bed and looked for clothes. He thought he'd dropped his shirt in the lounge room.

Greaser, by the door, looked away as he pulled his jeans on.

'Where's Sandgate?' he asked.

'North-east; by the sea. Maybe an hour with the traffic. It's easy to find, but. You just take Sandgate Road as far as it goes. If you hit the water, you've gone too far.'

Too late for that, Kevin thought. He was already out of his depth.

ELEVEN

Felicity was gone when a telephone call woke Reece an hour before dawn. He showered and shaved and, feeling only slightly rumpled in his stiff black GS uniform, made his way through Thorn. He wasn't convinced what had happened between he and Felicity was anything other than stress relief, but he had no regrets.

Forty years he'd been in Maximilian's employ, a rare beast indeed: brought in by Mira, installed from the start as a Hunter and her personal favourite. It had made him unpopular with pretty much everyone. With Mira off the board, chickens were coming home to roost. It was only the tacit agreement not to admit that Mira would not be coming back from her bedlam that forestalled more serious repercussions for Reece. The Old Man had not accepted his daughter was lost; her favourite could not be too seriously impugned.

But he could be demoted, to the Gespenstenstaffel – an elite unit of mostly vampires and red-eyes under Heinrich's command.

So the pre-dawn phone call was a strange one. Marshall Jane Smith, in charge of Thorn's far more mundane security concerns, wanted to see him. Down he went to her office on the second floor, at the opposite end of the building to Mira's sequestered chambers, never the twain to meet: access to the Strigoi's section was strictly limited, red lift only, and a pass-controlled set of fire stairs.

Had the special treatment for the Strigoi rankled? Oh yes. Had the Strigoi cared? Not one jot. Was Reece expecting to have his nose rubbed in her fall, and his? Most definitely.

A man in the crisp, olive-coloured uniform of Marshall's VSS – Von Schiller Security, guardians of all Maximilian's facilities – looked up from his computer screen as Reece entered the reception. The man's eyes flashed the tell-tale crimson of a red-eye.

'You took your time,' Marshall's Familiare told him, his voice as sharp as the sword-shaped letter opener on his desk. In fairness, they had told him to report ASAP, which to his mind allowed for a shave and a quick wake-up coffee and a smoke.

'Got lost,' Reece said. It'd been meant to be a thinly-veiled insult about being on their floor, but there was a deeper truth to the statement that made him blanch. Suddenly, he was too tired to trade insults with the officious red-eye. 'I can come back if she's busy.'

The man sniffed and pressed an intercom to announce Reece's belated arrival. Then he stood and opened the door, closing it behind Reece with a soft click, surprisingly similar to a weapon being cocked.

Windowless, the room had all the charm of a cell, the air conditioning set to chilly, the décor to cheap motel. Filing cabinets, bar fridge, microwave, several changes of clothes for different occasions hanging in plastic from a naked rack. Two computer screens. A muted wall-mounted television set to a 24-hour news channel, a transistor radio whispering to itself. The room stank of cigarettes. Homely, Reece thought.

Marshall Jane Smith stood as he entered; walked around to

shake his hand with a firm grip, then indicated a chair before returning to her desk and clicking off the radio.

Marshall, as she was known, was about his height, stocky, toned, hair trimmed to a low-maintenance bob. She clearly hadn't given up the good things in life. Some did, gradually letting the blood take over, and ended up looking like a walking advertisement for anorexia, hunger on legs. Marshall wasn't that much older than Reece, in unnatural terms, and still retained curves and complexion.

She flicked open a cigarette packet and offered him one, which he accepted though he found tailor-mades unpleasant in both taste and smell. She lit it for him, then one for herself. An ashtray in the shape of Australia sat brim-full on the desk, the acronym ASIO carved in the lip.

Marshall blew smoke at the ceiling – there was an exhaust fan there, he could hear the quiet whirr, a subtle reminder that power came with privileges.

'Busted, eh, Lieutenant Reece.'

'How so, Madam Marshall?'

'Please, just Marshall. This is an informal chat.'

He sighed blue breath, not having had enough sleep for jousting, and waited. He was due to be at some bullshit orientation program soon, but she'd know that, putting him under subtle pressure. Maybe he shouldn't have had the coffee after all.

'Takes a while to get used to uniform again, doesn't it?'

He nodded. She was in a suit jacket and white blouse, the top button undone; he'd noted the blue jeans, tight around the thighs, and RM Williams boots.

'This gunfight at the tattoo parlour in the Valley. How concerned should I be?'

'That would depend on how long Kevin Matheson stays at large.'

'Explain.'

'Matheson wants to take out Mira. He's looking for access.'

73

'Access.' Marshall tapped ash. 'The late Jack Flash was a known associate of the villein known as the Needle, was he not?'

'That is an avenue of–'

'That bloody spook. Got his fingers in more pies than we do. Could he get the assassin in?'

'The question is, would he want to?'

She was quiet then, just the sound of them drawing in breath and exhaling smoke, and the exhaust fan. If she was feeling the weight of the new day breaking outside, she gave no sign.

Reece leaned forward to ash his cigarette. He noticed a folder on her desk, the heading, and caught her eye.

'Fronds: the new casino at Coolum,' she confirmed. 'We're handling security, naturally.'

'I liked Coolum, back in the day. Quiet.'

'It won't be once this gets going.' She indicated the folder with her cigarette. 'The council's already jockeying to see who claims grazing rights.'

By council she meant Maximilian's board of department heads and favoured vassals, each doing their bit to ensure his empire ran smoothly. The actual municipal council would've had little say in the matter, once Maximilian had made up his mind about the development. Money talks, especially when backed up by the promise of immortality and the more mundane threats of early death and financial ruin. Big business, immortal style; gave the futures market a whole new meaning.

'I'm surprised anyone would want to leave Brisbane.'

'Come on, Reece. An hour out of town, away from the Old Man's gaze, and all those hopeless, desperate losers chasing a promise that's unlikely to ever happen. Throw in backpackers and holidaymakers and the entire Sunshine Coast to nibble on; it's a bloody smorgasbord.'

He gave a nod, conceding, as she analysed him, green-eyed, through the smoke. 'The Old Man does like his casinos. Casinos and brothels.' Both gave perfect exposure to powerful men with secrets to keep, as well as losers no one would miss should they get an offer they couldn't refuse. 'Who's the frontrunner?'

'The Toffs, maybe. Campbell thinks it'll shore up their support. Give us a few more inroads into the finance world.'

'You don't want it?'

'And give up all this?' She slipped the folder into a drawer and locked it. 'You ever think maybe Danica was right?'

'How's that?'

'We don't belong anymore. We shouldn't even try; just slip away, under the surface.'

'Could you do that?'

She dug out a folder from a tray and passed it to him. 'What do you know about this chap?'

He flicked through the papers, paused at a head-and-shoulders shot of a young man in a VSS uniform. 'I heard about it. Briggs, private, one of yours. Head cut off, hands and feet removed.'

'ID'd by DNA. Found among what's left of the mangroves under the expressway. Crabs had taken a nibble; fish too, maybe.'

'Just before the Debacle,' Reece said, noting the estimated day of death.

'Check the picture of his back. What does that suggest to you?'

He dug through the glossies until he found the photo: the mottled, pale skin, an ulcer-type wound on the right shoulder blade. He held it up to the light. 'A patch of skin taken off? A tattoo?'

'Tell me again about your interest in the Needle.'

He paused, studied the image. Couldn't fault her intelligence gathering. Couldn't see any point denying what she already knew. 'You think Briggs leaked the information about Jasmine Turner setting up shop out west to the Needle. Then was silenced by whoever told him in the first place, because no way could a VSS private know about it off his own bat.'

'Leaving me with the shit sandwich.'

Reece sat up straight, handed back the file, ground out his cigarette in the ashtray. The room had become quite cold. 'Why are you showing me this, Madam Marshall?'

'He should've watched his back.' A tight grimace at her word play. 'I think there's something in that for all of us. You'd better run along, Reece. You don't want to be late for your reorientation.'

He got as far as the door when she said, 'And perhaps it might be best if you keep me in the loop on this Matheson case. I'd like to know I've got a wolf at my door before he eats the baby.'

TWELVE

Kevin pulled the Monaro to a halt in a car park atop a bluff. It wasn't yet eight, but he felt as if the night had lasted a month already. Through a screen of pine and gum trees, he could see the ocean, dark and ominous and palely ruffled. A timber pier stretched out like a bony arm, sickly yellow in the electric wash of its lights. The swollen moon hung high over the water.

The only vehicle in the car park was a motor home covered in graffiti. A blond teenager in a trench coat lounged against the Winnebago's wall, smoking; light showed behind the vehicle's curtained windows.

Mel got out and popped the seat forward to let Greaser scramble after her. Blondie knocked on the Winnebago's door, then flicked his cigarette away as Kevin locked the car.

Mel led him over, saying, 'Argent, this is Kevin. The Needle's expecting us.'

The boy stared at Kevin, eyes showing silver. He opened the door. A teenage girl stood there, submachine gun pointed at them. She lowered it when she saw Mel. A silver tattoo – some creature's scaly tail – curled down her left side from under the ragged hem of her short singlet to disappear into her cut-off shorts. Another sliver snaked up her throat, vanishing behind her ear. Like the boy, she wore her peroxided hair short. Her eyes reflected a mercury sheen – contacts, Kevin realised. He was willing to bet they were both red-eyes.

Herbal scents floated out from behind the girl; there was the smell of antiseptic and a trace of blood. Kevin steadied himself, pushing away the recent blood memories from Ambrose and Mel.

This was the vehicle he'd seen in Greaser's blood; this was the Needle's mobile base. Finally.

Argent patted Kevin down, then said, 'He's in the back.'

'We'll wait,' Mel said, and the girl said she would put the kettle on, and showed Mel and Greaser to a cosy dining area up the front before pointing Kevin toward a curtain closing off the rear.

He was acutely aware of being unarmed as he pushed the cloth aside to reveal a couch similar to a dentist's chair, complete with overhead light. There was a basin and a UV microwave thing. A bank of shallow drawers labelled in print too fine to read at this distance.

His focus was on the man sitting on a wheeled stool behind a narrow bench. He wore scruffy blue jeans and sneakers. Green-glowing eyes blinked at Kevin, from the shadow of a voluminous hoodie, and changed to frosty blue.

The man pushed a takeaway meal to one side. Fresh blood scent tweaked Kevin's hunger.

'Sit.' A thin hand, the fingernails glinting like mica, pointed to a plastic chair.

Kevin sat. 'You're the Needle?'

'And you're Kevin Matheson, mechanic extraordinaire.'

'Not any more.'

'Who referred you to me?'

'No one, really. There was a guy mentioned you. Bhagwan. Up Rocky way.'

'I know of him.'

'He said you told him Jasmine Turner was setting up out west.'

'Did he?'

'Not in so many words, but that was the gist.'

'Ah, *the gist*. And what else did he intimate?'

'It means you know someone inside the VS operation; someone well connected, who could help me.'

The Needle leaned forward, as though bringing Kevin into focus. The movement offered a better view of the man's face, the suggestion of criss-crossing scars on nose, forehead and cheeks; of thin lips and sharp-tipped teeth; an appearance rattish and avaricious. Kevin could imagine that pointed nose twitching, those eyes blinking, the claws preening whiskers as he weighed the amount of cheese to be gained against the obvious risk of the suspected trap.

'Help you to get inside Thorn to kill the Strigoi. Is that right?'

'Blake tell you that?' Kevin asked.

The tattooist waved an enigmatic hand. 'Assuming I can provide you with the connections you need. What's in it for me?'

'How about, no Strigoi?'

'There is barely any Strigoi now. Since returning from her escapade in the west, she has fallen into bedlam. She is no threat to anyone.'

'What? Are you sure?' Kevin sat back, rubbed his face. He knew the dangers of bedlam. But Mira had seemed so *alive* when they'd last met. Crazy, but alive.

'You didn't know?'

He shook his head.

'Does this change things?'

Did it? He didn't know. 'Can she come back?'

'If anyone can, she can. I gather it's a little like being in a whirlpool. Throw someone a rope, they might be able to climb out.'

'Bedlam or not, she's still got something I want.'

'Are you sure she's in a position to give it to you? Or, for that matter, that you're able to–'

'I have to try!'

'Sounds to me as if you might be caught in a whirlpool of your own.'

'Just get me inside Thorn. I'll worry about getting myself out.'

The Needle leaned back, crossed his arms. 'In a fortnight or so, me and mine will be expected to provide Maximilian with a sample of our blood – a show of fealty. His ersatz bloodhag – Mira's apprentice, if you like – will sift those samples, potentially revealing this meeting. Just talking to you puts my life on the line.'

Kevin stood, straining ears seeking sounds of betrayal.

The Needle sounded tired as he gestured toward the door. 'Go home, boy. Live your life.'

'I have no home.'

From under the cowl came the hint of a grim smile. 'It's where the heart is.'

Kevin leaned on the back of the chair, his grip tight, and said, slow and low: 'Mira killed my mother. In cold blood. Just because she could.'

'Mira has killed many mothers. And fathers, and children.' He paused, as though distracted by something at the corner of his vision, something out of place he'd just noticed. 'Tell me about Danica.'

'She's not on the table.'

'I have a friend who would like very much to meet with her. To put to her a proposition. It would be in her favour, from what I gather.'

'I'm not in a position to speak for her.'

The Needle raised a finger. 'But you are in a position to set up a meeting. Give and take, favour for a favour: that's how our world turns, Kevin the mechanic. Some favours are worth considerable risk.'

The deal sat between them, slippery and pointed, a black snake with two heads.

Voices murmured on the other side of the curtain. The waves rolled hypnotically on the shore. A seagull called; further away, a plane droned. The everyday world filled the silence as Kevin and this strange man discussed something far from the everyday.

Kevin slipped back into the chair. 'She won't kill anyone,' he said, hoping to disappoint.

'That is not her talent.'

'I could ask her, I suppose. But she'd need more information; she won't see just anyone.'

'You get me a meeting with Danica, and I can ask my contact about getting you inside Thorn to kill her daughter.'

Kevin flinched. The brutality smarted. Maybe it was as well his parents couldn't see him, this thing he had become. They would want justice, though, wouldn't they? He forced himself to calm, to un-fist his hands.

'What if she won't agree to meet your friend?'

'The risk to me is great. If Maximilian were to find out I had helped you when he's given express orders for your capture?' He made a sudden chopping motion across his own throat. 'No, in this present unsettled climate, I cannot afford to take careless risks. You are a wanted man, after all.'

'Wanted by who?'

'Whom. You've been in the papers. The police, VS, others looking to please VS: they all want you.' He shook his head, as though the idea amused him.

Kevin studied the man, but he was contained, impenetrable. 'You didn't set me up, did you? At the tattoo shop?'

'If I wanted to deliver you to Maximilian, I would have done just that. Most likely, your enquiries reached ears other than my own. Only the snitch and Johnny Slick know who betrayed you.'

'The Fonzie dude.' Kevin nodded, seeing a way forward. 'Okay, where do I find him?'

'You think he'll tell you who he was working for?'

'One way or another, sure.'

'Very well. Flash was a friend of mine, and a damn fine needle man. He taught me a lot. Slick's gang runs on the south side. Melpomene will show you where. I suspect they've gone to ground. Maximilian won't be happy that he crossed the river without permission – assuming he didn't have permission, of course. But I doubt the Old Man would've sanctioned it when he could've just sent his own troops to bring you in. No, there's a snake in the woodpile. Go, flush it out, and let me know what you find. Just remember – in a fortnight, I'm expected to tithe, and by doing so, or not doing so, I will be just as wanted as you.'

'You'll do that though. You'll help me get Mira?'

'One step at a time, boy. You bring Danica to the table, and yes, I'll help you. Just be sure you can live with the consequences.'

Kevin held out his hand. The Needle shook it. Just like that, the deal was done. He should've been happy, right?

THIRTEEN

Kevin found the others outside. Greaser and the boy were throwing rocks at low-swooping flying foxes.

'Fucking foxes,' Argent said. 'We'll have to move on soon.'

'Should they be doing that?' Kevin asked as Mel stood beside him.

Mel twisted her lips, as though the answer was something caught in her teeth.

'There are foxes, and there are foxes,' Greaser said.

'You'll get your ears clipped one day,' Mel warned them before hustling Greaser to the car.

'They're spies,' the Needle's girl said from the motorhome's doorway, and when Kevin turned to her with his best *what the fuck* expression, she added, 'Kind of like drones?'

'Jesus.' Kevin hunched against the flapping of wings as he strode to the Monaro.

'All good?' Mel asked.

'Good enough. Strange-looking bloke.'

'That he is.'

'He was eating something disgusting.'

'Probably *sangue reale*. A kind of calzone made specially for him. He did the restaurant owner a favour once.'

Kevin unlocked the car.

Mel, looking across the roof at him, asked, 'So what now?'

'Do you know where I'd find the Viscounts?'

'Oh,' Greaser said.

'Are you asking me to come with you?' Mel asked.

'The Needle said you might.'

Greaser clambered into the back seat. 'Blake won't like it.'

Mel grinned. 'Well, in that case: better get our skates on.'

They drove across the soaring southbound arch of the twin Gateway bridges, the river far below. Blue light washed over them as they went through a toll point. A sign told him the number to ring to pay if he didn't have a pass.

'You're quiet,' Mel said.

'Just thinking.'

'It'll get ya down,' Greaser said.

'What do you know about this Johnny Slick?'

'He runs the Viscounts,' Mel said. 'They're von Schiller's *villeins*. Like the Needle's Snipes.' She gestured with a thumb to Greaser, who waved an acknowledgement. 'They pay tribute to Max in return for being allowed to live in Brissie.'

'What kind of tribute?'

'A tithe, they call it. Once a month – more often now – the blood van does the rounds, and everyone, vampires and red-eyes and hangers-on, gives up a pint or three for the Old Man.'

'And what does he do with it?' Kevin asked.

'Sifts it. Think of it like drug testing athletes. Keeping tabs on who's doing what, and who wants to do what. Hard to keep secrets in the blood.'

'The rest gets made into brew,' Greaser said. 'Feeds the troops.'

'So if everyone just didn't turn up–'

'The penalty for not paying the tithe is death,' Mel said. 'Although you've arrived at an interesting time. Max is short of two things, thanks to you: cow's blood and soldiers. They mix bovine blood with human blood. Helps it go further. He's got his claws in the blood banks, the hospitals; his own blood bags, obviously, but still, he's got a lot of mouths to feed. When you took out Jasmine Turner's farm, coupled with the loss of Bhagwan's, well, supplies have been running low. There have been a lot of blood drives in the media, lately, as well as the tithes among us nightfolk.'

'The natives are getting restless,' Greaser said. 'They don't like being tapped so hard.'

'And Max has even fewer troops to enforce his law,' Mel said. 'The Debacle took out a bunch of his best troops. So now he's short on soldiers and short on food. He's on shaky ground.'

'Why not just make more vampires?' Kevin asked.

'He can't make just anyone. He likes men and women who are used to working in security, who are used to taking orders and keeping their mouths shut. Soldiers, police; skills he can use immediately.'

'Thugs,' Greaser interjected.

'It takes a while, as you can appreciate, for a newborn to come into its abilities. Families, friends, lives, all those loose ends; out with the old, in with the new. No, Kev, you have dealt him a serious blow; so serious, it just might've made the cracks in the operation you need to slip in and finish the job.'

'I just want justice. That's all.'

'You like Metallica, don't you, Kevin?'

'Yeah, sure,' he said, taken aback by the sudden change of direction. 'The early stuff. Up until the Black Album; they kinda–'

'All I'm saying is, you want *Justice for All*, sometimes you have to *Ride the Lightning*.'

FOURTEEN

The car park was perhaps half full. The way the vehicles were clumped around the stadium entrance suggested a drive-in theatre. Adding to the impression was the high concentration of classic vehicles: plenty of fins and white walls and wide American grilles.

People clustered around the front doors, lit by an outline of naked bulbs: some goths, and boys with slicked-back hair and rolled-up sleeves and girls in billowing skirts, their hair coiffed in rolls and waves and fringes.

'No guns,' Mel warned.

'That's not good,' Kevin said, thinking of the weapons in the boot, feeling naked as they got out of the Monaro.

'I'll stay with the car, eh,' Greaser said.

'Keep the motor running.' Kevin passed her the keys.

'Greaser really likes your car,' Mel said as they walked toward the arena.

'She can take a number.'

The gaggle at the entrance gave them the once over. Mel caught the bulk of their interest and Kevin didn't mind. *Forget me*, he willed them. *I'm nobody.*

At the door, a guy in a tight shirt with a tattoo of a hot rod on his upper arm stopped them and pointed to the cashier.

Mel pulled her necklace out and dangled the pendant in front of his eyes like a television hypnotist. A rose with a ruby, or some red stone, in the centre.

The guy huffed and said, 'What about him?'

'He's my plus one,' Mel said, and assumed the crucifix position so he could pat her down.

Kevin followed suit.

Having found nothing, the guy waved them through. He spoke into a walkie-talkie once they were past.

'See if you can find Slick,' Mel said. 'He might be keeping low after last night's adventure.'

'You're certain he'll show?'

'There's Rabbit, his squeeze.' She pointed out a woman in a skimpy fluoro green outfit and wig. She was whizzing around the rink with a pack of skaters in pursuit. 'He'll be here.'

'Maybe we should've waited till the show was over,' Kevin suggested as they moved through the crowd. The rink was circled with bleachers. Some braver fans sat on the edge of the rink with only a rope between them and the action. 'What's to stop Slick from taking another shot?'

'Not in front of this many witnesses. I hope. But I agree, the sooner we're out of here, the better–'

'Fuck!' Kevin swore and dragged Mel behind a hotdog stand.

'We're in serious shit. That's Hunter. One of Mira's men.'

The bastard was at the entrance, flashing an ID at the bouncer. He wore the same tired long-coat Kevin remembered from out west; possibly the same rumpled suit, though both would've been the worse for wear after their run-in. Must have a boring wardrobe, Kevin thought, though he supposed his own wouldn't have offered much variety: check shirts, black T-shirts, blue jeans.

'His name isn't Hunter,' Mel said.

'That's what I call him.'

Hunter had a woman with him, also in black, but a lot smarter dressed; her suit shiny, and not a hair out of place in her severe bob cut. She didn't look the sort to let herself be patted down. And sure enough, they weren't, Hunter leading her toward a private box high up on the other side of the rink. Tinted glass turned the occupants to mere shadows.

'Damn it, he's probably heading for Slick,' Kevin said.

'We might have to settle for second best,' Mel said. 'Rabbit's been subbed off. Shall we pay our respects?'

They made their way to the team's area, ducked under the rail and pushed their way through the huddle of players to where the girl with the green boob tube and hot pants sat on a chair behind the rope "suicide line".

The girl watched them, her eyes shaded by the fringe of her wig and outlined in glittery green paint. Sweat glistened on her flesh. She still wore her knee and elbow pads, the outline of her helmet indented in her fairy floss wig. 'What are you doing this side of the river, Mistress Mel? Didn't pick you for a derby fan.'

She seemed nervous, flicking her gaze toward the box at the far end of the rink. Her eyes glazed red as they caught the side light, then flicked back to their native blue as she focused on Mel. A tattoo of a dancing skeleton in a top hat stood out amid the reds and greens and blues of Betty Boops and blue birds that sleeved her arms and shoulders. A white bunny peeked out from behind the boob tube.

'Okay, Rabbit?' another girl asked as she handed her an American-style bowling jersey.

'Fans,' Mel said.

Rabbit confirmed with a tight, 'It's cool', as she stood to shrug the jersey on.

Mel leaned in close and asked, 'Who sent Johnny northside last night, Rabbit?'

'I dunno what you're on about.'

'Mind if I take a sip, then?'

'Are you kidding? Johnny will have your guts for garters if you so much as nick me!'

'Johnny's in hot water, Rabbit. Tried to take the head off my chum here. And now he's got the VS hunting his autograph. See?'

She waved at the box, where Hunter and his partner were badging a Viscount guarding the door.

'If you cause any trouble here, you'll be in it just as deep,' Rabbit said, her voice trembling.

'That we will. But you won't be around to see it.'

The woman paled. 'You wouldn't dare.'

'I take headhunting very seriously. So does my friend, especially when it's his head. Now who sent Slick after him? C'mon, it'll be our little secret.'

'Shit,' Kevin said. 'I think Hunter's seen me.'

The cop had walked to the rail and was staring at him. His partner was at his shoulder, seemingly torn between joining him and keeping an eye on the box. A waiter in white pushed past the woman, a tray of drinks balanced in both hands. Hunter walked toward the stairs, his partner hesitantly following as she peered in Kevin's direction.

The box exploded.

The hum of the crowd, the nasal commentary, ceased. A skater tripped and fell, tumbling across the track as the others pulled up in a confused mob.

Smoke poured from the shattered stand. Hunter sagged across the rail. There was no sign of his partner.

Rabbit tottered forward a few steps. 'Johnny? Oh my god, Johnny?'

A drink seller in white trousers and shirt tossed his paper hat, pulled a handgun from his tray of goodies and shot two men guarding a side door.

More shots crashed the numb silence.

The bouncer went down.

The competitors scattered in a clash of skates. People screamed. A few, then a herd charged toward the doors.

'Grab her,' Mel shouted at Kevin as Rabbit pushed past, screaming, 'Johnny!'

Kevin snatched, got a handful of hair, only to have it come off in his hand. Bloody wig!

Rabbit collided with a fleeing person, caught her balance, made to set off.

Kevin snared her top and reefed her down on her back with a whuff of air.

Mel decked Rabbit's friend as she moved to help. 'Grab her! This way! Out the back!'

He grasped Rabbit under the arms and hauled. Mel cleared a path through the exodus.

More shots sounded and a nearby window shattered. Shards flew from the wall: Hunter, pistol in a two-handed grip, trying his luck as he fought through the chaos. Had his hands not been full, Kevin might've flipped him the bird. Any doubt that VS knew he was in town had been extinguished.

The surging crowd swept him outside. Taipan's instincts overcame Kevin's, leaving his consciousness sidelined, while his maker's muscle memory raced him through the throng: punching, blocking, dodging.

Rabbit twisted and yanked in his grip; the crowd jostled them. Someone darted at him, a knife flashing. He decked him in a crunch of bone, a reflex both wonderful and terrifying.

When Kevin reached the Monaro, there was blood on his hands, but he still had Slick's girl, struggling and swearing and very much afraid.

Greaser hauled the door open and pushed the seat forward. 'You're making friends, ain'tcha?'

Kevin shoved the girl in the rear and locked the seat in place as she flew at him, nails flashing, screaming to be let go.

'Where's Mel?' Greaser asked.

'She's... she was right behind me.'

They looked toward the stadium: smoke spilled from one end, gunshots sounded. Cars revved around them. The air was filled with smoke and exhaust and screams.

'Shit, I'll have to go back.'

Sirens announced that might not be a good idea. Greaser said, 'Don't be an idiot. She can look after herself. We need to clear out.'

She glared at him and added, 'But man, if anything's happened to her, I'll kill you myself.'

FIFTEEN

Reece sat back on his haunches beside the body, holstered his pistol and pulled out his tobacco pouch. Sweat dripped from his nose, stuck his shirt to his skin. Around him, cars streamed for the exits; bees fleeing the hive in a buzz of motors and shouts, exhaust hanging thick and choking in the humid night air.

Felicity hobbled over to where he sat outside the entrance Matheson had disappeared through. Her left arm was propped inside her tattered jacket, making her look like a Napoleon who'd been through a blender. Half her face was a raw swipe mark, the other half soot-stained and splattered with blood. She stank of burned hair and raw offal – something she'd stepped in, perhaps. Her vest had offered some protection from the blast.

'Slick?' he asked.

'Bits 'n' pieces. After the waiter went boom, some massive motherfucker in a Driza-Bone did some slicing and dicing. Four arms. You know him?'

'*Four arms*?' Always a new surprise in this job, but this was a new kind of special.

'Uh-huh. Took Slick's head with some kind of machete.'

Reece mumbled an expletive and finished rolling his cigarette. Johnny Slick hadn't been particularly forthcoming during their short exchange. Maybe having Reece's pistol pushed up under his jaw might've had something to do with that.

'How's the head, Slick?' he'd asked on entering the booth.

'Dunno what you mean,' Slick had replied, barely looking up from his blood soda. The greaseball looked plenty pale. A round through the head would do that. He was lucky it hadn't done permanent damage, but then, with mutts like Slick, you could never be certain.

'You've been out of bounds.'

'Prove it.'

'I was there, sport. I traded slugs with your merry band of fuck-knuckles. I've got you on film. You don't want me to call in the full GS, do you? Maybe spread the headaches around?'

'As if you could. The Old Man's losing his grip. He's toothless. You're toothless.'

'This isn't.' He pushed Slick's head back with the gun.

'You won't get three steps,' Slick muttered.

'There's no guarantee you will, either. Not at this range. Probably take out your spine. Maybe the brain stem.'

Felicity stood at the door, covering the muscle.

'Now, who sent you to do over the tattooist?'

He'd looked at Reece, then at Felicity, then back to Reece, and smiled.

'I did it for the money.'

Then Felicity interrupted: 'Is that the grease monkey over there? Hassling Slick's squeeze?'

'What's that?' Slick said, and Reece had backed away with a warning about making any sudden moves.

It'd been Matheson, all right. With some goth chick.

'One of the Romantics,' Felicity told him. 'Blake's moll.'

Reece headed for the stairs and Matheson spotted him. Then

the waiter had pushed past with an order, and he'd heard Slick say, 'What the fuck's this? We got our drinks already,' and there was a gunshot, and then the explosion.

And here they were. Slick in bits 'n' pieces, Felicity out on her feet and Reece feeling decidedly seedy.

They'd been lucky; albeit inadvertently, Matheson had saved their lives.

'What've you got there?' Felicity asked as she holstered her weapon.

'Blake's moll.'

He'd found her in the chaotic exodus of rockabillies and bobby-soxers. Staked her, right through the fucking heart. But Matheson had got away.

Sirens approached. The car park emptied.

'We're going to lose, aren't we?' Felicity said, and he heard, saw, the fear. Ever since he'd been convinced to serve Mira, he'd had the underlying belief that he was on the wrong side. He could imagine, though, how the realisation must've come as a shock to Felicity.

'The game's not over yet,' he said. 'Little miss eyeliner here is an accessory after the fact. I'm sure Maximilian will get something out of her.'

'Poor bitch,' Felicity said.

SIXTEEN

Heinrich and two of his personal bodyguard from the elite Fallschirmjaeger – crème de la crème of the GS, eagle flashes on their shoulders marking them as the truly obnoxious – were waiting with a trolley when Reece and Felicity arrived at Thorn. With the streeter strapped down, they rode the express lift to 13. Reece hated going to 13. It's where the reality of the city was most tenuous. That Heinrich's bulk filled the lift didn't help. Maximilian's right-hand man said nothing, just stood with his feet apart and hands behind his back, staring at the doors as though daring them to stick and give him an excuse to tear them apart.

The doors opened and the troopers wheeled the trolley down a softly lit hall to the conference room. Through the windows, traffic pulsed like corpuscles, all red and white, running in and out through the city's dark veins and arteries.

The troopers took guard at the door. More eagle flashes; Heinrich's men.

Reece helped himself to water from the cooler and studied the view. He could see the room reflected in the window. Felicity seemed unsure what to do; she smoothed Melpomene's skirt, though it didn't need it, and then walked over as though to also pour a drink but then changed her mind. The burn had left an ugly mark across her cheek and ear; it'd be a day or two before it was fully healed.

Maximilian entered. He stalked over to the girl on the trolley and studied her. The stake glinted amid the black material of her dress.

'This is not the mechanic,' he said, sounding confused. 'Nor is it Johnny Slick.'

'Slick's dead,' Reece said. 'This girl was with the mechanic.'

'She's Blake's progeny,' Felicity added. 'The villein who runs the Romantics.'

Maximilian fixed her with his gaze. 'I know who Blake is. What I don't know is what his *Blütkind* was doing with the mechanic.'

'Blake does dirty deeds for the Needle,' Felicity said.

'Ah.' Maximilian stroked the girl's hair, almost paternally. 'So this girl is our bridge, from Blake to the Needle to the mechanic. She can carry our message. And what of the leak?'

'We have a possible conduit, but we still don't know the source.' Reece looked at Heinrich, who stared through him at the city. 'Someone who doesn't want the Strigoi to recover, would be my guess.'

'She was not popular, my daughter,' Maximilian said. 'She wore her power boldly; brashly.'

He called Heinrich over and concentrated on the girl, patting her cheek, her hair.

Heinrich told Felicity she'd been seconded to the Gespenstenstaffel, and with what seemed a glint of relish in his eyes, ordered Reece to report to the second floor. 'It's ticket collecting for you, *Private*. Maybe you can manage that.'

'The leak?' Reece asked.

'No longer your concern. Now that you're fodder. Give Marshall my regards. I believe you two have established quite the rapport.'

A guard opened the door. Reece and Felicity stepped through to the foyer, almost running into two Hunters.

'Step aside, old timer,' one said.

'Why, if it isn't Laurel and Hardy,' Reece replied.

The two men paused, blocking their way: Newman, with his no neck and vulpine eyes, his designer suit crisp and shiny; and Petersen, older but no less rapacious with his hatchet face and balding head and slightly rumpled suit, a ruffled rooster full of piss and vinegar.

'You're out, Cagney and Lacey,' Newman said. 'Time to let the professionals take over.'

Reece felt Felicity bridle, but he took her forearm and led her away. Two GS troopers were at the lift, waiting to make sure they left.

'Great,' Felicity said as the doors slid shut. 'Fucking great.'

'Sorry. Looks like you're riding the soup vans for a bit longer.'

'Not your fault.' She caressed his arm, her fingers lingering. 'I can't believe he busted you to Security.'

'See out my days behind a desk. Checking the doors. Patting down visitors. Not so bad.'

'You'll hate it.'

He shrugged. 'Bar?'

'Shouldn't we report?'

'He wasn't specific on the when.'

'You're going to be cleaning latrines by the end of the week.'

'It's all just shovelling shit.'

She laughed. 'Sure. Let me freshen up first. Half an hour?'

He let her out on the sixth floor, where the Hunters had their quarters, and he realised with a sense of surprise that he would miss his room on 3.

He went back up to 11, and got as far as the observation room, and only then because he knew the nurse. 'Absolutely no visitors', she said, by order of the Hospitaller himself, Herr Doktor Tran. She spoke into a phone once she'd left him.

It didn't matter. Mira was in no condition to talk. He eyed her through the thick one-way glass. The walls were padded, the minimal furniture and bed shaped from moulded plastic. She wore a white gown, her hair black amid the white. Her arms had been covered in protective sleeves to prevent her from gnawing herself.

It was a far cry from the Mira he knew. Her flesh, cold and tight, and then running hot and soft with his blood. How, in those early days, when he'd drunk too much, and spewed, and depending on her mood, she'd mocked him, or sympathised, or been angry at the waste, as though his inability to hold his drink was a personal insult: 'Do you squander my gift?'

And that laugh, and her fingers in his hair, and on his cock, and her legs opening to him, though it meant little to her, not after the blood, though sometimes, sometimes he thought maybe, just maybe, he'd touched her, that the groan was real, skin on skin rather than blood in vein. Love in vain. Old habits.

Mira looked up from where she sat on the hospital bed, staring, as though she could sense his presence.

Maybe she could, at some level of awareness. Her left arm still held several rings of scar tissue showing her active blood links: one for Vee, one for Kevin Matheson, one for Reece, one for Felicity. In anyone else those links would've dissolved by now without fresh blood to renew them. But Mira was Strigoi, a bloodhag of the highest order.

He could still feel her, way down in his system; forty years of mutual feeding didn't just evaporate. But her blood had lost its potency. He was in menopause, slowly reverting to merely mortal as the vampire essence failed to fight off normal aging. He was slowing down. Maybe a desk job was all he was fit for.

She stood, making him frown. She was in bedlam, trapped in the tempest of all the lives she'd imbibed, her sanity being torn apart by the ghosts of those she'd taken into herself. Preservation, to some; collection, to others.

Once, Reece would've called it murder.

She shouldn't even know he was here. She shouldn't even know where *she* was.

And yet she hobbled to the mirror and raised a hand, then two, and laid her face against the glass so her cheek pressed flat and distorted in his vision. Her lips were cracked, her fangs out, her eyes swirling with purple and green in the subdued light of her room.

In his mind, he saw a car. Yellow, with a thick black stripe on the bonnet. *A classic.*

He smiled, held his fingers to her lips, and turned as the door opened and the orderlies arrived. 'By orders of–'

'Yeah, yeah.'

At the lift, security men in olive uniforms waited to usher him to his new quarters. The lift stopped one floor down. Marshall got in, the Green Shirts got out.

'I hear you're one of mine, now.' Her smile chilled him.

'The intimation was that I already was.'

'The mechanic will come for the poet's girl, you think?'

'He came for his mother and his girlfriend out west. That didn't end well. For anyone.'

'Then we'd better find him, hadn't we?'

'I was told I was off the case.'

'I thought you were told you were working for me.'

He watched the numbers count down. The lift felt like a vice, closing in on all sides.

'You like him,' Marshall said.

'*Like* is too strong a word.'

'Respect, then. Pity?'

'Do not doubt that I will do my duty, Madam Marshall.'

'Not for one minute. File a full report to me, then get some rest, Reece. I've got you on the day shift.'

He groaned.

'Since The Debacle, we've been on twelve-hour rotas,

stretching the manpower. Besides, it won't hurt for you to be off the night shift's radar for a bit.'

The doors slid open. Marshall got out. The lift continued its downward journey.

SEVENTEEN

Kevin pulled the Monaro into a side street. Houses slumped behind sagging fences; yards were overgrown, walls stained, windows curtained.

The scent of blood and gunpowder filled the car. Hunger and adrenaline had reduced Kevin's vision to shotgun barrels. Greaser hugged her door, Taser in one hand as she watched his every move.

Rabbit hunched in the back seat, her face smeared with tears. 'What are you going to do?'

'Get your skates off the seat,' Kevin told her, needing to be brutish, afraid for Mel and afraid for this girl. His voice grated out, strained by the dryness of his mouth, the effort of control.

She lowered her feet, her knees pressed tight together, hands balled in her lap.

He tried to block his senses, to still the hunger that had pricked at the smell and sight of her fear and blood and sweat, the hammer of heart and pulse of artery.

Ride it, he told himself. Use it. But don't give in to it. He gripped the steering wheel in both hands and found Rabbit's eyes in the rear-view mirror.

'Tell me who sent Slick to capture me, and you can walk. That's the deal.'

'I don't know what you're talking about.'

Kevin turned, appraising her through the gap between the front seats. His gums ached momentarily as his fangs extended. 'Your blood won't lie.'

She shivered, her arms locked across her breasts, her legs twitching.

'Think of the upholstery, Kev,' Greaser said, her voice tight.

'Someone inside Thorn,' Rabbit said. 'High up, Slick said. Cocky, he was, like we was finally getting some recognition. Maybe even make the jump to vassal. Sky's the limit, that's what he said. I'd be a made girl, he said.' Tears tracked her make-up. Her lip trembled. Glitter sparkled in the smudged eyeliner around her eyes. 'Do you think he's... Oh god.'

'Can't you tell?' Greaser asked. 'You're his moll, after all.'

'I can't feel him.' She rubbed her arms. Her voice cracked. 'I can't feel him at all.'

'Did he say who?' Kevin asked. 'Think. Who sent him after me?'

'Just someone close to the top who needed a favour. Snatch and grab; or decap, if it came to it. I told Johnny it was a bad idea. Out of our league, I said.' She rubbed her face, sniffed. 'He didn't agree. The bloody idiot.'

Kevin stepped from the car, walked around and got Greaser to let Rabbit out. The roller girl hesitated; he gestured angrily as though he might change his mind. She clomped, ungainly on her skates, onto the grass verge, keeping as far from him as she could.

A glint on her jacket caught his eye: a dancing skeleton brooch. He stepped closer, pointing. 'Slick had this design on his van.'

Rabbit cupped a hand over it. 'It's mine.'

'Her badge,' Greaser said, and flicked one amid the cluster on her own jacket: a long-nosed, long-legged bird that Kevin had mistaken for a kiwi though now he could see they were nothing alike. 'Mine's a snipe, see? Shows I run with the Needle's outfit. Dancing skeleton means the Viscounts.'

Kevin pulled Rabbit's hands away. She fell to her knees and he tore the brooch from the material.

'Well,' he said, pocketing the brooch, 'you won't be needing that, wherever you're going.'

'Who were they?' she asked. 'Who did this to us?'

'You don't know?' Kevin asked.

She shook her head, then reached to him; he helped her up.

'What's so special about you?' Rabbit asked. 'That you're worth dying for?'

'Nothin', as far as I'm concerned.'

'Is that Snipe your top girl?'

'I don't have a top girl,' he said, disengaging himself.

She bit her lip, tugged at her clothes to straighten them, pushed her matted fringe from her forehead with shaking fingers. 'I know people. I could help you.'

Greaser sneered. 'Aren't you all cut up about your boyfriend?'

'He's, he's gone, and I'm... I've got no one.'

Greaser snorted as she got back in the car.

'The other girls hated me for being Johnny's. I don't have anywhere to go.'

Greaser stuck her head out of the window. 'There's the factory.'

The pleading gave way to mettle. 'Do I look like a dairy cow to you?'

'Sure.'

'I should rip your tits off, Snipe.'

Kevin sat in the driver's seat and Rabbit tottered behind him, more assured on bitumen. She caught the door before he closed it. 'Wait.'

He stared at her.

'I'm a good top girl. The best. We could look after each

other. Better than any Snipe. She's not even a red-eye, just a chewie.'

'Greaser's not my top girl. I don't keep favourites. You should get out, while you can.'

She let go the door. 'You'll be sorry. They'll take your head, and I just hope I'm there to see it!'

In the rear-view mirror, Kevin saw her hugging herself as she watched them drive off. Then she turned and started trudging in the opposite direction.

'Will she be all right?' he asked.

'That sort always is. She'll find someone new to abuse her.'

Greaser gave him directions to get back to the northside.

Once he was on the main drag, he asked, 'So who do you think put them on to me? Someone going behind Maximilian's back?'

'You should talk to the Needle or Mel about it. They're up with all that stuff.'

'I might just do that,' Kevin said. 'So you're not a red-eye, eh.'

'I'm just a Snipe. Eyes and ears for the Needle. Errand girl.'

'Chewie?'

'Don't get any ideas. No one slurps on me.'

'I said I was sorry.'

'Whatever.'

'I've just not heard of a chewie before. So Mel isn't one of the Needle's Snipes. She's with Blake and his bunch of–'

'Romantics.'

'Yeah, real romantic. Why do you do it, then?'

'The Needle's a good man. He keeps us safe.'

They hit the Story Bridge, lanes of traffic thudding across under the skeletal twin peaks. The city rose to their left, the shorter, shadowed Valley waiting to their right.

'Mel's kind of friends with everyone,' Greaser said. 'It's the way she is. I hope she's okay.' She pulled out her phone and made a call. 'The Needle says to go to ground till we hear from him.' She pointed to the left. 'Maybe swing past Blake's; see if Mel's got in touch. He should know where she's at, given their blood link and all.'

Kevin followed the sign to the city. 'As long as he doesn't want me to recite poetry.'

EIGHTEEN

He was going to be late for drinks.

The security men marched Reece to the quartermaster's office on 2 where he was issued new interim ID. He'd also had to forfeit all false documentation for dealing with the mundane world, but he didn't mention the off-the-books dossiers that he considered to be his insurance policy, tucked away off-base at several bolt holes. No point dealing with forgers if you couldn't get the occasional favour done.

He wasn't allowed to return to his room. A carton of his belongings was delivered for him to store in a locker in the barracks. Half his clothes, none of his books and a few of his CDs arrived.

'Where's the rest of my gear?' he asked the orderly, who admitted that the cleaners had thrown out his "musty old books" and that was all the music that had been found. 'Who the hell uses discs these days?' the whippersnapper said as though by way of explanation. No grog, either, and his laptop had been repossessed. They'd never been as quick to issue equipment; things obviously went faster going downhill.

He collected his over-starched olive-green uniforms and

leather boots, new and squeaky and uncomfortably pinchy. Stared at them, realising only now just how low he'd fallen. He squared his gear away and headed up to 14.

Felicity was at the bar, either being hit on or being quizzed by an off-duty guard. The guy shoved off when Reece approached, his curiosity or his hopefulness not stretching that far. They had a drink, he told her about his books and the barracks and his fear of snorers; she touched his hand and told him she was sorry, and admitted she had yet to be evicted from her room on 6. She was still a Hunter, however long her secondment might last.

'So you've still got a room?'

'Sure.'

She touched his hand again. They went to her room, and he made sure he was gone by morning.

NINETEEN

They carved through the city, headed west along the river, into a hilly area where the streets were narrow and lined with trees and parked cars, and the peak-roofed cottages were dug from the slopes or projected out on stilted platforms.

Kevin parked on the footpath where Greaser indicated, outside a high-fenced property with a strip of unkempt lawn shaded by a mango tree, a rattan sofa on the front porch, cobwebs curtaining the balustrades.

Kevin got his gear from the car, feeling better for the comforting weight of pistol and Staker around his hips; the sword he left behind.

The gate opened with a quiet protest, one hinge gone, as they entered. Candlelight glimmered through a crack in a curtain.

Greaser bashed on a lion-headed knocker.

Blake opened the door, releasing a waft of incense and some soft instrumental tune, the strings rising and falling like surf.

'You've got a nerve.' Blake clutched his cane in one hand, the fingers stained with red and black ink. His face twitched, as though threatening to change shape. His shoulders slumped and he gestured helplessly as he told them, 'Maximilian has taken Melpomene. I've *seen* it.' He pinched the bridge of his nose, as though to drive the image away.

'Fuck,' Greaser said, and Kevin looked away, swearing under his breath, feeling the gauntlet of despair squeezing his heart.

Scarlet dotted Blake's cravat, his shirt cuffs. 'Got her up in the tower as we speak, I suspect.'

Visions of being interrogated by Mira rocked Kevin. Her nails, her fangs. The way she'd taken him into her, the way she'd invaded him and turned him inside out, shaken out his secrets and left him empty and soiled. He grabbed the door frame, pushing down the sudden rush, locking it away. And now they had Mel.

'We got separated. There was an attack–'

'Vultures, maybe,' Greaser added. 'They might've killed Johnny Slick.'

'*Maybe; might've.* You are a fucking gold mine of information, Snipe.' Blake pointed his silver-headed cane at Kevin as though the blade was already drawn. 'And you are bad news, chum. I've been asking about you, and the word is, everyone around you loses their head.'

'Not everyone,' he said softly.

'I've got a good mind to shop you, chum, an even trade: my muse for the bad penny.'

'I wouldn't do that, if I were you.'

'And why's that, then?'

Kevin smiled at him in what he hoped was a scary fashion. 'Because they're frightened of me, and they aren't frightened of you.'

'I don't follow.' But Blake stood back, the tip of the cane falling away, propping him up once more.

'They know why I'm here, and it scares them. Help me, and not only will we get Mel back, but we'll tear that tower down around their ears.'

'The way you tore down Jasmine Turner's farm? The tower ain't no squatter's humpy, chum. It's fuckin' near impregnable. You know how many fangers they got in there?'

'A lot less since they tangled with me. Surely you heard how we kicked their arse?'

'Sounded more like a draw, to me.'

'I'm still standing.'

'There's only one of you.'

'There's only one of everyone.'

Greaser thumped the door to get their attention. 'Can we maybe discuss this inside? I need to piss.'

Blake pointed with his cane. 'Loo. We'll be in the drawing room.'

Greaser went off down the central hall while Kevin followed Blake into a candlelit room. The walls were lined with piles of unshelved books. The only furniture was a small, upright desk and a high-backed stool before it.

Bella lay on a beanbag by the window, her corset torn loose, cuts in her breast and throat. Roses lay about her head.

'Is she all right?' Kevin asked.

'Of course. She's modelling as Erato. Don't disturb her.' Blake's gaze flitted to the desk. Papers covered the surface, and were scattered all over the timber floor. 'Why are you here?'

'If Max does have Mel, I want to get her back. Interested?'

Blake waved with his cane. 'Me and my murder are at your disposal.'

Kevin resisted the urge to choke the living shit out of the poet. 'You haven't infected that girl there, have you?'

'Infected?'

'Made her one of us; whatever you call it.'

'Giving someone the night without Maximilian's express permission is punishable by incineration. Balance of trade and all that.' Blake leaned his cane against the wall and fingered his fountain pen.

'Listen,' Kevin said. 'Someone in the tower is working against Max. I need your help to narrow down the field of possible suspects. Who might want to replace Maximilian?'

'Short answer: everyone. Except Heinrich, the Preceptor. He would die to protect his boss. Old, old blood buddies, they are.'

'Can you be more specific?'

'Fine.' Blake grabbed a sheet of paper, flourished his pen and scratched out a rough family tree. 'Max has five lieutenants, each responsible for a different part of the operation: supplies, business, security, that kind of thing. There's Heinrich, his loyal stooge, and four others. That's the Von Schiller Corp board, right there.

'They've got their own sergeants: Familiares, PAs, whatever they want to call them, right; all keen for the big kiss – the goodbye daylight, hello eternity.

'Out here–' he dashed off two Xs, one big, one small '–is the Strigoi and her Seer – daddy's girl, forget about her; if only you could, right? Ha!

'But her offsider,' he scrawled a big circle around the smaller of the two Xs 'is a strange egg. That one, gives me the willies. So who knows? Power corrupts and all that.

'And then there's the rest of the council – what they call vassals: gangs who've got down on bended knee in return for scraps from the table. And then there's the villeins, which is all the rest of us streeters – most of them would give their left nut for a seat on the council.'

He scrawled a mass of violent Xs across the page, ending in a brutal jab that ran out of ink, tore the paper and broke the nib. The diagram looked like a game of hangman played by a maniac.

'What would you give for a seat on the council?'

'Me?' Blake's hand went to his throat as though he was choking. 'I'm an *artist*, not a politician.'

Kevin pointed at the mess on the page. 'Someone in there

tried to sabotage Jasmine Turner's operation and then made a deal with Johnny Slick to bring me in. I need to know who!'

'Strange, innit? You'd think they'd hold the door open for you, let you top Mira. Although if she's in bedlam, what's the worry? Maybe they've got more to gain from handing you over.' Blake crossed his arms. 'Now, there was talk of getting our dear Melpomene back.'

Greaser entered and ran across to Bella. 'Jesus, Blake, what've you done to her?' She held up the girl's limp hand, fingers pressed to her wrist, then her throat.

'Strawberry girl,' Blake said, as though it was obvious. 'Like a taste?' he asked Kevin. 'Love lies bleeding? Such sweet sorrow?' He groped at the air as though catching moths.

'Just see if you can find out who Slick was working for,' Kevin told him. 'Find them and we might have an ally inside the tower. Someone who can help us rescue Mel.'

Greaser snorted. 'I think he's already casting for a new muse. Bella?' She shook the girl, who lay unmoving.

Blake ignored her. 'The enemy of my enemy is my friend. And yet,' he pointed his pen at Kevin 'you lose my Melpomene and you refuse my hospitality. I'm getting the feeling we're not friends.'

'You find out what I need to know, and we will get Mel back. I promise you that.'

Greaser swore. 'Kev – I think she's dying.'

Kevin went across to Bella. Barely any heartbeat. Next to no breath.

'Hold her mouth open.' He pulled his knife and sliced his wrist, forcing the blood to flow, a trickle he fed into the girl's mouth as Greaser massaged her throat. His body fought him; it didn't like giving up its vitality.

'Idiots!' Blake said. 'There's no beauty in this!'

'We should take her with us,' Greaser said.

'I'm not the safest person to be around.'

'Safer than his nibs there.'

'Yes,' Blake hissed, 'you should leave, and take that blood sack with you. Thoroughly *uninspiring*. And now you've gone and polluted her with your rural taint.'

'Is he all right?' Kevin whispered as they heaved Bella to her feet.

Greaser raised her eyebrows, a universal sign for *fucked if I know*.

Blake thrust papers into his leather satchel. 'Let's reconvene tomorrow night, what do you say? Maybe dream up a new plan?'

Kevin hefted Bella into his arms. There was colour in her cheeks, a flush in her throat. One pink nipple pointed up at him from the mess of her chest. He ground his teeth against the desire to take back what he'd given, to bite into that tender flesh and drink his fill.

'Just see if you can find out who Johnny Slick was working for, Blake. We'll be here after dark.'

'Not here! No, that will never do,' Blake muttered. 'VS is a ponderous beast, but it won't be long before they have a good snifter of our Melpomene's claret and come a'knocking. It won't do to have you here, in revolutionary discourse. No, that won't do at all.' He tapped his chin, stared at the ceiling, mumbled, then raised one finger in a eureka moment. 'Toowong! Let us converse with the spirits, seek inspiration among the whispers of the dead, those silent, blind witnesses to our talk of treachery.'

'You talkin' about the cemetery?' Greaser asked.

'The Mayne crypt. An hour after sundown. Enough time for you to fly from your belfry?'

Kevin looked at Greaser and she answered, 'That's doable. I can show you, Kev.'

Blake snapped the satchel shut with a flourish. 'My, aren't you quite the little tour guide.'

'Mel's my friend, too.'

'Yes, and I have remonstrated with her about the low

113

standards of company she keeps. I do hope I get the opportunity to say, "I told you so".'

'A charmer, aren't you, Blake,' Greaser said as she followed Kevin to the front door. She hauled it open for him.

Blake followed them and stood at the door. He rubbed his hands as though wiping off his guilt.

'At the graveyard, tomorrow,' he called. 'We three can meet again. *Fair is foul, and foul is fair*.'

TWENTY

'You want me to drop you two off somewhere? Hospital?' Kevin asked.

'You juiced her up; she'll be fine. You trying to get rid of me?'

'What Blake said was true. VS will be after me for sure.'

'You don't get off that easy. I'm sticking with you till we've got Mel back. Besides, where would you go?'

He hesitated. 'Back to base.'

'Don't be a dickhead. They got Mel. Chances are, they know your shoe size by now, not to mention whatever she took outta your blood at the Poeticals. You go back to the coffee house and you'll be Max's daily blend, for sure.'

'You have a better idea, obviously.'

'I know a place.'

'Even after I got Mel captured?'

'Because you said you'd get her back.'

'You got any ideas about how to do that?'

'No. But we can sleep on it, yeah?'

He drove, following her directions back toward the Valley.

'One thing,' she said.

'What's that?'

'Keep your fangs to yourself. You get peckish, you get your own.'

'I'm doing my best.'

'Dude, half-cut the way you are at the moment, you're no good to anyone. I see you go off into delirium; I see you eye everyone you meet like they're a rump steak on special. You need to feed if we're gonna save Mel.'

Bella groaned and prised herself up off the back seat. Her eyes flashed red as they caught the glimmer of passing street lights. Greaser filled her in on recent events.

'He called me Erato,' Bella said. 'He gave me roses. Do you think he wanted to bring me across?'

'He was killing you,' Greaser said.

'For rebirth.' A hand fluttered at her throat, her lips. 'Oh.'

'God,' Greaser said. 'Honestly, that lot should be called the Melodramatics.'

Kevin laughed.

'We'll drop her in the Valley,' Greaser said. 'She's strong enough to make little dove noises, she's strong enough to catch the train home.'

They watched the girl totter off on her high heels into the station. Then Greaser guided him into a nearby northern suburb.

They pulled up at a long, thin building holding down the corner of a whole row of copycats. Whirly gigs dotted the tin roofs at regular intervals. The roller door was down but there were cracks of light around the edges and the sound of mechanics at work: metal banging, a radio, bursts of conversation, bad karaoke and swearing.

Greaser rang the bell.

Silence fell behind the wall. The light went out.

'It's Greaser,' she shouted.

A door opened; footsteps approached from the lane; a man in overalls appeared, wrench in hand.

'It's late, Greaser.' He looked around and then caressed the Monaro with his gaze. 'But that's worth it.'

'Not for sale,' Greaser said. 'I need to garage it for a few days.'

'I don't have room for that.'

'We'll make it worth your while.'

'We?'

'My friend and I.'

Kevin rolled down the window. The man stiffened. Probably no stranger to people with funny-coloured eyes, then.

'He doesn't have a name,' Greaser said. 'One of them amnesiacs.'

'As long as he remembers where his wallet is. C'mon round the back. We'll make room. But two nights. I got orders to fill.'

'You're a sport, Barnie.'

The workers pawed the Monaro, a late-model Mazda sports car momentarily forsaken in its advanced state of dismemberment.

Kevin said nothing to anyone. His palms itched to get to work, to bury himself in that simple process of fixing something. It took all his concentration to stop from slipping into delirium, the memories of working in the garage teasing – him and his father, the smell of grease and oil, the chatter of the radio, the banging and swearing. Gone. All gone.

He grabbed the rest of his gear from the boot, satisfied the sword was hidden inside a blanket, and followed Greaser up the stairs.

'Barnie lives here, but he won't mind us spending the day as long as we're quiet and don't drink all his beer.'

Kevin scouted the flat: a lounge, a kitchen, bathroom, a bedroom, and another room filled with pieces of motorcycle, the walls plastered with semi-naked women draped over fast cars and newspaper posters of a football team.

Greaser told him to dump his gear on the sofa bed in the man cave.

'I'll dig you out some blankets and a spare pillow. You should be right here if we pull the blinds, eh.'

'Where will you be?'

'On the couch. No wandering.' She pulled the Taser from her pocket and waved it at him.

Kevin held up his hands in surrender. 'One problem, though. I've got nothing to pay your mate with. I'm totally skint.'

'I'll add it to your bill. Now make yourself comfy while I duck out for some takeaway. You'll need your wits about you.'

'You don't trust Blake?'

'I don't trust anyone,' she said. 'Except for Mel.'

'We'd better get her back, then, eh.'

TWENTY-ONE

No rest for the wicked. Nor for those on the shit list. Demoted last night, on shift this morning. But Reece didn't mind. Much. The image of the Monaro was stuck in his head. Sure, there were other images there: Mira in her asylum, Felicity in a state of undress; the ridiculous amount of shoeshine on his GPs. But today, it was all about the car.

They put him on roving patrol, a truly dull and witless routine of checking doors and hassling employees and visitors not displaying the appropriate security pass. He took it upon himself to sneak off his round to get some extra learning.

There were only two men in the security room, keeping watch on a bank of CCTV screens – mono internals, colour externals – and monitoring entry alarms. An old fella and a newbie; so many newbies, since the Debacle.

The promise of an early lunch break got the old fella out of the room without much argument, while Reece politely pestered young Kratzmann into showing him how to operate cameras and log reports. Even if he hadn't been up all night, he'd have been yawning regardless, but he tried to look interested, hoping the old fella wouldn't rush back. Reece dropped a pen, asked the kid to pick it up from the floor, since it was under his chair. Just as Kratzmann was lifting out of his seat, the leather as squeaky as Reece's new boots, Reece said, 'Did you see that?'

'See what?' The kid sounded nervous, sceptical even.

'That car. That's the third time it's circled the block in the past twenty minutes.'

'What car?'

'So you didn't see it? It's probably nothing.'

'No; nothing can get you killed.'

Reece could hear the drill sergeant's voice coming through the kid's.

'Don't worry about it.'

'What was it?'

Reece made a point of conceding. 'A yellow car. Plenty of them about, right.'

'A cab?'

'Our Yellow Cabs are orange. You ever wonder about that?'

'Not really.'

'Anyway, I'm pretty sure this was a Monaro. An old one.'

'Got a thing for cars, have you?'

'Not especially. But you know, Monaro: classic. Let's not worry about it.'

'I can run the tape back.'

They still called it tape, even though the cameras were all digital. Old habits. Oh, he knew about old habits. If he found the cunt who'd turfed his paperbacks, he'd revisit some of the more violent ones. Note to self: reorder his Spillanes.

'Nah, who would drive something that obvious if they didn't want to be seen, right?' he said.

'I can run a trace. See what's around.'

'Can you do that?'

'Sure. Here.'

And the kid showed him how to put the description in. Reece didn't provide a rego number. For starters, Matheson probably would've changed the plates, but mainly, he didn't want to flag the vehicle as hot.

'There,' Kratzmann said. 'It's in the police system now. A 1968, '69 Monaro coupe, yellow in colour, with black hood stripe. Unknown Queensland rego. Can't be too many of those around. We'll get a ping if anything shows up.'

'They'll just report it, right? I wouldn't want some poor

car lover to get the full stop 'n' search just because he drove around the block looking for the casino.'

'All good,' Kratzmann said. 'Just a matter of waiting to see if Traffic Branch spot it. They'll send it to us to action.'

'Keep me in the loop. Could be a leg-up for the both of us if it turns out to be something.'

Reece had had a bulletin out for just such a car since the Debacle, but it had got him nowhere. Maybe a fresh appeal would sharpen everyone up, especially now that Matheson was in the metro area. A lot more eyes, reporting much more quickly than out in the boondocks.

When the old fella finally returned, Reece gravely reported that there was in fact nothing to report. Kratzmann frowned at him, but Reece gave him a look and the kid kept quiet.

Reece resumed his duties. It was going to be a long day, waiting, hoping, for the Monaro to land on the radar, but he was very good at waiting.

TWENTY-TWO

During the day, Greaser had run an errand or two. There was a new Lexus in the chop shop and an Esky of plasma taken from Christ knew where. 'You owe me,' she said, and Kevin wondered how to repay larceny and whatever favours it took to find blood, even as he demolished the packs.

Showered, with a change of clothes, the hunger manageable if not sated, weapons prepared, he was ready to leave for their meeting with Blake at the cemetery shortly after sunset. He'd surprised Greaser by waking before sundown: a legacy of his maker. The older vampires Greaser knew of didn't need as much sleep, but relatively new ones like Kevin could snooze all day.

'You get any rest?' he asked as they drove out.

She yawned, said she'd got enough, used to working split shifts, and then skolled a can of Red Bull pulled from one of her pockets.

They skirted the CBD and drove west, winding through back roads to the cemetery, and parked up the top where residences crowded in. The cemetery sprawled across several hills, spotted with stands of trees and crossed with scrubby gullies. It was littered with a veritable city of gravestones and tombs. Stars strained through the dusky light pollution, the air warm but slowly thinning with a touch of the approaching autumn. The almost full moon made the headstones glow, dappling the boneyard with stark shadow.

The gates were shut, but the fence was nothing to speak of, just two rails made of steel pipes.

They crept in, sticking to the high ground as they wound their way through the graves. The stones were weathered and streaked with bird shit, fungus and mould.

Kevin kept one hand on his pistol; almost drew on a plover that gave a warning cry as they passed. He willed himself to be invisible, his skin crawling under the suspicion of watching eyes.

Greaser pointed out the highest hill. Grand monuments silhouetted on the skyline showed where the *fancy pants* were buried. There was a corridor of trees; people went there for picnics, she said, day and night.

Tonight wasn't going to be a picnic.

Nice try at lightening the mood, though, he'd give her that. She pointed out the white smudge that was the monument where they were to meet Blake and then fell silent as they sneaked down the slope.

It was about halfway up the hill, beside a road.

They found cover where floppy rubber-leafed bushes had taken root in crumbling graves. Kevin regretted having strapped on the sword as he adjusted the scabbard so he could crouch. More hindrance than it was worth.

The crypt was made of large bricks, its flat top bordered by a short, decorative stone fence more likely to be found on an Italian-style house's verandah. Inside that, there was a taller fence of wrought iron topped by what looked like arrowheads. A statue of an angel stood inside a structure reminiscent of a cathedral's spire. Her back was turned, showing Kevin her wings.

Fruit bats flapped overhead, black darts against the moon. Greaser eyed them suspiciously. 'Might be spies from Thorn.'

'What is it with you and the fucking flying foxes?'

'There's a fella called Batcatcher. He can see through their eyes.'

'Bullshit. There must be hundreds, thousands–'

'Not all of them, obviously. Trick is knowing which ones.'

'So what's the trick?'

'Search me. I just hate 'em all.'

'Well, we've got more to worry about. Here comes Blake.'

The poet walked up the road as though out for a weekend stroll in his long coat and top hat, silver cane catching the light from step to step. Three gothlings followed in his wake: Ambrose and Bella, and a tall, thin lad in leather pants and sleeveless top.

'Let's test the water,' Kevin said, resting his pistol on the ground within easy reach. His vision blurred as he summoned his doppelganger, projecting his senses down the slope. His temple throbbed with the effort; his blood ran hot.

A second Kevin appeared beside the crypt, standing still, hands by its side.

Greaser whispered, 'Whoa,' but he ignored her, concentrating, his pulse racing as he dug deep into his bloodstream for the power.

Kevin whispered, 'You're early, Blake,' and the doppelganger repeated it, the voice carrying in the night air in a strange stereo effect he still hadn't got used to.

Blake pointed his cane. 'Take him!'

The three offsiders drew handguns and blazed away. The doppelganger stood its ground. The sound of the shots rolled away down the gully. Raucous crows arced up and the bats circled like carrion around a carcass.

'What the fuck?' Blake said.

His offsiders changed clips.

'Did you aim for the head like I told you?' Blake's voice quivered, with anger or fright or both.

'Can we try this again?' Kevin asked, and then flinched as he heard – *fuck!* – footsteps, crunching in gravel.

Behind him!

He rolled. A gun thundered. Dirt plumed where he'd been lying. He rose to one knee, reached for his pistol. A second shot smacked him in the chest and he tumbled backward down the slope.

When he found his feet, chest in agony, ears humming, Blake's people had bolted like a flock of startled crows. Greaser was crouched behind a headstone, Taser pointed at the figure that loomed over her. The man was well over six feet tall, and two axe handles wide. He wore a heavy overcoat to the ankles and carried a sawn-off pump-action shotgun. Greaser fired a dart trailing a thin cable into him. The man jerked back, dropping the shotgun, then yanked the dart from his coat. She tried to dodge, but his foot caught her in the guts and sent her rolling.

The man advanced on Kevin. His face was scarred, glittering with embedded metal. He had massive fangs, like a panther. No hair.

Kevin drew his sword. The man's jacket opened and Kevin damn near dropped the sword in shock.

Two extra arms dangled from the bloke's ribs, the hands pawing weakly as though to massage Kevin's face. Steel tips glittered on the ends of each finger. That would be a nasty shave.

The two men circled each other, stepping warily on the sloping ground littered with twigs.

Shots cracked in the night. The man stumbled. Kevin darted forward. Stabbed. Up through the throat, into the head.

The man wavered, his punctured brain taking its time to work out what had happened, and then collapsed.

Kevin looked up the slope to where Greaser still pointed Kevin's pistol at the fallen giant, her other hand pressed to her stomach.

'What the fuck is this thing?' he asked.

'Beamer,' she gasped, then answered his confused look with, 'Body modifier.'

'No day job, eh.'

She coughed. 'A gang of them got a patch on the north side.'

Kevin toyed with his sword: should he stab the monster again? Take its head? The guy was about the size of one of the gunmen he'd seen at the roller derby, but the arms: he would've remembered them. Maybe they'd been tucked away, out of sight.

A voice shouted, 'Freeze!'

Greaser groaned.

Hunter was coming down the slope. A man in a drab green uniform kept step to one side. He had an assault rifle and a clear line of fire.

Elsewhere, there were shouts. Shots. Engines.

Reinforcements.

'Hunter,' Kevin said.

'Matheson. Stand still. I'm taking you in.'

'You'd better shoot straight.'

'At this range? On your feet or on your back, it's your choice. Same applies to you, young lady.'

Kevin held his hands away from his body. His sword was no match for the handgun. He'd tasted Hunter, had fought him. He knew the red-eye couldn't miss.

Greaser placed the pistol at her feet. She had a little trouble straightening.

'How's Mira?' Kevin asked.

'She's looking forward to seeing you. You and Danica.'

A motorcycle engine whined. Hunter looked toward the noise.

A headlight flashed at them. Kevin threw an arm up, his vision already wiped.

A burst of automatic fire made him duck. He groped hopelessly for the sword.

The engine howled as the motorcycle charged up the slope. Hunter dived behind a headstone as bullets sprayed his position. His mate tried to stand his ground, swing his weapon toward the new threat. He fell in a spray of blood and the thup-thup-thup of multiple impacts that tore through vest and flesh alike.

The bike pulled up, the rider in black leather snapping shots at Hunter from a machinepistol.

'The Needle sent me,' he said to Kevin. 'Get on.'

'Can you take us both?' Kevin asked.

'Just you.'

Kevin handed Greaser his keys. 'Can you get to the Monaro?'

'Sure, if no one kills me.'

He pushed her toward the bike. 'Get her to the top there,' he told the rider. 'I'll follow. Meet at the garage, Greaser. Look after her for me.'

He holstered his sword and pistol. Then he snatched the shotgun from the fallen beamer's groping hand. He shot the vampire in the head, and then fired at Hunter, bullets chipping the headstone.

The motorcyclist swore; hauled Greaser on board and took off.

The bike bounced onto the road and roared away.

Troopers were well spaced out and heading up from the gully. Others circled down from the top of the slope.

Kevin worked his way uphill, crawling, crouching, sprinting from headstone to headstone. This was Taipan's natural environment; channelling his maker, Kevin barely made a sound as he crept along. But soldiers were everywhere, searching methodically.

Kevin lay on the ground as two troopers approached. They

127

were too far apart for him to take them both. He'd have to hide. Now.

Kevin summoned Taipan's gift and reached down, down into the soil. A didgeridoo wail filled his ears; cockatoos screeched in the distance, echoing and ghostly. The earth opened under him. It rubbed like sandpaper as he sank. He fought back a moment of panic, for all that he'd practised this, as earth filled his nose, buried his senses.

Not too deep. He couldn't afford to give in to the feeling of security. Couldn't afford to get lost down here.

The thuds of cautious footsteps vibrated down to him. He imagined thrusting out, like a diver surfacing in an explosion of dirt, to drag the Gespenstenfuck down. But he stayed still, letting his senses range, until he felt they'd moved on. He rose, the soil sloughing off, the smell of it clinging.

All clear. He gulped fresh night air, tasted dirt on his lips. A cautious survey: the searchers' dark shapes, ghoulish creepers hunched amid the headstones. Headlights on the roads that criss-crossed the cemetery.

Kevin ran with Taipan's light stride to find Greaser and the biker waiting at the Monaro. An olive-uniformed body lay nearby.

Greaser was just puncturing a second tyre on a black BMW parked near the Monaro. 'Enjoy the walk, Gespenstensucker.'

Kevin clambered onto the back of the bike and wished her luck. She brandished the car keys and, as the bike powered off, he wondered if he'd ever see her or the car again.

TWENTY-THREE

Reece was leaning on the bonnet of his car, smoking his second cancer stick, when Felicity walked out of the graveyard. She was in uniform, her sword hidden poorly under a long coat. Lights were on in the houses around them; a few braver, more curious souls stood on landings and verandahs, peering toward the cemetery. Sirens filled the air. A helicopter thundered overhead, searchlight searing down. Red and blue strobes on nearby cop cars painted houses, fences, trees, gravestones. Cops kept the more inquisitive at a polite distance. Reece was clammy with sweat, his coat heavy on his shoulders. Fuck, it was hot.

'Kratzmann's dead,' Felicity said.

Reece nodded. 'I told him to stay behind; little bastard insisted. Chasing a promotion, I guess.'

'How did you even know to be here?'

'Vehicle trace. Then I got wind of this op, Green Shirts drafted in for back-up.'

'You must have a death wish. Why can't you just let it go?'

'No one seems overly concerned about Mira's bedlam. I'm wondering why that is.'

'No one?'

'No one important.'

'Maximilian is concerned.'

'He's so far removed from the world, he doesn't even know what century he's living in.'

'He still loves his daughter.'

'Loves?'

'Well, you know.'

'So how's life in GS?'

'After the first twenty-four hours: busy. You know that Heinrich is demanding the Hunters be placed under his control?'

'Bishop won't like that.'

'She doesn't.'

'So Heinrich believes there's a leak.'

'Maybe he is the leak.'

He flicked ash. 'How did you lot know about this?'

'Blake was sent the message: if he wanted his girlfriend back, he had to hand over the grease monkey. Batcatcher tracked him, just to make sure the poet was playing it straight.' She pointed to the still-circling flying foxes.

The grease monkey. That was Mira's pet name for Matheson. He was doing a fine job of making *them* all look like monkeys.

'You were too far back,' he said.

'Wasn't my call. They were afraid of scaring Matheson off.'

'He knew it was a trap but he came anyway. Cocky.'

'Or reckless.' She raised an eyebrow, to draw a comparison, he suspected; he ignored the suggestion. 'I wouldn't have thought Blake would be able to get the beamers on side,' she said.

'I'm not certain he did,' Reece said. 'Not his style.'

'That four-armed dude was the same one who did Johnny Slick at the roller derby.'

'Exactly. Why would Blake even care?'

'Freelancer? And what about the biker who killed Kratzmann?'

'More hired help, maybe. Hired by who, is the question.'

'Another city, muscling in while the boss is under-strength? Sydney?'

'Possible. Whatever it means, we need to get Mira back sooner rather than later.'

'You'll be lucky to keep your head at this rate.'

'I'm menopausal and being retired, Flick. What the hell've I got to lose?'

She touched his cheek, but didn't kiss him. People were watching.

TWENTY-FOUR

There was a saying, that those who didn't pay attention to history were doomed to repeat it, or something to that effect. That, and absolute power corrupts absolutely, were two of Kevin's father's favourites, usually in the context of politics. But sitting on the back of a motorcycle being driven by a killer, again; being driven to someone who promised to have all the answers, again; before going to battle against Mira, again; he wondered what lesson he was meant to have learned.

To pick his friends more carefully? To get the fuck out of Queensland?

Having lost his family, did he have to give up his home as well?

Kevin Matheson, the parochial vampire.

Last time he went head-to-head with Mira, she had escaped and he'd been forced to bring Kala across to save her life. He hoped to have learned enough to do better next time.

The rider weaved across the city's north side. Once, Kevin thought he might've been either shaking off a tail or had taken a wrong turn, because they seemed to loop around. He finally turned in to a shopping centre.

The complex covered a city block, surrounded by a mostly deserted car park and thirsty-looking hedges. The only activity was a cluster of cars around the entrance to a grocery store, and the biker steered well clear of that as they headed into the underground car park, where seemingly endless vacant bays stretched away in fluorescent-striped rows.

Had the rider forgotten to get milk on his way back?

They zigzagged toward an area where *Staff Only* signs and hazard warnings dotted the concrete pylons. The teenage boy Kevin had seen at the Needle's mobile studio sat at a roller door, smoking. Argent stood as the headlight found him, clearly showing him speaking into a walkie-talkie. The rider flipped up his visor. The kid looked him over, then at Kevin. He nodded and told the walkie-talkie to 'open her up'.

The door rattled up and in they went.

The lad's mate waited for them on the other side. She was kitted out in a bulletproof vest and stiff guards, like hockey greaves, on her ankles and wrists. The silver tattoo on her neck glowed in the harsh light, so liquid it looked alive.

'You weren't followed?' the girl asked.

'What do you think?' The rider's voice carried a soft American accent. He slipped off the helmet, allowing long hair to flow freely over the collar of his leather jacket. He took his sword, complete with scabbard and belt, from a specially made sling at the side of the bike. A machine-pistol hung there, too. He slung the sword over his shoulder, then removed his gloves and extended a hand to Kevin.

'We haven't been introduced. Yoshi Kohito.'

'Kevin.' Good, solid handshake on the fella. Eyes flashing green. No surprise there, the way he'd handled himself.

'Is the boss at home, Silver?' Yoshi asked the girl, and she told them to follow her. But first she took Kevin's sword and pistol. He handed them over reluctantly; she all but tapped her foot while she waited, hand out.

They passed several khaki-green crates carelessly covered by a canvas tarpaulin.

'Look familiar?' Yoshi asked.

Indeed they did. Taipan's gang had been flush with guns and ammo in much the same kind of military packaging. But Kevin kept his reply to a grunt, then asked, 'Isn't it dangerous, having them out like this?'

'Boss has got an arrangement,' Silver said.

'I'll explain when we get there,' Yoshi said.

Silver led them down wide, heavily scuffed cream-coloured corridors to a service lift and up one floor. Polished tiles reflected the minimal lighting. Shapes lurked behind glass storefronts: staring mannequins, glinting racks of toys, blinking lights. The ceiling was like something out of a science fiction movie, the inside of a space ship perhaps, all beige sheeting and recessed lighting, as though the crew were in deep freeze and about to be awoken to face the alien peril.

They moved on, almost silent on the tiles, to a section of lofty ceiling where skylights let in an ambient city glow that didn't quite make it the floor. Stalls in the centre aisle hunched secretively under sheets; here sushi, there a cobbler, and there, something twee in rounded lettering that could've meant anything. Kevin's attempt to read the jellybean script was abandoned when Yoshi said, 'Here we are'.

Light spilled from a doorway: a timber facade, tables and chairs stacked in the aisle. Coffee smell hung in the air. Kevin shivered, almost tripping as he fought back flashing experiences, of the coffee factory in the Valley, and further back in time to that infernal espresso machine his parents had at the servo, the one that had driven him to distraction, much to their never-ending amusement.

'Okay?' Yoshi asked.

Kevin nodded, clearing his mind of the vestiges of the life before.

Silver had walked ahead to announce their arrival.

At a table inside the cafe, the hooded figure of the Needle sipped a short black in a dainty grip. His long, curved nails made the act seem equal parts menacing and absurd.

Silver motioned them to sit, then went behind the counter to make herself a drink. There came the crunch of the portafilter, a whoosh and burble.

Kevin sat opposite the Needle. 'Late-night shopping?'

'Limited natural light. A general atmosphere of distraction. And, at certain times of the day and night, intensely crowded.' The Needle smiled, all fangs and twisted lips. 'A shopper's paradise. Would you like a *sangue reale*? I've just had a box delivered.' He pointed to a carton with a foil lid, a spill of tomato red around the seal.

'There's more on the table than a feed, though, right?' Kevin said.

Yoshi asked, 'How much has the Needle told you about my offer?'

'You're the friend who wants to meet Danica?'

Yoshi inclined his head. 'An emissary. You noticed the weapons in the basement, right? That's a sign of good faith. Same kind of gear I gave Taipan. Same deal, pal. Introduce my boss to Danica, we give you more. Enough to bring down a king.'

'So who's your boss?'

'It's not appropriate for me to say at this point in negotiations, but rest assured he's no pal of Maximilian.'

'Well, you can *rest assured* that Danica's made it pretty bloody clear she isn't interested in playing these games, okay? So I don't think I can help you – or your boss. All I want – all I need – is for someone to tell me how to get to Mira. I can do the rest.'

The Needle batted Kevin's argument away with a chop of his hand, as though backhanding a ping-pong ball.

'Removing Mira isn't enough. She's as good as removed already, due in no small part to the action you took out west. You should listen to Kohito-san. His offer is a good one, with no risk for Danica.'

'Please, just Yoshi.' His American accent was more pronounced now they were talking business.

'There's no such thing as no risk,' Kevin said. 'I promised Danica I wouldn't tip her in the shit. Besides, I don't even know where she is. We didn't part on the best of terms.'

'She didn't support your desire, your *thirst*, for vengeance,' the Needle said.

'No. So I don't know why you think anything you have to say would be of interest to her. She wants out. She is out. End of story.'

'Then you have a problem,' the Needle said. 'You want something no one has any reason to help you attain, and without help, you really are up shit creek without so much as a paddle. What's more, your friend Melpomene is spilling her every corpuscle into one of Maximilian's goons as we speak, no doubt indicting the both of us as conspirators against his lordliness. Just how do you propose to make that up to me?'

'There are other cities.'

'I like this one.'

The teen behind the bar interrupted. 'Question?'

They all looked at her, sitting on the other side of the counter with one hand on her cup, the other raised in the air.

'Yes, Silver?' the Needle said, his tone that of a school teacher holding out for the final bell of the day.

'Why did they try to grab the bumpkin at Flash's?'

'VS, looking to take out the threat,' Yoshi suggested.

'But why use the Viscounts?' the Needle noted. 'They're just villeins from the south side. It's not as if VS don't have troops of their own; depleted, certainly, but more than enough to take care of one rogue vampire.'

'What if it wasn't VS?' Silver said.

'Good point,' Yoshi said. 'Who else could get something out of icing our young friend?'

'Slick's moll told me he'd been promised a big promotion,' Kevin said. 'Sky was the limit, she said.'

The Needle nodded, obviously warming to the theory. 'So the Viscounts were being used by someone in a position to make, and presumably keep, big promises. Someone who thought capturing or killing Kevin was worth the risk. But wanting to keep their role under the radar.'

'There is a price on his head,' Silver said, and the way she said it made Kevin wish he hadn't given up his weapons.

'Not *that* big a price.' The Needle studied Kevin, squinting, as though through a microscope.

'Danica,' Yoshi said. 'He's our only connection to Danica.'

'Because Mira's in bedlam,' the Needle nodded. 'They want to woo Dee back; to save her, or replace her.'

Kevin dredged up a memory. 'In the gorge, when we fought, Mira said something about Danica being able to cure her.'

'Max, then,' Yoshi suggested, 'but not wanting to risk any more of his troops, using his ersatz soldiers instead.'

'For something as important as saving his daughter, he'd send the Gespenstenstaffel at the very least,' the Needle said.

'But what if it was someone who doesn't want Mira cured? Someone who, say, let it slip to me that Jasmine Turner had moved out west, and was vulnerable there. A someone who hoped to lure Taipan to her, in the hope of damaging Maximilian's operation, and perhaps drawing Danica out into the light. They must be very happy indeed with how that all worked out.'

Yoshi leaned toward the Needle, his voice low. 'Don't suppose you know who set you up, hey, pal?'

'The source of that particular piece of information has since expired.'

'Interesting.'

'Isn't it?'

'Let me get this clear,' Kevin said. 'Maximilian probably wants me alive. Someone inside his operation probably wants me, and Danica, dead.'

'So it would appear.'

'Then no way am I bringing Danica into this. I owe her that much.'

'Under the circumstances, I concur,' the Needle said.

Yoshi seemed about to argue, but the Needle motioned him to silence before turning to Kevin. 'If you want to free Melpomene, I suggest you talk to Blake. He's her maker. His blood link will help you find her. How you get access to her is your business.'

'I want to talk to him anyway,' Kevin said. 'Thank him for tonight's not-that-much-of-a-surprise party.'

The Needle fingered his takeaway, as though the box held an answer if only he dared to open it. 'As you wish. I need to pursue the matter of a faction within Maximilian's operation. Perhaps the rot inside the tower will bring von Schiller down, if we but give it a helping hand.'

'What makes you think the new chief won't be as bad, if not worse, than the previous?' Yoshi asked.

'Oh, I have my own ideas about that. Silver, show Kevin out. And tell Greaser to keep her distance. And give up her badge. For the time being, she's officially no longer a Snipe.'

'Have you heard from her?' Kevin asked. 'Did she get away?'

The Needle lifted the lid on his meal, a faint ghost of steam and blood rising. 'She did. I think this needs to be reheated.'

'I'm going with him,' Yoshi said, standing with Kevin.

The Needle questioned him with a look.

'He's my only link to Danica. You might not need him, but I do. If you don't mind me riding shotgun, Kevin?'

'You saved my arse in the graveyard. You want to give me a chance to even the score, sure. But Danica's off-limits. Just so we're clear.'

'It's my experience that, when things go pear shaped, nothing much is clear. But for now, let's go reel in this Blake guy and see what he can tell us.'

TWENTY-FIVE

Reece paused outside Vee's apartment. He adjusted his tie and his shoulder holster. A pattern of scarlet dots and lines covered the door. He'd heard housekeeping hadn't been happy about that, but there was nothing they could do. Power came with privileges, and graffiti was one of them.

There was no buzzer. Reece knocked and waited. He was about to knock again when he heard the slither of cloth and the clunk of a lock.

Vee opened the door, stood with one knee poking through the split of their kimono, one hand holding the door. The sleeve pooled at the elbow, revealing a black and purple snake tattoo circling their forearm.

'Not a surprise, and yet, surprising.'

They stood back to let him enter. The living room was candlelit, the flickering flames haloed in the incense cloaking the room. Book shelves covered one wall; a huge cabinet of weird shit another: animal and human skulls, puppets and dolls, an array of jars, coloured beads. Where most people would've had a television, there was a terrarium of branches and platforms, home to a mass of creamy coils. The python raised its head, tasted the air, yawned as though Reece's arrival was of no consequence, and tucked itself back into slumber.

'This won't take long,' Reece said. Sweat beaded on his forehead. How the fuck did Vee breathe in here? He adjusted his tie again.

Vee stood at the terrarium, talking to the snake. 'You want to know if I tasted the poet's woman.'

'I thought she might've known something about the mechanic's whereabouts.'

'All this fuss about a grease monkey.'

'He wants to kill the Strigoi. Doesn't that worry you?'

'How can anyone with a blood link not be worried?'

Vee stared at Reece, unblinking, and he felt a flush of heat in his throat where Mira's mark had once indicated her ownership. The two scars had faded over the past month, but he still felt them.

Vee waved one hand, as though clearing smoke from the air between them. Maybe they were, their green eyes glowing in the dimness.

'The Hochmeister conducted the interrogation himself. It seems all those favoured by the Strigoi are, shall we say, less involved than we once might have been.' A smile flickered across their thin lips. 'You must be feeling it, the separation.' They held up a hand, fingers open, palm up. 'Your time is running out, Reece. Tell me, what does it feel like?'

'It's Mira's time I'm worried about. Can you bring her back?'

'Dr Tran and I are doing what we can, but you have to realise, she has quite the history. A lot of voices in there.' Vee tapped the side of their head. 'The cacophony is deafening.'

'So you're saying there's nothing to be done.'

'I'm saying there's nothing for you here, Hunter. But I can assure you, if anyone wants to kill the Strigoi, they will have to go through me first.'

'I can live with that.'

Vee smirked. 'Can you?' They opened the door. 'So nice of you to visit.'

Reece poised in the doorway. 'You cut any deals with the rockabillies lately, Vee?'

'Really. Do I look like a bobby-soxer to you?'

'I don't know what the fuck you look like, sport.'

Vee gave a condescending smile and pushed on the door. Behind them, the snake yawned again. 'Give my regards to the other one.' The door closed.

Reece stood in the hall, catching his breath, the sweat cooling. He should've known the freak wouldn't help him. Their rivalry, their antipathy, ran too deep.

Interesting, though, that Vee was as much on the outer as he was, with no knowledge of Matheson's whereabouts and no apparent reason to have tipped off Slick.

He snorted. *The other one.* Flick would love that.

TWENTY-SIX

Yoshi parked in the shadow of a multi-storey building surrounded by chain-mesh fencing. It had boards fixed across its windows and doors. With the bike parked out of sight in a rutted driveway, they huddled at the corner of the property from where they could see the front of Mel's apartment block. They'd agreed to wait until early morning before making their visit, mainly to ensure that the poet was the only one to get a rude shock, assuming Kevin's theory about Blake's location was correct.

Kevin gestured at Yoshi's sword. 'You ever get pulled over because of that thing?'

'The cops haven't caught me yet.' He grinned. 'I only carry it when I'm working. It has a certain intimidation factor. Plus you get stuck through the heart with this, you stay stuck, right? And when it comes to the coup de grâce...' He drew a finger across his neck. 'So what makes you think Blake will come to his girlfriend's?'

'He'll be too scared to stay home, now that his trap has failed. Too scared of me and VS, probably. Plus, if Mel's that important to him, he'll want to feel close to her.'

He knew what that felt like, that yearning for contact, to hear that one voice, to see that one smile. All gone now. The empty street, the silent buildings, closed around him. So desolate. Sepulchral was the word that came to mind; it wasn't one of his. And not likely to be one of Taipan's; he'd done his damnedest to reject the education Jasmine Turner had forced on him. The word was more likely Mira's, or someone she'd eaten and liked enough to keep.

His head swarmed with the ghosts of other people's lives. Danica had shown him how to stop them from overwhelming him, from sending him into bedlam, but there was leakage, usually in response to something like this: some emotion that sparked a vivid memory from his life or someone else's, and pulled it unbidden into consciousness.

'That beamer in the graveyard. Did you see him?' Kevin asked, keen to shake the phantoms in his bloodstream.

'Mister ambidextrous? Hard to miss.'

'You ever seen anything like that?'

'Nothing that freaky. I've heard of similar, though, body modifiers who try to use implants and whatnot to reshape the flesh.'

'Like growing extra arms?'

'That's, kind of extreme,' he shrugged. It didn't look like it was working very well. Kind of fighting biology there, not to mention nerves, muscles, whatever. It's a pretty painful process. Lots of traction and re-breaking of bones to overcome our super healing. I heard of this one guy–' Yoshi gripped the hilt of his sword. 'Car coming.'

A taxi pulled up in front of the apartments. Blake stumbled out like a drunkard.

'Well guessed,' Yoshi whispered.

'Let's grab him.'

'Wait for him to get upstairs. Comfy. Safe. Might shake him up a bit.'

'He looks pretty shaken up already.'

'A little more won't hurt. Not easy to interrogate fangers; you need to get them off-balance, hope they slip, or that you can find something in their blood.'

'Risky, isn't it?'

'Last resort, sure; the chance of anyone other than a bloodhag extracting the right information is pretty remote. I'll be interested to see what the Needle can do.'

'You think he's a bloodhag?'

'He's got something going on.' He smacked Kevin's arm. 'Come on. Let's go chat with our pal.'

'Wait,' Kevin said, holding him back. 'Look there.'

A flying fox winged low across the roof of the departing cab, then circled while Blake fiddled at the front door. It flew to a nearby gum tree and settled upside down; wings wrapped around its body like a cloak.

'That's a big motherfucker,' Yoshi said.

'Let's go round the back, see if we can find another way in.'

They vaulted a back fence into an overgrown yard. A tumbledown brick structure showed where a presumably communal barbecue had once stood; a vandalised Hills Hoist stood like the mast of a ghost ship, arms bent and wires dangling, a single tattered singlet hanging forlornly.

'What's with the bat thing?' Yoshi asked.

'Maximilian uses them to spy on people, apparently.'

'Cheaper than helicopters, I guess.' Yoshi shook his head, and Kevin wondered how long he'd have to survive before nothing could surprise him; to get a handle on this bizarre world of monsters he'd been dragged into.

A crack, and he realised Yoshi had already grabbed the handle of the back door and heaved. The frame was splintered, the handle hanging loose, but the way was clear.

'Top floor,' Kevin said.

They took the stairs. 'Whew,' Yoshi said as a rank, stale smell cloaked them. The dim sounds of life carried: televisions and babies, a cat mewling.

Outside Mel's, they heard a piano being keyed, plunk, plunk, plunk.

Yoshi tested the door. Locked.

He rapped with a single knuckle.

The piano stilled.

Incense filtered out, the earthy, floral scent reminding Kevin of Mel.

'We know you're home, Blake,' Yoshi yelled. 'We're here to help.'

'Who is it?'

'Just let us in, pal.'

The door opened, just a few inches. Blake looked puzzled as he studied Yoshi. Then he saw Kevin and his eyes widened. He tried to slam the door. Yoshi pushed and Blake lurched back. Blake fumbled with his cane and Yoshi knocked it from his hand, sending it rattling down the hall.

'Rough night, pal?' Yoshi asked as Kevin followed him in and shut the door, slipped the security chain across.

'Rather,' he said, and retreated to the living room. He slumped into a stuffed sofa.

Shadows cloaked the room, lit only by the dim city glow through the windows.

Yoshi hit the lights and went around the room, picking up things and putting them back down again.

'So what have you been up to, Blake?' Kevin asked.

'It's your fault. Had she not run off with you–'

'I want to get her back,' Kevin said.

Blake looked desperately at him. 'I can barely feel her.' He held out a hand, palm up, fingers spread wide. 'She's slipping away. She's slipping away.' The hand clenched to a fist. 'What are they doing to her?'

'Nothing nice,' Kevin said. 'So the sooner we free her, the better. Do you know where she is?'

'I was going to trade you for her. Now – now it's too late.'

'This is beautiful,' Yoshi said. 'An original?' He stood with a finger pressed against a small, framed painting. A couple in period dress, like characters in a Jane Austen TV show. Blake? And Mel?

'Buck was quite the admirer,' Blake said. 'In our sunlit days. You know of him?'

'Sure. I know a bit about art.'

'The muse; it changes. After you've been given the bite. You know?'

'I know.'

'Blake! Do you know where Melpomene is?' Kevin repeated.

'Slipping away,' Blake said. 'Out of reach.'

Kevin grabbed the man, shook him until his eyes focused. 'Do I need to open a vein?'

'No, no,' he said, eyes bulging. 'After you escaped from the graveyard, they sent a message to my house. A brick through the window. Stylish, as always.'

He dug a crumpled piece of paper from his pocket and held it out, a child offering a bully his pocket money. 'For my failure to deliver you, she is to be sent to the coast. In the morning.' His eyes lost their focus once more. 'She always did like the sea; always at night, even before–'

Kevin snatched the paper.

Last chance to deliver the mechanic. At 9, she's on her way to hang 10 with the meter maids.

Yoshi read the note over Kevin's shoulder. 'They left out the bit about it being a set-up.'

'It's between the lines,' Kevin said. 'Fuck.'

'What are these meter maids?' Yoshi asked.

Kevin shrugged, but Blake tuned in. 'Lovely girls. And boys.

On the Gold Coast. They more or less run the joint. Vassals, of course.'

'Can we intercept them before they get there?' Yoshi asked.

'You could just give yourself up,' Blake said.

Kevin ignored him. 'Stake out the tower? See who leaves? Run them off the road?'

'At nine in the morning?' Yoshi said. 'Gonna be hot out there.'

'Maybe the Needle would like to volunteer some red-eyes. A little bit of sunburn won't worry them too much.'

'He was pretty clear about not getting involved. I could have another word to him – if you were prepared to meet our terms.'

Kevin shook his head. 'What about your mob, Blake? They happy to take some risks to get Mel back?'

'We're poets. Writers. We can't go up against Maximilian's stormtroopers!'

'What happened to the pen being mightier?' Yoshi asked. 'No matter. I've got a couple of crates of the best "swords" money can buy. Max won't be expecting that.'

Kevin dug Rabbit's dancing skeleton brooch out of his pocket and weighed it in his palm. 'Gather your Romantics, Blake. It's time to stick it to Maximilian.'

TWENTY-SEVEN

It was oh-five-hundred plus a coffee, and Reece sat alone in the cafeteria. The place was less than half full, a sorry sign of their depleted numbers and the difficulty of recruiting mercenaries for an organisation that had to make allowances for ops that were blacker than black. The eggs were rubbery, the toast cold, the bacon like slivers of steel. He heard his name, looked up and lost whatever appetite he had.

Petersen and Newman were manoeuvring through the tables with a familiar young man in tow.

'Nice uniform, Reecey,' Petersen sneered.

'Just right for a bus driver,' Newman said. 'You got a job. You and your mate, here.'

The kid, fidgeting in his VSS private's uniform, stepped forward and waved a hazy hello. 'Nigel. From out – you know.'

'I remember you, Judas.' The surfie had run with Taipan's gang until he'd sold them out to Mira. Reece couldn't stand snitches, as much as he acknowledged their usefulness. He'd heard Mira had repaid his treachery with a job in the garage. Nigel was a passing good mechanic, by all accounts.

The kid blushed.

'They let you keep your surfboard?' Reece asked.

'Not much time for it, y'know.'

Newman clapped a hand on Nigel's shoulder. 'Which is why we thought the private here might like a nice drive to the Goldie. Maybe you could take the board, eh?'

'What's this about?' Reece asked, tired of the bullshit and happy to let it show.

'You two have been requisitioned,' Petersen said. 'For a job.'

'Marshall know?'

'Your boss's got no say in it,' Newman said. 'This is from the top.'

'So why isn't the top doing it?'

'You got the skills,' Petersen said.

'Yeah,' Newman said. 'You two were the first names to come up when we were looking for volunteers. Being old mates, and all.'

'Prisoner transport duty to the Gold Coast. Cushy. Right up your alley,' Petersen said.

'Who?'

'The poet's squeeze.'

Oh, shit, Reece thought. 'I heard I was off that case.'

'You're whatever the boss tells you, Reecey,' Petersen said.

'Dunno if driving a van amounts to being on the case, so much as being along for the ride.' Newman picked up a piece of bacon and nipped off the end. 'Not quite the same as the tucker upstairs, is it?'

'Have it; I'm done.'

'You certainly are, sunshine.'

TWENTY-EIGHT

Reece and Nigel, wearing civvies and issued with false driver's licences, waited in the office of the VIP section of the basement car park under the watchful gaze of a GS staffer. Their ride was parked outside: a modified four-wheel-drive van, riding low on its boosted suspension due to the weight of armour. The Hunters had taken Reece's and Nigel's phones, on the pretence of a possible security leak. To which Reece called bullshit, but was powerless to overturn.

'Keys,' he said.

'Petersen gave them to me,' Nigel said.

Reece snapped his fingers.

Nigel moved his shotgun to the other shoulder so he could fork them out.

'You loaded for bear?' Reece asked.

'Huh?'

'Are you carrying high explosive for that cannon?'

'Yeah, yeah. That's what Petersen said.'

'Petersen gave you that?'

'With the keys. Told me not to shoot my dick off, the wanker.'

'Give it here.' Reece checked the load. 'Looks okay.'

'Why wouldn't it be?'

Reece concentrated on extracting a semi-drinkable coffee from the machine to go with his cigarette.

Nigel swore, mumbled something about being treated like a mushroom.

'Is it everything you expected it to be, Judas?' Reece asked as the machine vomited froth into the plastic cup.

'Better than out on the road, an eye over your shoulder all the time.'

'But was it worth selling out Taipan's gang?'

'They were about to replace me with that Matheson guy. I did what I had to.'

'That what you tell yourself?'

'It's the bloody truth.'

The lift doors opened. Petersen and Newman escorted two troopers wheeling a gurney. A girl was strapped to it, a hood over her head, a hospital gown open at the front where a silver stake poked out of her chest.

Reece pinched out his cigarette as they arrived, then lifted the girl's hood.

'Satisfied?' Petersen asked.

'Always like to check the cargo,' he said, and nodded for the troopers to load the gurney into the van.

'No stopping for snacks,' Newman said, managing to make it sound salacious. 'Straight to the Goldie, undamaged.'

'Expecting trouble?' Reece asked. The soldiers wore flak jackets and carried automatic rifles.

Petersen sneered at him. 'She's on ice, but we understand your previous history with prisoners isn't the best.'

Reece made a promise to himself to flatten Petersen the next chance he got. The troopers strapped down the gurney, then perched on fold-down seats on either side.

Reece shut the doors. 'You boys aren't coming?' he asked the sneering Hunters.

'We've got *important* work to do, cleaning up your mess. Have a good trip, boys. Don't forget the sunscreen.'

Fuck you, Reece thought. As a red-eye, it was true his tolerance for direct sunlight was much, much higher than a vampire's, but prolonged exposure still hurt like a bitch as the sun triggered nasty reactions with the vampire blood in his system. The result was nicknamed *wolfbite*, for the red rash it caused. But he had a lot more to worry about on this trip.

Reece and Nigel clambered into the front. It was dead on nine. Reece fired up the truck, let it idle while he checked the radio – direct to a GS operator, despite the fact the squad were all Green Shirts. Marshall had been cut out of the loop.

'You've been here a month,' he said to Nigel. 'You recognise those guys in the back?'

'Nah. Should I have?'

'Probably not. They aren't red-eyes, though.'

'Is that a problem?'

'No, they're no problem at all,' Reece muttered, and relit his cigarette. As an afterthought, he offered his tobacco pouch to Nigel, who waved it back.

'Just means I don't like our chances of reaching the coast.' He slid open the slit window in the compartment door between the cab and the rear. 'Good to go?' One gave a thumbs-up. Reece checked the lock. The soldiers could bail out the back if they had to, but no one was coming up the front without his say-so.

Nigel stared at him through the wreath of cigarette smoke; hand tight on the shotgun at his side. 'What do you mean, you don't like our chances? What's going to happen?'

Cigarette held in his lips, Reece put the truck into drive and headed for the gate. 'She's going to be rescued. And we're going to be killed to make it look good.'

TWENTY-NINE

The lookout, positioned across the road from Thorn, reported a van leaving. A photo followed by text message.

'That's it,' Kevin said, recognising Hunter at the wheel. He couldn't make out the passenger behind the windscreen glare.

A motorcycle tailed at a distance, confirming the van was taking the most direct route along the M3, before merging with the M1. Traffic was moderate. Keeping tabs on the vehicle wasn't difficult as it trundled along the highway at slightly under the speed limit. The bike reported a police helicopter keeping pace.

'That could be a pain,' Kevin said.

Blake, next to him in their stolen Commodore, groaned. The poet had insisted on being in on the rescue and had complained the whole time about the formless attempt at sun-smart clothing, the heat, his thirst. Fair call – Kevin felt as though he was in a sandwich toaster, ham and cheese bubbling away, tomato gushing out the seal – but there was nothing to be gained by whingeing about it.

He'd rather Yoshi came along, but the vampire ruled himself

out of a daylight operation. 'Think of me as back-up,' he'd said as the team set out from Brissie in the wee hours.

Blake had mustered four red-eyes, including Ambrose and Bella, and a few more wannabes; and Greaser had found a few friends among the Snipes willing to risk the Needle's disapproval to rescue Mel. They'd all been kitted out in long pants and tops, gloves and balaclavas. Blake had foregone his cane and carried a rapier and a long, thin dagger. He'd been offered a gun but refused. 'Garish,' he said.

They had a good half hour to wait, now that the route had been confirmed. Parked near a boat ramp on the southern side of a bridge over the Logan River, they were separated from the highway by a row of trees. Traffic hummed. A boat had puttered down the river but paid them no mind as they'd slithered down low behind the dash until it passed.

They'd stolen two other vehicles: a hatchback to provide an escort, and a delivery van to get Melpomene away. The Commodore's job was interception. Kevin couldn't afford to fuck this up.

'Time is very slow for those who wait,' Blake pronounced, wiping his eyes for the umpteenth time. They were cooking, the sunlight wearing them down.

Ambrose and Bella, in the back seat, were feeling it too; patches of exposed flesh showing the mottled crimson of wolfbite. They stretched, trying to ease the ache in their joints and spines as the sun teased at the vampire taint in their blood.

The phone rang – the bike, reporting the VS van's approach.

'Time to go,' Kevin said, and Ambrose joined the group in the hatchback, Bella the delivery van.

Greaser's voice jagged from a walkie-talkie. She was among the trees, keeping watch. Kevin had sent her up there to keep her out of harm's way. She wasn't vampire and she wasn't a red-eye; she would have no chance against either if it came down to a one-on-one. She had used up her luck in the cemetery; he didn't want another life on his ledger. 'I see them,' she said.

Kevin wheeled the Commodore around as a shadow passed overhead, the chopper just audible over the traffic and the motor and his thumping heart. The delivery van and the hatchback pulled into position, one on either side of the Commodore.

'They're speeding up!' Greaser reported. 'Go–go–go!'

Kevin planted his foot. The Commodore jumped forward. He tore through a gap in the scrubby wattle and slammed onto the highway. The impact threw him and Blake against their seat belts.

The VS vehicle, in the far lane, sped past.

Kevin swore, stomped on the accelerator. They leaped across the distance, clipped the van's rear. It swung in a wild waltz as metal crunched; the Commodore bucked, the wheel wild in Kevin's hands.

Kevin jammed the brakes and swung the wheel, pulled them up just short of the barrier.

The van careered into the concrete divider with an almighty smack.

The air filled with the stench of burned rubber and hot oil.

Cars screeched to a halt as two Romantics in fluoro vests with stop signs waved down traffic. One car zipped through the litter of metal and glass. It pulled up further down the road. The driver's door opened.

Someone fired a couple of shots.

The driver got back in, powered away.

'Quite a ride,' Blake said, fumbling with his seat belt.

Kevin dropped Rabbit's brooch on the seat, threw open the door and heaved himself out. The sun hit him like a branding iron, scorching through his hoodie, his sleeves, gloves, jeans, sneakers. The ground could've been on fire. Bright lances stabbed into his eyes. He heard shots and cars braking and tyres squealing. Shouts. His group's hatchback pulled up and disgorged gunmen. The VS van rocked under their fusillade as it sat with one ruined wheel up on the barrier. Metal popped. Glass shattered.

The gunfire subsided.

Their van pulled up, reversing, and Kevin clung to the cover it offered with his pistol at his side, the weapon too heavy to lift. His vision was awash, like staring at sunshine reflecting off a salt pan.

The rear doors of the VS van opened, pockmarked with bullet holes like the worst case of acne. One hit the ground with a chunk and the other closed again and did not reopen.

As Snipes and Romantics crept forward with guns pointed, a gurney slid out. It bumped hard and almost overturned. Then it trundled like a wobble-wheeled shopping trolley toward their van. The Snipes regarded it suspiciously until it thumped into the van's wheel.

Greaser checked the swaddled figure strapped to the trolley. 'It's her!' A bunch of them hefted the trolley into the van. Someone heaved Kevin after it and closed him into the merciful shade.

The southbound highway had become a car park behind them, the bridge filling as motorists pulled up. The northbound lanes slowed as rubberneckers gawked at the van mounted on the intervening barricade.

The chopper kept its distance, though its side door was open and a man sat clipped there with a rifle in his hands.

The hatchback escorted them south along the empty highway.

'We got everyone?' Kevin asked, and was told yes, everyone had got away.

The helicopter swooped down and kept pace as they drove, the only cars on their side of the highway. The helicopter gunman swapped bursts of fire with them and their escort vehicle. The van filled with the thunder of gunfire, the stench of gunpowder, but no one accomplished anything before the vehicles took the first exit.

The chopper backed off, prevented from getting too close by the presence of passers-by and the clutter of roofs and power lines. Romantics and Snipes, a threshing machine of arms, legs and prattle, freed Mel from her cocoon of blankets. She was in underwear and a hospital gown, her skin paler than the bleached material, her body covered in bites and marked by a couple of fresh bullet wounds. A spike glinted in her chest.

'How is she?' Kevin asked.

'She's alive,' Greaser reported. 'Nothing a good meal and a lie down won't fix.'

She beamed at him and he smiled back, thinking a feed and a nap would be just the ticket. But they weren't out of the woods yet.

'Get that spike out of her,' he said.

They'd been expecting her to be on ice. The spike came out in the grip of pliers, and she gave a tiny mew, a flicker of her lashes. The Romantics siphoned blood from bags into her, and colour crept back into her cheeks, her lips, her fingertips. Wounds closed, but very, very slowly. A flattened bullet thunked on the van floor and Greaser pocketed it. A Snipe pulled out a dress and straw hat, ready for the next leg. It'd be dangerous, but VS would never expect it, not in the daytime.

'Mel? Mel, you're safe,' Greaser said. 'We've got you.'

The van drove into shadow; the sound of the chopper diminished. The driver shouted, it was still there, hovering above the shopping centre they'd driven under.

Mel didn't move.

'Mel?' Greaser's voice edged higher as she cradled Mel's head. 'Mel!'

'What is it?' Kevin asked. 'I thought you said she was okay?' If their own side had tagged her, a bullet causing irreparable damage to her brain or spine…

'Shit, man,' Greaser said, voice catching. 'She's in bedlam.'

THIRTY

Rescuing Mel was the first part of their problem. The second was getting away.

They'd chosen the shopping centre for two reasons: the undercover parking meant VS could not track them once they'd ditched the vehicles. They could be driving out, walking out or even bussing out; their movements perfectly hidden. Or they could change out of their battle-tainted clothing and take the covered walkway to the train station adjacent to the centre. Which was exactly what they were about to do.

The chopper could wait impotently for the cops and VS to respond, while they were safely, albeit uncomfortably, riding the train back to Roma Street, there to wait out the day in the cafés and backrooms of the huge station. They hoped VS would consider the train the least likely option at this time of the day.

They were about to find out.

Kevin rolled his balaclava up and stowed it in a coat pocket. It was easier to function inside the shopping centre, the air conditioning chilling the burns he'd suffered despite the layers of protective clothing. His eyes still played tricks, throwing blind spots and mirages when he least expected. But he could function, and he could concentrate, which he needed to do if he was going to pull this off.

While Blake and the rest kept watch, Kevin helped Greaser manoeuvre Mel into a parents' room in the shopping centre where they stripped the hospital gown. He turned his back while Greaser, all but sobbing at the task, searched Mel for tracking devices on or in her.

As Greaser washed her hands and then her face, snuffling, Kevin turned his attention to the problem of a blood trace. They had to assume that Mira's understudy had her knack of hitching a ride in a blood link.

He took the leather pouch from around his neck and upended it. The *putsi* fell into his palm. Danica had made it for him, because, she said, a person couldn't be too careful where Mira was involved.

The Strigoi had a blood link on him, though after all this time, it would be weak. Ordinarily, without replenishment, it would fade to nothing. But Mira hooked him when he was in the change from human to vampire, and something of her stuck, a permanent burr in his new DNA. Only death would sever the connection.

This piece of mojo was meant to fuzz that signal. The pendant was based on a flat disc of silver with a five-pointed star etched on it. Tradition, Danica said; might as well use it. A small locket was soldered shut in the centre of the star.

Now, copying a ritual he'd seen Taipan use little more than a month before, Kevin cut Mel's hand and waited for the blood to flow. He needed only a little.

None came. The wound healed. He cut her again. The flesh parted, a colourless, toothless mouth that soon sealed over.

'Body's in lockdown,' Greaser said.

'Damnit, I need her blood! Can you help me cut—'

'No fucking way. Not after what I just did to her. You do it.

You've got the equipment.' She made a snarly face and put two fingers up to her top teeth.

'Just a little, and hold on tight. There's no telling what's going on in there.' She turned away, swearing. 'Knew it was too easy. The bastards.'

Kevin cut Mel's palm, let the knife go in deep, and then brought the wound to his mouth. His fangs extended at the first touch, and he bit into the flesh. He sucked on the wound, feeling resistance, like a fish pulling against a hook. The first drops came, and then a red trickle bubbled up. He pulled back at the first tentacle touch of the lives careening through Mel's bloodstream.

A mere glimpse, a snow globe filled with a town's worth of experience, bombarded him. Deaths upon deaths, dreams upon dreams, despair upon despair. He saw Melpomene in an alley of cobbles and gas lamps, wreathed in fog. He saw her in a darkly timbered room, a man forcing her to drink from his breast. He saw Danica, on a wagon under moonlight, saying, 'I always knew it would come to this. But her, too?' And a hooded Mira, turning, questioning, as if to say, 'to whom are you talking, Mother?'

When Kevin surfaced, he was on the floor with Greaser leaning over him. There was blood on his lip, his chest. He spat Mel's blood onto the talisman and watched as it sank into the amulet. Warmth washed over him. Blood spotted brightly on the floor. Greaser handed him a wet towelette.

'Max did this to her,' Kevin said. Ghosts ran screaming through the hallways of his mind. He slammed doors behind them; a machinegun beat shoring up his sanity. And that, just from a touch. What must it be like for Mel?

He prayed she'd found a quiet eye amid that cyclone. That would be the only chance of ever bringing her back.

'Maximilian did this to her,' he said again as he hung the *putsi* around her neck. 'Because he could.'

Greaser helped him stand, and for a moment they were eye to eye.

'Are you so sure, Kev, that Mira's the one you should be going after?'

He couldn't answer her. All he could hear was Danica, saying to him before he'd left Cairns:

Vengeance isn't just a two-edged sword; it's a whirlpool.

THIRTY-ONE

With Mel dressed and a wheelchair sourced – Kevin didn't ask, the red-eyes didn't tell – they scarpered, as casually as they could, for the train station. Blake slunk along behind the group, looking like a reject from a cricket team in cream chinos and long-sleeved shirt and vest, a broad-brimmed canvas hat. He'd been dirty that Kevin hadn't let him into the change room; hadn't let him see what they'd done to Mel. Bella lingered with him, looking forlorn. Ambrose reported that, despite the time lost dealing with Mel's bedlam, they were on schedule for the next train.

The chopper still hovered outside, the air full of sirens. But no one hassled them as, after a short, tense wait, they swiped their cards against the readers and boarded the train, hefting the chair through the door rather than wait for the driver to furnish a ramp.

'We'll never get her back,' Blake said. 'There's no return from bedlam.' He reached toward Mel, and then pulled back, as though afraid she was contagious.

'You've still got Bella,' Kevin said, to be rewarded with a

scowl from both of them. He said to Bella, 'I can't believe you went back to this loser after what he did to you. *Erato.*'

She looked away, but Blake met his eye, smirking at Kevin's apparent naivety.

'Your vision is limited, grease monkey.'

Kevin's eyes narrowed. 'You're not the first one to call me that.'

Blake played with his collar, as though missing his cravat. 'A common appellation, I'm sure.'

'I saw a movie once, where they called hitmen mechanics. Weird, huh.'

'Fixing things, I would assume.'

'I guess. You looking to fix me up, Blake?'

He stared at Melpomene. 'I just want her back.'

'So you can dump Bella back on the pile.'

Bella walked away. Blake concentrated so hard on Kevin, spittle collected pinkly on his lips as he said, 'There is a place for Erato in our existence, grease monkey, but make no mistake – Melpomene is queen.'

'I get the feeling she's a bit tired of wearing your crown.'

'She's mine. Make no mistake about that, either. I made her. We are bonded – forever.'

The train pulled out of the station. The other passengers gave them a wide berth where they clustered around the wheelchair.

'We should've taken a car,' Blake said. 'Or even a boat down the river. We're too vulnerable on the train.'

'Only if they know we're on it,' Kevin said. 'With luck, they'll think we're either hiding at the shopping centre or already swapped cars and driven away. That's right, eh, Greaser?'

The girl might've nodded. She hadn't left Mel's side. Kevin had to hope that the Needle knew what he was doing when he'd suggested this.

They huddled inside their hoods as sunlight lanced through the windows and suburbs passed by. The heat stole any remaining exuberance; their silence became one of anxiety and weariness and growing discomfort. By the time they got to the city, he and Blake and the red-eyes were patched with wolfbite, their exposed skin flaming, joints aching. It took all of Kevin's will to stay awake, to not curl up on the floor in any shade he could find and close his eyes.

They made one concession to Blake's fears. Greaser put in a call, and they rode the train one station past Roma Street to Central. Rather than wait for nightfall, they exited by a pedestrian tunnel to Anzac Square. Kevin, Blake, Bella and Greaser escorted Mel in her wheelchair; the rest jumped trains or used the station's many exits to vanish into the city.

Palm trees in the square threw little shade; the lawn crackled underfoot. Blinding midday heat radiated from concrete. A bronze statue of a mounted soldier looked ready to drip.

A van was waiting on the street. Silver and Argent heaved Mel in and Kevin crawled in after her. He lay on the floor, gasping, his face and hands feeling baked even though he wore gloves for the dash across the square. Blake flopped on the floor beside him, a blood sheen on his face, his white clothes turning pink, deepening to scarlet, where they stuck to sweaty flesh. Greaser sat with Mel; Bella was near the doors, eyes closed.

Finally, they arrived at the shopping centre, a heavy darkness closing over them, bringing small relief from the sun. Silver and Argent unpacked them next to a delivery door.

The car park was busy. Shadowy figures moved in the greyness, weaving through the vehicles, pushing shopping carts and prams, or laden with bags.

'You look like hell,' Silver said.

Kevin tried to ignore the pulse in the boy's neck as Argent helped him to stand.

'The Needle has a little something for you,' Argent told him, as though detecting Kevin's thoughts.

He tried to walk tall, but bravado got him only so far. He felt the stares of passers-by as they pushed through the shopping centre's bright, crowded corridors; Silver pushing Mel in her sun hat and wheelchair; and he, blistered in jeans and hoodie, an arm around Argent's shoulders; Blake limping behind with Bella; and Greaser hovering like an expectant father on the way to the birthing suite.

They entered a massage business. Water trickled. Air conditioning chilled him. Fragrant incense spiced the air. The manager left the counter to flip a *Back in 10 minutes* sign on the door and then ushered them through to the rear. Argent might've introduced him, but the man's garbled name was lost under the roar in Kevin's ears.

'Keep watch,' Argent told Greaser. She stared daggers at him, but stayed in the reception.

The Needle and Yoshi awaited in a back room, sitting on a padded bench, blinking like owls.

'You look like hell,' the Needle said.

A woman entered the room, middle aged, as tall as Kevin's shoulder.

'Go with Kim,' the Needle said. 'I'll check Mel over.'

'Don't take that necklace off her,' Kevin said, each word a hot stone.

'She's lost,' Blake said. He slid down the wall, leaving a pink smear. Bella reached for his hand but he pulled away.

The woman walked Kevin to the next room. She sat him on a bench and lifted his feet so he was prone. The manager entered. He'd changed into a black smock, to match the woman's; they both wore cloth masks over mouth and nose.

Was Kevin to have his nails done?

But no. The woman unbuttoned her top until the garment hung open to her navel. He smelled massage oil and a sweeter scent from a burner on a nearby bench, heard the ethereal breath and hover of a shakuhachi flute from the speakers in the corners of the room. It was meant to be relaxing but Kevin's senses sharpened with each extra square of flesh, the plane of chest, the swell of breast, the black material of bra, the slight paunch of belly appearing from under the cloth. The stem of her throat, the bobbing veins, loose hairs dangling along her jugular, fine age lines across her carotids. The flute gave way to the taiko beat of her heart, the incense to the aroma of flesh and blood.

She leaned forward, face averted from his.

'Drink,' the man said. 'But not too much.' A Staker glinted in his fist.

Kevin drank. He submerged himself in her bloodstream, her life playing out before him, through him, and her heart, thudding, her breath gasping. It reminded him of being underwater, hearing his heart in his ears, the splashes of other swimmers, all cocooned in warm liquid.

'Enough.' The manager's voice reached Kevin like a distant shout, muffled but urgent.

The absence, the loneliness, the need... He floated like a jellyfish in the surf, rudderless, her life buoying him.

Another woman came, younger, smelling of jasmine.

And then a young man, smooth and muscled, smelling of green tea and the ubiquitous massage oil and, if Kevin wasn't mistaken, Vegemite.

Taipan loomed, shark-like, his white teeth outlined in crimson:

Fresh from the vein, fella.

Kevin lolled, his body heavy, the pains eased, the hunger stilled.

'Restroom, this way,' the manager said.

Kevin saw no sign of his three donors as he tottered to the room, pissed a pink stream and washed. There was a bundle of fresh clothing: cargo pants, a white T-shirt, a long-sleeve chambray shirt, a cane hat best seen on a Volvo-driving fisherman.

He opened the door, refreshed but tired, to find the manager waiting.

'He will see you.'

There was a kitchenette at the back of the parlour. Yoshi dozed in a chair; the Needle read the newspaper, a mug of blood on the table beside him. A serving from the same young man who'd bled for Kevin, if his nose told him true. No sign of Blake.

'Relaxing, isn't it?' The Needle closed the paper and pushed it aside. 'Nothing like a massage to get the kinks out.'

Yoshi opened his eyes and sat up straight, yawning and stretching, hands above his head.

'How's Mel?' Kevin asked.

'Blake and Greaser are watching over her,' the Needle said. 'We got her body back, but her mind is totally immersed. I can't help her. No one can.'

Kevin slumped against the wall. 'Danica might.'

'She might,' the Needle conceded with a nod.

'Do you think the girl is the trap?' Yoshi asked.

'I've seen VS do this before,' Kevin said. 'They put a blood trace in. Follow along behind. Wipe everyone out.'

'Your amulet has deadened any signal, though,' the Needle said. 'Plus, I've worked a little mojo of my own. My tattoos don't just look pretty.'

'I hate to say this,' Kevin said, 'but the risk is too great.'

'There is another consideration,' the Needle said. 'I believe you're right, that Maximilian put her in bedlam. She's awash with Max's blood and all the lives he's taken. Who knows what secrets slipped out with the rest of his evil old life? You want a way into the tower? You want to know who the enemy of your enemy is? She can tell you. Maybe. If she's brought back.'

'My offer still stands, pal,' Yoshi said. 'My boss can keep Danica safe.'

'Why would he, or she, do that?'

'He. He hopes her famed blood-magic can find someone who's missing. No one else has been able to.'

'Did you ask Mira?'

'Before the bedlam, you mean? Danica is, by all accounts, the more powerful. Besides, my boss and Maximilian have history.'

'And what are you offering?'

'Haven. If she agrees to meet my boss, regardless of whether she can find his missing person or not, he will help her re-establish herself anywhere in the world. Or, if she wants to work with him, she will have his absolute protection.'

'I don't think she's the lackey kind of woman.'

'Haven, then. That's got to be attractive to someone who's lost everything and is on the run.'

Kevin looked away, a vision of Mel in front of him, her pale skin pockmarked with bites and bullet holes, her eyes staring. His fault.

'And I get as much firepower as you can supply.'

Yoshi nodded.

'This missing person – what's the deal? Danica won't help your boss hunt someone's head.'

'The details are only for Danica.'

'Listen,' Kevin said. 'I'm stumbling around in the dark here. No one is telling me jack shit and it's getting people killed. Killed, and worse. If you want me to help you convince her, then I need to know what your boss wants. It must be important if he's willing to risk going up against Maximilian.'

'He thinks so.'

'Well?'

'It's a long story.'

'We've got all afternoon.'

Yoshi held up his hands in surrender. 'Okay, have it your way. It's like this: my boss, Rodan, had a sister. *Has* a sister; called Brigitte. A long time ago – a very long time ago – she and he were made vampire. But she was the squeeze of an asshole by the name of Uhgrau. He's a magician, of sorts. He feeds on the blood of witches, preferably ones from his own family. Yeah, I told you he was an asshole. The short of it is this: Uhgrau holds Brigitte as security; Uhgrau does little jobs for Rodan, Rodan does little jobs for Uhgrau. What Rodan would really like is to find Brigitte and cut his co-dependence on Uhgrau entirely. He's hoping that Danica will trace Brigitte's location.'

'She'd need a sample of her blood, for starters.'

'Rodan has it. To prove that Brigitte is still alive, Uhgrau gave him a special kind of jar with her blood in it. While it glows, she's still alive. But no one has been able to use it to track her down.'

'And if Danica can? This Uhgrau isn't going to give his edge up without a fight.'

'Danica has only to find her. Rodan will worry about retrieval. Which will be interesting.'

'When you people say things are interesting, that usually means all hell's about to break loose.'

'Fucking A.'

'It's taking a big risk, isn't it, pissing off Uhgrau *and* Max?'

'Rodan will piss off anyone if it means even half a chance of getting Brigitte back. That's what families do, I guess.'

'I guess so. I'll ask Danica. But I hope you've got a plan B, if she says no.'

THIRTY-TWO

That night, Kevin went up to the shopping centre's roof – it felt important to have open sky above him; he would've loved to have had earth under him, too, but there was nowhere nearby he could sit and be sure of being undisturbed. The sky would have to be enough.

Legs crossed, hands in his lap, he closed his eyes and focused on Kala. His blood was in her, and they'd agreed that, while no phone numbers would be exchanged, the blood link between creator and created would remain open. He couldn't think of her as his daughter, or his servant; he didn't know how to think about her, now she was *blood of his blood*, as Danica so poetically described it.

He reached out, feeling for Kala's presence: her breath, her voice, her essence. And found her – on a beach under the sharp leaves of a melaleuca, watching white caps by moonlight, her two red-eyes playing guitar by a campfire on the beach.

His forehead throbbed with concentration, his blood churned as he manifested his doppelganger. He'd never tried this over such a distance.

The serenade stopped on an abrupt off-note as the red-eyes

scrambled to their feet. They were hazy on the edge of his vision, but Kala was more solid: cut-off shorts, singlet and jacket, fringe playing across her forehead in the breeze. She looked beautiful, arms around raised knees; moonlight striking an emerald gleam from her eyes. He remembered – felt – being with her, in her, her blood and body as one with his. But that had been before the showdown with Mira. Before Kala had gone over the cliff and he'd had to bring her across to save her. He still wasn't convinced he'd made the right decision.

He walked the doppelganger toward her, hands by his side, palms out. The fake Kevin flickered as his concentration ebbed and flowed.

'Hey, Kala.'

'Still kicking, then.'

'Still pissed with me, then.'

She huffed.

'You aren't still in Cairns.'

'Of course not. We left as soon as your tail light had gone round the corner.'

'I'd never betray you.'

'You've still got blood in your veins, haven't you? Look, just forget it. What do you *want*?'

'Well, there's this bloke in Sydney called Rodan.'

'I've heard of him. Their version of Max von Shitter.'

'He wants to ask Danica a favour.'

'Tell him to send her an email.'

'Please. It's important.'

'Gonna help you on your crusade, is he?'

'There's a problem.'

'Of course there is.'

'There's this girl–'

'That was quick work.'

'It's not like that.'

'Of course it isn't.'

'She's in bedlam.'

'So?'

'Danica could cure her.'

'Maybe. Why should she?'

'Protection. Rodan's offering a ticket to anywhere. If Dee helps the girl, and if she hears – just hears – Rodan's offer.'

'So this girl, she isn't actually Rodan's project. She's yours. Another casualty of your vengeance kick. We told you–'

'It's horrible, Kala. Max did it.'

'He did, did he?' She looked through the doppelganger, out to sea. 'I'll ask Dee.'

'You want my number?' he asked.

'Oh, I've got your number. Fine, give it to me.'

He relayed the number of the mobile the Needle had provided. She repeated it.

'Go away,' she said.

He did.

She rang in the morning and told him where to meet and when.

She hung up before he could say thanks.

THIRTY-THREE

Reece remembers the heat. Trapped in the cab of the broken-down four-wheel-drive, run out of *something* due to sabotage, the heat slowly roasting… her.

The hunger is hotter than hot. It ravages her where she lies on the back seat, cooking from the inside, cooking from the out. Her body is a mass of pain, broken bones without the wherewithal to heal; sliced and bruised skin. The sun sears through the windows. She is a husk, home to hunger; to that incredibly hollow need that only the red rush can fill.

Reece sits up front, vile cigarette smoke invading her nose and throat and lungs, a clogging cancer. There is dust in her wounds and her mouth, her eyes. She is the earth after drought, after bushfire.

She needs the red rain.

How they clamour, those ghosts within. Her control seared into nothing; they ravage and roam, a furious mob chanting for blood.

If only she'd taken Mother when she could. Drunk on victory, cruel with lust. Take the victory; rub the defeated faces in the glory later.

She knows he knows, can smell the fear, the alertness, the gun oil. His tension vibrates through the seat, through the floor, through the air.

She will not kill him. She will not sate herself with his blood. Not his. Not after all these years. It would be like eating a pet dog.

The heat increases. The hollowness increases. The need increases.

He gets out of the car. Hot air rushes in, a flash of brightness. She moans. Is surprised to hear the noise.

A car. Voices. She coils. She hopes, in her desperation, that *he* isn't the one to open that door.

A shout. The door opens. Pure sunlight blasts her. She lunges. And there is molten heat in her mouth and under her claws. She is swimming in the sun. She sinks, and sinks, and sinks.

Around her in the redness, the ghosts dance like solar flares.

They will have blood.

Reece surfaced.

The solar blindness shrank, to reveal cream walls, ceiling, sheets.

Hospital.

He retched, reached for water and drank straight from the plastic container. When he lowered it, a crimson drip splashed into the water and evaporated into nothingness. And then another. He wiped his nose and the back of his hand came away smeared red.

There were two tubes in his arm: one clear, one scarlet.

He was on the eleventh floor of Thorn; Hospitaller Tran's kingdom. There, only three beds away, was the door to the isolation area where Mira was housed. In the bed next to his, Nigel flipped through a magazine of surfboards and girls in bikinis.

'Welcome back, boss.'

Boss. Better than dude.

'The other two?' he asked.

Nigel shook his head, flipped a page. 'Like you said, boss – they weren't red-eyes.'

A nurse approached. 'Awake at last.'

She checked his tubes. His temperature. His blood pressure and pulse. Maybe the anaesthetic had run out, because in the time it took her to ask him how he felt, his body went from general numbness to feeling as if he'd been caught in a hail storm of cricket balls. But hot.

He'd been dreaming; of being Mira in the outback, after they'd been done over by Matheson. She'd never let on just how close to the edge she'd been. Not until Felicity had arrived with the reinforcements, and Mira had killed the first trooper to open the door. It'd taken four of them to get her staked out. By then the soldier's throat was a ragged mess, his blood soaking into the dry earth. And when they'd taken out the stake, back here in that security ward, she'd been gone. Deep, deep in bedlam.

'Click here,' the nurse said, pushing a handgrip into his palm. 'It'll help.'

'You right, boss?' Nigel asked.

Reece clicked. The nurse smiled encouragement. 'It's okay, you can't OD. It's measured.'

He clicked again, then asked Nigel, kind of hazy in the brightness, 'And the girl?'

'They got her, just like you said.'

The nurse said, 'Well, I'll leave you to talk.'

'How long?'

'About twenty-four hours, boss. They tagged you good.'

'I remember... You dragged me across the road. Through the traffic.'

'Yeah. Once they had the girl, they kinda lost interest. Quick thinking, that, pushing the trolley out. Guess that's why you were a Hunter, eh?'

'I guess.' He fell back against the pillows and hit the button a couple more times, waiting for the meds to kick in.

When he opened his eyes again, Nigel was gone and Marshall was standing over him.

'They told me you were awake.'

'They lied.'

She sat on the edge of the bed. The nurse hurried over, exchanged glances with Marshall; the nurse left. Marshall's fingers thrummed a discordant beat; she wanted a cigarette, he guessed. A bourbon, too. He reached for the water jug and she poured him a glass. In this light, her eyes were a deep brown, hard as timber. The real stuff. No veneer.

'We were never going to come out looking good on this one, Reece. It was only luck that I heard you'd been seconded and was able to get a support team sent out in time.'

'Nine lives, that's me.' Which struck a chord, a memory, of Petersen. When? *More lives than a black cat, Reecey.* When? Downstairs, arriving? Or up here in some post-surgery, post-transfusion haze?

'I don't suppose you know what happens next?' she asked.

He didn't, and she topped up his glass.

'Petersen and Newman have been reassigned to special duties. A squad of GS has been sent on a mission too secret for me to know about. And Heinrich is pissing blood about something to do with his Fallschirmjaeger.'

'Petersen? I think he came by to gloat. Cleaning up my mess.'

'I wouldn't bet on it. He'd been staking out that abandoned coffee roasters' warehouse in the Valley ever since the poet's moll spilled the beans.'

Reece pulled himself upright. 'Not the sharpest pencil in the box, but his kind always survives.'

'We may have another problem. This was found at the scene of the ambush.' She showed him a silver brooch in the shape of a dancing skeleton with top hat and cane.

'Viscounts? I didn't think there were any left.'

'Rebuilding, it would seem. And helping the Romantics; or fucking them over. We know that Melpomene helped Matheson kidnap Rabbit from the roller derby.'

'So did that Snipe of the Needle's, I bet. She was there at the tattoo shop; she was there at the cemetery. No, this is the Needle at work. Sowing red herrings.'

'That a pun, Reece?'

'Yeah, I'm in stitches.'

She smiled, and it touched her eyes, a trace of honey. 'Good to see you haven't lost your humour. You'll need it.'

'Oh.'

'Officially, you're on sick leave. Unofficially, I agree with you. The Needle is up to something. We also found this at the scene of the ambush.' She unfolded a piece of paper from her pocket. A photo printout of a gun lying on bitumen with a yellow square with a number 14 next to it. 'From the same batch as the ones you identified from the Debacle. Whoever armed Taipan's gang to go up against Jasmine Turner also armed the streeters who rolled you yesterday.'

'I traced those guns – they were meant for a military depot outside Sydney. Rodan?'

'Troops depleted, no Strigoi…' Her gaze flicked to the isolation ward and back to him.

'And the vultures are gathering,' he finished. 'Any idea about where Four Arms fits into this?'

'He's got no form. I can't even imagine where you'd hide a *thing* like that.'

'And then there's the motorcyclist from the graveyard. More skill than most streeters.' He sought out his med unit and gave it a jab. 'Do you get the feeling that there's more than two sides to this coin?'

'There always is in our world. Boxes within boxes within boxes. You know, no one would think the worse of you if you took retirement – voluntary retirement. Not after what you've been through.'

'Matheson is still out there.' He paused, clicked the pain meds again, dying for a smoke. 'So, what do you want me to do?'

'First things first.' She stood, looked around, then turned off the drip and pulled the needle from his arm. She kept one finger on the puncture. She raised her other hand to her mouth. A wet ripping sound, like someone biting into a soft apple, and then she was offering the wound to him, blood seeping along the edges. 'Here, Reece, have some of the good stuff.'

It was very good indeed.

THIRTY-FOUR

The van was nondescript, white, with rust around the wheel arches and the beginning of a knock in the engine that Kevin found unsettling. He did not want to be riding in a vehicle that broke down in the middle of the day. He'd had quite enough daylight for the time being. He could not forgive poor maintenance. Still, the rendezvous Kala had outlined was less than four hours north of Brisbane and it would not require them to travel in the daytime. She had been that kind.

Bella drove and Ambrose rode in the back with Blake and Yoshi. The red-eyes wore bulletproof vests under their shirts and coats. They had the windows wound down, warm air blasting through in what passed for air conditioning in the vehicle. Greaser had wanted to come but the Needle had overruled her – the job needed red-eyes, he said. Besides, she would be more use in the city; he had tasks needing doing, suited to her skills. Melpomene was Blake's offspring and his responsibility; it was a job for the Romantics.

It sounded like someone washing their hands, but Kevin kept his mouth shut.

They drove north after sunset, past pine forests and cane farms, the highway narrowing as they left the Sunshine Coast's outposts to a lane each way with nothing but a white line separating them. The traffic lessened the further they got from Brissie, but it was early enough that the trucks hadn't taken over entirely.

There were ghosts on the highway, flashing past like roadside reflectors, glaring white and red in the headlights. Taipan's life. Kala's. Maroochydore, Nambour, the slow wind through Gympie, then turning off through Maryborough's quiet streets and lonely traffic lights; heading toward the coast.

Kevin clamped down, willing the restless blood to be still.

Taipan and Kala had met near here; Taipan had grown up at *this* farm.

They pulled up at the end of a zigzag series of narrow bitumen roads hemmed by barren cane fields, lined with dry grass and crooked power poles and stunted wattle trees. The eastern horizon glowed like a false dawn with the long, thin strip that was the seaside town of Hervey Bay; the dim parabola of its poor inland cousin Maryborough lit the west. The full moon was climbing high, its light rendered irrelevant by the cities' sickly wash.

'This is it, huh,' Yoshi said, eyeing the house from behind Kevin's shoulder; and Blake asked with unmistakable nervousness, 'Are we there?'; and Kevin told them both, 'Yes.'

The farmhouse sat in a bare field, the sparse sticks of sugar cane brown and fallen. A tall mesh fence surrounded the building, as though trying to keep the decrepitude out, but the slack wires and leaning poles suggested a dereliction of duty. True, the outbuildings were peeling, and machinery stood flat-tyred and rusting, trapped by rampant grass, but the house endured with valiant charm, an elderly woman dolled up to receive visitors who'd never come. Except, here they were.

Kevin's senses shimmered as he looked at the place.

Taipan's lifestream bubbled through his, connecting to this place. Loathing flowed through him – loathing and despair. It was here that Taipan had first failed his sister. Here that he followed her into the eternal night. Here that he pledged to free her from Jasmine Turner, who had taken them – twice stolen – and made them in her ever-hungry image.

'Anyone home?' Yoshi asked, and Kevin couldn't tell if he'd been asking about the house or just calling him to attention.

Kevin shook himself free of Taipan's phantoms. He had enough of his own to contend with. 'I'll have a look.'

A wide door under the house swung open, big enough to drive a car through. A woman walked to the gate.

'Li Li,' Kevin told them. 'One of Kala's red-eyes. Found her and her boyfriend in Cairns.'

'AC/DC, huh?' Yoshi said.

'Just red.'

Li Li held up a hand to the headlights and Bella dropped the lights to low beam. Li Li's eyes glowed crimson as she guided the van into the space under the house. They manoeuvred Mel out. She stood limply, draped between Blake and Ambrose.

'Upstairs.' Li Li was in jeans and long-sleeved checked shirt, a pistol holstered at her hip. She pointed the way with a broad-bladed cane knife. Impacts on the floorboards above their head suggested someone moving to the front door.

Kala met them at the top of the stairs in jeans and sleeveless top. Kevin still wasn't used to the green vampiric flash of her eyes. She stood, hands on hips, accentuating the thin strip of flat stomach where shirt and pants failed to meet.

'Is she worth it?' she asked with a nod at Mel.

'Isn't everyone?' Kevin answered.

She bit her lip. Introduced herself and Li Li, coming up behind; and Williams, broad-shouldered and sun-blond, at the door with a rifle held at ease.

Kevin returned the introductions, then asked, 'Where's Dee?'

'Somewhere safe. I'll take you there tomorrow night, if nothing happens.'

'Interesting choice of hideout.'

'Didn't think they'd look here. Besides, it's only for tonight.'

'May we take Mel inside?' Blake asked.

'Sure.' She stood back to give them room. 'She should be right at home in this madhouse. But there's a condition. You won't like it.'

THIRTY-FIVE

They faced off on the verandah. It had been closed in with louvre windows, but the space was filled with a miasma of stagnation: sugar cane as pungently sweet as death, the graveyard reek of stagnant mud holes and rotting leaves. There wasn't a lot of room to move, the two parties squeezed in among an ancient day bed sagging under the weight of dust, several wicker chairs and a large pot sprouting a long-dead plant.

'You're pretty game, making demands when you're outnumbered three to one,' Blake said.

'It's my way or no way, Kevin,' Kala said.

'So what is your way, Kala?'

'I taste you. All of you. The nut job, too.'

'Don't call her that,' Blake said, holding Mel tighter.

Bella and Ambrose lined up against Li Li and Williams, but neither looked confident.

'C'mon, Kala,' Kevin said, 'you ain't a bloodhag. You're just as likely to get memories of our first pet as you are about whether we're setting up Dee.'

'Nonetheless, you will each bleed for me. As a sign of good faith.'

'This is insulting,' Yoshi said, 'but under the circumstances, I offer you a vein. Sure you can handle it?'

'I'll take my chances,' Kala said as he held out his forearm.

She drank, stumbled a half-step, her front teeth darkly rimmed in the uncertain light.

'See anything you like?' Yoshi asked.

'Yeah, I love Asian. It's the ginger. Poet – give it up.'

'This is a disgrace,' Blake said. 'Give me a vessel. I won't have fangs in me.'

'You got something to hide, mate?' Kala asked.

'Do I get your blood to compensate me?'

'You get to stay with your girlfriend. The price is a taste, straight from the vein.'

'If those are your conditions, I will demur, but under protest.' He propped Mel on the bed and rolled up his sleeve, reciting, 'Love seeketh not itself to please.'

To which Yoshi said, 'Love seeketh only Self to please.' Blake scowled at him, and Yoshi smiled.

Kala bit into Blake's arm and sucked. He shivered, and she gave him such a look of sour pity that he turned away, to roll his sleeve down and check on Mel.

'Careful,' Kevin cautioned as she went to taste Mel. 'It's a shit storm in there.'

Kala paused. 'Dee's relying on me, Kevin. If VS has had this girl, there's no telling what they've done. Dee will have to taste her; they know that. Better me than her.'

Kala bit, hesitantly, and Mel's eyes flickered at the contact. She moaned like someone in her sleep.

Kala slumped back, rubbed her temples.

Blake covered the wound protectively, though the flesh was already sealing over the tear. His two red-eyes stood close.

Kala hefted herself up, using the foot of the bed for support.

'My turn.' Kevin held out his arm, but she refused.

'I think we know each well enough. But your myxos can make a donation.' She nodded at Bella and Ambrose.

'They're mine!' Blake said. 'Vein and soul.'

'You need to share if you're going to get your girlfriend back. But you've certainly got time to get back to Brissie before sun-up if that's too much to ask.'

Blake waved her on. Kala tasted Bella, leaving her flushed, then Ambrose, who gave the slightest whimper. Li Li and Williams shifted where they stood watch, hands opening and closing on their weapons.

Kala wiped her mouth, more from reflex than need. She'd spilled barely a drop. 'One of you can plaster them,' she said, her gaze sweeping the three vampires. 'I'm not giving them my blood, not even a smear.'

'Only a nip,' Ambrose said, one hand to the leaking wound in his arm. 'It won't take long to heal.'

Bella licked her bite mark like a cat cleaning a paw.

'Did we pass?' Yoshi asked.

'You'll do. This way.' Kala led them into the living room, where the furniture was covered in dust sheets, and told Williams to light a gas lamp. 'I trust you've eaten?' When Kevin assured her they had, she gestured to a table covered in clothes, like something from a flea market of last season's tourist chic. Shorts, T-shirts, towelling hats with the names of popular tourist towns on them, Hawaiian prints.

'Take whatever fits, for the girl, too.' Kala indicated Mel, who was being settled on a couch, its dust sheet bundled under her head for a pillow.

'Everything you're wearing, right down to jocks and socks goes in here.' She held up a garbage bag. 'This, and your car, will be left in a car park in Hervey Bay. You can collect it after.'

'Is this really necessary, pal?' Yoshi asked.

'If you want to see Danica, yes.'

'I have to see her,' Yoshi said. 'That's the deal.'

'You can't write it down, *pal*?'

Mel spoke, her voice cutting through the tension. 'Write it.

Make it all right! My kingdom for a nib, oh poisonous ink, inconstant scribe, to bare my secrets thus on the page, writ large.'

'What the hell?' Kala said.

Everyone stared at Mel. Blake kneeled next to her, a hand on her forehead. 'Melpomene, what is it?'

She stared at him, as though seeing him for the first time. 'O rose thou art sick!'

'Melpomene!' Blake shook her shoulders, called her name.

'What's she on about?' Kala asked.

'Dunno,' Kevin said. 'First words she's said since we got her back. Blake, lay off her, eh. You'll knock her block off if you shake her any harder.'

'Leakage,' Yoshi said. 'Sounds like songs or poems, bits of old conversations.'

'What is it?' Blake said. 'Talk to me, Melpomene. My journal – where is my journal? My pens? I need to write this down!'

By the time Ambrose had fetched the poet's satchel, Mel had fallen quiet again. Blake crouched next her, wringing his hands in a fine display of artistic agitation. He stroked her arm, as though wanting to feed, but thinking better of it.

'Let me see those,' Kala said, and to Blake's consternation, pored over the bag, unscrewed his fountain pens and shook ink from each, tore the spine from his journal.

'You have no soul,' Blake said as he reassembled his kit.

'Yeah, well, I'm not the one she was calling a sick rose, am I? Maybe you should stay here.'

'I'm not letting Melpomene go anywhere without me,' Blake said. 'She's my muse. I need her.'

'We're not wired,' Kevin said.

'I'm not taking the risk.' She pointed to the pile of clothing. 'Strip. The lot of you. And give me the keys to that rust bucket you arrived in.'

They did as she said. Blake insisted on undressing Mel,

with Bella's help. Kevin and Yoshi turned their backs. Yoshi asked Kala what he should do with his weapons – a shirt was hardly going to hide his katana the way a trench coat did – and she said they'd find a duffel bag big enough for it and Kevin's sword. Or perhaps a fishing rod bag.

'I should get you a camera, too, eh?' she said. 'Help you blend in.' She held up her hands as though taking a photo.

Yoshi stared at her and Kevin felt a shiver: she was pushing Yoshi, hard; what would happen if he pushed back?

Williams gathered their guns.

'You can keep your blades, in case you get a visit from VS,' Kala said. 'But the guns go with us. I'll be back once I'm sure you haven't been followed, and then I'll take you to Danica. Sleep tight.'

Kala and her red-eyes left.

Yoshi said to Kevin, 'Nice girlfriend you got there.'

'She ain't my girlfriend.'

'Did she seriously think the Needle would have us bugged? Or that we'd be carrying a wire for VS? She knows that just by being with you, our heads are on a plate, right?'

'That's what she's worried about.' Kevin looked at where Blake sat by Mel's side. They'd dressed her in light pants and a pullover. The *putsi* was a dark splash against the cloth. 'There's no chance VS implanted some kind of homing signal on her, is there?'

'We looked, your pal looked. Besides, our bodies don't take kindly to foreign matter. Takes will to reshape them, even something as simple as an earring. No way could someone in bedlam maintain anything in their body.'

'I can't allow anything to happen to Danica.'

'Nothing will. We'll make sure of it. In fact, Rodan's offer might be the safest thing for her.' Yoshi collected his sword and headed for the hall. 'Might as well make ourselves comfortable. Blake, your red-eyes can keep watch, hey, pal. Just in case.'

THIRTY-SIX

As good as new? Reece was too old to believe that. His body was starting to agree with him, although outwardly there were few signs of having been almost shot to death the day before. A few scars, some stiffness, pains that went all the way to his spine. Thing was, he'd been sucking down vampire blood for four decades. His body was starting to say, enough. It would take more than a grease and oil change to get him back in peak condition, and he wasn't sure he'd take the option of a complete refit, even if it were offered. Forever was an awful long time to regret.

He spent the day beating the bushes, rousing every contact he had at all rungs of the criminal and civic ladder. Contacts made carefully as he'd been introduced back into society as his friends and acquaintances, mostly coppers and crims and layabouts from his Special Branch days, had died off or moved on.

The conversations went more or less the same, with the level of coarse language varying to suit the occasion: 'You seen the Needle, sport? The tattooist, him of the silver fame. You know where he is? What's he look like – think of a badger's face painted on a plate; now drop the plate and glue it back together, messy-like: that's what he looks like, sport. What about his gang? Snipes, little long-nosed birds on their lapels. Their fucking *collars*, all right? If you see him, tell him I'd like a chat – just a chat. What about a vampire with four arms – you'd know him if you'd seen him. No? You see any of them, here's my card. Don't fucking lose it; I have to pay for them myself.'

He'd put out a bulletin for the Needle's mobile studio; he'd searched the man's registered address and a rumoured address; he'd rousted two known associates who were so far down the chain they didn't even know the Needle had gone to ground. Then he'd had a late afternoon kip, a feed of steak at a place that was not the canteen, and started over again with the night people. The swearing increased, the success rate stayed firmly at zero.

It was as hot as buggery, which didn't help his mood. He had to keep his jacket on because wearing handguns in public was a bit of a faux pas. His jocks, his trousers, his shirt, they all dragged him down with what felt like his own bodyweight in sweat.

It was past nine and the humidity hadn't dropped, the temperature was still tropical. Fucking February.

He found a seat at the bar at a pub near the show grounds. The room was air-conditioned; water beaded on the sides of the glass. The pokies were locked away in another room, a few suits laughed too loudly in the beer garden. He could smell their hair cream from here, not a bad effort over the stale beer in the carpet and the sickly perfume clouding around the barmaid.

The loo didn't smell any better. Someone had added a fanged smiley face to graffiti reading *Suck My Cock* over the urinal. He was still in the Valley; neutral ground, though every gang in the city wanted a slice. A melting pot of musicians and homeless and yuppies, transients and a few ancient residents who could remember when there was a tram line to the city.

Reece had ridden that tram, remembered the big shopping emporiums that had been the heart of the place; back before the decline of his policing years, when the shops had moved to the burbs and the scum had risen to the surface, the gambling joints and the bordellos doing a roaring trade in brown paper bags to the coppers. The rules had been simple back then; you knew when to keep your mouth shut when rules were being broken.

A man came in and stood next to him as Reece washed his hands. A look passed between them. Reece's mitt was still dripping when he went for his gun, but the guy was quicker, trapping his hand outside his coat, pinning him awkwardly against the basin so he couldn't use his left hand, either.

'I thought you just wanted to talk,' the Needle said.

He was in a hoodie and cargo pants, his eyes mere pin-prick glimmers in the dunny's blue light. A girl in a hooded army jacket stood with her back to the door.

'Sure,' Reece said, forcing himself to relax. 'Buy you a beer?'

The Needle let him go. 'Why not?'

They sat at the bar, the girl keeping her distance. It was the Snipe he'd seen with Matheson at the tattoo shop and at the graveyard.

'Where's the grease monkey?' Reece asked the Needle.

'I can't tell you that.'

'How about who sent that sap to you with the gen about Jasmine Turner's little foray into the livestock trade?'

'I won't tell you that.'

'Did you help spring the poet's chick? I almost got killed.'

'But you didn't. And no, I won't tell you that, either.'

'So what can you tell me?'

'How about the location of the four-armed vampire?'

THIRTY-SEVEN

The girl, Greaser, guided him. She kept her mouth shut except to tell Reece where to turn, but he took a shine to her. His cop nose told him she was one of the good guys, a rare straight-up type in a two-faced world.

'You haven't taken the blood, have you?' he asked at one point, and she told him the light had changed to green.

'Scarface look after you Snipes okay?'

'Take the next left.'

'You hear from Matheson lately? I like the kid, for all that he's tried to kill me a bunch of times. And vice versa.'

'It's coming up on the right. There. See it? The dojo.'

He drove past, slowed to allow himself a decent gander, then pulled up around the corner. They both got out.

'What can you tell me about it?'

'There's a basement. You can see it through a broken window down there.'

'Handy bit of vandalism, there.'

'City's gone to the dogs.' She leaned against the wall, arms folded. 'He isn't alone.'

Reece crossed the street, trying to look casual as he kept his hand near his pistol. When he looked back, Greaser was gone, but he figured she would be watching: some window, some rooftop.

The rumble and squeal of a suburban train blotted out his hearing as he made his way toward the crumbling, two-storey building at the corner. There were a few cars parked in the street, presumably for the dojo or the nearby Chinese restaurant with the dripping ducks in the front window. Other businesses were either shut or vacant; all needed a coat of paint. Reece made a point of eyeing the restaurant's menu, then strolled around the corner. As Greaser had promised, there were windows down low facing the side street. They'd been painted over, but still cast rectangles of dim light on the footpath.

He looked, listened and then crouched where a fist-sized hole in a pane allowed a brighter beam to escape.

Half a dozen shirtless freaks were gathered inside. They stood on a white mat spotted with blood, four red-eyes taking turns to belt two vampires with various hammers and bars, smashing their faces before inserting various bits and bobs arrayed on a table. Silver was the metal of choice. Some had pictures to guide them, either from movies or simple sketches of the new dream visage.

And there was Four Arms, at the front of the room with a table between him and the others. He had only three arms now; the fourth lay on the table, like a fish about to be scaled, the flesh grey and withered. Reece thought, *I'd've thrown that one back.* There was a massive wound in Four Arms' side, like a shark had taken a chomp in passing. Four Arms bellowed and put down a bloodied knife, and the red-eye next to him, all pierced and weird looking but not so much that he wouldn't get bar work, jogged across the room to where, after some craning and squinting, Reece could just see a body hanging from the ceiling, dribbling blood into a bucket. The red-eye filled a tin cup and ran, more cautiously, back to Four Arms, who skolled it with a grimace. Two more bodies were chained to a wall; both clothed, both alive.

The beamers howled and chortled, slurped on sports drinks that spilled red in their rush to knock them back.

Reece backed away to the other side of the street and called it in. He'd need serious back-up for this one. The duty sergeant reckoned an hour. Reece swore at him to speed it up, but was told half the squads were unavailable: some special op out of town. Reece rang Marshall. She didn't pick up, so he rang Felicity. She answered, her tone hushed against a background of indistinct male voices.

'What is it, Reece?'

'You okay?' he asked.

'Kinda busy just now.'

'You on this special op?'

'Aren't you in hospital?'

'You haven't visited.'

'Not in town, okay? What is it?

'I've got Four Arms in my sight and need back-up. You can't swing by, I suppose.'

'Hardly. You ring the–'

'He said an hour to muster up.'

'Patience is a virtue. I gotta go.' And then, almost as an afterthought, 'What are you doing out of bed, you crazy bugger? You want to lose your head?'

'I was missing you. Watch your back, Flick.'

'You too. And Reece – I'm sorry, all right. I wish you were here for this. Bye.'

No 'don't call me that'. She was tense. Not in town – where was she? *Wish you were here*? Were they on Matheson's tail? Had Petersen and Newman tracked the kid when Reece had failed? He stared at his phone, wondering who to call and what such a call might achieve.

Could he get a message to the kid? Tell him to come in where Reece could protect him, cut a deal; get Danica to heal Mira and everyone can go their merry way. Yeah, right.

He pocketed the phone, took a deep breath to still his nerves.

Nothing he could do about it. But if they did get Matheson, they were a step closer to Danica, and that meant Mira was either a step closer to being cured or forever damned. He needed to bring in Four Arms and find out who he was working for. Doubtless his employer and the person plotting against Mira were one and the same.

One thing Maximilian could not tolerate was disloyalty. Four Arms was the key to unveiling the traitor inside Thorn and the best bet for saving Mira. Hell, if it weren't for the bedlam she'd probably be dead already, and Reece with her.

He went back to the window. Four Arms was on his mobile. The freak looked around, suspiciously, and Reece ducked back, holding his breath. When he peeked again, the phone was gone and Four Arms had a briefcase open on the table, the lid facing Reece and the other beamers.

'Who was it?' one beamer asked, voice muffled on account of having few teeth; and Four Arms – he could speak, who'd have guessed – said it was his girlfriend, in a *fuck you* tone. Speaking was one thing; a girlfriend was quite another. Reece's instincts screamed trouble.

Four Arms closed the briefcase. He'd taken nothing out, just fiddled with something inside. He left the case and grabbed his tent-like Driza-Bone from a hook on the wall.

He was leaving. Reece withdrew. Had he missed something? A handgun from the briefcase, perhaps? Was Four Arms on a mission; Matheson, perhaps?

Reece got around the front and across the road in time to see the vampire emerge from the dojo and lock the door behind him. Then he got into a four-wheel-drive.

Luckily, he drove off in the direction of Reece's car. Reece jogged after him, hoping he wasn't watching in the mirrors.

The dojo exploded.

By the time Reece picked himself up, the building was well alight, and Four Arms long gone.

THIRTY-EIGHT

In his dream, Kevin sees Hunter in a bed made from a book; something about a postman. He can't quite make out the words where the cover lies rumpled around Hunter like a doona. The bed is in the centre of a bookstore; Kevin knows the place instinctively, a shop the red-eye frequents. He had tasted Hunter out west, still carried vague impressions of the man's life in his blood. Hunter leaves the bed to search shelves that stretch to the whitewashed horizon. Kevin finds the book first. Its title, written in liquid silver, is *Strigoi*. Kevin flicks through the pages and ends on one showing a colour plate of his mother. She's behind a window at their house, looking out, as though waiting for a visitor to arrive. Kevin tears the page out, scrunches it into a ball, and eats it. Hunter snatches the book. Kevin grabs for it, hungry for more pages. The shelves topple. He is crushed to the floor, buried under books as heavy as boulders, as suffocating as earth.

Kevin jerked awake. Still alive. He rubbed his chest, feeling the absence of Danica's *putsi*. Had he lost its protection now that Mel wore it? Could Mira sense him? Could she use her blood magic to implant her strange visions in his sleeping mind?

It was the only explanation, because vampires did not, *could not*, dream.

In which case, what kind of dream was that to send? Was she teasing him? *Threatening* him?

'Hey.'

'Huh?' Kevin jerked out of his doze, feeling disoriented as he tried to anchor himself.

Secrets among the corpuscles. The books Jasmine made him read, the diction, the schooling. Breaking glass. The earth under his feet. The fury

Blake's pen, scratching at the edge of perception.

Hunter, browsing paperbacks at his favourite book store

A girl on a farm outside Rockhampton, throwing a textbook against her bedroom wall in frustration

'You were bloodwalking,' Yoshi said, and Kevin mumbled an apology as he forced the ghosts to settle back into his bloodstream.

'Want to talk about it?' Yoshi asked.

Kevin shook his head, and they were quiet for a bit, just Blake's pen breaking the silence, like a chook scrabbling in the dirt.

They'd turned off the gas lamp and opened the curtains. The night was still and silent, except for the occasional car on the main road.

Kevin, Yoshi and Blake were sitting in the living room, the smell of dust and mould heavy in the air, the tease of blood like a mote glimmering among them. Blake scribbled listlessly where he sat at Mel's feet, but she hadn't uttered another sound. The red-eyes slept in one of the bedrooms, getting their rest before they took the day shift.

'She's only fresh, I take it,' Yoshi said.

Kevin's forehead creased in confusion. 'Eh?'

'The girl who isn't your girlfriend,' Yoshi said. 'Newborn.'

'Yeah. She wasn't always like that,' Kevin said. 'Kala, she was nice.'

'The change affects everyone differently,' Yoshi said. 'Takes a while to find your feet. It's not an easy thing.'

'You've been, y'know, for a while, I take it.'

'Just a decade or so.'

'How long you been in Aussie, then?'

'All of that time. My sponsor brought me back with her. Clean break and all that.'

'Sponsor? I haven't heard it called that before.'

Blake looked up. 'Artistic, or more like a Twelve Step program?' he asked with a twitch of a smile, somewhere between jealousy and insult.

'Maybe both.'

Blake huffed.

'Where in the States are you from?' Kevin asked.

'Seattle,' Yoshi said. 'My parents worked for Boeing. Mom and Dad wanted me to follow in their footsteps, but I went to art school. Wasn't terribly good at it, so I wrote about it instead.'

'A critic,' Blake said, scorn dripping from his tongue.

'That's what killed me,' Yoshi said. 'There was an exhibition, minor stuff, but it caught my eye. I wrote it up for a journal, saying how the artist was ripping off a dude who'd been dead for three hundred years. Only to find out it was the same dude; testing the water after a bit of a break.'

'Could he do that?' Kevin asked.

'As it turned out, no. The inspiration, the *talent*, was gone, you see. He could replicate his previous style, but he couldn't evolve it. Couldn't apply it elsewhere, or differently. He'd lost his vision.

'My boss – not Rodan, but my actual boss, my sponsor – she says there's a fine line between creativity and cunning, and us lot, we fall on the animal side.'

Blake said, 'I don't believe that. We are vital, living beings. We think. We create.'

'We *re*-create. We don't dream, pal. *Can't* dream. All our memories and dreams, they're all stolen from people we eat. We just take it in, mull it over and shit it out again.'

'Our experience is unique. Our vision. Mortals can barely comprehend what it is like for us.'

'And there's an entire level of our society aimed at keeping it that way. That painter – once my piece ran, even though only a dozen students and the editor probably read it – he vanished. Gone. Maybe he'll surface in another couple hundred years, still churning out the same old stuff. The ultimate retro knock-off artist. Can an artist plagiarise himself?' Yoshi smiled, which Kevin assumed was all the answer he was expecting.

'Melpomene opens my mind,' Blake said. 'She's unique, an angel, a muse. She lets me imbibe the creative spark, she opens the window to my vision, she guides my hand and my verse with the world she sees through her unique eyes.'

Yoshi shrugged, as if to say, whatever.

'I cannot lose her,' Blake said, brandishing his pen like a sword. 'I simply cannot.'

But the sad fact was, if Danica couldn't, or wouldn't help Melpomene, she already was lost.

THIRTY-NINE

Reece sat on the back stairs of his house – his family's house – on Hamilton Hill, quietly smoking as he surveyed the city before him; the rising sun throwing dirty pink light over the buildings, traffic streaming over the twin arches of the Gateway bridges, the river a silver snail trail meandering across the gloom.

He wasn't meant to visit; too compromising, his all-but-ageless face poking around his old neighbourhood. The corp kept the yard tidy and the mailbox empty, just enough to keep the neighbours from complaining. Usually VS would've just taken the property and given him some cash or just a howdy do, but Mira had seen to it, calling it his retirement package.

He liked to come here regardless. It was a chance to clear his head away from Thorn's stifling air conditioning and bland corridors.

Last night had been a disaster. Four Arms on the phone, presumably a tip-off; no trace of him since. No word from Felicity. No mention of Matheson's arrest. Just a sense of expectation, of desperation. A hush in the corridors of power.

He hadn't slept well, had awoken in a sweat, flushed and dry-mouthed, heart thudding. He'd been plagued by a familiar dream, one reluctant to release him, and all the more powerful for its repetition.

Mira, tied down, and Hospitaller Dr Tran reaching with his upright fisted hand, blood in the hollow of the thumb, telling her there'd be no dessert if she didn't tequila. Taking his blood, feeling it worming through the noise, a banshee ripping open doors in an asylum, the corridors echoing with piercing wails and the screams of the dying; faces and entrails floating down the red-lit halls.

Reece wiped his face, aware of the shake as the dream flashed across his vision again.

He felt the weathered timber of the stair under his hand, the heat of the cigarette burned down almost to his fingers.

Sunlight, lancing across the city, struck sparks from the towers. He imagined the shutters closing on Thorn's windows. Imagined the vampires settling in for the day.

Tonight, there would be the toast of allegiance, the in-house tithe in which most of Maximilian's fangers and red-eyes gave up an offering of blood and received a serve of vampire and cow blood in return. Familiares of board members were usually exempt, relying on their bludgers for sustenance. Tonight, though, they were sure to bleed Reece, simply for the joy of being able to, now that Mira was locked away.

Which gave him today. The best part of thirteen hours between now and sunset. He squinted at the breaking day, feeling the warmth, the turning from night cool to day heat.

He rolled and lit another smoke, his thoughts following its tendrils into phantasmic futures, the all-too-real past.

His mother had died here, of complications due to alcohol abuse; her body hadn't been found for the best part of a month and the papers had been outraged at this sad indictment of the breakdown of community spirit. Didn't people know their neighbours any more? There was no denying he'd felt bad that VS hadn't been on top of it. She was, after all, his mother, and they were meant to be monitoring such possible Achilles heels. Maybe that was why she'd lain there for *only* a month.

The house had been empty since. It was on the side of the hill overlooking a bend in the river, the city in the distance, salubrious suburbs on the opposite bank. He could see cruise liners dock at wharves that hadn't been there when he was a kid and this house had been worth a bit, but not the mint it was now. A lick of paint, some new iron on the roof, wouldn't go astray.

He wasn't supposed to visit the family graves, either, though that hadn't stopped him. But he'd found the headstones offered no comfort. The house was a little better. He could reach back to the heady days before the noises in the night, before the bruises around his mother's eyes and along his sister's veins. Back when it was good.

The city had been smaller then, in geography and outlook.

He liked to come here to remind himself of that, of them. He wouldn't often go inside, but rather, would sit here looking at the city, imagining his retirement once Mira was gone and he'd been cut loose. He wondered whether they'd allow him to slowly moulder or help him on his way; VS didn't like loose ends.

How long would it take to find his body, if anyone did?

He had a cache here, one of a couple. It was tempting to pry up the floorboards in the granny flat under the house, take the ID and the money and split. But the fact remained that Mira was in bedlam, and that was a hell of a thing.

Kevin Matheson held the key to saving her and possibly Reece as well. If anyone could overcome his menopause, it was she. Mira was one of the most powerful bloodhags known, only a shade weaker than her mother, Danica. Vee had nothing on her; if he discovered that Vee had leaked the information about Jasmine Turner, had led to Mira's bedlam in an effort to take her place, he'd happily take the freak's head and what happened next be damned.

He'd been there when Mira had bought Vee – firmly a him back then. A rare overseas journey, Reece accompanying Mira to a slave auction from a reputedly cruel and, in the flesh, distasteful vampire by the name of Laurie Lee. The bloodhag was incumbent in New Orleans, a place she liked to visit once in a while and raise some Caine. This time, she'd raised Vee, himself a bloodhag of promising power, but one she was happy to part with for a princely sum to allow a relocation to another country for another spell.

'People tell such tales,' Mira had told him when Reece had broached the subject of Laurie Lee's entertainments: blood fresh from the vein, extracted indelicately, in rites that could only be classed as torture. There was talk of organs and puree and freshly squeezed.

Mira had laughed, there among a mere half dozen others gathered for the bidding. 'They can imagine worse horrors to explain the simple ones, and yet, the ones they imagine somehow never surpass the reality of their own cruelty.'

'Slavery is cruel,' he'd said.

'Oh, I agree.' Mira put on a passable Southern accent. 'I prefer to keep my herd in line through kindness.' She touched his cheek in a way that repelled him and made him shiver.

Before the night was over, Mira had added a blood band to her wrist, a sign of her link to Vee, now her apprentice; and they'd quit the city for the long, uncomfortable, island-hopping flight home. VS's resources did not stretch to a private jet. The journey, albeit in business class, occurred mostly at night.

New Orleans had been hot, he recalled. As hot as Queensland. This was his home and he wasn't going to leave it. Not for anyone. Mira needed him, and it was perhaps testament to her kindness that he left the tin box under the floorboards, deliberately squashed out his cigarette and drove back to Thorn.

The toast of allegiance was tonight, when von Schiller's minions would bleed and let Vee taste their lives, and the freak was welcome to his.

As long as they had Mira, he wasn't going anywhere, even if it was the death of him.

FORTY

Bella roused them mid-afternoon, sunlight lasering through the dusty air from behind blinds and curtains, the heat making the house creak like an old man's joints. Even the crows sounded exhausted.

'Company,' she told them, and shortly after, from the doorway, Li Li said, 'We've gotta get moving. Clock's ticking.'

Wrapped in blankets, they followed her to the bottom of the stairs, where she told the vampires to hop into a beaten-up Land Rover, and Bella and Ambrose to take the rear seat of a sedan.

'No,' Blake said. 'I need them.'

'What's this about?' Kevin asked, aware of Yoshi gripping his sword; that Li Li was well within striking distance.

'The red-eyes are staying elsewhere,' Li Li said. 'They can pick you up when we get back.'

'We didn't agree to this,' Kevin said.

'You want to stand out here and debate it?'

Blake indicated for his followers to do as Li Li said. The car drove off as soon as the doors closed, leaving Li Li to drive the Rover and Williams to ride shotgun.

The rest crawled into the back of the four-wheel-drive, grateful for the shade offered by a canvas tarpaulin.

'Just like old times,' Kevin said.

Kala grimaced. She sat at the cabin end, wrapped like a lonely jillaroo in Akubra and Driza-Bone.

'Those red-eyes could've been useful,' Yoshi said.

'We got enough myxos,' Kala said.

Myxos – Taipan's term for red-eyes. She'd been one once, had hated the derogatory term. Point made, then, Kevin reckoned. 'So where are we headed?'

'We're going to drive around for a bit, just to flush out any tails.' She checked her watch. 'We've got almost two hours to kill before the last barge.'

'Barge?' Yoshi stared at her, fist tight on his katana's scabbard. 'You didn't tell me we were going across water.'

'What's wrong, pal? Can't swim?' Her jibe lost some of its effect as she reached to hide a yawn.

He shook his head and sat back, jaw rigid.

'Don't worry,' she said. 'It'll be dark when we get where we're going. Meantime, stick your letter opener in this.' She nudged a long Cordura bag across the floor toward him, a logo with a rod and line painted on the side. 'And the rest of your blades, all of you. We're going fishing.'

FORTY-ONE

They drove off the ferry. Under the dual weights of sunshine and suspicion, they kept their heads down. From inside the vehicle it sounded as if they were part of an invasion: shouts, the whine and thump of the lowering ramp, the revving engines and growl as they convoyed off, the clouds of fresh diesel exhaust mixing with the heavy scent of brine. Seagulls squawked and a pelican grated out a protest.

The Rover ploughed through sand. Late afternoon sunlight striped the canvas with shadows. Kevin peeked through a curtain draped to separate the cabin from the tray; they were driving along a narrow trail almost arched by trees. The sand was the colour of bone and ash. Vehicles had dug deep ruts in the track. The Rover wallowed in places where the sand was soft. From the angle of the shadows, he figured they were heading more or less north.

'Welcome to K'gari,' Kala said. She wore sunglasses despite the canvas gloom.

Yoshi looked bewildered.

'It used to be called Fraser Island,' Kevin said. 'Biggest sand island in the world.' He shook his head. *A bloody island.*

'There are wild dogs here, right?' Yoshi said. 'They bite people.'

'Stupid people, who think dingoes are tame.' Kala looked at Kevin. 'Stupid people feed the dingoes and then other people get bitten.'

'Leave the mutts alone, huh?' Yoshi said.

Blake patted his brow with a kerchief; the cloth came away smeared with red sweat. 'How much farther?'

'We'll be there about dark.'

It couldn't come soon enough for Kevin. The sun weighed him down, burning his flesh and glazing his eyesight, filling his joints and bones with fever pain. Thirst provoked equal parts desire and fear.

'Aren't you worried about being trapped here?' Kevin asked Kala, desperate for distraction.

She turned to Yoshi. 'How old are you?'

'What do you mean?'

'How long have you been one of us?'

'Ten-year anniversary is coming up.'

'That's tin,' Blake said. 'You get tin for ten.'

'I'm not married,' Yoshi said.

'There are two ways onto K'gari: boat and plane. We were just on the last barge of the day, and what air strips there are aren't equipped for night landings.'

'But you've got to get off again,' Yoshi said.

'How many times you been on a boat since you got munched?'

'Never.'

'And why's that?'

'I've never been into boats, much.' She dared him with a look, and he conceded, 'I don't fancy drowning. Over and over again. Waiting for some shark to come put me out of my misery.'

'Same for VS. Even if they did have the balls to cross the water, as Kevin the walking tourist brochure pointed out: this is the largest sand island in the world. Good luck finding us, and even better luck stopping us leaving.'

They drove on, just the rattle and thump and sway of the vehicle, nervousness rising as the light faded.

The Rover pulled up at a Y junction. Li Li spoke to someone who emerged from the scrub. The man, face shaded by a broad-brimmed hat, slapped at his neck.

'Only bloodsuckers are the midges,' the man said.

'Eyes open,' Li Li told him. 'It's getting dark.'

The man brandished a walkie-talkie by way of farewell before slinking back into the bush. The Rover moved on.

'Only way in,' Kala said.

'Only way out?' Kevin asked.

'We've been on the run for decades, Kevvie. We're not stupid.'

The Rover eventually nosed out onto the beach. Sunset pierced clouds with golden beams that sparkled on the water. The sand glowed deep orange. Bathtub waves lapped the shore.

'Should be just up ahead. A gap, there; see it, Li Li?'

The driver followed Kala's pointing finger. A track led between dunes taller than the Rover, the sand matted down with grass and vines and scrubby she-oaks. They entered a sparsely treed bowl backed by another, taller dune. A camper van was parked with its nose pointing toward the gap. A table, chairs and gas barbecue sat under an awning. A middle-aged woman with a shotgun watched them arrive.

'You've made friends, too,' Kevin said.

'We needed bodies,' Kala said.

'Can you trust them?' Yoshi asked.

'More than I trust you.'

'Well, I guess that'll have to be good enough.'

They parked and piled out. Williams put the bags containing their weapons on the table. Grey twilight settled upon them with a chill. The mainland was a dark line on the horizon.

Seagulls called and the sea made the barest of lullaby lappings. The trees were still.

Kala dropped the tailgate to make it easier to haul Mel out. They sat her in a chair.

The shotgun-toting woman watched them, her fingers flexing on the weapon.

Kala kissed her and called her Edie. She smelled of suntan lotion and mosquito repellent and wood smoke. 'All clear?'

'No one's come by since you.'

'Let's do it.'

Edie pulled a whistle from her pocket and blew it.

Kevin winced.

From the underbrush up the slope behind the camp came a single yip, and then Byely and Cherny came pelting out of the bush, ears back and tails wagging. They sniffed around the new arrivals, then came to Kevin for an ear rub. Byely huffed at Blake, who stayed close to Mel, cane in hand.

Danica came at a more leisurely pace. She'd dreadlocked her hair since Kevin had last seen her, the strands just visible under her shawl. Bangles and pendants glinted in the twilight. She carried a pair of riding boots, her bare feet visible under the hem of her black, beaded abaya. 'No trouble?'

'Thanks for agreeing to this,' Kevin said. 'If you can help her–'

'Did Kala explain my proposition?' Yoshi interrupted.

'I am familiar with the head of your house, Kohito-san, and will consider the details. One thing at a time.'

Danica kneeled in front of Mel and held her face gently so she could look into her eyes. She handed Kevin his talisman. Their fingers touched.

A flash in his mind, transporting him: of her dripping his blood into a vial in that incense-thick room, and later, of Mira reefing the pendant from his naked chest, and Kala snatching it back, clasping it in her bloody fist. He had thought at the time it had been a sign that she'd wanted to live. Maybe he'd misinterpreted an accident for purpose.

'Max, you said?' Danica asked.

'What?'

'Max did this, you said.'

'I believe so.'

'Why?'

'Punishment for helping me.'

'And me,' Blake said. 'Her defilement cuts to my very quick.'

'Or because they knew you were the only person who had any chance of curing her,' Kala said, and looked to the sky. 'Do you hear that?'

'A plane,' Edie said. 'The come over all the time, heading into the Bay.'

'Let's take her into the caravan where we can have some privacy,' Danica said. 'The sooner we get started, the sooner we can all leave.'

'I'm coming too,' Blake said, and she shot him a look. 'I am her–'

'You can wait out here. Your presence upsets my dogs; it upsets me.'

'I really don't like this,' Kala said.

Kevin looked up, the sky filled with stars, but no sign of hazard lights. 'I can hear a plane, too.'

'Is that something flapping?' Kala asked.

'Seagulls?' Yoshi suggested. He crossed to the table, and Kala said, 'Hey, we're not done yet,' but he dug his sword and a submachine gun from the pile of equipment as Li Li and Williams covered him.

'Bloody big seagulls,' Kevin said.

Mel, standing with Danica at the stair into the camper van, looked over her shoulder and cried, 'The invisible worm has found out thy bed of crimson joy!'

Blake grabbed Danica's arm. 'Please, heal her – heal her now!'

Mel, off balance, stumbled, would have fallen to the ground had Edie not caught her.

Danica pulled herself free. 'It's not like throwing a switch. There's no simple antidote. It could days, weeks, months, to drain Max's poison, and do it without destroying her sanity.'

'Guys? I think there's something up there.' Kala hauled out her walkie-talkie.

Kevin ran to Yoshi's side and armed himself. Kala's red-eyes faced the beach, weapons poised. The dogs growled at the waves, barked, as though picking up on the nervous tension. Or something else.

Blake sat with his back to the camper, Mel clutched in his embrace.

Kala said, 'There's definitely something out there. Get Danica to the Rover. Call in the boat in case we need a fast exit. Damn you, Kevin!'

A shadow moved across stars, faster than a cloud. There was the sound of cloth flapping, a flag in a strong breeze. A very big seagull indeed.

'Bats?' Yoshi said, sounding desperate.

'No way a bat could've kept up with us,' Kevin said.

He heard a thump, like a bale of hay hitting the ground. Rustling, like someone making a bed, flipping out the sheets.

The dogs barked and capered, muzzles raised as though biting at sand flies.

'Let's get the fuck out of here,' Kevin said.

FORTY-TWO

The toast of allegiance was a grand event that took place once a fortnight. The board oversaw the proceedings. Mira randomly sampled the blood of the assembled faithful; the Strigoi had the authority to taste anyone outside the board and their Familiares at any time, but this was done with pomp and ceremony. She often made a comment on what she'd seen, the more embarrassing the revelation the louder her voice. And then the troops lined up in order of rank: Heinrich's small cadre of elite Fallschirmjaeger, the Hunters, the GS and the handful of lowly VSS red-eyes waiting until last. There was a speech. Then the filling of the chalice, a spill from each member of the board, and each soldier in turn approached the dais and drank the cocktail that kept them in peak condition.

It was a sombre occasion. Tonight was damn near a wake, with only a fraction of the usual bodies in the room.

And no Mira.

No Hunters.

None of Heinrich's Fallschirmjaeger and very few Gespenstenstaffel.

Standing in for Mira, Vee did not taste anyone.

Maximilian von Schiller told the gathering to hold the line. That they were the chosen ones, bloodied, depleted, but they would rebuild, they would rise and conquer. Their brothers and sisters in the field were embarked on an important mission that might, by morning, yield a major triumph. Drink and be ready to build on their success, he said.

The board didn't look too convinced. Several conspicuously eyed their watches as two nurses wheeled out the urn – an antique bowl and ladle from which the brew would be dispensed.

Hospitaller Tran invited the troops to come forward.

Reece was one of the last to go up; even Nigel went ahead of him.

Reece had spent the day asking questions without getting answers, of being stonewalled and insulted. And that'd just been inside Thorn, as he tried to find out what was going on with the Hunters, to get a fix on Matheson or the Needle. He just needed a lucky break; none had come. There were no suspects to verbal, no witnesses or snitches to lean on. Being among the last to drink tonight was the perfectly crap end to a perfectly crap day.

Tran ladled blood into a pewter chalice and offered it to Reece. 'A bit different to straight from Mira's tit, I don't doubt.'

'You tell me, Doc.'

Tran frowned.

'I wouldn't let the Old Man catch you swapping bodily fluids with his daughter, if I were you.'

'How–' Tran's eyes narrowed. 'The day is coming, Reece, when you might regret not having been more friendly.'

He withdrew the chalice before Reece could taste it, and motioned the next man forward.

Fuck Tran. Reece surveyed the board, found Vee smirking from what should've been Mira's place next to Maximilian. Hunger made his guts growl. Usually, after the ceremony, Mira would summon him for a private tasting; her eyes bloodshot, her lips twisted in that deadly razor smile by all the secrets she'd imbibed. But tonight Vee was in Mira's place; and the only blood Reece got, would normally have got, if he hadn't insulted Tran, was *goon* – that vapid mix of watered-down vampire blood that kept the wolf from the door, but lacked the personal touch.

The rim of the cup was so cold; always cold. The blood barely warm, thick, gelatinous, with no heart to push it hot and foaming into his mouth. Hard to go back. Very hard. Harder still to know it was all coming to an end. Even if Mira had torn open her chest and said, here, straight from the heart, it wouldn't have mattered in the long run. The blood had lost its potency, his body worn out from it, running hot for far too long. How he missed her. And how he hated Tran for noticing.

As the last red-eye wiped her mouth on the cloth held out to her by Tran, the board began filing out; the gathering was dismissed almost as an afterthought.

'Why the rush?' Reece wondered, only then realising he'd said it out loud.

'They're going to the war room,' a nearby GS told him. Always keen to show their superior knowledge, the Black Shirts, especially to a recent reject. 'It's been all hands on deck all day. The balloon's going up – tonight by the sound of that speech.'

'Any idea where?'

'North, is the whisper.' He lowered his voice, 'It might be Dee. Picking up where you left off, eh, *Private*.'

His reputation had preceded him.

'I wish them luck.'

'How long has your lot been hunting her?'

He smiled. 'All my non-life.'

'Looks like you might need a new hobby. Bullet catching, maybe. Look, here's your target practice buddy.'

The man laughed and moved off as Nigel approached. He slipped a note into Reece's palm. 'One of Marshall's Familiares gave me this for you.'

'You read it?'

'Course not!'

Not even a text message? How paranoid was Marshall getting? Reece flicked the paper open. 'Closing in on D. Need N to name names NOW.'

'There goes my night,' Reece muttered, crushing the note.

'Bad news, boss?'

'Just some hatches to batten down.'

'Thought you were still on medical leave.'

'More fool me, eh?'

'Yeah, boss; never figured you for a bunny, but I guess this place–'

He clapped Nigel on the shoulder. 'Brilliant, Nigel. I'd better go hop to it.'

FORTY-THREE

Kala's walkie-talkie kicked into life. A male voice:

Something on the beach. Moving toward you. Maybe four–

And then a woman's:

On the beach. Can you see anything? Bruno, can you–

'Bruno?' Kala said. Then louder: 'Bruno? Are you there? Skip? What is it? What did you see?'

'Move out,' Kevin yelled, gun drawn. 'Get Dee away from here.'

Williams ushered Danica toward the Rover. They'd covered half the distance when he grunted, threw up his hands and fell to the ground. Danica slid down next to him.

Yoshi fell down. Edie stepped toward Danica and collapsed, leaving a bloody splash on the side of the camper.

Kevin crouched, gun poised. The dogs, barking furiously, stood guard over Danica.

Li Li crouched near the camper, confused as to where the danger was coming from. Blake clutched Mel like a shield.

The shots sounded like blasts of compressed air; Kevin heard the metallic snick of the bolt and ejector after each one.

Yoshi hauled himself to his knees only to be knocked down a second time. Kala crouched behind the overturned table, gun out. Holes appeared in the table, crunching through like bites in an apple. Kala sprawled backward, her chest bloody.

Kevin looked to the beach and saw a muzzle flash on the crest of the dune. He went down without firing a shot.

But he heard gunfire, like being in a barrel with firecrackers. He heard men shouting. One, Blake maybe: 'Don't touch her!' And someone else: 'Take him down! Get the bloodhag!' And: 'Take out that motherfuckin' snipe–'

Volleys of automatic fire, fading, and the crack of a large-calibre rifle.

Blake: 'What about us? You can't leave us–'

And then came a distinct thump, like a cricket ball thudding into the ground.

A blast of heat and sound rolled Kevin in the sand. He came up on all fours, only to be rolled by a second blast, one that came with slicing pain in his legs and back.

The Rover was on fire.

A gunshot sounded from the dune at his back, and a figure in black that had been kneeling near the gap in the dune went down like a sack of shit. Blake lay at the edge of the camp, cane sword glinting by his hand. Mel had been rolled under the camper.

Yoshi was dragging himself to his feet, Kala too. The three red-eyes lay still; Williams' body was on fire, giving off a gut-churning stench. And there, just reaching the beach, two men in black were dragging a limp Danica.

Kevin found an assault rifle, pulled himself up onto his elbows and fired long bursts at the retreating figures. A line of winking lights returned fire.

The beach behind the attackers came alight with red flares. A two-engine airplane touched down on the hard sand and came to a whining standstill, props whirring. Soldiers retreated toward it.

The side door opened. A man in a suit stood in the gap,

waving, shouting, 'Bring her, bring her, *raus schnell* you bastards.'

Yoshi crawled over to Kevin as bullets flew around them. The camper rattled with hits. The dogs whimpered, rubbing their heads in the sand, pawing at wounds.

'I count maybe nine, plus whoever's in the plane,' Yoshi said.

'We can't let them take her,' Kevin said.

'I don't know we got a lot of choice, pal.'

'Grenades on that dead dude there.'

'Not even we can throw that far, even if we could get to him before he gets up again.'

Kevin looked around for options. The two dogs whined as they crawled through the sand toward the plane. Blake was stirring.

'Make sure that cunt doesn't get up,' Kevin said.

Yoshi shot Blake.

Kevin shimmied across to the dogs, tore into his arm, and let them both lick at the cut.

Fuck, it hurt, those tongues pushing into the wound, lapping at blood he couldn't afford to lose.

He reached out through the blood, calling on Taipan's presence, channelling the memory of his maker summoning cattle...

Bush tucker

...and he felt the connection click with Byely and Cherny. They understood. They were willing.

Yoshi and the sniper were still firing, and Kala had joined them. Several attackers had fallen, but others had formed a ragged arc in front of the plane while two figures tried to get a struggling Danica up and in. Bullets dug up sand, pinged on the plane's fuselage. The podgy suit at the door ducked back and Danica sprawled on the sand.

Kevin hustled the dogs forward as he charged at the downed

trooper. The man stirred. Kevin shot him in the head. The dogs barked. Kevin flopped down beside the body, and the dogs followed suit, one on either side.

Yoshi dug into the sand on his left side and fired a burst. 'What now?'

Kevin pulled two grenades from the soldier's webbing.

'Any idea how long these fuses are?'

'Six seconds, maybe? Eight at the most, I'd guess.'

'It's gonna be tight.'

'No way can you throw that far. It's gotta be seventy, eighty yards.'

'I'm not going to. We need to give the dogs their chance.'

He gave each dog a grenade. They bit down, understanding, linked by blood. He pulled both pins, and told them, 'Go!'

'Hope the release doesn't go early,' Yoshi said as he changed magazines.

'Cover them,' Kevin said, and began snapping off shots.

The dogs bolted, like greyhounds out of the box, low to the ground, sand flying up from their paws.

Kevin summoned a doppelganger. It was bloody hard work, with the noise and the fear and the anxiety; his wounded body protesting at being forced to concentrate. The figure appeared, wavering, ghostly, on the ocean side of the plane, and some men turned to it, shouting in surprise, and fired. It vanished, Kevin unable to keep up the illusion. Hot liquid ran from his eyes and nose.

The dogs had spread out, Cherney going in hard and straight, Byely, a little slower, limping slightly, going wide.

A trooper fired from the hip. Cherney sprawled as though she had hit a trip wire, rolled and flopped at the man's feet. An explosion threw the trooper back and knocked another off his feet. The plane rocked as sand and smoke sprayed up. Shrapnel whirred.

Byely jagged around a gunman and ran for the plane. Two soldiers were lifting Danica up to the suit. Byely knocked them down as he leaped for the open door. The man in the suit fell backward out of sight. Danica fought to free herself from her captor's grip as the dog tried to scramble into the plane.

'No,' Kevin shouted. 'That's not what–'

An explosion blinded him. Danica, the dog, the soldiers, vanished in the flame, the roar.

The plane's wing collapsed; the fuselage flickered with flame. The plane edged forward, pivoting on its left side where its landing gear was stuck, the wing digging into the earth. And then the fuel in the plane's wing exploded, and the rest went up.

The troopers still standing were bowled over.

'Let's get in there,' Yoshi said, 'before they recover. I don't want to face those boys in hand to hand.'

He and Kevin ran across, firing at anyone who looked remotely mobile. They decapitated them all.

For a long moment, they caught their breath, swords and guns dangling from their hands.

'Fuck.' Kevin surveyed the wreckage; desperately hoping Danica had survived the blast. 'Fuck!'

'Sorry, pal.' Yoshi squeezed Kevin's shoulder. He rolled a body onto its back. 'So who are these guys, anyway?'

'Gespenstenstaffel?' Kevin suggested. 'Max's stormtroopers.'

The men wore black jumpsuits, combat boots and bulletproof vests. They had eagles embroidered in black on their shoulder tabs. 'Though the ones I've seen have a little GS logo on their collars. Maybe these blokes are something different.'

'Well, they're ex-whatever now, bud. All vamps, though.'

Kevin swore, again, one more hearty 'Fuck'.

'Come on,' Yoshi said. 'There's nothing more to do here. Let's head back.'

They found Bruno, a hunting rifle slung across one shoulder, emerging from the scrub at the base of the dune, and Kala checking their dead. Blake and Mel sat against the camper. It was hard to say who looked the more dazed.

'Where's Danica?' Kala asked.

Kevin turned away from her. 'Gone.'

'Gone where?'

He pointed to the burning wreckage. Was that a piece of dog he saw there? A hindquarter? Bile burned in his throat.

'What happened to the plane?' she asked.

'We blew it up,' Yoshi said.

She slumped to the sand. Then stared at Kevin. 'I hope you're satisfied. I hope your revenge was worth – this.'

Kevin turned his back and stared out to sea as the grief and anger threatened to pull him under. Tears stung his eyes.

Blake stood, wiped sand from his hands, and then slunk across to survey the mess on the beach. There were bodies everywhere.

He grabbed Kevin's arm. 'What about Mel? Who will cure her now?'

'No one, Blake. No one will cure her.'

'No, no, no.' He released his grip, his arms dropping as though made of straw, and he stumbled to the nearest chair still upright and slumped into it, head in his hands. 'They were meant to take us with them. To heal her.'

'You gave us up?' Kevin said.

Blake took his fountain pen apart and placed the ink canister on the table, then took off his boot and slammed the heel on to it. Pieces of metal lay amid the black splatter.

'You gave us up!' Kevin hefted his sword.

Kala seized his wrist. 'Enough!'

'I just wanted to save her,' Blake said

'I might have a way,' Yoshi said.

All eyes turned to him.

'A man in Sydney. A sorcerer, I guess you'd call him.'

'Not that fella Uhgrau you mentioned?' Kevin asked.

'That's the one. He works with blood magic. Different to your bloodhag, but still, he's pretty darn powerful. If anyone can fix her, he can.'

'Why on earth would he–'

'You can't take her!' Blake said. 'I need her.'

Kevin pulled his pistol and shot Blake through the head.

Mel blinked. A fresh trickle of blood dripped from her nose, across her lips, down her chin.

'Jesus, Kevin,' Kala said as she wiped the girl's face.

'He fought 'em off,' Bruno said, cradling his rifle. 'They was gonna finish you all, but he went to town with that rapier of his when they tried to get at the girl. Between him and ol' Winnie here, we kept 'em off youse.'

The sentry from the road ran up, panting and sweaty, as a small boat appeared from the north.

'That's your ride,' Kala told Kevin.

'Shit,' Yoshi said.

'We'll clean this up best we can, take the camper, catch the barge to Inskip.'

'Where will you go?' Kevin asked.

'Do you really expect me to answer that?'

'Don't stay here too long. They'll send someone. Might even be watching the barges.'

'For you. Not us.' She looked at the smear of Edie's blood and brain on the camper. 'Bring me some water, Bruno. Let's see to our people. VS's spin doctors can handle the rest.'

'At least we've already got a fire lit,' Bruno said.

Kala took in the entire scene of devastation. She nodded once and looked away. But not before Kevin saw the tears brimming so dark and glistening, red on red.

'Kala?' he offered.

'End of the line,' she said, her eyes flaring green as she turned her back on him, tears withdrawn behind that icy glimmer. 'You'd better get started. It's a bit of a trip. Skipper will get you to the mainland okay. I'm sure you'll be able to find your own way back to Brisbane.'

Kevin and Yoshi helped Mel down to the water where the boat had anchored. The tide had started to come in; the boat pointed out into the bay as though eager to leave.

They scrambled aboard.

A shout from the shore: 'Hey!'

Kala ran after them. 'Aren't you forgetting something?'

Kevin and Yoshi looked at each other; shook their heads.

'The bloody poet!'

'He can make his own way back,' Kevin said. 'Or call his VS mates for a lift.'

'He knows me, Kevin.'

'It's your call, but remember this, Kala – VS already knows you. You're no safer than the rest of us. You're just further down the shit list.'

'I'd better keep my head down then, hadn't I?'

'It's not the end of the line,' he said, his voice drowned by the ignition of the twin outboards. 'Not while Mira's alive.'

Skipper pulled up the anchor and hurried back to the console to get them underway. Overhead, the sky was filled with stars. Kevin did not look back.

FORTY-FOUR

They huddled in the boat, aware that there was precious little shelter from the sun should they get caught out. The boat bobbed with the waves as Skipper steered south.

'Where are you taking us?' Kevin asked.

'Over the side if you don't let me concentrate. The Strait is a bitch at the best of times. At night–' She indicated her irritation with a violent shake of her head.

'We'll need a car,' Yoshi said to Kevin. One hand held the side; the other supported Mel's head pillowed on a life jacket beside him. The hull crunched on a wave, showering them with a fine spray of salt water. 'I can drop you in Briz-bane and keep going. I'll have her safe in Sydney in two days tops.'

'Sounds good,' Kevin said. 'Though I'm not sure why you're doing this. Or why this sorcerer of yours would help.'

Yoshi shrugged. 'Uhgrau will cream his pants when he knows that Maximilian did this to her. Who knows what he'll find. A few of Max's secrets might keep my big boss happy; considering.'

They were silent for a time. The smack of water on hull, the whine of the motors marked their progress.

'How long?' Kevin asked Skipper.

'We'll be there well before dawn, don't worry. I'm not all that keen on a dose of wolfbite myself, y'know.'

'Where's *there*?'

'We're going all the way up the river to Maryborough. It's a small place, quiet, lots of dark hidey holes, and, y'know, there's people.'

'People?' Kevin said.

'I don't know about you,' Yoshi said, 'but I could sure use a snack.'

'Can you drive a boat?' the red-eye asked.

'No.'

'Then eyes front. This trip doesn't come with meals.'

'I couldn't eat anyway,' Yoshi said, his knuckles white on the side of the boat.

'You really don't like boats, do you?' Kevin asked, though he was sure his grip was just as tight.

'Never interested me. I'd go out with friends, sure, but I was more of an indoors kind of guy. If I had to get fresh air, I preferred the mountains. I like ground under my feet. And now, well, the thought of being down there...'

Kevin checked the tie on his life vest.

The only time he'd been on a boat had been a tinnie on the river back home. This was not particularly pleasant. How the red-eye was steering, he had no idea. Islands slid by in the night, little more than shadowy shapes; and there were areas of white froth she said were reefs and sandbanks. She had some kind of GPS – a depth sounder, perhaps – but mostly steered by instinct.

Back in the day – before he'd been liable to shrivel up and die – this might've been fun. But at night it was interminable, and now all he could think about was being tumbled on the seabed, like some old-time diver without a suit, drowning for eternity.

Less than two months ago, he'd been a mechanic working for his dad. Now, well, drowning and gunfights were the least of it. Now, Danica was dead, and it was his fault.

He clenched his jaw and waited to land. He'd rather face another batch of Max's goons than spend any more time out here.

FORTY-FIVE

The name of the woman at the front desk was Cheryl, but everyone called her Amelia. She didn't seem at all happy to see him, which was not the level of customer service he'd expected.

'Phillip Reece. Haven't seen you in, like, forever.' She seemed distracted, as though she'd left the oven on.

'I've been out of town a lot.' In truth, this wasn't really his kind of place. He'd been here on duty rather than to see the escorts; he'd always preferred roll-your-owns.

'I heard that. Travel hasn't been kind to you, huh?'

'It can be wearing. But you do appreciate coming home, don't you?'

'What is it then: business or pleasure?'

'Is there a difference?'

'There is for you.'

'I heard you had a new girl. I'd like a half hour of her time.'

'Got a couple of new faces, Phil. You got a preference?' Her nails tapped on the desk, fumbling at a pen.

'One I want is called Rabbit.'

She shook her head, brow creasing, but he cut her off to save the pantomime. She wasn't very good.

'I'm going through an Alice in Wonderland phase,' he said. 'Just a quick talk, Cheryl. No one needs to know.'

The pen rolled across the desk and she slammed a hand down on it. He could see her, turning over the ramifications. He'd never used her real name before. She still had family.

'I think she's busy.'

'I'll pull up a pew then.' He strode to the waiting room, aware of Cheryl making a phone call, and arrived in the room in time to see Rabbit getting up from the bar, something pink in a martini glass behind her, and the barman setting a phone back on the wall. She wore stilettos and a black negligee, stockings, fingerless gloves to the elbow. Her hair was copper now, but there was no mistaking the silver Viscounts tattoo on her upper arm.

'I've been looking for you, Rabbit,' he said, and she said, with what she probably thought was Lauren Bacall but came across as Paris Hilton, 'Let me guess: all your life?'

'Just most of the night.' He flashed his ID and watched the mask change.

'I know you. I seen you; at the rink.' The puff went out of her, leaving wariness.

'Hey,' the bartender said. He wore just trousers and waistcoat, his arm showing a silver tatt of a broken heart. The Needle's work was everywhere, even here in one of Maximilian's key strongholds. If only those tattoos could talk.

Reece flashed his ID at the bartender. 'Rum, neat.' He gestured Rabbit back to the bar. 'C'mon, finish your drink.'

She settled, eyeing him as she sipped through the straw. His drink arrived, none too gently. 'Now get lost,' Reece said. Rabbit nodded an affirmation and the bartender got busy unstacking a dishwasher at the far end of the bar.

'You've done well for yourself, Rabbit. From streeter moll to Petite Morts, no less.'

'I'm a survivor, Hunter. I do what I have to.'

'I'm sure.' No point in setting her right. She might be less forthcoming if she knew he was just a glorified security guard.

'I realise you're on the clock, so I won't take up much of your time.'

'I've got twenty minutes yet. He's nice. A banker. Plays the international markets. Or something.'

'So how did you come to land on your back, Rabbit?'

She screwed up her face at him. 'After Johnny, um, after Johnny bought it, I was ready for a shift. I bumped into one of the girls, she said I had the pins for it. I thought, why not?'

He listened to her retro speak, and played along. All those hard-boiled novels were good for something.

'So when you were auditioning your *pins*, you didn't happen to mention that you knew who sent Johnny after the mechanic, hey?'

She smiled slyly as she swizzled her drink. Crossed her legs. Oh yeah, she had the pins for it. Maybe even the smarts.

'I really don't know what you're talking about,' she said.

'That why the mechanic took you for a drive, the night Johnny bought it? To see if you knew nothin'. What did you tell him?'

'Nothin'. I told him nothin'.'

'I found you, Rabbit. You think the mechanic won't?'

She spilled a little of her drink, the straw flicking out of her fingers.

'Scarlet?' the bartender asked.

'Back off, sport,' Reece told him. He lowered his voice, his face right next to hers. 'What will you pay me to keep your little secret, *Scarlet*?'

'A dame. Johnny said a dame came to him with a photograph, a time and a place, okay.'

'A "dame"?'

'A *woman*, okay. A *Thorn* woman.'

'Marshall?'

'No. This broad was just some go-between. Sky was the limit, if he took the grease monkey's head. That's what she told him.'

'In those words?'

'Huh?'

'I know you still got a bit of the Viscounts' retro lip, there, Rabbit, but it's important. Is that what Johnny told you the go-between said? In those exact words?'

'I don't know. That's just what he told me, all right?'

'And who was she working for?'

'He didn't say.'

'But you suspected. He gave you a hint. "The sky's the limit" he told you.'

She pulled away, then, and the bartender stood up close, saying, 'That's enough'.

Cheryl came in. 'Private Reece, is it? I have someone on the phone for you.'

The bitch had done what she should've done in the first place and checked him out. *Oh Cheryl, I thought we were friends.*

'Private?' Rabbit said.

He shrugged and started to walk out. 'Some of us land on our back, others on our arse.'

'Do you really think the grease monkey will come back? After everything that's happened?'

'Pretty sure.' He followed Cheryl toward the front counter; before the door shut behind him, he heard Rabbit asking the bartender for a rum and Coke, a double. Didn't hurt to keep her on edge, should he get the chance to continue their little chat.

There really was a phone call waiting.

Cheryl stood by his side, arms crossed, but at least she wasn't tapping her foot as he picked up the handset, an antique thing in ivory and chrome.

231

'You chasing *eine kleine nachtmusik*, Reece?'

Marshall. Sounding not quite amused.

'Yeah,' he said. 'It's quite the wonderland here.'

'I got a call from Treasurer Campbell, asking what you're doing darkening his doorstep.'

'*His* doorstep?'

'The Petite Morts do fall under his aegis.'

'Still–'

'Doesn't matter. I've been ringing you for hours.'

'I haven't listed my new number yet. Petersen took the old phone before the Gold Coast caper and, I'm told, it has been misplaced.'

'Fuckers. Hope you didn't keep your dirty pictures on it. Get your clothes on and get back here, pronto. Danica is dead. Maximilian wants a word. In person.'

FORTY-SIX

Motoring up the Mary River was excruciating, nothing but pale fields and dark mangroves and occasional specks of farmhouse lights until they'd reached the outskirts of Maryborough. Darkened houses loomed on the right bank. The barking of dogs carried across the water. Kevin hunched in the bow as they pushed upstream until a well-lit bridge appeared, like an ancient fortification bathed in orange lights. Skipper slowed the already excruciating putt-putt to a mere burble and nosed past small yachts and motor boats as she headed for a dock on the town side; the other side was a muddy bank lined with mangroves giving way to a low, barren flat of fallow fields.

Skipper tied up at the dock. The only movement was the gentle roll of the moored boats.

'End of the line, boys,' she said, by way of wishing them luck, and walked away with hands in pockets.

Kevin and Yoshi struggled to get Mel up the dock's ladder. The night was still and silent, save for the slurp of water on hull and, somewhere, a wood duck giving voice to a bad dream.

Kevin huddled with Mel behind a hedge. The street might've been a graveyard, edged in stone, two- and three-storey buildings. Businesses, by the look, all sightlessly staring.

Yoshi returned to report that many were vacant. A heritage or tourist precinct, he said, with a nod to the ornate lamps that cast small pools of radiance on the tiled footpaths on both sides of the road. 'There's a good-looking one at the far end.'

They walked Mel down. Their shuffling footsteps sounded incredibly loud.

Yoshi ripped boards off a window at the rear of the building, and shattered the glass with the tip of his scabbard. Kevin winced at the noise, but there was no apparent response. The building stank of damp and grease and oil. An old engineering works, a sign said.

They were in an office, glassed off from the rest of the building. Through the dusty panes, Kevin saw a roller door; a bare floor with bolts sticking up and faint lines in the concrete where machinery had once been anchored. A cobwebbed pulley system hung from thick beams in the ceiling.

'Should be dark enough to wait out the day,' Yoshi said.

'And then what?'

'Then we get cleaned up. We can't go anywhere looking like this.'

'Yeah, we look pretty beat up, huh.'

'I just mean the clothes. They're pretty terrible.'

Kevin chuckled. 'Fair enough. I got sand in me sand.'

'You thought about finding our ride?'

'If VS tracked us to the house, then they might've followed the van. We'll have to start again.'

'What about Blake's red-eyes?'

'Who knows? I've got no way to contact them, even assuming VS hasn't caught them.'

'So, we're on our own. First, we need clothes. Don't suppose anywhere will be open this time of the morning.'

'You'll be lucky to find a petrol station, I reckon.'

'A felony it is, then. And then we have breakfast. I don't know about you, pal, but getting the crap shot out of me does wonders for my appetite.'

FORTY-SEVEN

One of Maximilian's Familiares met Reece in the car park. Her gaze took in his utility belt, his rumpled suit. She straightened his tie and pursed her lips slightly as she took in her handiwork, a clear sign she'd done all that she could, and led him to the lift.

'We're on our way up,' she said, and Reece realised that she was talking to her mic, not simply stating the obvious.

He did the math on how long he'd been awake as the floors ticked over. Lost count, confused by the flashing numbers, stifled a yawn and ascribed it to tiredness, not nerves.

The bell rang. Round one, he thought, though it felt like maybe thirteen. Fitting. He'd been to this floor more in the past week than he had in the past year. Fucking-up will do that.

They tromped down the familiar hall to the boardroom, where his escort removed his weaponry and locked it away in a drawer. She straightened his tie again, which he'd managed to knock out of line in some reflexive attempt to avoid choking.

Preceptor Heinrich and Treasurer Tony Campbell stalked

out of the room. The door slammed behind them. Both shot him filthy looks: laser vision set to evaporate.

The Familiare swiped her ID card and thumbprinted to unlock the door. She did it all with a certain mechanical prowess that suggested someone who had yet to tire of feeling special by having access to people deemed important. She led him across the boardroom to a doorway flanked by two vampire guards wearing Maximilian's personal sigil.

Shit, he was going into the sanctum sanctorii. Was he to be a midnight snack? The Old Man might be disappointed with the vintage.

The Familiare ushered him inside the office but didn't follow. The door shut softly.

Maximilian stood at the far end of the darkened room, staring out the window. His hands were clasped behind him.

Reece could sense rather than see clouds massing darkly over the mountains to the west. There was a storm coming, of that he had no doubt.

The room was dominated by a desk, the heavy, dark timber like a monument – an altar, perhaps; and lined with bookshelves. A display case held a battered shield, a selection of bladed weapons.

A woman sat on a chaise longue off to one side. Bald. Wearing a smock without sleeves. Pale.

'Drink?' Maximilian asked, indicating the girl.

'No, thank you, my lord.' Reece tried to keep the confusion out of his voice; had the Old Man mistaken him for someone else?

'I've asked Dee to join us.'

'My lord?' No hiding his confusion this time.

Maximilian turned, looked around, as though surprised to find himself in the room. 'Out,' he snapped at the girl, who stood, curtseyed and disappeared through a rear door made to appear like wood panelling. It was half hidden behind a drape, one which Reece eventually recognised as an old, threadbare banner still attached to a pole with a splintered tip.

'Memories,' Maximilian mumbled as he adjusted the hanging material, fondling it like the hem of a mistress's negligee. 'What I wouldn't give for one bloodless dream.'

The silence stretched out.

'Things move so quickly now. Have you noticed? Like a carousel; faster and faster. You know, I once had an enemy, a man – just a man – who thwarted me; a business arrangement, a trifle, really. On his deathbed, I showed him the documents, how I'd destroyed his fortune, bankrupted his family, reduced his line to ash. I waited his entire life, Hunter Reece, to reveal my vengeance.

'I wonder did I move too fast, or too slow, for Danica to want to stay?'

Reece stood at attention, feeling the sweat bead around his collar, on the small of his back. The air conditioning was chill on his flesh.

Any minute now, the Old Man would get to the point.

Maximilian bent, the movement so sudden Reece flinched. He skimmed a folder along the table toward Reece. Papers spilled out, and photographs, white against the dark timber, the brightest things in the room. Kevin Matheson's mugshot stared up at him.

'Tell me about this cub; this *grease monkey*.'

'You've read my report, I take it.' Reece gestured toward the dossier. Maximilian preferred paper. Someone had tried to offer a briefing on a tablet, once; it'd taken days to find all the pieces of the device.

'It's a competent report of the Jasmine Turner Debacle, but it doesn't tell me about the boy. Who is he, Hunter Reece, that he can lead us all on this merry chase?' The desperation in Maximilian's voice was unexpected, disconcerting; his flesh so drawn, so grey, his face all angles and hollows.

'I'm not a Hunter anymore, my lord.'

'Don't quibble with me!' Spit flew from his lips. Fangs flashed.

'He's not even two months into the night, my lord.'

'And yet he remains at large. And yet, my best cannot reel him in.'

'Luck of the devil.'

'Perhaps.' He mulled it over some more, rubbed at his face as though to slough off his frustration; that hint of appalling weariness. 'Perhaps of two devils: Taipan and Danica.'

He looked at the view, then, and Reece stood at ease, unsure if he'd been dismissed or what. Was Maximilian working out if he could throw Reece through the plate glass; guessing how long it would take for him to hit the ground?

Then Maximilian spoke, his voice as low and dry as drifting sand. 'You might have heard: there has been another debacle, Hunter Reece.'

'I thought Petersen and Newman were on the case.'

'Petersen is dead. So too is my best pilot and all our Fallschirmjaeger. And Danica. All dead.'

'That's not good, my lord.' *And the prize for understatement of the century goes to...* And he'd never got to give Petersen his comeuppance.

'Enemy losses: three squires. *My best troops*, Reece – for three squires. And Danica gone. And with her, my best hope to bring Mira back.'

Reece kept his mouth shut. The Old Man was as tight as a tow rope, fraying in the middle. If he snapped, he could bring the whole building down.

Maximilian turned to him and his eyes were blazing green, his jaw tight, his hands fists on the table as he leaned toward Reece. 'The scales are shifting, Reece. I can *feel* them. It feels like Tannenberg. Like Stalingrad. Who *is* this pup; this, this *harbinger*?'

'He's a mechanic, my lord.'

Maximilian shook his head, then slumped, drained, into a seat at the table. 'Sit. Tell me about this mechanic. Tell me how you can kill him, before he kills us.'

It was after oh-two-hundred when Reece was dismissed. In the outer office, he paused, undid his tie. The Familiare appraised him with one raised eyebrow as she handed back his weapons. He helped himself to water from the cooler. Wished her a good day as he threw the crumpled cup in the bin and made his way to the lift. Hit 3 out of habit, stabbed 2. The lift stopped on 7. Heinrich got in. Reece decided out was better, but Heinrich blocked him. The door shut.

Heinrich threw him against the wall. Locked his forearm across Reece's chest. It was a manoeuvre Reece had used many times in asking a suspect some pertinent questions. He did not like being on the receiving end.

'What did the Old Man want?' Heinrich demanded as the lift continued its descent.

'Tea and scones. I was fresh out.'

'Don't play smart with me, Hunter. You don't have the years.'

'I'm. Not. A Hunter.'

Pressure built as Heinrich leaned into him. 'What. Did. He. Want?'

'To share the bad news. From the island.'

'Why you?'

'He likes me.'

It felt as if his chest was about to cave in. Fireworks flashed before his eyes. He struggled for breath.

'Do you really want me to take it from your blood?'

'He wanted to know about Matheson. I had nothing. It's all in the dossier.'

Heinrich pushed Reece's head to one side to bare his throat.

Fetid breath blasted over his face. Fangs glinted, shining with drool.

The lift stopped with a ding.

'Gentlemen.' Marshall, with both her Familiares.

For a long moment, no one moved. Then Heinrich stepped back.

'Get out, Private,' Marshall said, and Reece stumbled from the lift as a glaring Heinrich swiped to descend to the restricted basement level where the board had their private chambers.

'Come.' Marshall headed for her office, the two guards virtually pushing Reece along behind her. 'I'll buy you a drink and you can tell me what that was all about.'

FORTY-EIGHT

They waited till after nine o'clock, when they were certain the shops would be shut. Mel murmured inanities, but she was content to simply sit like a doll. They debated tying her up, staking her, but she showed no sign of wanting to do so much as move, let alone run. As long as the pendant masked her from any blood trace, they figured it was safe to leave her. Danica was dead. Did anyone care what happened to them now?

The streets were empty. The buildings, few more than two storeys, showed an uncomfortable mix of old and new. Glass-fronted shops squeezed into the ground floor while the original stone facades glowered above with dark windows. It reminded Kevin of his home town, although the streets were narrower here. Out west, progress had largely passed them by; here, it felt like an imposition.

Silence reigned above a low electric hum of street lights and transformers, the electric tock-tock-tock of an unused pedestrian crossing. They had to duck for cover once, hiding in a bus shelter as a taxi cruised past.

Kevin kept watch while Yoshi broke into a clothes store.

The American sniffed, muttering about the fashion time warp. They washed in a staff bathroom, grabbed a change of less touristy fare and hit the street. There were no sirens, no obvious alarm.

'Now, for some takeaway,' Yoshi said, and walked toward a splash of lights further up the road. Kevin caught up with him as he reached the corner.

There were only a few cars out the front of the pub. Chalkboards boasted of a beer garden and pool tables, and $10 steaks on Wednesdays and ladies night – first drink free – on Thursdays.

'What's today?' Yoshi asked.

Kevin had to think about that. 'Tuesday. I think.'

'Oh, well. Maybe we can get a different kind of special.'

'Is this a good idea?' Kevin said, but Yoshi was already crossing the street, and Kevin realised just how famished his companion was, and how much worse that seemed to make his own hunger.

A few drinkers, all middle-aged, all men, lined up at the public bar watched them enter, smirked, or simply looked through them, before returning to their conversations or stolid cricket viewing.

The clink of billiard balls drew them through a side door into an open area, with several pool tables on a wide, roofed verandah; the rest of the space taken up with tables and potted trees, a closed serving area on the far side, but a bar still operating. It backed onto the public bar, the one tightly T-shirted barmaid serving both between chews of gum, her lashes like Venus fly traps, her lips painted pink to match her inch-long nails.

Two girls and three lads stood around the tables, smoking, drinking, holding cues. The girls both had long hair dyed three different shades of blonde, tight jeans, open denim jackets. The boys wore old jeans and either tight T-shirts or checked shirts.

'Maybe we should wait outside,' Kevin said quietly, but one of the lads overheard.

'What's ya problem, mate? You and your chink mate too good to drink with us?'

'Just lookin' to have a quiet beer,' Kevin said.

The kid looked them up and down, a terrier of a lad in his Jim Beam T-shirt and shark tooth necklace, a stud in one ear and a respectable mullet warming the back of his neck.

'Ya not faggots, are ya?'

'Why?' Yoshi asked. 'You need a date?'

One of the girls hooted before slurping from the neck of her rum and cola, and her mate said to her, 'Good one, eh, Jessie. You need a date?' And snorted.

'Funny little chink, ain't ya,' the terrier said.

'Ya want a ladyboy, do ya, Woz,' Jessie said, causing a snort from her friend.

'You wanna go outside, do ya?' Woz continued. ''Ave a go?'

One of his mates hollered, 'Wanna give him a blow job, Woz?', and the other mimed fellatio on a pool cue.

'Fuck you, Billy,' Woz said. 'This cunt can suck my dick.' He puffed out his chest and danced up to Yoshi on the balls of his feet, his puffy eyes glinting; close enough together to give him the appearance of a tropical fish. 'How about it? You wanna go?'

Yoshi hit him. The terrier folded up like a camp chair and fell in a heap.

'Hey, enough of that,' the barmaid shouted, and the drinkers and the kids stared, all suspended in a moment of disbelief.

And then the lads put down their drinks and charged.

'You take the Nip, Streak,' Billy shouted. He was short but solid, with pinched dark eyes shaded by a curly mop of black hair. He steamed into Kevin, grabbed him by the collar and pushed him against a pool table.

Kevin's arms came up, breaking the hold, and then he

punched Billy square in the nose. Bones broke. Blood gushed. Billy's head snapped back like a Pez dispenser and he bounced along the floor, out cold.

Yoshi took to Streak like the boxing bag he resembled, breaking ribs and rupturing internal organs with a series of blows that left the lad crumpled on the floor, able only to moan.

Jessie shouted as she smashed her glass on the table and drove it at Kevin. He blocked the blow with enough power to crack her forearm. She dropped the glass. His right hand found her throat, lifted and dropped her on to the pool table in a smooth motion. Balls rolled away from the impact. He ripped out the side of her throat. Blood and booze surged through him. It had been days since he'd fed. He'd been boiled in the back of the Rover, shot and blown up. The blood hit him like a flash flood, sweeping him away.

Jessie's life submerged him: experiences, feelings, bobbing like flotsam caught in the current.

An impact roused Kevin. Something across the shoulders.

He stood in time for the baseball bat to explode against the side of his head. He fell to his knees, aware of Jessie's legs parted above him, her pants dark with piss, the smell swirling with booze and blood.

Men shouted. Bodies fell.

A man stood above him. The light shifted as he raised the bat over his head.

Kevin punched the man's knee and was rewarded with the snapping of bone, a scream. The man fell next to him, hands to his ruined joint. His bat rolled on the floor.

Kevin got to his feet to find three men swarming Yoshi. Another lay on the floor. Kevin grabbed the nearest still standing and hurled him across the room, scattering a table and chairs like ten pins. A second man turned to face him and Kevin broke his jaw with a punch, then sent him to the floor with a blow to the guts and one to the back of the head on his way down, just for good measure.

Yoshi felled the last punter then munched on his throat – just a quick skoll more out of spite than need. When he'd done slurping, he stood, unsteady, and only then pulled a pocketknife out of his gut. He dropped it to the floor. It stuck, point first, juddering.

Yoshi wiped his mouth on his sleeve. 'That didn't work out quite the way I planned.' Blood soaked his shirt; his face was flushed, his voice slurred. He weaved to the nearest pot plant and pissed a red stream, gave a sigh as he zipped up.

Kevin couldn't talk yet, just nodded, slowly, his head aching. Two, three of the guys on the ground were bleeding from nasty gashes.

'I'll get a jug for Mel.' Yoshi went to the bar where the barmaid cowered out of sight. He reached across to jerk something from her hand – a telephone – and traced the line to the base where he ripped the cord out. 'Something with a lid,' he told her. She crawled to a fridge and handed him a bottle of soft drink. He emptied it on the floor as he walked back, retrieved the pocketknife and made a hell of a mess bleeding one of the men into the bottle.

Sirens sounded by the time he was finished. The bar girl had fled.

Yoshi stood at the pool table, feeling for Jessie's pulse.

'Okay?' Kevin asked. He knew she was a nice enough girl, worked part-time at a servo on the edge of town, fucked Billy regularly and Streak occasionally, liked to sing karaoke – could've been all right if her parents had paid for lessons.

Her throat was a ruined mess, the table dark with blood.

Yoshi shook his head. 'We can't leave her looking like this.'

A man groaned and Yoshi told Kevin to see if he had wheels.

'Beggars can't be choosers,' Kevin told Yoshi, holding up a set of Ford keys, in time to see him grinding a broken glass into Jessie's wounded neck.

Yoshi licked his fingers, wiped his bloodstained mouth. 'Time to go.'

'Should we, you know, clean up?' Kevin asked.

Yoshi shook his head. 'Give VS something to do while we make our getaway.' He winked.

Kevin's gut lurched. He was happy to get out into the open air.

'Glad we took a change of clothes.' Yoshi pulled at his sodden shirt. 'These didn't last long.'

They found the car easily enough, a sedan with a dent in the rear panel.

Kevin drove the short distance to their hideout. Mel was exactly where they'd left her, staring at the sky through a barred window high on the wall. They fed her the blood, which she drank with little evidence of tasting and even less effect. Kevin cleaned the spill from her cheek and throat. He thought she might've noticed him, as he touched her, a look of pleading, of desperation, but then the shutters came down again. She shuddered once and let herself be led to the car and made to lie down on the back seat.

'How long to Brisbane?' Yoshi asked.

'Three, four hours if we take the highway, but I think we should go the long way. They'll be looking for this, once the driver tells them.'

'And you're sure you want to go back?'

'That's where Mira is.'

'Is she worth all this? Those people on the island, your friend in the back here?'

'They're the reason I can't stop.'

'If you change your mind, I think Rodan would offer you haven. I'd vouch for you.'

'So I could kill for him?'

'It rarely comes to that. Besides, for him, for you: what's the difference?' Yoshi glanced at a passing car, lowered his gun as it went past. 'What are you going to do if you manage to kill Mira? You thought about what comes next?'

'I'll worry about that when it's done.'

'Think about my offer, pal. Eternity's a long time to carry a grudge.'

'This won't last that long. I can promise you that.'

Kevin drove west. The temptation to keep driving and not stop until he'd reached home was magnetic. But there was nothing for him out there, and Yoshi's offer had less appeal. All that mattered to him was in Brisbane. He owed too many people to turn back now.

Once he'd put a good distance between them and Maryborough, he turned south for the big smoke.

Mira was all he had, now, but Yoshi's words haunted him. What would he have when she was gone?

FORTY-NINE

Reece tried not to yawn as he waited in the reception on 13. He'd got bugger-all sleep. Thorn was an angry ant nest, the death of Danica and the Fallschirmjaeger having dropped a massive shit brick right in the middle of it. He'd been on the streets all day, hunting the Needle, Matheson, anyone who might shed light on what the bloody hell was going on. That he had Maximilian and Marshall breathing down his neck and Heinrich, Campbell and half the Hunters all trying to wring it, didn't help. He almost envied Mira her bedlam; or at least the isolation it provided from the septic politics of Thorn.

Speak of the devil. Campbell, a sneer behind his smile, entered the room, with the head of Public Relations, Monica Bishop, in tow, like a dag on a sheep's arse. Their Familiares accompanied them – personal assistants in Campbell-speak. But then, Campbell was the sort of poser who wore glasses when he didn't need to, all part of his corporate facade. Bishop paused, wiping a lick of bleached fringe from her eyes, to say hello. 'How's life on two treating you, Reece? Too bad about that; you were a good Hunter, even if we didn't see much of you.'

Hypocrite: Bishop had hated that Reece, nominally a Hunter, had effectively been seconded to Mira's service from the moment she'd brought him into the organisation. A loose cannon, he'd been called.

'I heard Petersen bit the dust on Fraser,' Reece offered.

'No concern of Security, I assure you.'

'No, it was a GS operation, wasn't it? Although, were your Hunters calling the shots?'

She glared, and he had to give her points for retaining her composure in the face of an epic failure. But then, she was head of PR: hiding shit under rugs was her job.

One of the Familiares – like penguins, they were, almost identical in corporate chic suits and haircuts – tapped the tablet he cradled. 'Almost seven.'

Campbell asked the Familiare behind the desk: 'He in?'

'Waiting. You're the first to arrive.'

The group had reached the boardroom door when Christian Jensen bustled in, also trailing a suit with Bluetooth headpiece and tablet.

'Got enough toilet rolls?' Campbell asked. 'There's shit all over the fan.'

Jensen actually looked up at the ceiling. As Trappier, the organisation's logistics were his concern; his finger was on every ream of office paper, every loo roll, every box of ammo that entered the building. With his short-cropped blond hair artfully tousled and his jacket pulled tight across his narrow shoulders, he tried to look nonchalant despite his gaffe, but he couldn't stop playing with his cuffs and adjusting his tie. Another military failure must've put a dent in his balance book. Marshall's arrival saved him from trying to find a witty rejoinder to Campbell's remark.

'We having the meeting in the foyer?' she asked, and winked at Reece as she followed the others in. Jensen, the oldest of the bunch, barely came up to her shoulder.

The door had shut when Hospitaller Tran, a Familiare and

Vee arrived. Tran made small talk with the Familiare on desk duty about who was and wasn't in already, and what mood the Old Man might be in. Vee hovered, as expressionless as a mannequin, matching Reece's stare.

'Are you refreshments?' Vee asked finally.

'Cleaner, I think,' Reece said. 'You know how messy the Old Man gets when he's angry.'

Tran stiffened and pointedly ignored Reece as he led the other two toward the boardroom. Vee had not been assigned a personal assistant.

Reece wanted to ask how Mira was, if there'd been any improvement, but he wouldn't give them the satisfaction of ignoring him.

They went in.

The Familiare resumed her typing – the von Schiller machine, churning twenty-four-seven. Always night-time somewhere. Reece checked the time.

The meeting should've started by now. No Heinrich. Had he entered by another door?

If not, the Old Man wouldn't be impressed.

Reece had arrived early, just in case; as well as to get a bo-beep at the board, try to gauge the lay of the land. Not that he had expected any great revelations: they'd had too much time to perfect their poker faces.

Then the door was hurled open and Heinrich charged past, no lackey in tow, clearly not happy with the hand he'd been dealt. There was shouting from behind the boardroom door, words indistinct: might've been Crete, crate. Casualties, definitely.

The shouting stopped. After a while, the Familiare's phone buzzed. She answered. 'They're ready for you.'

He went in.

The room was thick with tension.

Maximilian sat at the head of the table, facing the door

along the length of the table. The shutters were closed behind him, cutting off the city view.

An empty seat occupied a space to his left. Mira's customary place: not a department head, per se, but as Strigoi, she sat at the head of the table with her father. Vee stood behind the chair, a sure sign Maximilian had yet to give up on his daughter's recovery. Reece suppressed a smile, imagining how much the slight must've rankled Vee. Before she'd done a runner, Danica had occupied the post at Maximilian's left. That she would never do so again made the emptiness palpable.

No one looked at that chair, not even Vee, who kept their hands in front of them and expression suitably downcast. They could afford to be reverent, with the role of Strigoi so much closer in the aftermath of last night's disaster on Fraser Island.

Heinrich sat at Maximilian's right. Arranged around the table were the rest of the board: down one side, Campbell, Tran and Bishop; and facing them, Marshall and Jensen.

Familiares stood in the wings, tablet computers and Bluetooth headsets at the ready. Maximilian was the only exception: he also had two vampire bodyguards. Both wore combat armour and had Gothic crosses on their lapels, the ends shaped like sword tips.

Jensen gave a dry cough; rings sparkled in the downlights as he motioned for his Familiare to top up his goblet. *Lazy git*, Reece thought.

'Hunter,' Maximilian said, his words echoed by the soft tapping of a typist's fingers where she recorded the minutes. Quaint; the room was bound to be wired for sound and video, but Max was old school.

'We were discussing the matter of Kevin Matheson. In fact, there will be an extraordinary council meeting in two nights' time to discuss certain events directly related to him. We were thinking of offering a seat on the council to any peasant who can bring him in; on ice.'

Reece said nothing.

'What do you think?' Maximilian said into the silence, spitting out *think* as though it had tobacco on it.

'An effective bounty, my lord.'

Marshall looked up from the pen that had been occupying her attention. 'Do you think he will come here? His maker was Taipan, after all: a nomad.'

Heinrich said, 'A nomad who eluded Bishop's Hunters for thirty years.'

'It was more like forty, wasn't it?' Marshall said, off-handedly. Jensen stifled a chuckle.

Bishop shrugged, as if to say, what's a decade between vampires.

Campbell reminded them that they still had men in the field, looking for Matheson.

Maximilian said to Reece, 'He *will* return, won't he?'

'I should think so, my lord Hochmeister,' Reece said.

'And why is that?' Marshall asked.

'Two reasons, Madam Marshall. The first: he blames Mira for the death of his family. And secondly: he has nowhere else to go.'

'Then we kill him,' Heinrich said, 'With Danica dead, the boy is no longer of any use to us. He is just a threat. Put the word out to all the vassals, all the villeins. More territory, or a council seat for whoever brings us his head.'

Campbell, smiling, wiped his glasses with leisurely swipes of his handkerchief, said, 'All in favour?'

Hands went up. Heinrich leaned back, apparently satisfied. 'It's unanimous, then. Kevin Matheson is now persona non grata. By Thursday night's council meeting, he will be a prisoner or dead.'

FIFTY

The morning was deep, dark, quiet when Kevin pulled into the car park of a shopping centre in a northern suburb of chain stores and car yards. He got out, stretched.

'You be all right?' Yoshi asked as he took Kevin's place in the driver's seat.

'Sure. What about you? Only a few hours till sun-up.'

'We'll be fine.' Yoshi looked into the back seat, as though to make sure Mel was still under the blanket they had stolen along the way. 'Call me when you're done and I'll let you know how she's going.'

'Take it easy,' Kevin said.

The car reversed, turned and was gone; heading toward the west to avoid the highway and the toll roads where detection would be more likely.

Kevin found a working pay phone and dropped coins taken from the console of the stolen car.

Greaser answered just when Kevin was about to hang up.
'It's me.'

'Hello, me. I thought you might be dead.'

'Sorry to disappoint you.'

'Early days. I might get to keep the car yet.'

'You're a macabre little fucker, aren't you?'

'Big word for a bumpkin. You been swotting up on the beach?'

'I do read, you know.' Comics and car magazines, mostly, but he wasn't letting her know that.

Greaser asked where he was and he told her, and she said she'd be there in forty at the most.

It was a long wait. Vehicles cruised by occasionally; once, an ambulance with lights flashing but no siren. Two teenage boys walked with hands thrust in pockets and heads down. If he was a smoker, this would be the time, but he wasn't, so all he could do was slouch in a doorway and try not to think too much. Keep looking forward.

Easier said than done when ghosts lived inside him. Ghosts so real they might have been flesh and blood, their lives overwhelming. The girl at the pub – he could feel her dying. The only consolation was that she would fade; he hadn't taken her soul. Not like Nicola, the girl at Rockhampton.

He could, with the flick of a mental switch, cast himself into Nicola's life; incidents, moments. The sun on her face, a lover's hand, the taste of fairy floss at the local show, the smell of horse after a day's riding, the burn in the muscles of her legs.

Kevin rubbed his eyes, so tired; pressed against his eyelids to drive Nicola from his mind.

Yoshi had been manic. *He* had been manic.

Is this what vengeance – justice – looked like?

Danica had told him not to go. Now she was dead. Kala had washed her hands of him. Who was left to see, let alone care, if he lived or died?

A black Monaro pulled into the car park. It flashed its headlights, but Kevin was already on his way. It felt good to move, to focus. Greaser sat behind the wheel, smiling like she'd just bought *the best Chrissie present evah!*

'What do you think?' she asked.

'It's black.'

'Good job, eh?'

She'd put a scoop on the front, a wing on the back.

'Yeah,' he said. 'Good job.' He dumped his sword in the boot, then told her, 'Shove over.'

She grimaced, but did as she was told. 'Where's Mel?'

'With Yoshi. Danica; it didn't go well. Yoshi knows someone who might be able to help. A long shot, but at least Mel will be safe.'

'Oh.' She turned away, wiped an eye, and her voice was subdued when she said, 'He was all right, eh, for a Yank.'

'I need to talk to the Needle.'

'That's a bit of a problem. He's missing. None of us knows where he is.'

Kevin sat, hands on wheel, mind paralysed. All avenues seemed to be dead ends. 'You've really got no idea where the Needle is?'

'I've spent the past two days checking all the haunts. Nothing.'

'But you don't think he's shot through.'

'We were his family; that's what he called us. He wouldn't abandon us.'

'And you would've heard if he'd been caught, right?' he said.

'I guess.'

'Okay.' *Breathe. Think.* 'Back to the start,' Kevin said. 'The mole who told the Needle about Jasmine. Heard anything more about that?'

'Nup.'

'Two of Bhagwan's people had silver tattoos. Who else has them?'

'Just about every streeter has Needle's tatts. They like to wear their allegiance close to the bone, you know. But the VS aren't allowed. Contamination, they call it.'

'Are you absolutely sure no VS got a tattoo from the Needle recently?'

'I'm not his secretary, all right, but I know who would know: Silver and Argent.'

'Let me guess: they're missing, too?'

'No. They're with the studio. Up on the mountain.'

Kevin put the car into gear. 'Let's go then.'

FIFTY-ONE

Reece was dismissed and told to wait in reception, but the meeting didn't go much longer. Marshall collected him on the way through and he fell into step beside her, her Familiare trailing behind.

'What did I miss?'

'Heinrich posturing about the loss of his precious Fallschirmjaeger, threatening to clear the streets with a *whiff of grapeshot*. Campbell pushing to get more villeins upgraded to vassals as a way of boosting our forces.'

'Foxes guarding the hen house.'

When they reached the lift, she told her Familiare to take the next one. Then she asked Reece if he'd had a chance to read the reports she'd emailed him during the day.

He had, in the pub where he'd had his lunch. The first was a weighty dossier about the "engagement on K'gari/Fraser Island". The second, a string of incident reports about gang violence and vampire-suggestive graffiti in the city. The street art was adolescent strutting. The bashings, a somewhat more serious sign of Maximilian's control being undermined.

'I have three men on 11, all beaten to within an inch of

their lives – by Bogans and Batemans, mostly. What do you make of that?' she asked.

'Campbell, extending his influence, keeping your troops spread thin and distracted.'

'Campbell? Why make the Old Man dislike the villeins any more than usual when he's pushing to get them on to the council?'

'Who else can gain?'

She raised an eyebrow.

'It could just be the streeters flexing their muscles,' he said.

'Oh, come on. It's that damn three-sided coin, Reece. I can't pick it.'

When they reached her office, Marshall retrieved a bottle from a filing cabinet and poured two fingers of neat bourbon for each of them.

'So, a manhunt for Kevin Matheson. What are his chances of being brought in alive?'

'Depends who finds him,' Reece said. 'We can presume Max's ploy of using Blake's moll to force contact with Danica worked. That they still have the girl suggests they still hope to save her from bedlam.'

'A long bow, you're drawing. They might just be nice boys not leaving anyone behind.'

'Hope springs eternal. The fact they are in contact with Rodan adds weight.'

'The Japanese?'

'For starters. But someone doesn't want Mira to come back. It was interesting that no one at the meeting mentioned the four-armed assassin and which interests he might be serving.'

Marshall sipped, watched the ripples in the top of her glass. 'You think me cowardly for not challenging Campbell.'

'Without evidence? Sensible, given what Rabbit told me about Slick *doing it for the money*.'

'Treasurer.' She rubbed her temple as she ingested the accusation. 'Treasurer Campbell, the slimy bastard. And he's got Bishop on his side; probably Tran as well – he's the one who called for the extraordinary council meeting.'

'Doing Campbell's work for him. Which means Campbell needs Heinrich, you or Jensen to swap sides to give him control of the board.'

'Jensen might. He and Max do go back a'ways, but he's always looking for a bigger slice of the action. Logistics is important, but ordering groceries doesn't carry a lot of prestige. The casino could just sway him.'

'I think Bishop might have expectations there; it's right up that cockatoo's alley. She's all facade; with her running the Hunters, we spent more time covering shit up than tracking down the perps.'

Reece swallowed a mouthful of bourbon, enjoying the hit, wanting it to cleanse him of the bitter taste Bishop's PR bullshit left in his mouth. But Bishop wasn't their biggest problem. 'So, if Tran called the meeting at Campbell's say-so, then it's likely that's when Campbell will make his move.'

'As soon as he has enough of his pet vassals installed on the council to give him the majority; for certain. This crisis is giving him the opportunity to stack the meeting, regardless of Jensen's support.'

'He won't be able to shift Maximilian, surely.'

'Everyone knows Heinrich is doing most of the chairman's work without having the title. Campbell could easily shift Maximilian to being just a figurehead and take the chair for himself. That'd sideline Heinrich at the same time. He's taking the empire, piece by piece. He'll be after my job next.' She huffed, drained her glass. 'I wonder why I care.'

'A shame to let the greaseballs win, Madam Marshall.'

'Pride before the fall.' She contemplated her drink, considering. 'We need proof, Reece. We need the Needle to testify to the council. If he can vouch that Campbell betrayed us by leaking the information–'

'There's no guarantee he knows that for a fact. And I don't

think we can trust Rabbit to stand up. She's in Campbell's pocket.'

'Still, wouldn't hurt to bring her in. Vee might be able to extract something useful. All we need is to stir up doubt over Campbell's loyalty to prevent his takeover bid.'

'A hostile takeover?'

'That remains to be seen. We've got two nights to prevent it. If Campbell wins, we all lose our heads.'

He stood, knocked back the last of his drink and headed to the door. 'I'll get to it, then.'

Reece sat on his bunk while he ran through the files – printouts, easier to grasp; solid. But there was sweet FA about the Needle, his haunts, his known associates.

The aircon was on the blink again, the barracks thick with body odour and stale socks. He tossed the papers back in their folder and took them with him to the rec room, where he ordered a beer before stepping out onto the balcony. The air was still, the city sluggish, a cabbie below too tired to even honk at the car in front idling at a stale green light. Reece sat at a table, both it and the chair bolted to the floor. The only other people out – a couple, he behind her, pressing her to the rail as they took in the view – soon left.

On the street, a tree itched with crickets, the racket reminding him of camping trips and the deafening scratch of cicadas; and at the family home too, trees thrumming with the noise of them, the sound of summer if ever there was one. Nights like this, he and his sister used to sleep on thin mattresses on the verandah, the unmoving, damp air thick with the reek of mosquito coils and the whine of the defiant bloodsuckers taking a chunk of foot and finger where the single sheet didn't cover. And his mother would be there, nightie wet and discoloured and clinging around her neck and chest as she rolled a cold stubby or tall glass across her forehead – depending on whether it was a beer or g&t time of day – and she'd tell them to get some sleep because the cool change was gonna come. They'd watch the storms charge down from the ranges like angry Apaches in a John Wayne film, all roiling and arrowful with lightning, hollering fit to make the house shake, and that cold, wet wind would charge ahead, chilling his puckered flesh like that of a chicken straight from the freezer. His mother would study the clouds with a knowing squint and pronounce it a bad one, 'get the car under cover, there's hail in that one'. And the green rotten-meat glow would indeed foretell a next-day front page of gushing streets and suits huddled under uplifted newspapers and inside-out brollies and someone showing off a bucket of hail stones as big as golf balls or cricket balls.

Reece ran his stubby across his forehead, the cold shivering his skin and provoking a minor headache. There were clouds on the mountains and the air was thick with swamp heat. The city sweated, waiting for the cool change.

Gonna be a bad one, all right.

He flicked through the files again, careful to keep the papers away from the pool of condensation where the stubby had sat. They'd got sloppy, Newman and Petersen, more interested in stray fanny and big-noting themselves than doing their job; too reliant on the blood to reveal trouble in the making.

But blood in Reece's world was after the fact; it was evidence. The Needle was a fucking phantom. The Needle was a master of disguise. The blood didn't lie, according to the vampires' mantra, but in his case it said nothing. Nothing at all. The biggest lie: the lie of omission.

Reece gathered the papers and drained the stubby. Cast a last resigned look over the railing at the waiting city.

Nothing for it but to hit the streets and hope he got lucky.

Reece had a list of likely suspects. Emergency workers and janitors, taxi drivers and prostitutes and hobos. Vampires and red-eyes and hangers-on close enough to the Needle's gutters to be worth paying a visit and leaving a card. There were others, of course: socialites and recluses, businessmen and eccentrics who could get away with partying at night and doing business behind curtains during the day. But they weren't the types to get shiny tattoos, however novel.

No, it was the streets for him: greasy spoons and soup kitchens, brothels and servos – a tedious night of question and answer, with only the amount of aggro to differentiate one from the other.

He was on his fourth door-knock of the night and contemplating a morale-boosting beer when he got the call from Marshall: shit had gone down in some town called Maryborough. Newman was there, covering it up like a good Hunter should. It sounded like Matheson and Rodan's Japanese muscle, following on from the clusterfuck on Fraser Island the night before. She was sending him an email with what little details she had.

Reece knew of Maryborough, about three hours' drive north of Brissie. Taipan had grown up near there, under the dubious patronage of Jasmine Turner. Was it coincidence that Taipan's offspring, Kevin Matheson, had returned to the area? Should Reece have expected that?

He went to the nearest pub, a favourite haunt near the showgrounds, and got the bartender to click to a news channel where the blaze was still getting airplay. Nine people dead in a hotel fire, only a day after a light airplane crashed into a four-wheel drive while attempting a beach landing on the island – yeah, that was news, all right.

Double tragedy on Fraser Coast the ticker tape read, as footage alternated between a burned-out plane wreck awash with waves, and the burning pub with smoke and flames leaping through its blackening frame.

He drank a beer with a rum chaser and watched the footage, tried to avoid thinking of things he might've done differently or not at all. He had taken a severe dislike to Johnny Slick for fucking up his collar at the tattoo shop, but realised he was really just angry at himself. Getting old. Old and slow. And people were dying as a result.

When the news moved on, so did he, and there would be no time for another drink break. If Marshall's info was accurate and Matheson was involved in that fire, it meant two things: the kid was getting desperate, and he was on his way.

Reece had to reach him first.

FIFTY-TWO

Greaser and Kevin backtracked along the roads Kevin and Yoshi had followed into the city's northern outskirts. The winding road up the mountain seemed interminable, the farmland below a mottle of open paddocks and lightly-forested areas in the glow of the waning moon. At this time of morning, few lights showed, except when they neared the peak and the road afforded glimpses toward Caboolture and the coastal towns.

They turned off, away from the ocean, following a ridge. They entered forest, trees and scrub making a dark corridor of the narrow road.

'What makes you think the twins will tell you anything?' Greaser asked.

'Maybe they won't have a choice.'

She grimaced.

The trees fell away on their right, to reveal a cleared park with covered tables and a toilet block near the road. The Needle's Winnebago was parked on the far side.

'Look all right to you?' Kevin asked. His senses went into overdrive as he shut the engine down. Earth and wattle, the gentle whisper of trees in the breeze, a distant trickle of water. A plover. A fall of bark, clacking through the branches.

'C'mon, night's wasting.' Greaser got out, worked the slide of a pistol and tucked the gun into a pocket before resuming her familiar slouch.

They walked over, shadows grey and indistinct before them.

Kevin's back itched, his ears strained.

The motorhome's door opened. The rectangle filled with the shape of a blonde-haired girl. 'Why, if it isn't country mouse and city mouse. What do you two want?'

Greaser waved a greeting. 'You got the kettle on, Silver?'

'Long drive, Greaser? Thirsty, are ya?'

'What's with the aggro, Silver? We're just lookin' for the Needle.'

'You and everyone else. Guess you'd better come on in. Make the place look untidy, hanging about.'

Kevin's nose twitched. Something in the air. An excitation. An expectation. A hunger.

He paused, but Greaser was already up the steps. He followed her inside the dimly-lit vehicle. Dirty dishes were piled in the sink; the room stank of stale blood and pasta. The smell of ink and disinfectant pushed through from the studio on the other side of the closed curtain.

Argent guarded the studio. Silver shut the door and leaned back against it.

Kevin cursed silently. He moved Greaser to one side, so he stood between her and the two streeters.

'How long did you know we were here?' he asked.

Argent gestured at the walls. 'Listen to that.'

'I don't hear anything.'

'Exactly. So much as a roo farts, we know about it long before we smell it.'

'Good sense of smell, have you? Good hearing? Better than before?'

'If you say so.'

'Do you miss the bright colours, though?'

'Huh?'

'When did he turn you?'

'Is it that obvious?'

Argent took a step forward, into the moonlight coming through the window, and his eyes glazed green.

'Oh, shit,' Greaser said, stepping well back.

'I just want some information,' Kevin said. 'If any VS goon got a silver tatt, maybe, six to eight weeks ago. I need to know who they belonged to; who sent them.'

'Shall I consult the appointment book?' Argent said.

'No need,' Silver said with a wave. 'It's *verboten* for any VS trooper to be tattooed by the Needle.'

'That's right,' Argent said. 'They lose their pension.'

'And their head,' Silver added with a knowing leer.

'Listen to me,' Kevin said. 'I can help the Needle. We can help each other. We both want to same thing: to stop Maximilian.'

'I thought it was Mira you had the hard-on for?'

'Mira, Maximilian: it's all the same. Take them out and the whole bloody lot comes crashing down. That is what the Needle wants, isn't it? That's why he told Bhagwan about Jasmine Turner. The Needle knew Bhaggy would see her as a rival.'

'The boss's reasons are his own,' Silver said. 'We just follow.'

'You're his Familiares; you can't be that ignorant.'

'We call it polite. Not talking about others' business.'

'His business is mine. VS is hunting me, too.'

'Did they follow you?'

'Smell any farts?'

Argent snorted. 'Still can't tell you where the Needle is.'

'But,' Silver said, 'as it happens, there is something you can do for us.'

'Blood?' Kevin asked.

'For starters.'

They leaped. Greaser swore; Kevin fired.

Argent went down – not out, just down. Silver was too quick. She hit Kevin side on and they crashed against the table. Her hand pinned his wrist; he couldn't bring the gun to bear. Her fangs gnashed at his throat as he held her other claw away from his guts.

Greaser shot her, again and again. Silver stumbled against the door, holding her stomach as though winded.

Kevin pushed Greaser through the curtain into the tattoo studio, yelling at her to get out the back.

'What back?' she shouted.

He followed her, his pistol levelled at the twins as they found their feet and advanced.

'He turned you, didn't he?' Kevin said. 'Sent you up here, away from everyone, until he calls you in. He's going to war.'

'Mighty hungry, waiting,' Silver said.

'Mighty hungry,' Argent repeated.

They both pulled handguns. Kevin shot them and ran. The curtain fell shut behind him, blocking the twins from view. A body lay on the tattoo lounge, mauled and bloodless.

'Through the window, Greaser. Now!'

Greaser bashed at the rear window, the little sign that read *In case of emergency, push out.* Kevin charged through the cramped room and threw himself against the panel.

The window popped under the impact, and he hefted Greaser up and out.

The twins scrabbled after him, popping off wild shots. He fired back, making them duck. It gave him enough time to leap out, chased by bullets. Greaser was running for the Monaro.

Kevin sprinted after her. The motorhome door clanked open. Gunshots. Bullets chewed earth at his feet. One hit him in the back. He stumbled, but kept running.

The Monaro roared to life. Greaser swung it around. Kevin

fell into the passenger seat and slammed the door. A bullet struck the car and he winced. Then they were away, gravel rattling against the guards as Greaser planted her foot.

'Are they following?' she asked.

'In that thing? Built for comfort, not speed.'

She eased back on the pedal.

'Wasn't really worth it, was it?'

'If I understood those two weirdos correctly, whoever spilled the beans on Jasmine is dead.'

'So what now?'

'Back to Brissie, I guess, and hope that the Needle turns up.'

'You don't mind if we stop along the way? I'm starving. What about you, Kev? Are you hungry?'

'I'm doing okay.'

'Uh-huh.'

'Somewhere with drive through, eh? It's getting late. I might have to jump in the back.'

'I could really go a pizza, but I guess it'll have to be a burger. No one else is gonna be open this hour of the morning.'

'Wait a minute. Those things the Needle liked. The calzon-ee. Where did you say he got them from?'

'Georgina's. It's on the north side, by the river.'

'Two birds with one stone, then.'

'Huh?'

'You get a pizza, and maybe we find our Needle.'

Dawn's pink fingers poked the Monaro when they hit the city. Following Kevin's hunch about the Needle's location would have to wait. They got drive-through, the smell of burned, fatty meat filling the car. They left the windows down when they parked at the chop shop.

Kevin whiled away the day in fitful sleep, haunted by images of violence and the faces of dead people. Mira, too. Hunter. His mother.

With a whole day to wait, doubts resurfaced. Maybe Yoshi was right. With Danica gone, maybe Kevin was no longer on the radar, just an annoyance to be scratched when the opportunity arose.

He could leave. Go west, north, even south; find someplace monster free, and make some kind of life with a red-eye to watch over him and a rotating roster of willing blood addicts to feed him. *A murder* in Blake's words; *a family* in the Needle's. Neither sat well with him.

Time droned on: traffic, the tinny radio and the conversations of the men working in the garage beneath them, the crunch and ring of metal. The urge to run warred with the need to get to the Needle, to get access to Thorn, to destroy everything in sight. Hunger scratched at his guts.

The sun lowered, heat lingering like a threat. Finally, Greaser came to him in the grey glow of sunset. She'd brought him a change of clothes and more ammo. No blood, though. Her suppliers had dried up ahead of the big meeting at Thorn tomorrow night. 'An emergency council meeting,' she said with a dramatic roll of the eyes. 'Everyone will be there.'

'Really?' he said as they headed for the car. 'Everyone?'

'Everyone important. And they've got all the streeters out hunting for you. They've upped the reward, big time. VS wants you bad.'

'Well, they might just get what they want. They mightn't like it, but.'

'There's that death wish. Do you think you should at least have a feed first? Last meal of the condemned man and all that? I can look the other way while you snack. We've got time,' she told him, but he didn't agree. He needed to find the Needle. He needed to end this.

FIFTY-THREE

Another night, another board meeting. No wonder nothing got done. Reece had barely slept, having spent all of the previous night and most of the day fruitlessly shaking the bushes for word of the Needle or Matheson. His attempt to bring Rabbit in had failed, too; she'd been tucked so far behind the skirts of the Petite Morts he couldn't get to her.

Now he was wasting time sitting in Marshall's reception room, where she'd told him to wait for her. It'd been an hour so far. He and her Familiare made a good effort of ignoring each other. A bloke, tonight. He guessed the woman would be with Marshall. Most of the board had at least two Familiares to cover the night and day shifts. Plus, variety, he supposed.

Marshall slammed through the door like a wrecking ball, making both the Familiare and Reece jump.

She turned to the man behind the desk – his hand was already poised over the telephone.

'Trappier Jensen is dead. Butchered with his lover in his love nest.'

'I'll–'

'GS is handling it,' she told him. 'Put our people on alert. Tell them to drink more coffee, because no one's getting any sleep. Reece – with me.'

In her office, she poured generous shots.

'Do we know who?' he asked.

'Campbell's blaming Matheson. Reckons he's coming for us, one by one. Tran's afraid to step outside of Thorn.'

'As if the good doctor ever leaves the building anyway.'

'Still; what do you think?'

'It's possible. But likely? I couldn't say. Matheson's interest is in Mira. Unless the incident on the island has changed that in some way, made him expand his vendetta.'

'They've put your partner, um...' She prompted him with a gesture.

'Felicity.'

'That's the one. They've put her on the case, until the other Hunters get back from the island.'

Reece nodded, drank. Tried to work the angles. Drank some more.

'The Old Man's losing it. He looked bereft, once the anger passed. And fucking Campbell was all about who would take Jensen's place as Trappier.'

'Did he have a candidate in mind?'

'A matter for the council, but he's dropped a couple of vassals' names. They're going to run a special tithe before tomorrow's meeting, try to keep a lid on the streeters.'

'Good luck with that. Treasurer's done a great job of stirring up trouble to help get his measures through.'

'Do you have any good news?' Marshall asked, though her tone suggested she already knew the answer.

Reece had just about finished reporting his own lack of progress when his phone vibrated. He pulled it out, waited for Marshall to indicate he should go ahead, then checked the text message.

'Urgent,' he read, heart accelerating. His pavement pounding finally paying off? Or was even more shit hitting the fan?

He rang in, and frowned. Batcatcher wanted to see him at the rookery – urgently.

'I need to follow this up,' he said.

'I think we're done,' she said, making it sound like a dismissal and a broader statement.

Reece strode for the lift. When word got out about Jensen, the tower would become a madhouse of rumour and ambition; even more so than usual. If it was Matheson who'd killed Jensen, he'd done a fine job of putting a cat among the pigeons. But he'd also greatly reduced his chances of being brought in alive.

And that worried Reece, because the grease monkey was the only person he knew who had even a possible link to a cure for Mira. And as long as Mira remained in bedlam, his own life wouldn't be worth shit.

Whatever Batcatcher had to say, he hoped it was indeed bloody important. Life-saving, in fact.

FIFTY-FOUR

Kingsford Smith Drive was clogged as Kevin did a drive-by of Georgina's restaurant. There'd be no quick getaway there. It was a relief to turn out of the crawling lines of traffic and find a park in a residential street at the back of the restaurant. A driveway opened onto the small customer car park, with a lane running up one side of the building to the main road. A busy night, judging by the amount of cars. Stairs led to a second floor above the restaurant; there were lights behind the curtains. Steel bins smelling of garbage and wet cardboard walled in a door underneath the staircase.

Hunched and wary, he and Greaser used the cars for cover as they approached. They'd entered the lane when a door opened, emitting warmth and the clatter of cutlery and hubbub of conversation. They both jumped, enough that the man stared at them before walking toward the car park. Greaser pointed to the door but Kevin shook his head and they continued to the main road. Traffic crawled past, growling under a choking exhaust stench. Kevin eyed the restaurant through the front windows, trying to be casual about checking the menu while Greaser extolled the virtues of the scaloppine.

Georgina's was nestled at one end of a row of shops, a picture framer sharing one wall and a bicycle shop on the other side of the alley. Across the street, the river view was blocked by a conglomerate of dark concrete boxes assembled to form an apartment complex with spotlighted palm trees poking above the perimeter wall. Further down the street, where a massive fig tree shaded the bank, a CityCat ferry pulled in, its mast light blinking white, and disgorged pretty young things in party clothes, headed for the pub across the road or one of the many restaurants on nearby Racecourse Road. Some posh nosh there, Greaser told him.

Georgina's wasn't posh, what with its butcher paper tablecloths and a few Kmart pictures on the whitewashed walls. It was, however, an attractive bolt-hole, in terms of exit points. Access to main roads was good, with the highway and several of the city's main arterials within a short drive.

Kevin hoped the Needle was here, or the restaurant could at least tell him if they'd delivered any of their blood-filled specials lately, because damned if he knew where else to look.

He told Greaser to wait out the front and she scowled. 'The food's wicked good.'

'I'll bring you a garlic bread,' he said, and she flipped him the bird.

He slid the door open and stepped into the humidity of kitchen and bodies. The place was crammed with families, suits, a cluster of shrieking teenagers. An old fella sat by himself, reading the paper in another language, a tiny cup in front of him. The din echoed around Kevin, pummelled him. Something sizzled in the stainless steel maze of benches and shelves behind the counter on the far side of the room. The smell of garlic, cheese and tomato enveloped him as he walked between the tables.

A waitress asked if she could help him.

His hunger stirred and he cursed the Needle for leading him here. He was always hungry. Always.

'I'm looking for a guy called the Needle. I thought he might be here.'

She shook her head. 'Strange name. The Chianti is on special before seven, though.'

'I'm his friend. It's very important I speak with him.'

Behind the counter, sheltered by a stack of takeaway pizza boxes, a cook with a white towelling cap spoke into a phone on the wall.

'Would you like to see our takeaway menu?' the waitress asked.

'You got *sangue real – reale* – on it?'

The waitress stared at him, blank faced.

The cook gave Kevin the once-over, then returned his attention to the phone. Nodded. Hung up. 'Come with me,' he said, 'I have a table out the back,' and the waitress walked away without so much as another glance.

Kevin followed the cook through a door marked *Private*. The man pointed up the stairs and went back inside. At the top, Kevin paused, scanning: a television, omnipresent traffic, the smell of food and detergents.

The door opened at his first knock. A dark-skinned teenager held a pistol by his side. 'No one followed you?' the Snipe asked. 'No one knows you're here?'

'Only Greaser, out the front.'

'Come in,' the Needle shouted from another room, and the kid showed Kevin through.

The tattooist sat on a sofa, the television news turned down low, a glass of thick, red liquid in one hand, a paperback in the other. A Snipe sat beside him; legs tucked under her, a handgun on the coffee table within easy reach. Everyone was quiet as the Needle dog-eared the page and placed the book on the table, next to the pistol. He asked Kevin, 'Can I offer you something to eat?' The wave might have taken in the girl, might've meant the kitchen.

'I've eaten,' Kevin mumbled.

'You need to get over your reluctance. The hunger must be sated. Accidents are best avoided.'

Impatient, Kevin asked, 'Is this all the men you've got?'

'Straight to the point. You really should eat. You'll think clearer.'

'I'm thinking clear enough to find you.'

'That you are. Take a seat.'

The other Snipe finished doing the rounds of the windows; double-checked he'd locked the internal door behind Kevin. 'All clear.'

The Needle didn't acknowledge the lad, just motioned again for Kevin to sit.

He took the armchair opposite. 'Will you help me?'

'To do what?'

'I was thinking I could just sneak inside the tower and take out Mira. But I've realised that isn't enough. For anyone to be safe in this city, in this state, Max has to go, too. I doubt I can do both.'

'Still suicidal, hey.'

'I don't think so.'

'What will you do after you've brought down the house? Have you thought of that?'

'Not really.'

'You should. You don't win a chess game by thinking only of the next move.'

'This isn't a game.'

'Of course it is. Politics is the grandest game of all, never ending, always fascinating – if you can see behind the scenes.'

'Will you help me?' Kevin asked again.

The Needle steepled his fingers in front of him. For a man hiding in a restaurant with only two red-eye teenagers for security, he seemed very sure of himself. 'What have you got in mind?'

'Like I said – sneak into the tower, take them down.'

'Take them down?'

'Mira and Max.'

'Kill them, you mean. Can you do that? Given that you're too squeamish to even feed from the vein.'

'Mira killed my family. You bet I can kill her.'

'And what about those between her and you? The secretaries. The guards. The office worker who turns the corner at the wrong moment. What if their families want to hunt you down afterwards?'

'I guess that's their right.'

'Ever wonder where that ends?'

'It ends when I'm dead. There's no one to come avenging me.'

'Ah, the man with nothing to lose. Not as trustworthy as the man who has everything to lose. You might be prepared to die, but I'm not. Nor am I prepared to sacrifice my people unnecessarily.'

'Get me inside. Keep the troops off my back. Just give me my damn shot!'

'A full assault on the tower.' He indicated the two Snipes. 'I think we're a little undermanned, don't you?'

'I found Silver and Argent. Saw what you'd done. How many more have you turned?'

'Clever,' the Needle said, 'but you still aren't seeing the big picture. Killing the Old Man will not stop his troops from coming after you. You need to replace him with someone the troops will follow. Heinrich, perhaps, or Marshall.'

'Okay. Would they do that?'

'Perhaps. Things have been happening while you've been on the road. Did Greaser not tell you?'

'She said there'd been trouble, that you were on the run, that she'd been doing some shit-stirring with the gangs and they were out of control.'

'The gangs are very much in control, actually. Although

the Romantics have been a concern. There was a gathering but then–' He raised his fingers, exploded them with a silent *poof.* 'My dear?'

The female red-eye shook her head. 'Sent a Snipe to the site of the last blip, but haven't heard back. None of them on the streets, either, boss. Just kind of vanished.'

'Without a trace.' The Needle rubbed his scarred forehead, regarded Kevin, but Kevin could only shrug. He had no idea where Blake's *murder* might be hanging out. Possibly driving to the island to fetch their leader. Assuming Bella and Ambrose hadn't been killed or captured, and that VS hadn't caught Blake by now.

'Relax, Kevin. We can do business. I'll help you stage your coup. Now, why don't you have a drink and we can see if we can't figure out a plan that won't end up with all of us dead.'

FIFTY-FIVE

Reece wrinkled his nose against the cloying mustiness of fruit bats. The rooftop park shared space with the helipad and antennae and industrial boxes, the branches of a Moreton Bay fig out of place against the city skyline. The air hummed with motors. Reece picked his way across the artificial lawn. A couple of benches were splattered with figs, as though the flying foxes had been playing paint ball with the fruit. The ground was littered with droppings. Twittering flying foxes hung in the branches, bulging eyes watching him like CCTV cameras.

Batcatcher looked a lot like his pets: long pointed ears, round eyes, protruding fangs, ochre fur cropped short over head and neck. He stood up stiffly from a banana lounge. He wore Bermuda shorts and a tropical shirt open to the waist, revealing a short down of dark, reddish fur. Elongated, slender fingers wrapped around a tall glass of some off-red liquid, with bendable straw. On the table next to him sat a creased Batman graphic novel titled *A Death in the Family*. A subtle message or just coincidence?

'What is it, Batcatcher? You said it was urgent.'

Batcatcher tsked. 'Always in a rush, Reece. Stop and enjoy

the moonshine.' His head cocked to the side like a Labrador. It felt more like he was trying to get a better approach angle to Reece's throat.

Reece stepped back. 'Some of us are busy.'

'Too busy to see what's under your nose.' He touched his own, that flattened protuberance that gave him the appearance of having run into a glass door.

'Bat shit?' Reece walked to the glass fence at the edge of the park.

From below came the traffic rumble and hum, voices shouting and laughing; mundane stuff he could barely imagine. He couldn't see anything suspicious.

'The Strigoi was always close to my heart,' Batcatcher said, beside him.

Reece flinched, and the rail cut across his ribs. He hadn't heard Batcatcher approach. A bat stretched its wings and something plinked on the ground.

'Taught me to handle all those furry friends talking at once.' He gestured toward the trees, the sky.

'How many do you have?'

'We are quite the family, my pets and I. And one has followed the vehicle of your interest.'

'The Monaro?'

'Is that its name? Hornet-coloured?'

Reece stepped closer to Batcatcher, the constriction in his chest more powerful than the waft of the man's stale breath: carrot and blood? 'Where is it? Is Matheson with it?'

'With Danica gone, who then to help the Strigoi?'

'Who indeed.'

'But the boy; he might, yes?'

'He might know someone.'

'The Japanese? On the motorcycle?'

'Someone.'

'Your people, they think my bats are blind. But they are foxy, my bats. No echoes do they chase, but they follow their noses, oh yes. And their eyes, Hunter. The Snipe took the car, from the boneyard, to a garage. And there it received a new skin. It left town last night, further out than my wings could stretch, but now it has returned.' He pointed downriver, across the city toward Reece's house. 'Over Hamilton way.'

'Fancy,' Reece said.

'I tell you first, as her favourite; as one who cares when all else have turned their back.'

'Is the Snipe still with him?'

Batcatcher's nostrils flared. His eyes closed momentarily. 'I believe so. The smell; yes, it's likely.'

He pointed to a flying fox, in time for Reece to see it unfold from its perch and flap leisurely up to circle overhead. 'Kirk will guide you.'

'As in captain?'

'Doctor.' A goofy smile.

Reece shrugged it away. 'Tell no one. And thanks.'

'Godspeed, Hunter.'

'I'm not – never mind.'

He rang Nigel as he waited for the lift. 'You back on the roster?'

'Yeah, boss, it's all go here. Council meeting's got everyone in a flap.'

'You got any cars on the dock?'

'One.'

'I'll meet you in two minutes. Grab the keys. No paperwork.'

Nigel started to ask something, but Reece ended the call and tried not to run.

FIFTY-SIX

Reece let Nigel drive, because keeping an eye on Kirk was a right pain, even when he knew roughly where they were going. Near the river, Batcatcher had said, and so they followed the main drag, out onto Kingsford Smith Drive, two lanes each way tracking the Brisbane River. The bat veered when they reached Racecourse Road but they were in the wrong lane to make the turn. At the lights, facing the river, was an Italian joint he'd been to once. And there at the front, looking pissed off with nothing but a menu and passing cars to stare at, was the Needle's Snipe. He was sure of it. Bingo.

Nigel leaned over the wheel, looking up at the bat where it circled over the restaurant.

'I can do a blockie,' he said, and Reece assured him that would be fine.

He made sure his face was turned away and low as they passed the restaurant. He made Nigel go all the way up to the next set of lights and turn. The kid made no comment. Why would he? When they worked their way back down the next street running parallel to the river, to the spot where Kirk circled overhead, they found the Monaro.

Hamilton was a posh suburb; streets lined with jacarandas and poinciana, the houses large Queenslanders or brick mansions barricaded behind high walls and hedges rubbing shoulders with cramped McMansions and compact slabs of apartments.

It was bold of the Needle to hide in one of the city's richest suburbs. Admittedly, there were empty or rundown houses here; his own further up the hill was a case in point. Not everyone could afford to knock down and rebuild. Not everyone wanted to take the money and run. But there was no guarantee the Needle had been that obvious. He could be in that three-storey monstrosity, or that quaint post-war cottage on stilts, or that rather tastefully restored mansion on the corner with the mango tree in the front yard. The slippery bastard could be anywhere the sun didn't shine.

Was the Snipe on a tucker run? Then why not wait inside? Only way to find out was to ask. Nigel parked farther up the street, away from the nearest street light. Plenty of cars for cover.

'What now, boss?' Nigel rubbed his neck, as though to indicate he'd done his bit tonight, clearly uneasy about being off the books without explanation. Kirk hung from a nearby jacaranda, apparently off the clock as well.

'Stake it out.'

'Huh?'

'The Monaro. Didn't you notice it?'

Nigel craned to check behind them. 'Fuck me, is that–'

Reece's phone rang. Felicity. He toyed with not answering.

'Boss?'

He hit the answer button. 'Flick?'

'Where are you?'

'Went out for a pizza.' Shit, he shouldn't have said that. 'Why?'

'Jensen is dead.'

'I heard. You're there?'

'It's a fucking mess. Went out for a little cheer-me-up and lost his head. I'm not sure if it's good news or not, but the building security footage suggests it wasn't Matheson.'

'Who, then?'

Her voice lowered. He could imagine her cupping the phone to her mouth like an illicit cigarette. 'It's hard to tell, but my money's on that four-armed freak. The shape's about right, even without the extra limbs.' She sighed. 'I could use you on this one. I'm the only Hunter in town.'

'I'm on sick leave.'

Silence. He could almost hear the cogs turning. 'What's going on, Reece?'

'Indeed.'

'You should be champing at the bit to get your teeth into this.'

'I'm off the case, Flick.'

'What are you up to?'

'Nothin'. You just keep your eyes peeled. Gotta go, they're calling my order.'

He signed off. 'You got a phone?' he asked Nigel, who nodded.

'Give it to me.'

'Why?' But he handed it over.

'Mine's gone flat.' Reece opened the door.

'What the hell are you doing? I thought we were on stakeout.'

'I'm gonna go in for a closer look. You stay here. If that car moves, follow it.'

'How can I call you?'

Reece pointed to the bat, slammed the door, aware that Nigel had got out and was watching him across the roof of the car. He could feel the kid fuming. The night was still and hot, the air pressing down under the weight of clouds that made such a sickly ceiling above them. It gave him an excuse for the clamminess he felt.

He checked the Monaro, nodding at the tasteful bodywork; noted the rushed paint job, the mud sprayed up the sides, the faint warmth from the bonnet. Scowled at a fresh bullet hole. Memorised the new plate.

There was a lane of sorts, opening into a bitumen car park, a toilet block, another entry lane between wall-to-wall businesses lining Kingsford Smith Drive. He approached the back of the restaurant, ducked behind a car as two women came out a side door and dodged potholes to the loo. There was a staircase to a landing, and a curtain, dim light behind. He saw nothing untoward. He walked across, aware of the crunch of gravel under his boots, the smell of cooking oil and spoilt garbage.

A loo flushed, the sound muffled by the concrete, and he made up his mind. Up the stairs. He knocked.

FIFTY-SEVEN

One of the Needle's Snipes was pouring a baggie of heated blood into a glass for Kevin when a knock at the back door interrupted him. Everyone drew weapons in the sudden silence. With a gesture from the Needle, the male Snipe sneaked to the back door and peered through the spy hole.

'A whitefalla in a suit,' he whispered. 'Looks like a copper.'

'Just the one?'

'Looks like.'

The cop's voice carried as he said, 'Phillip Reece. *Hunter* Phillip Reece. I'm here to talk to Matheson.'

Kevin scrambled to his feet but the Needle waved him back and told the Snipe to let Reece in. Kevin tucked his pistol behind his leg.

'If *he's* found us...' Kevin said, nervousness putting a shake in his voice.

'We'll hear him out,' the Needle said.

The girl Snipe retreated to the far side of the room, her weapon ready for business, and the boy showed Hunter in.

Hunter forked his revolver out with his fingertips, and then a small one from his ankle, followed by the Staker from his belt, and the lad piled them on the kitchen table. He patted him down, finding nothing more, and then brought him into the living room.

Hunter gave Kevin a nod. 'Matheson.' He turned to the Needle. 'Well, this is nicer than a urinal, isn't it?'

The Needle gave a small inclination of acknowledgement. 'Bold, coming here by yourself.'

'I think young Kevin and I have a bit of an understanding.'

'You're still alive,' Kevin said, 'so I guess we must.'

'We probably don't have a lot of time, sport,' Hunter said. 'I've got a feeling my people are on their way.'

'Tipped them?' Kevin asked.

'I suspect they've been tipped for me.'

'Interesting colleagues you've got there,' the Needle said.

'Keep me on my toes.'

Kevin tapped out a text message on his phone, feeling pressure closing around him, jackboots thumping on the stairs. 'I'll tell Greaser to keep an extra eye out.'

The Needle sent his two Snipes to keep watch and then asked Hunter, 'So what's the reason for this little tête-à-tête?'

'I wanted to ask young Kevin here what happened to the Romantic, the one in bedlam. I know Danica didn't make it off the island. But where's the girl?'

'She's safe,' Kevin said.

'And her condition?'

'Ah,' the Needle said.

Kevin shrugged.

Hunter looked at him, at the Needle. 'Is she being treated? Because if she is, I was hoping you might tell me where.'

'Not a chance, sport,' Kevin said.

'Mira's case is much worse,' the Needle said. 'She purposefully consumed her ghosts, purposefully took them within her. Those life streams are embedded in her core, not like Melpomene's. Hers are a flash flood that will abate, albeit leaving her scarred; Mira's are a lake in which she's constantly drowning.'

'Lakes can be drained. Drowning swimmers can be saved,' Reece said.

'Dangerous, giving mouth-to-mouth to a snake.'

'Old habits,' Reece said, lowering himself into an armchair, looking tired, looking – *old*.

'There's no way I'd help Mira,' Kevin said. 'You must know that.'

'But you didn't kill me out west when you had the chance. You fed from me. Could've taken me all the way. But you didn't. I still haven't been able to work out why.'

'Maybe you just weren't my flavour, Hunter.'

The man raised an eyebrow.

Kevin rubbed his eyes, his face, wishing for water and a towel and somewhere to sleep. Sleep for a year. 'Maybe I'd just had a gutful of killing.'

'And now?'

Kevin looked away. That was the question, wasn't it? How much was enough? How many deaths would it take for him to be truly free? Was it even possible?

'Kevin – give it up, sport. Danica is dead. Mira's in bedlam. Your parents, my mates, your mates. It's enough, isn't it?'

'More than enough. I want to make sure there's no more.'

'That your job?'

'It's got to be someone's.'

'Yours?' Hunter asked the Needle, looking at him with fresh eyes, a policeman's perhaps, searching for something beneath the surface.

'I'm not making any promises.'

'You wouldn't. You think young Kevin is going to give you an advantage? Or are you holding on to him for the reward?'

'Reward?' Kevin stood.

'Maximilian wants you; badly,' the Needle said.

'That's not news,' Kevin said.

'Badly enough to give a council seat to the person who brings you in. That's a lot of prestige,' Reece said.

Kevin studied the Needle, who met his gaze unflinchingly. He didn't strike Kevin as the kind of guy who gave a damn for prestige. No, Hunter was up to something. Well, Kevin wasn't falling for it. He'd already tasted Hunter once and knew the copper hadn't liked it.

Kevin bent over Hunter, hands either side of him on the arms of the chair. 'Where's Mira?'

'You can't get to her, sport. Just give it up.'

'If I can get to her, it'll be in your blood.'

'Or you could get the last time I played cricket.'

'You played cricket?'

'Thought you might've seen that, last time.' He kept his eyes on Kevin's, measuring him. 'Like I said, never can tell what you'll get.' A sigh as Kevin didn't move. 'Preferred rugger, but yeah, police shield champions, 1969.'

'We made the state finals, once, a couple of years ago,' Kevin said, standing away from Hunter. 'Played up the road at Allan Border Field.' He gestured at a wall, not sure he had the right direction, more a reflex.

'Didn't win?'

Kevin shook his head.

'Opposition's tougher this time, sport. Believe me. It's an attacking field, and the quicks, well, you haven't seen anything as quick as them.'

'Still, you pad up, don't you? Give it your best shot.'

Kevin's phone rang, the bass hook of Deep Purple's *Black Night* thumping. 'It's Greaser. People moving in.'

'Got VS, far end of the car park,' the Snipe in the kitchen said.

'Tell your friend to run,' Hunter told Kevin.

'Already running,' Kevin said.

The Needle pointed to the back door. 'Out!'

Kevin paused to exchange a glance with Reece, the man hauling himself to his feet with what looked like sheer force of will.

'Go,' Hunter said. 'Keep going. Because if you come for Mira, I will stop you.'

'Unless I stop you first. You think of that?'

Hunter lifted two fingers to his forehead and flicked him a salute.

Kevin gave a curt nod and ran. He reached the landing in time to see the Needle's Snipes vaulting down the stairs. Figures at the far end of the lane shouted as they jinked forward, from car to car, guns aimed.

The Needle jumped on to the rail and then leaped for the roof. Grabbed the creaking, bending gutter and hauled himself up. Kevin jumped, too, grabbing the brickwork, driving the toes of his boots into the mortar and shinning up, fingertips as sure as picks.

Bullets chipped the wall as the Needle hauled Kevin onto the roof. The shooters were using silencers, lending the violence an air of eeriness.

From the roof, Kevin could see the suburb meandering back from the river, the taller buildings of the main shopping street upstream. The cityscape a long way away, the stream of traffic running beside the river. And carving in toward the jetty across the road, a CityCat with a huddle of passengers at the bow.

'Meet up at Mel's,' the Needle said.

He ran downstream across the roof, jumped the lane and kept running. His Snipes had, Kevin thought, gone in that direction, VS well behind.

Kevin ran across the roofs, upstream.

Shouts and shots followed him, but he gained the street, using a handy sapling to swing down outside a 7-Eleven aglow on the corner. He ran through the traffic to the ferry landing. The gangplank was down, passengers alighting, others lined up on the pontoon to board. He pushed through the new arrivals and got to the boat just as a crewman was about to raise the bridge. He raced aboard.

'In a hurry, mate?' the man said, sounding annoyed. Kevin ignored him as he darted for the cover of the cabin.

The crewman waved to the captain upstairs and the catamaran pulled back, then powered away, followed by shouts from the bank. Kevin watched from the doorway as the first of his pursuers reached the dock. One was talking on a phone.

'Where does this go?' he asked the uniformed woman taking money for tickets.

'All the way to the uni,' she said. 'You a tourist?'

'Sure.'

She pointed to a map. 'Where do you want to get off?'

The route criss-crossed the river. Mel's place was on this side. The second stop would be as close as he could get to her apartment. Question was, how long would it take VS to stake out each ferry stop? Or could they react faster, maybe send a boat to intercept? He asked how long the trip took and tried to factor the fractions.

He forked out change to pay the fee, then went to the back of the boat. They were midstream, the bank dotted with leisure boats, some meccano cranes further away, the banks lined with sparkling buildings, the city spires a backdrop to the west, the Gateway bridges to the east. He could just make out one of the peaks of the Story Bridge ahead, projecting above a bend. A jumble not so much of hiding places, but ambush points, and Kevin had no idea how it all fitted together.

The first dock was Bulimba. They pulled in almost directly opposite the wharf where he'd boarded. It was tempting to get off and find another way to get across the river. Steal a car or a boat, or hitch a lift, maybe hail a taxi. Surely VS couldn't monitor every cab in the city. How long would the drive take? How long would the Needle wait for him?

He braved out that first docking, watching closely the few that boarded. A couple stood nearby, but soon moved inside, perhaps convinced by the diesel fumes, perhaps by his brooding presence. Others huddled on the bow. Most seemed satisfied to stay inside the cab.

The ferry finally started its approach to the next dock, bobbing floodlit around a point. A concrete building squatted on the peninsula – he thought from the bulk of it that it was the theatre he'd seen from Mel's. People sat at a cafe just above water level. Behind the dock was a park bordered with fig trees. He immediately checked the sky, but couldn't see any flying foxes following him.

The boat was going slowly, much slower than it had on its first crossing to Bulimba. Maybe because they were going up-river, now, nose into the current. But really slow. Another ferry came down, travelling much faster. A bat swooped overhead, a gentle whoosh of wings. Kevin looked away, shoulders hunched. How good were the creature's eyes? Assuming it was one of Max's spy animals, probably better than average. Or could they smell him? The animal swooped away, scribing a big arc. He knew, he realised, nothing about flying foxes except they were hated by orchardists and stank of piss.

As the boat idled back and the crewman went forward to prepare his ropes, Kevin sat on the side and, when he was certain no one was watching, eased himself over and kicked away. He bobbed in the boat's wake, dog paddling, afraid of making telltale splashes. With careful effort, he pushed through the water to a navigation buoy and clung, sodden, in the red wash of its warning light.

A car pulled up at the dock, brakes squealing. Men piled out. The boat nudged into the dock, people got off, more got on. Men worked their way through the arrivals, boarded.

Kevin's wet clothes dragged on him and he sank as low as he could. The men spoke into phones and then got back in the car and left. The ferry resumed its journey, twin engines churning, rocking the buoy.

He clung for a while longer and then swam for shore. Had the Needle got away? Had Greaser? Greaser wouldn't know where to find them, and his phone was saturated. Would it work? No doubt the Needle would have a way of contacting her. The important thing for him was to get to the rendezvous. If he could avoid drowning or being shot. If he could trust the Needle not to have sold him out.

FIFTY-EIGHT

A wobble of light from behind, the ring of a bell, the whirr of tyres on concrete.

Kevin stepped off the path as a bicycle sped up, its rider hunched over the handlebars, Lycra-clad legs pumping, a light strapped to his helmet. Kevin stiff-armed him as he drew level. The man went down in a mess of arms and legs and bloody teeth. The bicycle clattered into a bottlebrush tree on the sidewalk. Kevin, uncomfortably wet, hungry, eyed the groaning rider, considering: blood scent and sweat.

He turned from the cyclist and grabbed the bike. It'd been a long, long time. He pushed off. Mel's wasn't too far away, but this beat walking. In sight of Mel's apartment, he hid the bike behind a fence and made a cautious approach.

The building was bone white. There were no live voices: no arguments, no conversations, no children; just televisions and radios. No fresh cooking smells, but blood and piss and shit; that familiar miasma of death overlaying the mould and rot and human odours. The stench leached out of the bricks like a sick fog. He could imagine the walls dripping with ichor.

The front door wasn't locked. He opened it slowly, standing

back, one hand pushing with the fingertips, the other clenched on his pistol. Electric whispers floated out, accompanied by blood trace, sinuous and teasing.

Feeling like a fish following a lure, he crept up the stairs as the eerie, peopleless silence settled around him. There were scuffs and spots on the stairs, like a stale line of bloody breadcrumbs. The more he listened, the more ominous the silence grew; the televisions and radios so banal and oblivious in their self-importance, music little more than beats, repetitious and irrelevant. There wasn't even traffic noise.

Mel's door was shut; the dark timber, the loose number, felt like a trap. Muted music sounded, undiscernible but for that heartbeat of bass. The stench of blood radiated from behind it. He wouldn't have been surprised to see blood under his feet, welling out from under the door. But the boards were clear.

He reached for the doorknob and paused at the first contact. Sticky. Blood. More, there, on the jamb. And another smell – burned flesh; charcoaled. Lucky the joint had no fire alarm system.

He turned the knob and pushed. The door swung open on the dark apartment.

The curtains at the far end were closed but there was a lamp, one with a burgundy shade and hanging fringe; its reddish light illuminated the swirls of patterned wallpaper.

He crept down the hall. Checked the bedroom, found the four-poster's curtains torn down and cast over a mound of bodies. They lay on the bed, on the floor, on the small chest of drawers: pale, streaked with dark blood, unseeing eyes. Patches of flesh missing – arms, chests, ankles. One, half her back flayed off. Throats a bloody ruin, their clothes stiff with the stuff.

Romantics; he recognised some of them. A corset, a cravat. A coach hat, flattened on the floor. Silver pins.

The barbecue stench hung thick.

The bathroom was next. Blood splattered the white surfaces like mould. A black dress, the velvet suggesting it was one of Mel's, hung from the curtain rail. The bath overflowed with limbs; the floor was covered in an untidy pile of semi-naked bodies, as deep as his waist. Old people, young people, children. Bloodstained jugs lay haphazardly on the floor and in the sink.

Kevin covered his mouth and nose, fighting the sensory assault and the memory of his night here with Mel.

There was music. Louder. Closer.

In the living room, Ambrose lay sprawled on the floor with his shirt torn open, a silver stake in his chest, mouth open, fish-like, a frown etched into his frozen brow, eyes staring at the ceiling as though trying to understand some vague truth just outside the edge of his understanding.

Blake sat on the lounge with Bella sprawled in his lap, her long hair spilled over his knees. Her top had been torn open, her bra pulled down to reveal her breasts. Her chest was covered with blood and bites, the flesh pale like raw chicken. The ornate hilt of a dagger protruded from under her ribs; blood had flooded from her mouth.

Blake's eyes shone green in the lamplight as he stared into a space close to the ceiling near the centre of the room. Kevin could see nothing there.

The song ended and began again, a moan of male vocals, a tragic air to the drum machine and guitar swirl. One name, floating over the insistent beat: Alice.

Melpomene's human name.

In the kitchen, on the stove, a fry pan sat piled with crisped strips of flesh. Next to it, a bowl overflowed with the blackened, curled stuff.

'What the fuck have you done?' Kevin said.

'You.' Blake's focus locked on Kevin. 'You!' He jerked to his feet, tumbling Bella to the floor with a solid thunk of skull on timber.

'See! See what *you* have done!'

He snatched up his cane – a thrust – and Kevin's pistol was knocked from his hand. A smooth twist, and Blake pulled the blade free. He flew at Kevin with jabs of the scabbard, stabs of the sword, punctuated by ranting.

'I can't write any more, don't you see?

'When she died, my muse died, too.

'No one can take her place.

'No one.

'And it's. All. Your. Fault!'

Kevin pedalled backward. Bumped into a cabinet, grabbed a carved bust of some old man and smacked Blake across the side of the head with it. The poet fell to all fours. Kevin considering smashing Blake again, but he simply dropped the bust. The sword was in his guts. He pulled it out slowly. Two fingers higher, it might've got his heart.

Blake leaped at him. His white sleeves were dyed rusted burgundy, his face and throat covered, hands smeared. A blow jarred the sword from Kevin's hand.

Blake's fingers closed around Kevin's throat with manic strength. They crashed over a coffee table and rolled onto the floor. Blake came up on top, straddling him, gouging into his throat.

Kevin punched, a clumsy blow from this prone position. Blake tried to thump his head through the floor, in time with his repeated question, 'Where? Where? Where?'

Kevin scrabbled at Blake, raking his face, his throat. One hand jagged on something in Blake's pocket. He wrenched it out as his eyesight dimmed and starred, the only vision that of Blake's face, mouth flecked with pink foam, drool looping from his fangs.

Kevin flicked the lid off the fountain pen with one nail, reversed his grip and drove the pen into Blake's eye. The man reeled.

Kevin dived for the pistol.

Snatched it up.

Rolled.

Blake had pulled the pen free. Something gelatinous and red coated the tip.

Kevin fired. Blake collapsed in mid wail and lay still. Kevin retrieved the cane sword and drove it into the man's heart. He felt the tip hit the floor as he thrust down.

Once he'd got his breath, he went to Ambrose and then Bella. He pushed their lips up so he could be sure. Both had been infected.

He was kneeling beside Bella–

'Kev!'

He turned toward the shout.

What the fuck now?

FIFTY-NINE

It took a split second to process. Greaser stood in the doorway, with a man behind her. She was terrified and he was tall and broad, a hand on each of her shoulders, and *another* hand resting on her head.

The beamer threw Greaser to one side. She thumped into a shelf and crashed down amid a tumble of CDs and books.

The beamer charged.

Kevin wasn't even fully upright before the man hit him. They went down. The beamer was incredibly strong. His fists landed like sledgehammers. His third hand, poking from the front of his shirt, did little more than wobble and clasp. But it was distracting, scraping across Kevin's face and chest with metallic nails.

A massive thump to the ribs sent Kevin tumbling. He went with it, making the most of the space. Gun out. Gone in a flash of fist that left his fingers numb. Something broke inside with the next hit.

Greaser appeared. A tongue of flame flared.

'Run,' Kevin told her. 'Get away!'

She hit the button on the spray can again, a cigarette lighter out in front, and blasted another flame at the beamer.

The beamer shrank back, shook his head as the air filled with the stench of burned eyebrows.

Greaser triggered a third jet. The beamer reached through the flame, grabbed her hand and crushed it around her lighter until she fell to her knees.

Kevin yanked the sword from Blake's body and stabbed the beamer. The man whirled. Greaser was sent somersaulting across the sofa. Kevin ducked a wild backhand, dodged behind the beamer and launched himself at the man's back. He grappled him around the shoulders and buried his fangs in his neck.

The man reared up, drove backward, rammed Kevin hard into the wall. Again and again.

Kevin's fangs tore loose from the man's flesh, and he shouted again at Greaser to run. He dug his fingers at the beamer's eyes as he was rammed yet again into the wall. He lost his grip and slipped down. Took an elbow to the face, a knee to the guts. Slumped. The man loomed.

Kevin grabbed the beamer around the legs, managed to jerk him up and back. Twist. The window shattered. The man seemed to hang against the curtain for a moment. Hands flailed for the frame. The curtain tore. The third hand grabbed Kevin's shirt, more a tangle than a grip.

Kevin clawed for purchase, found none, was hauled up and out and down.

A whirl of city lights, lawn, sky. He smashed into darkness as solid as concrete.

SIXTY

When Kevin could see again, he was on his back on the ground. The Hill's Hoist was at a marked angle, and the beamer was skewered face down through the guts on the pole, saved from total impalement by the struts of the clothes line's arms. The man flailed against the tangle of wires and bent metal as he fought to free himself.

The hoist groaned, tilted. Kevin saw his slim chance.

He climbed up, an ungainly balancing act, and straddled the beamer. He grabbed a loose wire, wrapped it around one fist and then the other, and then noosed it around the beamer's throat.

With his knee in the man's back, he pulled with all his might, sawing the wire. The man roared, the sound ending in a choke and spray of blood. All three hands clutched for the wire that was slicing through his windpipe. Kevin's fists burned with an acidic agony, but he kept sawing.

The wire struck bone. The beamer's third hand flopped uselessly. He rocked side to side. Kevin fought to keep his balance. He pulled and pulled. One final heave and the beamer's vertebra gave, the wire finding the gap and slicing through, like a saw through a sapling suddenly finding only the final skin of bark.

Kevin tumbled from the hoist as the wire pulled clear. He sat, weary, hands paining, as blood bubbled from the stump of the beamer's neck. The bald head lay nearby, staring at him.

Movement caught his attention.

A man in a long black coat stood by the back door, arms folded, scowling.

Greaser bolted through the door.

Kevin cried 'no', but the man had already snatched the girl's hood and pulled her almost off her feet, reeling her into his embrace. A dagger appeared in the man's right hand; he held Greaser's chin with the other.

A flash of silver. Greaser's neck parted in a torrent of dark flood. She looked startled in the moment before he threw her to the ground.

Kevin started moving toward him, hands fisted.

The man pulled a pistol, bulky and undeniably ugly. The first round streaked toward Kevin like a laser beam; he was lucky to avoid the hit. The bullet sparked off the Hill's Hoist. Kevin, unarmed, took cover behind the lump of ruined barbecue as a volley of phosphorous sparked around him. He ran, making the most of the change of magazine, just got over the neighbour's Colourbond fence, feet punching dents as he hauled himself over the top of the sheeting, only to have bullets punch holes behind him.

He sprinted across the backyard, along the side of the house, leaped the fence.

More rounds chased him. Not all phos, he realised, as one pushed him into the footpath.

A car pulled up in front of him, smoke clouding from its tyres. The back door opened. The front passenger blazed at the gunman. Kevin threw himself in the back. The car took off. The door smacked against his legs, then slammed shut with the momentum of the car's acceleration as he pulled himself in. Bullets thudded into the vehicle. Someone grunted. The car kept going.

The passenger leaned around the seat to face Kevin. 'Hello again,' Argent said.

Silver parked on top of a cliff. They'd crossed the Story Bridge and doubled back to the river bank; the bridge was to their right, a solid flow of traffic crossing with rhythmic thumps. The city blazed across the water.

'C'mon,' Argent said, hitting Kevin on the shoulder, and Kevin realised he'd been staring without really seeing. Just Greaser, and the blood, and the expression on the suit's face as he'd pulled the knife across: totally blank. Totally uncaring.

'Weren't you trying to kill me last night?' Kevin said.

'Life's funny, isn't it?' Silver said.

'No.'

'The Needle's waiting. You can philosophise later.'

Silver tied a length of rope to a nearby post and threw the end over the cliff. Kevin stood on the lip, fighting a touch of vertigo, to watch her climb down the stone face to an opening.

'You next,' Argent said.

Kevin considered taking off his boots and using Taipan's power to gecko his way down, but he was so very tired and the stone looked remarkably smooth. As good as he was, he still needed something to hold on to. He regretted the decision as soon as the rope touched his injured hands. It was like gripping barbed wire. But he got down to Silver and she helped to steady him. She'd opened a grate, the bars clogged at the bottom end with plastic bags, dead branches and other flood detritus.

'Storm water,' she told him as he stepped inside, barely having to duck. 'Only panic if it starts to rain.'

Argent arrived and they walked on. Their breaths echoed; water dripped; footfalls scuffed. Shadows danced in torchlight as Kevin followed the pair through a network of dank, mossy pipes.

They emerged into a large chamber with what looked like a set of steps at the far end, a series of tunnels above, a pool of water at its base. Gas lamps hissed in the stillness, the air thick with damp and mould. The Needle was waiting for them.

Kevin sat next to him, immobile, numb. 'Greaser,' he said.

'Yeah,' Argent said. Dry blood caked his arm.

Silver passed Kevin a plastic bag of blood. It slipped from his fingers.

The Needle lifted the bag up to him. 'Drink,' he said. 'You need to heal.'

Fresh welts lined both Kevin's hands. Bullets ached in his back. The blood was tainted with plastic; it contained no memories, no trace of a donor.

That was something.

SIXTY-ONE

Reece stood in Thorn's VIP car park with Nigel, watching the Monaro being unloaded from a flatbed. No keys, of course. History repeating, most annoyingly. Perhaps this time he'd get to keep it. It was a fine machine; an ideal retirement present to himself, if it came to that.

Felicity had been unimpressed, to say the least, to find him in the Needle's lair.

'Nigel said you'd gone scouting,' she said. 'I hope you didn't *spook* them.'

'Gone when I got here, not long before your lot.'

Her frown showed she wasn't buying it. 'Why didn't you report it?'

'I knew how thin you were stretched. Besides, I'm on sick leave.'

She'd sworn at that, but laughed when he excused himself to go impound the Monaro. 'Second chance, hey.'

'Everyone deserves a second chance.'

She hadn't reacted to that. What had he expected? That she'd confess? Beg forgiveness for betraying him; promise to make up for it somehow? As much as it hurt, he couldn't blame her for allying herself with the stronger side. Now, as the Monaro was pushed into a garage bay, he wondered: did any of them deserve a second chance?

'You get your phone back?' Reece asked Nigel.

'Yeah. What was that about, boss?'

'Operational necessity, sport. Trying to keep you out of the shit.'

'I had to call it in, boss. You know that, right? I was worried.'

'Yeah, we've got each other's back. It's all good.' Reece congratulated himself on maintaining a friendly tone, on not calling Nigel 'Judas'.

One of Marshall's Familiares approached. It was a relief to go with her. Whatever Marshall wanted had to be better than making small talk with Nigel.

'You could've rung,' Reece said as they rode the lift.

The woman wasn't up for small talk, either. There was sweat on her forehead; her jaw was tight with tension. She showed him into Marshall's office and closed the door behind him. Reece caught a glimpse of her taking position in front of the entrance as the timber clicked shut.

Marshall sat at her desk, collar undone, sleeves down, butts piled high in the ashtray. 'You lost him?'

'I got the car.'

'Jesus, Reece!'

The silence stretched out as she ground out a half-spent cigarette and promptly tapped a fresh one from the packet. Offered him one as an afterthought, which he declined.

'Roll my own,' he said.

She lit, inhaled, blew smoke. 'I wish you'd rolled Matheson.'

Silence again, but for her breath, pushing nicotine in and out of her lungs.

The alarm sounded. They stared at each other. Reece was reaching for his gun; she was ditching her ciggie, when the phone rang.

One hand covered her free ear; the other held the phone in tight. 'Heinrich?' she said, brow furrowed. 'Ambush? … The tunnel? … *Our* people?'

She stared at Reece over the phone, eyes blank computer screens behind which data would be tumbling like waterfalls.

'Get to cover,' she told the person on the other end of the line, then stabbed the connection and said to Reece. 'You heard?'

'Heinrich, ambushed?'

'In the Clem7. There was an incident, not long ago. An entire apartment building massacred. They're saying the grease monkey. Heinrich was on his way to check it out. Word is, it was Security that jumped him in the tunnel.'

Reece swore, stood by the door, gun in hand.

Marshall was rifling filing cabinets; pocketing thumb drives, tapping keys on the computer with precise stabs of her fingers.

A knock, a call: he opened the door. 'We're in lockdown,' Marshall's Familiare reported, 'but no one will tell me why.'

'Get out if you can, Sue,' Marshall told her.

The lift at the end of the corridor gave a muffled ding, and the Familiare gave a wry smile.

'Not taking visitors, madam?'

'Oh, Sue.'

The Familiare turned her back to the door, a hand on her holster. Reece closed and locked the door.

'They were too quick for us, Reece,' Marshall said, reefing her gaze from the blank door.

'That they were.'

'I must be slowing down, working to vampire time. You got a car ready?'

'No, but I'm sure you do.'

She cocked an eyebrow at that, a lift of the side of her mouth; most fetching. Human. 'Fancy a drive, Hunter Reece?'

Tempting. 'I'm not a Hunter anymore.'

He thought she was going to argue. But all she did was

nod, respectful, a little morose. And then, 'You've got my number.'

She left through the side door, which he knew would give her access to the red lift. She wouldn't be headed for the car park. More likely the executive basement floor, where there was rumoured to be an escape tunnel leading to various exits, some dating back to World War II; or, knowing her, striding with stiff back and not a care in the world, straight through the foyer.

A ruckus outside the door gave him enough time to holster his pistol, lean on her desk and pick up the phone.

The door splintered open. The room filled with GS. Newman pushed through the mass of black uniforms.

'Reece, I might've known you'd be here.'

'I could say the same about you, Newman. Back from the beach, I see. How was it?'

Veins bulged in the man's neck. He looked as if his bug eyes were about to pop out.

Reece hung up the phone and propped himself on the edge of the desk. His heartbeat was deafening, his shirt clammy with a sudden sweat. He was very much alone here. No one would miss him.

'You're dirty up to your eyebrows, aren't you?' Newman said.

'Well, I am off duty.'

Newman stepped in close enough for his breath to gust across Reece's face. 'Where's Marshall?'

'Dunno. She called me up to see if I could drive her, but she didn't say where. Something to do with the kerfuffle in the tunnel, I'd think. Or Jensen's murder. Duteous to a fault, Marshall.'

Newman hit him in the guts, an expert blow that stole his breath, but Newman thumped him again anyway. Reece slid from the desk, grabbed the edge to keep from going all the way to the floor. Then Newman ground the barrel of his pistol into Reece's neck. 'You aren't a Hunter any more, Reece. You're just shit on my shoe.'

Reece had no air, no ability to go for his own weapon, to even protest.

'Ten-shun!' A GS snapped his heels together at the door.

The rest followed suit. Newman reluctantly pulled back, leaving Reece gasping.

'At ease, at ease,' Campbell said as he strolled into the room. He wiped his mouth, then his hands, on a black handkerchief. He pushed his glasses higher on his nose. His cheeks were aglow. 'Problem, Hunter Newman?'

'One of Marshall's pets, covering for her.'

Campbell picked up the ashtray, shook his head in mock disappointment. 'Poor choice in women, Hunter Reece. A recurrent theme, I believe.'

Reece shrugged.

'Where is Marshall Smith?'

'As I was just explaining–'

'I *can* take it from your blood.' He put the ashtray down, nonchalantly, wiped ash from his fingertips. 'Or get Vee to do it.'

'Look, I've got no idea where Marshall is, all right? Check her diary.'

'For someone who is supposed to know everything, you're not impressing me.'

'It's not so much knowing a lot of things, but the right things.'

'Well, this is what I know: you're done.'

Campbell confiscated Reece's weapon, mobile phone and ID, and then told two Black Shirts to escort him to detention.

'Nothing too serious, Reece,' Campbell said as the guards bundled up his possessions. 'We're letting a few of you Greenies cool your heels in the cells, just till we've sorted out the mess. A dirty business, this.'

'On whose authority are you ordering the GS around?'

'Maximilian's. With Heinrich dusted, I'm acting Preceptor until the council meeting, when the new board will be decided.'

The Black Shirts led him out. Marshall's Familiare was dead, a gun spilled from her holster where she lay on the floor, throat torn out.

'What's happened to the Strigoi?' Reece asked the guards as they entered the lift. One man's eyes flashed red as he turned to answer. The other swiped his card and hit the button for basement level C – AKA, the Dungeon.

Reece hit him in the throat. The man fell, gagging.

Reece drove his elbow into the guts of the second man.

The red-eye was quick, though, managed to pull back in time to avoid the full force of the blow. But he was off balance, and Reece followed up, making the most of his advantage. A shoulder, a fist.

The soldier pushed back, gained enough space to claw for his sidearm.

Reece smacked his head into the wall, fumbled, then snatched the Staker from the Black Shirt's belt and rapped it hard, baton-like, against the man's knee. The man canted and Reece walloped him behind the ear, sending him to the floor. A twist to arm it, and he brought the Staker down on the soldier's chest. There was the soft whump of the cartridge firing the stake from the housing. The man went limp.

He pulled the soldier's sidearm and belted his mate behind the ear to keep him quiet, then cuffed him with the irons on the man's belt.

Reece fell back, exhausted. He allowed himself a moment to wipe his face as the adrenaline drained, leaving his muscles aching. He retrieved his confiscated gear, then snatched one of the guard's IDs, and filled his pockets with ammo clips.

The lift reached C, but he hit the close button and managed to get going again without anyone noticing his arrival. He pressed 11. He was lucky; the trip was uninterrupted. Lockdown was good for something.

The doors opened and he used a soldier's foot to prevent them closing. The hall was empty. He stalked to the ward, gun by his side, and squinted through the glass doors. *Shit.* Two GS vampires guarded the ICU. They were looking in his direction, too; had probably heard the lift arrive.

At least he knew Mira was being kept alive. He'd know if they killed her – the blood link would snap like a motherfucker. But they had her under guard, so she still had time. More than him.

He turned back for the lift, broke into a run as an orderly approached. One of the vampire sentries stuck his head out the ward door as Reece pulled the dead guard back into the lift and hit 1.

The lift stopped once, but he blocked the door, hand out, shouted 'medical emergency' and punched the close button until he got moving. Two very confused suits watched him leave.

On 1, he hit the button for the top floor and stepped out in time to avoid the closing doors.

It wasn't far to the kitchens. He walked quickly, and made a show of talking on his phone, using it to mask his profile when he met anyone. He ignored enquiring looks from the staff dutifully finishing their dinner preparation for the various mess halls – who the fuck would be eating in tonight, he wondered – and took the service lift to the basement car park.

He pulled a recycling bin into the lift door and crept out to a point from where he could scope the situation. Guards on the gates, of course. And on the main lift bank.

He wondered if Marshall had come this way. If she'd got away.

The Monaro had been offloaded. Nigel and the tow truck driver were sharing a smoke.

Reece forced himself to saunter; a belt of rum wouldn't have gone astray. At least the alarms had stopped.

'Hey,' Nigel said, and offered the packet. 'What's the story, boss?'

Yeah, they were best buds since they'd been shot up on the highway. Reece shook away the offer. 'Bit of a to-do about a fire in a bin.'

'Don't see why I can't leave,' the truckie said.

'Actually, can I hitch a ride?' Reece asked.

'I'm just goin' back to the depot. Bowen Hills.'

'Close enough,' Reece said, then told Nigel, 'I'm on leave, no pay, till things blow over. Watch the Monaro for me, eh?'

'I'll watch it real good,' Nigel said. 'There ya go, green light.'

A guard was waving from the exit.

Reece jumped into the cab next to the driver and they chugged to the gate. He endured a nervous wait, hand on pistol, as the guard came around to his side, but he gave Reece's stolen ID only a cursory glance before letting the truck proceed. Reece bailed with an awkward thanks at the first red light, and high-tailed it.

He had a bolt-hole, only a few blocks away. With Jensen and Heinrich dead and Marshall on the run, there was nothing to stop Campbell from taking over at the council meeting. Hell, he was more or less in control now, just waiting for his rubber stamp.

And then what for Mira? A hostage, or a martyr, or a scapegoat? None of those suited her, not one bit.

He had less than twenty-four hours to save her, and maybe himself, but he'd need help. What were his chances of getting in touch with young Matheson, he wondered. The grease monkey was probably his best hope, if he could stop him from killing Mira.

SIXTY-TWO

The Needle showed him photographs. The faces were vaguely familiar, but one Kevin recognised immediately: the sneer as the blade opened Greaser's throat, the cold stare through the glasses making him look fish-like, a barracuda perhaps. Tony Campbell, head of Treasury.

'Sure?' the Needle asked.

'Yeah. The beamer was working for him. Got the taste of that when I sank my teeth into the cunt.'

'Just the two of them at Mel's?'

'All I saw. Must've snatched Greaser outside the restaurant.'

The Needle gave a short groan. 'And I texted her to meet; I led them straight to you.'

Kevin shook his head, the closest thing to reassurance, to forgiveness, he could muster through another wave of loss; there was plenty of guilt to go around.

How much more guilt was to come before he had avenged his parents, and avenged himself? Rabbit had asked him what made him so special that he was worth dying for. He'd said 'nothing', and that was true. But justice – that was worth dying for. He just hadn't expected so many people to pay the price.

Danica had warned him about revenge being a whirlpool, and with Greaser's death, he felt more than ever like a leaf caught in the eddy, being sucked closer to oblivion.

He had to get to the end. He clutched at that belief. It was the only way to repay the dead for their sacrifice, to prove they had died for something worthwhile. He would have all the time in the world for guilt once Mira was dead.

Silver broke the maudlin silence. 'I'm surprised they didn't have back-up.'

'Wheels within wheels,' the Needle said. 'They put a squad of VS against us at the restaurant–'

'Knowing their Hunter was on the spot,' Silver said.

'But only the beamer for the kill. No prisoners. No leaks.'

'Trust issues?' Kevin suggested.

'Secrets, I think,' the Needle said. 'I just got word. Trappier Christian Jensen is dead, assassinated. Heinrich is dead, killed in an ambush; purportedly by VS turncoats. Marshall Smith is on the run.'

'Blake?' Kevin asked. 'I left him on ice.' Or had he?

'No idea.'

Kevin rubbed his temples; pressure pounded on the inside of the bone. 'What the fuck's going on?'

'Campbell has made his move. It's the whole *night of the long knives* thing.'

'What about Max?'

'My guess is: watch this space.'

'And Mira?'

'No word. But Heinrich? That shows the gloves are off. Positioning before the council meeting tomorrow night. A state of panic; the Old Man isolated.'

Kevin reached for the picture of Tony Campbell. The Needle pinned the snapshot with a nail. They locked gazes. Kevin took his finger off the photo and the Needle palmed it.

'What was your plan again?' the Needle asked.

'It's changed. Seeing Hunter made me remember something.' Kevin picked up a paperback and flipped through the pages before throwing it down on the table. 'I think him and me are about to reach a new understanding.'

SIXTY-THREE

Kevin had been a vampire for less than a week when he kicked piss and pick handles out of Hunter; bailed him up against a rocky outcrop in a gorge in western Queensland and tore a great chunk of flesh out of the fucker's throat. He'd drunk, and drunk, only just managing to avoid killing the man. Had, in fact, left him for dead. But Hunter was made of sterner stuff: Kevin knew that. He'd tasted it. Forty years of trading blood with Mira. Forty years of fear, and misery, and momentary ecstasy in her embrace. A little of Hunter had stuck in Kevin's lifestream; glimpses into his life as Mira's most favoured pet. Mira was paramount, already tottering on the brink of bedlam when they'd crossed paths, and Hunter sliding down the slope of menopause. An aging dog all out of new tricks, taking his pleasures where he could: a cold beer, Mira's blood, the occasional fuck. The Rolling Stones, Brian Cadd, Billy Thorpe. And Hammett, Spillane, Chandler.

Which was why Kevin was now standing in front of Pulp Reader, his face flushed with a touch of wolfbite from his late-afternoon surveillance of the bookstore. The rash darkened his reflection in the window. The displays meant little to Kevin but plenty to Hunter – enough to have stuck in his lifestream like a burr to a sock: Megan Abbott, James Lee Burke, Martin Cruz Smith; dark covers, shadowy figures.

Movement caught his attention: a customer leaving with a paper bag clutched under the arm, and a woman at the door saying goodbye. She glimpsed Kevin and stepped back, the door swinging.

Kevin caught it with an inch to spare. He felt the tension as the shop attendant pushed; Kevin thrust. The woman stumbled back and the door swung open. Kevin stepped in, closed the door and flipped the sign to *Closed*.

The attendant was middle aged, going grey, in slacks and open-necked blouse and cardigan.

'I don't want any trouble.' She strode behind the counter and dug in a drawer. Kevin slammed her wrist down on the counter, jarring the pistol loose. A plastic shelf of bookmarks shivered with the impact.

'I don't want to rob you,' Kevin said. 'Not that I'd expect a bookshop to have a lot of cash.'

The woman grimaced – from the insult or the pain in her wrist, who knew?

Kevin scanned the shop. Cosy, with bookshelves squeezed in so tightly two people wouldn't have room to pass each other. He almost missed the door at the back labelled *Private*.

'I just want a favour,' Kevin told the attendant. He let go her arm and walked around next to her. Shelves were lined with brown packets, with papers sticking out with names written on them, all in alphabetical order. He looked for the Rs. He always thought of Hunter by his rank, never his name.

'Reece,' he said, and the information bobbed to the surface like a cork. 'Phillip Reece. A customer of yours.'

'What if he is?' The woman rubbed her wrist. She eyed the office door behind Kevin, then the front door.

Kevin looked up at the ceiling. 'I thought you might know where I could find him. Or get in touch with him – a phone number, maybe.'

The woman looked confused, but not convincingly.

'Do you know where he is?' Kevin asked.

'Why would I?'

'Because,' Kevin said.

The woman shook her head.

Kevin checked the name on a bundle of books and then dropped it on the floor. 'Nope.' And another. 'Nope.' There was a computer on the counter, still bright, cursor blinking on some inscrutable form. 'Database?'

'No,' the woman said through clenched teeth.

'I don't want to hurt you.'

'No you don't,' said a voice from behind – Hunter's – followed by the metallic snick of a hammer being pulled back.

Kevin turned to face him.

'What do you want, Matheson?'

'*The Maltese Falcon.*'

Reece paused, then laughed, a rough hiccup like a car stalling, and safed the weapon; put it away inside his coat. He told the shopkeeper to leave, that he'd lock up, that there was no cause for alarm.

The woman scowled but left, still holding her wrist, taking a moment to stare through the window as though imprinting the store on her memory in case it wasn't there in the morning.

Hunter locked the door before leading Kevin up a set of stairs. 'Alley at the back,' Hunter told him as they passed a multi-locked door marked *Fire Exit*. They continued down a short carton-lined hallway; a toilet was signposted to the right, but they walked to a door marked *Staff Only*. Inside, the walls were lined with more cardboard boxes, shelves brimming with books. A window covered with a yellowed roller blind overlooked the street. A space had been cleared in the centre of the floor for a camp bed. A suitcase sat next to it, brown and dented and scratched, the kind of thing you'd expect a door-to-door salesman to have. Nearby a power cord snaked out from an invisible corner, sprouting a powerboard with a kettle, a smart phone and a radio scanner. The box blinked and crackled as they entered, telling them between scratches that 'soup can one' had left the kitchen, that 'soup two is rolling', 'can three is outbound'. An ashtray overflowed on the floor next to a stained mug, a tumbler and a bottle of Bundy rum.

'Pull up a pew, sport,' Hunter said. He poured himself a dram and sat on the nearest convenient carton. 'I'd offer you one, but I've only got one glass.' He tasted, winced. 'How did you know I was here?'

'I knew this was a hiding place for you. Thought it was worth a shot. So why are you here?'

'Things at the tower are a little tense right now.'

'Mira?'

'Still there. But the new management has called a council meeting for later tonight. I figure they're going to do your job for you. That is why you're looking for me, isn't it? To see if you can convince me to get you inside Thorn. Bedlam's not punishment enough.'

'Mira has my mother inside her. If someone drinks Mira, drains her...' He motioned with his hand, a circle going on and on. 'The blood is everything,' he murmured, reciting a different context, but it seemed to fit. He didn't want – didn't need – to explain. Hunter had been there. He knew.

'Yeah, I hear that every day.' He drained his glass and poured another. 'So, what was your argument, sport, to get me to agree to this suicide mission of yours?'

Kevin shrugged. 'I was just gonna threaten to kill you. But then, if things are like you say, if Mira is on death row, then maybe you might like to save her. From them first. Then from me.'

Hunter swilled a mouthful, sifted for hidden flavours. Swallowed. 'Sure.'

SIXTY-FOUR

Riding Yoshi's bike with Hunter behind him, Kevin couldn't help but remember riding as pillion to Taipan, carving through the outback by night. It might've been a thousand years ago, the memories of another person swimming in his bloodstream. He was no longer that young man, injured and confused and desperately afraid, still caught in the throes of the change from human to monster. He was all monster now, but still, he had to admit, confused.

He suppressed those memories. Charging through Brisbane traffic on a bike wasn't the best place for bloodwalking. Besides, he might've been in the driver's seat, but Hunter was far from a helpless passenger. They wove through the Valley, Kevin trying to remember the turns to get to the rendezvous with the Needle. He waited for Hunter to try something, though Kevin had taken his guns and Staker; expected at any moment a VS patrol to plough into them.

He rode with the helmet's visor up. Warm, wet air gusted through the opening; sweat pooled under his arms, on his back where Hunter pressed against him. There'd been clouds over the mountains, massive rolls of grey and black hiding the dying sun, as he headed out for the bookstore. But the sky over the city was still clear.

The Needle had told him, somewhat extravagantly, that the storm would crash down tonight, bringing cool relief in a violent cleansing of overflowing gutters and downpipes. The faraway look in his green-tinged eyes suggested he was looking at more than the weather report. Plunging through the choke of brake lights and headlights and reflecting bodywork, Kevin could see no relief here.

They passed the Brunswick Street Mall with its spindly trees and crowded cafes and floating homeless. Kevin scribed a u-turn through the one-way streets to circle the mall, then zigzagged to the narrow car park squeezed between pub and weatherboard apartment block where a gang of Snipes was waiting.

'Ah,' Hunter said, as though something had become clear. Kevin envied him his clarity, wished he'd share. He propped the bike on the broken bitumen and drifted after Hunter, feeling like a sidekick to the quietly confident hero who knew exactly what he was doing, and why.

SIXTY-FIVE

Reece stood in the car park, surrounded by Snipes. None had said a word since taking his gear from Matheson – even his phone, not that he had anyone to call. The Needle let him sweat for a good ten minutes, and he still had no idea how he was going to get out of this.

When the Needle finally deigned to grant an audience, it was over the bonnet of a car, with Reece's confiscated possessions spread across it. It was as though the Needle had been divining the future in them, like twenty-first-century entrails. He wore cargo pants and hoodie, with bulging pockets, more street warrior than mystic: and his cadre of black and camouflage-clad Snipes were likewise misshapen with barely concealed weapons.

Two white-haired bodyguards, looking like leftovers from a 1980s music clip, flanked him. They barely regarded Reece. All their attention was on Matheson.

Interesting. Something he could exploit? 'Where's Greaser? Spying?'

'Dead,' the Needle answered.

'That's a pity.'

'Campbell killed her.'

'Then I imagine you're keen to even the ledger. I won't stop you. But Mira's mine.'

The Needle looked at Kevin, then back to Reece, smirked, and declared, 'I have no interest in a strigoi in bedlam. Vee, however–'

'I have no interest in a strigoi's blood sack,' Reece said.

'No?' The man seemed amused, making Reece annoyed at his own apparent show of emotion.

Jealous? Mira would have said with a mocking twist of the lips; she liked to tease.

Reece turned away to regard the motley collection of Snipes. 'All red-eyes?'

'Most.'

'Fangers?'

'A few.'

Reece sucked in air through his teeth. 'I know VS isn't exactly at full strength, but still...'

The Needle gestured, 'We'll make do.'

'What do you want from me?' Reece asked.

'What have you got?'

He eyed his possessions on the bonnet, decided against mentioning the dagger strapped to his left forearm that Matheson had missed, then offered: 'Half a pack of tobacco and a buck fifty in change.'

The Needle smiled, a flash of fang, and lifted Reece's stolen security pass on a long fingernail.

'This might be a good start.'

'Probably been cancelled by now.'

It didn't matter, the Needle said. Reece's presence would be enough. 'There's a soup van nearby, enforcing the tithe before the council meeting. It's attracted a baker's dozen of northside streeters – Bogans, Batemans, even a few Petite Morts – possibly a few unmarked others.'

'Got an eye on them?' Reece asked, and the Needle replied, 'Of sorts.'

The gang stirred, scraping boot heels on bitumen, cupping flame-flaring cigarettes, eyeing Reece with alternating curiosity and hostility. Christ, they were young.

'Trojan horse, huh? I can probably help you out, sport. Get rid of some of the detail from the van. Assuming it's the one I think it is.'

'Why would you do that?'

'I have my reasons.'

Kevin broke his silence: 'You know *Flick* doesn't love you.'

'I know,' Reece said, 'but she's, well, she's okay.' *Mostly.*

Fucking grease monkey had thrown him with that; he had no idea how much of his life the kid had sucked down. Enough to know about the bookshop, that he had a thing for Flick; Felicity. How much else? That he was burned out, desperately running on impulse and a feeling best described as Stockholm Syndrome?

And yet, here he was, still standing, still pushing.

The Needle gestured for him to proceed.

'My phone?'

The Needle handed it over.

That was unsettling. Had the tattooist had time to hack his address book? What did it matter? Most everyone in it was, by the feel of things, either in the Needle's employ already, or dead.

He rang Felicity. 'Where are you?' he asked. She sounded tense. Big night, he supposed.

'Soup run.'

'Jamieson Street?' he asked, just to be sure he'd heard right on the scanner.

'Why? You want to donate? Plenty of guys here be happy to take a collection.'

'You don't think I – or Marshall, for that matter – had anything to do with the hit on Heinrich.'

'I don't know what to believe. The council meeting will settle things down.'

'Sure. How would you like to take Matheson to that meeting? Get yourself one hell of a promotion.'

'Are you serious?'

'I'm looking at him right now.'

The kid scowled, muscles tense. Strung out. Unpredictable.

'Where?' Felicity asked.

'Him and a couple of Snipes are in a huddle. The Irish pub at Strathpine.'

'Strathpine? That's Bogan territory. What are they doing there?'

'Dunno. They're out the back, in the beer garden.'

'Don't go anywhere. I'm on my way.'

'Bring a friend. The Snipes are showing green.'

Reece hung up.

'She believe you?' the Needle asked.

'She can't afford not to.'

'Let's go find out.'

'How about a weapon? Enemy of my enemy and all that?'

'Enemy of my enemy is still my enemy,' the Needle said, and Kevin laughed, a bitter sound that made Reece wonder what the kid had been through since they'd last met, to sound so cold.

SIXTY-SIX

Escorted by Snipes, Kevin and Hunter trooped a couple of blocks to a dead-end alley between the looming rear walls of buildings smeared with graffiti and water stain. A van, garishly painted with all the colour and shapeless enthusiasm of a kindergarten fence, was parked at the far end, blocking a loading dock lined with rubbish bins. A side panel was open to make a servery, but there were no cups or soup bowls, and inside it looked more like an ambulance with hanging plastic blood bags, a fridge and stretcher. The sign sprayed across the van said, *Knights of Solace*. Suns and moons and flowers surrounded the letters.

Vampires and red-eyes milled around it like hobos.

The scent of blood teased Kevin, reminding him how long it had been since he'd fed. He could taste the anxiety radiating from the gangers as they shuffled and stared. He eyed the narrow canyon of looming brick, aware of how distant the street noise was, how cut off they were. He gripped Hunter tightly by one arm and pushed him ahead, using him as a shield.

Kevin pulled his hood tighter as he and Hunter approached, their escort of Snipes following behind: what would the gangers do? The Needle had played his cards close to his chest, but he'd seemed confident. One alarm, one call, and it was all for nothing. If he wasn't the one to kill Mira, then he'd have no way of knowing she was really dead; no way of knowing who else might've drained her, and taken with her blood the last remnants of his mother's life.

There were two vampires on the van as well as two GS myxos. Of course there were. You didn't send just myxos to wrangle full bloods. Damn it; would Maximilian know? Mira maybe? The blood links were impossible to predict. Even Hunter was a risk with his link to Mira, but the Needle had been sure she wasn't likely to be receptive. Bedlam was a bitch.

On the plus side, when Kevin found her, she mightn't put up a fight. Would that make it easier? Could he do it – kill her in cold blood?

He thought of his mother, dead on the sofa, and his father, dead in the burning service station. He thought of Melpomene, plunged into bedlam, and Greaser, poor Greaser, killed for being surplus to requirements.

Could he kill as easily? He swore on those souls that he would try.

Reece stumbled but the grease monkey held him from behind, guiding him with an uncompromising grip. A few Snipes straggled behind them.

The Needle's information had been accurate. There was an uneasy mix of gangers – suited Batemans, Bogans in singlets and T-shirts, Petite Morts dressed for a hot night on the town, even the boys – all called in under Maximilian's need for fuel for his troops, to remind the streeters who was boss. Their chiefs would be gathering at Thorn to press their claims to territory in return for loyalty: blood for blood. Give a little, get a little.

The streeters milled in their groups, loitering, as though waiting for a signal: a thrown brick, a shot – anything.

Reece looked for escape routes. The loading dock, if he could get it open? The back doors of shops? Probably locked. Walls too high to climb. And a long, long way back to the street with very little cover.

No sign of Felicity, so she'd taken the bait. That was something. He'd hoped she might've taken the red-eyes or even a vampire with her, but no such luck.

He recognised the squad only vaguely, the GS never having been his preferred drinking partners. Two vampires at the van's back doors, armed with sidearms and swords, checking off the donors; while two red-eyes inside took the collection – a needle or, for the vampires, a simple slash across the wrist to allow the blood to flow. Donations were carefully labelled before the donors were sent on their way. Not so much as a cup of tea tonight. No need to put on a show for Joe Normal passing by.

Always a tense time, all that blood and resentment. But tonight? It wasn't just the humidity making him sweat.

What would the streeters do when the balloon went up? That was the question. Whose side would they come down on, if any? Because the Needle's red-eyes didn't have the numbers.

He reckoned there were at least a handful of vampires here, which was interesting in itself. Someone was either cheating or had been given dispensation to spawn, which meant favours were already being cashed in. The shit just kept getting deeper.

He scanned the streeters, noting the long coats, the packages, the cases for sports equipment and musical instruments. Armed to the teeth, waiting to hear the fallout from the council meeting, waiting for the chips to fall.

If Maximilian didn't handle this very carefully indeed, the entire city could end up painted red; the kind that even a PR guru like Bishop would be hard pressed to explain.

He was metres from the van, the GS fangers checking him. A flicker of recognition. He raised one hand.

The trooper rested his palm on the grip of the pistol at his waist, fingers flexing.

'You coming in, Reece? We got orders about you.'

The trooper's partner put down a glowing tablet, the better to stand ready, one hand on sidearm, one on sword hilt.

'Yeah,' Reece said, 'I'm coming in.'

And closer, enough to see the green sheen of their eyes, the two red-eyes in the van pausing from taking blood to observe, one reaching for a shotgun in a bracket.

'That's Matheson,' a voice shouted, and he recognised her, inside the van, her arms sliced and leaking red.

Rabbit, jack-knifing upright, pale hand pointing like a lightning bolt. 'It's him! The mechanic!' She struggled to get to her feet, long heels stabbing at the floor, a flat-bladed knife appearing from under her long skirt.

Reece had time to swear before he was propelled forward into the two goons. Guns fired. Hot liquid splashed his face and he fell.

Rabbit shouted. Kevin didn't see her, just heard her. The guards drew, so fast he could barely see. He hurled Hunter into them, enough of a distraction to make them stagger. One fired, the shot going wild, and Kevin shot the man once in the chest, once in the head. The other smacked his pistol across Hunter's temple, driving him to the ground.

Kevin squeezed off a shot, thought he might've winged the vampire as he darted to one side. Kevin leaped to his left, crouched. The trooper rolled, came to his feet, put two shots through the air where Kevin had been standing. Kevin returned fire, sending the man sprawling.

Bullets smacked Kevin. He staggered. The alley echoed with gunfire and ricochets. Brick sparked. Tin rang. Glass shattered.

Kevin lay on the ground, aware of muzzle flashes in the back of the van, of metal flying from the doors. Rabbit appeared through the mess and the noise, slithering out of the van, blade drawn, eyes fixed on him. He raised his hand to shoot her;

realised not only could he not feel his fingers, but he'd also lost the pistol.

Rabbit got to her feet and hunched over, picking her way past bodies toward him. She jerked forward, fell face down. The blade rang on the bitumen. Hunter had her ankle in his grip. She kicked him in the face with her other foot. He rolled away, gushing blood where her heel had opened his cheek.

Kevin groped for Rabbit's knife as she came at him on all fours. She reached for where he'd just found her blade.

'I told you–' she began, and then her knife cut her off, driven into her throat, popping out the back of her neck.

Silence fell with her. For a long, long moment, Kevin stared at her, at what he'd done. He hadn't needed to kill her. It'd been instinct. Taipan's? Mira's? His?

He rolled away, shaken.

The Snipes were dragging the dead myxos from the van. Others were disarming certain of the gangers, standing frozen in various poses of attack: drawing weapons, poised in the act of firing, or fleeing, mid-stride.

The Needle stood at a distance, his arms out as though appealing for rain. Blood dribbled from his eyes, his nose.

Argent staked the two GS vampires and helped Hunter to his feet, sneered at Kevin as he guided Hunter to the front of the van.

Kevin stood up, body flushing hot as his metabolism went into overdrive. Rabbit's blood had splashed warm and dark across his hand and he fought not to lick it, afraid of what that taste would trigger.

A nearby Petite Mort, identified by her pin, stood statue-still, bleeding from a tattoo on her neck, silver and red running in molten helixes down her skin. She stared straight ahead, forehead beaded with blood. Muscles quivered with the effort to move. Her eyes widened as a Snipe lifted a Staker to her chest and fired the nail home. The vampire collapsed.

A gasp and the Needle let his arms down. Silver lent him her support, then ordered a Snipe to the van to get blood.

Kevin licked his dry lips, his head swimming with the scent. The need in his guts sucked at his vision, his balance. Hunter re-appeared with Argent.

'Any word?' the Needle asked.

'Radio's quiet,' Hunter said.

The Needle smiled as he opened a vial of blood. 'On with the show, then.'

SIXTY-SEVEN

Reece got into the passenger seat, though he'd warned them his visiting privileges at Thorn were a touch dodgy. He'd answered their concerns, told them the scent of fresh blood probably wouldn't raise too many eyebrows, though gunpowder might if they encountered GS, whose senses were sharper than the mundane VSS schmucks. But most GS would be protecting the council meeting. His best guess was they wouldn't encounter resistance until they were inside Thorn and the damage to the soup van – mostly contained to the rear – was noticed.

By then, the Needle suggested, it would be too late.

To which Reece could only shrug. In the wake of the recent losses at Thorn, everyone would be on tenterhooks. You could get nailed reaching for a packet of ciggies, let alone running around in a shot-up soup van with a bunch of Rogues.

'There are,' the Needle said after a long moment of concentration, 'six, perhaps seven, Vultures escorting the other soup van. I can have a team intercept them. But there are others – Bogans, Batemans, Mods, Petite Morts – gathered outside

Thorn. Our people will have to contain them, especially if their chiefs aren't happy with how the cookies crumble at the council meeting.'

'Storming the Bastille?' Reece said.

'Do you care?'

'I'm wondering where you got the manpower to take out a soup van with a ganger escort.'

'Friends in high places.'

'And the mob at the tower?'

'Friends in low places. You'd be amazed what a gang will do in return for hunting rights in the Valley.'

'Dangerous game; prime territory that.'

'Compared to the Old Man's hold on the hospitals? The blood banks? Worth sacrificing for.'

'Refined palate, eh?'

'We will see. Now tell us what we can expect inside.' He checked his watch. 'Still a good forty minutes before the meeting. We might still be in time to save your strigoi.'

SIXTY-EIGHT

Kevin sat in the back with the Needle and his crew; one of the more conventionally dressed Snipes drove. Reece rode shotgun, but without a weapon. The constant wail of sirens penetrated the walls; their van's radio crackled with reports of violence.

'Let's hope they do not toll for us,' the Needle said, and then the driver reported that they were approaching Thorn.

Kevin flexed his fingers, so stiff where they curled tightly on his pistol's handle. Finally. His vision was edged in shadow, his heart thumping. Finally.

'Showtime,' the driver said as they turned into the access road to Thorn's car park.

'Can't you freeze the guards?' Kevin asked the Needle.

'Maximilian didn't want his people getting tattooed by me. A pity. I've always wondered if that was a sign that the Old Man wasn't as out of touch as people said.'

'So?'

'Push through. We need to get to the council meeting and, ahem, stake our claim.'

'You need more men,' Hunter said. 'You'll never get out of the loading dock once the alarm goes up.'

'We'll see. I've recently arrived at a new arrangement that might smooth our way. Unfortunately, it is a *very* recent arrangement. Things are uncertain.'

They pulled up at the security booth set into the building's wall, controlling a narrow strip of driveway leading into the basement. The barred entrance looked like a trap to Kevin. He gripped his pistol as Hunter leaned across the driver to talk to the guard, who was protected by a thick glass screen.

'You guys are cutting it fine,' the guard said. 'The gang's all here for the big meet; they're calling for the goon.'

'Well, we'd better get in there,' Hunter said. 'Can't have a party without the red.'

The radio squawked as the gate slid open. The West End soup van was under attack. The Needle's diversion, kicking in.

The guard opened the gates for them, distracted by his own radio.

They drove through. The gates slid closed behind them. No alarm. Or a silent one? The ambush ready to spring, now that they were cut off from the street? There were vehicles, workshops, a stairwell and banks of lifts. Plenty of places for troops to hide. Even here, the sirens reached, sounding as if the city was under attack. This was no shelter, though; this was the heart of the danger.

'Here it comes,' the Needle said.

Two guards split from a small group near the lifts and hurried to meet them at the loading dock. The Monaro was parked nearby, its bonnet up, a mechanic in overalls bent over the engine.

'Who the hell are you lot?' a guard asked as they piled out. 'Where's the goon?'

'Jesus,' said the other. 'What happened to the van?'

Hesitant hands reached for guns, uncertain.

Argent and Silver drew on them. Kevin stepped out to face the barrels of the two troopers, a sudden standoff. In his peripheral vision, he saw the men by the lifts fanning out, weapons drawn.

The mechanic put his head up from the car. 'Matheson?'

Fucking Nigel.

'What the fuck are you doing here?' Nigel said as he wiped his hands on his overalls. 'You catch him, boss? *All* of them?'

A guard reached for his radio. Someone shot him. The garage reverberated with a crackle of gunfire. Nigel ran. Kevin chased him through the brief, violent exchange.

Fast, the little surfie bastard, but Kevin was faster. Caught him near a lift where a guard slumped, blood smeared on the bullet-pitted wall behind him. Kevin pushed Nigel hard into the wall. The surfie crunched and bounced to the floor.

The others crowded around as Kevin pulled Nigel to his feet. 'Still playing master and servant, eh, Nige?'

'Still a loser?'

'Yeah.' He hit him in the face. Bones broke. Blood spurted. He had to hold himself back from thumping him into paste. He'd let Nigel escape once before, out at Jasmine Turner's; he had a bad habit of letting people off the hook.

Nigel went down on one knee, hand to his nose.

'That's enough,' the Needle said, and helped Nigel to his feet. 'Tell me – there seems to be a gathering of the night people somewhere above. Do you know where?'

'Sure,' Nigel grunted through his bloody fingers.

'Well then,' the Needle said, a hand on the back of the man's neck. 'Lead the way.'

SIXTY-NINE

The gang took the guards' passes and weapons and crowded into the nearest lift, but they'd made sure Reece remained unarmed. He was next to last in, managing to get the Needle's silver-painted gangers between himself and Matheson.

'Boardroom, I'm assuming?' the Needle said.

'Boardroom,' Reece said, and Nigel added, sycophantically, 'Thirteen,' and hit the button. Reece fought the urge to clock him.

Nothing happened.

Nigel swore. 'My pass won't take us that far.'

'Mine's no good either,' Reece said, 'but we can get some of the way.'

'Try this one,' the Needle said, handing over a pass from an inside pocket.

Friends in high places indeed, Reece thought.

'Which floor for us?' Matheson asked as Nigel hit the button again.

'Not that one.' Reece brushed aside the Snipe in the doorway, dodged Matheson's grasping hand as the doors slid shut.

Reece ran for the cover of a firebox; he could always use the axe in a pinch. He expected the kid to follow, but Matheson didn't need to, of course. Nigel would tell him about Mira's room on the hospital floor.

The lift moved off. The race was on!

Reece triggered the fire alarm. An ear-splitting woot-woot echoed around the car park. The lift would stop at the nearest floor. They'd need a high-level pass to get it moving again before the all-clear was given, and he was damn sure no one important had been taken down in the garage.

Weaponless, he ran to the stairs and cast his gaze up the central void. The steps receded above, naked concrete bathed in red emergency glow. Hellish, all ten – no, eleven – flights from here. He could just walk out, of course. Turn his back as the Needle and his cronies did whatever they were going to do and let the whole thing burn down behind him.

But he thought of Mira, and Matheson, and this was not the way for it to end. Not without him knowing. Trying.

Footsteps sounded in the stairwell. The Needle's raiders, heading upward. And Matheson with them, no doubt.

The mechanic had a head start. And was faster. Much faster.

Reece ran to a second stairwell at the far end of the garage. Just as tall, just as forbidding, but at least without a gang of raiders preceding him. His feet found the stairs and he began to climb, his lungs telling him he was very shortly about to regret a lifetime of smoking.

SEVENTY

Kevin didn't go after Hunter. The man had no chance of reaching Mira first. No chance.

'Where is she?' he asked Nigel, who told him and obediently punched 11. The surfie's face had a satisfactory bruise, though his myxo blood was already doing the business, turning the yellow and black to the traitor's usual half-arsed red-eye tan.

The alarm went off when they'd barely gone a floor. The lift jerked to a halt; the doors opened. Kevin elbowed his way out. A man in a uniform, submachine gun across his chest, looked at him in surprise. Kevin smacked him with the pistol, kept smacking him until he stopped moving. The rest were on their way to the stairs and he ran to get past them, imagining Hunter had already got ahead of him, sprinting toward Mira.

His legs were paining, his breath ragged, by the time he reached the eleventh floor. At least the alarm had ceased, leaving just the pounding of blood and breath in his ears. He was running on empty, body slow to adjust to the effort. Should've eaten. Useless, squeamish bastard: come here to murder, but too weak to take a slurp from some sonofabitch who probably – definitely – deserved it.

He looked over the rail, thinking of Nigel and the satisfying spray of blood across his face. Where was Hunter? Creeping along behind the Needle's gang? Or did he know another set of stairs, or perhaps a lift he could use despite the fire alarm. Was he already helping Mira get away?

Kevin cracked the fire escape door open to reveal a whitewashed foyer, the only colour a rubbery plant in one corner and the scarlet caduceus painted on sliding glass doors facing him.

He crossed the foyer and peeped through the glass. The ward was a shambles, sheets tugged from beds, stands of liquid spilled across the floor. Red lights flashed against the fluorescent wash. Window shutters were raised to reveal office blocks staring back at them. The nurses' station was empty, like a redoubt overlooking a battlefield.

And there was Mira's room, just as Nigel had described: restricted access, according to the sign.

He'd see about that.

Kevin walked slowly, picking through the wreckage. Bodies, still warm, and a fog of blood, saline, antiseptic rising from the floor. Eerie, that no one was here, that no alarm had been raised. Death had come quickly. He counted five all told, one a nurse, a huddle of white in a scarlet pool near the isolation ward's door. Was he too late? Had someone else hit Mira already? Hunter? Impossible. Even with the delay with the lift.

So what had happened?

He crept toward the isolation ward. Pushed the door open. Listened. Nothing. He entered a spartan office with a wide, deep window looking onto a hospital room. The door to the isolation room was open. Blood hung so heavy in the air he could've choked on it. An Asian man in a white coat, stethoscope on the floor nearby, was slumped in one corner. Kevin thought he was dead, crimson splashed over his face and chest, eyes staring, but he blinked when Kevin approached. His mouth fell open as though dumbstruck, fangs glistening with bloody drool.

Kevin's vision darkened, his pulse quickened; his body flushed with heat. Vampire blood, so rich and tantalising, teased at his famished need. But the man was in bedlam.

Despair and relief warred inside Kevin. Mira wasn't here. *Mira wasn't here!*

His hunger surged; blood everywhere, none to drink, and his body ravaged with wounds, his spirit caught between his desire for revenge, to end this once and for all, and the relief of not having to test his ability to do so.

Panting, footsteps. Hunter.

Kevin turned to greet him. Maybe Hunter could shed some light on this. Maybe they wouldn't have to kill each other yet.

SEVENTY-ONE

Matheson's eyes were wide and feral green. The ward was silent, the air heavy with blood and waste, a riot of scarlet and broken furniture. Their gazes locked. The grease monkey hadn't done this. The blood was already still, and besides, Matheson was too clean to have wrought this carnage.

'Where is she?' Reece asked.

'Gone. Just some bloke in bedlam in there. A doctor, I think.'

Reece swore. What now? This didn't make sense.

They both jumped when Reece's phone rang. They stared at it, as though it were some new technology, some mysterious box of noise. Friend or foe?

Reece answered, aware of Matheson's gaze boring into him, aware that the kid could definitely hear whatever he said. Might, possibly, be able to hear the other side of the conversation as well. He had no idea how sensitive the kid's hearing was.

Vee sounded strained. 'Where are you?'

'Thorn. And you?'

'I'm with the Strigoi.'

His grip tightened; he focused on Matheson, alert for

movement, for any hint of what the kid would do. 'Where are you?

A long pause. 'Your house.'

'Alone?'

Vee hesitated. 'No. I don't know how long we've got.'

'What condition is she in?'

'Not good. I only just got her away; I didn't know who else to call.'

'On my way.'

He hung up. Matheson greeted him with raised eyebrows.

'I need your help, sport.'

Matheson stared at him, waiting.

'I know where Mira is,' Hunter said. 'She's waiting for us.'

'Just us?'

'Just us. She isn't alone.'

'Of course she isn't.'

'Might take a gun this time.'

Matheson nodded and fished car keys from his pocket. 'But I'm driving.'

The kid wasn't stupid. He stayed behind Reece as they headed downstairs, the exertion sufficient excuse for Reece not to try to force conversation.

His guts were a hard knot: Matheson could change his mind, try to extract Mira's location from Reece's blood; even if he and his unlikely ally did succeed in rescuing Mira – now there was a turn-up for the books – there was still the question of stopping Matheson from killing her. And then there was the bedlam. He wished he knew the details of the deal Matheson had made with Rodan.

Things went surprisingly smoothly when they reached the garage – the area had been secured by a collection of Green Shirts and streeters, and once Reece and Matheson had made it clear who they were, they were allowed to leave with a polite refusal to provide back-up and a 'good luck' that sounded awfully like 'goodbye'.

The Monaro gunned across the city as Reece directed Matheson. It sounded magnificent. Reece said as much and shared a smile with the kid. He thought about icing him, or at least ditching him, but the fact was he needed Matheson to get to Mira.

Vee had warned him and whoever was with her had heard the warning. They knew he was coming, but he was superfluous: they were after the kid. Had Vee's captors not known he was with Matheson, he doubted he'd have received so much as a snide text message.

'Very nice wheels,' Reece said.

'A classic,' Matheson said.

SEVENTY-TWO

A cold wind was shaking the trees when they pulled up in the street a few doors down from Reece's house. Lightning stalked the sky and thunder rumbled like a starving gut that had caught its first whiff of fresh meat.

'Looks nasty,' Reece said.

The kid shrugged as he scanned the cars parked in the street, the houses.

It was still early; windows were lit. Cooking smells drifted; televisions murmured. Dogs barked. A plane droned overhead, running ahead of the storm.

'What's the plan?' Kevin asked.

They'd talked about it on the drive. Reece had given the kid a rough layout of the house and settled on two options: to try to sneak in through the granny flat underneath, or go in through the back door, all guns blazing. They didn't know how many they were up against, or whether they had vampires with them. It made it hard to plan. Now they were here, inspiration was still hard to come by.

'Let's find out what's what,' Reece said. 'And then, then we see, I guess.'

'You're sure something's up?'

'You bet. Whoever wants to run this town wants Vee's power. Without Vee, or Mira, there's no one to safely sift the blood tithes. No one to stalk the streeters' dreams. No bogeyman to keep them in line. There's a limit to how many fangers a town can support before it reaches critical mass; Brissie's bloody close. Max was keeping the lid on, imposing order, keeping the number of fangers to a manageable level. If he loses the vote this evening, and it seems he will, well, I wouldn't want to be around here.'

'Where would you rather to be?'

'Somewhere else. Let's move.'

He and Kevin stalked down the side of the Queenslander to the backyard. They heard voices, low and indistinct, in the back room. The lights were on, the curtains closed. Stairs came down from the rear landing. On the other side was the door to the granny flat under the house in which Reece had lived while his mother rolled around the cottage upstairs amid cigarette butts and gin bottles.

'Blood,' Kevin said, voice low and hoarse.

Reece could smell it, too; like mock orange on a still summer's night.

They crept up the back stairs to the deck where they had the height to look over the rear fence and the downhill roofs to see the full expanse of Brisbane city rearing from behind the sluggish curves of river, a glowing web of Christmas lights strung across a suburban patchwork of businesses and residences. The storm rose above it all like a tidal wave of violence.

Where would he rather be? He studied the house, his family's house. It was no longer familiar but a strange building, a place of threat and defilement. Anger sharpened his senses. Adrenaline pumped through him.

Reece clutched his pistol, the handle still sticky with its

dead owner's blood. He turned his back on Brisbane, content that any threat was contained inside the house in front of him and not lurking behind a neighbour's fence.

Windows stared at them from either side of the back door, its wood a little warped. Bloody thing always stuck. He should see about the swallows nesting in the eaves, too. He was glad his family, such as it was, hadn't survived to see it come to this. They'd had enough of their own demons to fight without worrying about ones made flesh.

He gestured at the back door to indicate they'd approach on either side. Go in hot and hope the grease monkey gave him the edge.

'Let's do it,' he whispered.

Matheson nodded. The kid's body was tight with suppressed energy.

Movement; at the window, open a bare inch. Reece threw himself down, too late – a flash; a punch in his guts. Sparks of phosphorous leaped at them, dragging the thunder of gunfire. Kevin jerked backward, hit the rail, toppled over.

The door flew open, banging in the buzzing of his deafened ears. Boots clomped on the timbers. He lay on the deck, fighting for breath, a knee in his back, a warm muzzle pressed tight into his nape.

'Gone,' a GS trooper in full kit reported. 'I filled him fulla phos, but he's gone.'

'Get after him.' Newman stood, releasing Reece, and Reece cursed, here with his cheek pressed against the rough wood, the weight of despair holding him down in the absence of Newman's knee. He pushed his pistol across the boards.

'Steady,' Newman said. 'The back-up, too.'

'Kid took it,' Reece said as he pulled himself to his haunches, hands pressed to his aching stomach where he'd copped a round, and his head woozy as his battered body called enough, enough.

'You're a pretty shit Hunter, ain'tcha?' Newman said, motioning him to get to his feet.

'How did you know she'd be here?'

'A little bird told me.'

'Vee? Why the hell would Vee call you?'

Newman left two men to hunt Matheson and ushered Reece into the lounge with those big windows curtained off from the view. Two more grunts stood guard at the door. A sheet lay rumpled on the floor near a sofa. Mira sat there, unrestrained but unmoving; and Vee sat in an armchair facing her, stakes in heart and forehead – a GS double tap.

Mira wore a too-large nurse's uniform, one bare shoulder showing where it had fallen. Someone had tried to clean her up, but her face and hands, arms and neck, her bare feet, were smeared with blood; her hair was clotted with it, her nails outlined in black. She stared at the floor, acknowledging no one.

Felicity sat with her. She had her MP3 player in one hand, turning it over and over as though it were a good luck charm.

'He got to you too, huh?' Reece said.

Felicity looked back stonily as she tucked the player into her pocket and picked up the pistol by her side.

'I ain't the one getting to anyone,' Newman said. 'It was your girlfriend's idea to call me in after you sent her on the wild goose chase. Just as well, too, because when Vee realised it didn't have your new number, who else was it gonna call but Mira's other best friend?'

'It's just business, Reece,' Felicity said. 'With Mira, Vee and the grease monkey, we've got all the aces. It's nothing personal.'

Of course it was personal. You didn't stick a gun in someone's face without making it personal.

Reece slumped into the dust sheet of another chair, the motes choking him. A shroud, he thought; he was sitting on a shroud in a mausoleum. Everyone who'd lived in this house was dead, except for him.

'You've been with Campbell since, let me see, since we offed Bhagwan?'

'Pretty much,' she said.

Reece rolled a cigarette, once Newman gave a nod of permission. Mention of the condemned man's last smoke wasn't uttered, but it was in the set of the man's lips.

'You know there's been a change of management back at the office,' Reece told her. 'You might've lost your desk.'

'With Matheson and Mira on ice, I figure I've got a good chance of getting it back. Somewhere. What's Sydney like, this time of year?'

'Given they've been arming Taipan's mob and helping Matheson, pretty cold, I'd reckon.'

'They'll want what we're offering,' she insisted.

'What's that? A Strigoi in bedlam in return for a new bludger for the pair of you?'

'Jeez, Reece, you shoulda been a detective,' Newman sneered from where he stood near the window, watching for his men to return.

Reece ignored him, studying Felicity. She didn't look comfy.

'You don't think you might be better off leaving town?' Reece sucked in smoke. Shit, his guts hurt.

'The game's not done,' Felicity said.

'Not for us, anyway,' Newman said.

A burst of gunfire came from outside. And another. And a third, short and sweet, truncated: a dying reflex? Or a coup de grâce?

The two soldiers at the door exchanged looks that said their confidence level had taken a southerly dive.

Reece put away his tobacco pouch, using the action to loosen the knife strapped to his wrist – Matheson didn't know all his secrets, and Newman, as usual, was too damn cocky to care.

Neighbourhood dogs went ballistic, and then a shudder ran through the floor as something hit the rear of the house.

'Where's that?' Newman whispered.

'Not the front,' Felicity said, staring at Reece, and then peering, frowning with concentration.

He could've told them it was the back door to the granny flat. That by now, Matheson would've crossed the one big room that made up the bulk of the space under their feet, and would be at the narrow, jerry-rigged stairs that led up to the hallway linen closet. His old man had installed them, much to his mother's objections, when he'd been making home brew in what he called the basement.

Reece'd put a lock on the downstairs door to keep his sister out of his music collection and his wardrobe, once the kegs were gone and the granny flat installed; to stop her stealing his ciggies and his grass and crashing the party when he had a sheila over.

Kevin would be unlocking that door now. Testing the stairs, one at a time. Third, no the fourth one, it creaked a bit.

The linen cupboard door.

The hallway.

'See anything?' Newman asked, wiping his forehead. A floor lamp bobbed where he bumped it with the butt of his shotgun.

'Nothin',' Grunt One said.

Grunt Two flexed his hand on the pistol grip of his submachine gun.

Felicity followed Reece's glance toward the hallway; hefted her pistol.

Newman crossed to Reece and levelled the shotgun in his face. 'Where is he?'

'Behind you?'

'C'mon Reece.' Sweat beaded Newman's forehead, his upper lip.

Felicity stalked to the hallway, close to the wardrobe and

the concealed staircase. Had he tipped her off somehow? A glance in the wrong direction? She'd taken off her boots; her bare feet made little sound on the carpet. She crouched against the wall, biting her lip. It might've been endearing.

The front door shuddered under a heavy impact.

Everyone jumped.

Fooled me again, Reece thought. What the fuck was the grease monkey up to?

SEVENTY-THREE

Kevin hit the ground. The impact was nothing compared to the pain wracking his body. The tracer rounds had torn massive wounds in him. They burned like coals.

But he couldn't lie here. They'd be coming to finish him.

He pushed through the agony. Desperation powered him. He called to the earth and it answered. He sank slowly into that gritty embrace, feeling the soil close around him, a dough made of gravel and broken glass. His ears filled with the familiar didgeridoo heartbeat, the hoarse shriek of cockatoos.

And slowly the pain in his body faded. Cool night pressed down on him in his cocoon of earth. How long? Seconds? Years? Was Brisbane as he'd left it, or had he travelled back through the roots and stones, to when it was swamp and forest? Or had the forest since re-emerged to cloak the streets and houses with branch and tendril, to heal this mighty wound even as his body rejected the damage, expelled the foreign matter? Was nature as hungry as he was, as keen to heal its hurt?

The slightest of tremors penetrated his fugue. Buildings falling? White men felling trees, making way for the future?

Or just the footfalls of a nervous gunman, looking for a body he couldn't – wouldn't – find?

Kevin followed his hunger back to the surface. Through the heavy scent of earth and grass came the stench of cologne and body odour, gunpowder, fear and blood.

He lay on the grass, staring up at a cloud-cloaked sky, the house a hard shape behind him, treetops a silhouetted frame. And there was the gunman, his back to Kevin as he stared out at the yard and the city, and on the other side of the stairs, a second, peering into the night.

Kevin rose soundlessly. Three steps and he was behind the nearest gunman. The man sensed his presence. Began to turn, to shout.

Kevin hit him in the side of the neck. Bones broke. He snatched the man's submachine gun as the body slumped. The second hood fired: too soon. Bullets streaked off into the trees, into the fence, the neighbour's house.

Kevin's reply sparked across the gunman's chest and blew off his bottom jaw. The dead hand fired another burst into the sky, a flare to mark his falling.

Kevin drank from the dead soldier at his feet, more interested in information than feeding. The blood was already still, the lifestream fading. But he was able to extract what he urgently needed to know: just Newman, Reece's ex-partner and two more hoods. Reece, a prisoner; Vee, on ice; and Mira.

They had Mira.

No telling where, now. The hood's memories were out of date.

He hefted the submachine gun.

What next?

How long before they killed their hostages? Before all the gunplay brought the cops?

The door from the verandah was too obvious. A window? Unlikely to be that easy. Front door was no good, not with the hallway to negotiate, a natural killing zone. The internal stairs from the flat that Reece had mentioned? Even if the top door was locked from the house side, it might give him the edge of surprise.

How long before reinforcements got here?

Down below, the oblivious city's lights blazed and a CityCat arced across the river, heading for the Hamilton wharf. It reminded Kevin of his aborted voyage on one of the ferries. He remembered the fig tree. He remembered the bats. And wondered...

You'd rather eat rats?

Taipan's mocking words came to him.

He needed to keep the gunmen guessing. Buy some time.

He kicked open the door to the flat. The whole house seemed to shudder. Mustiness rolled out. Crouched in the opening, he reached out, feeling for them; those furry little bastards, the stench of stale piss that clung to them. The bulbous eyes, the veins etching their membranous wings, the chitter of them in their roosts, the epic lines of them stretching across a sunset sky as they left for the nocturnal food hunt. He reached desperately for contact.

Bush tucker, Taipan said, in another time, another place.

There was resistance; not all answered the call. Some were already spoken for. He could *feel* the presence, holding the animals back; further west, toward the city. But he called and some came, a handful at first, then another, his reach expanding, shaking them loose from trees and foraging; drawing them to him.

He stumbled to the front of the house, straining with the bare threads of control as the cloud of flying foxes wheeled above. Damn it, he should've got in position first!

Some slipped from his control as he blasted the front door lock, then kicked it with all the force he could muster.

Two rounds thumped into the door from the other side.

Two more kicks, and it flew open with a crack of splintered wood. He twisted to the side to avoid another burst of gunfire. He sent the foxes in, a long stream of dark, flapping bodies.

Crouching, he followed them inside.

SEVENTY-FOUR

Newman swore as gunfire and heavy knocks came from the front door. Guns swivelled to point down the hallway.

Felicity snapped off two rounds.

The door shivered again. Timber cracked. Splintered. Then the door slammed open and thudded into the wall.

Newman's team opened fire.

Reece grabbed Mira and pulled her, unresisting, to the floor beside the sofa.

A flutter, like the sound of autumn leaves blowing along a street. And then: wham!

The hall, the room, filled with a chaotic blast of darting shapes.

Newman and his thugs recoiled, crouched, arms up as the bats ricocheted around the room.

Wings brushed Reece's shoulders where he lay across Mira.

Newman screamed at someone called Gaz to kill Reece and the bitch.

Reece dropped the dagger from his forearm sheath and crept

to the edge of the sofa. Just in time. The thug approached, crouched like Quasimodo.

Reece stabbed. The blade sliced into the man's knee. The thug stumbled. Reece pulled him down by the gun arm, one arm locked around the wrist. He stabbed again, hit vest. The thug fought for his weapon. Reece could feel his grip giving way. He stabbed again, desperately: into the neck. The man flopped to the side, gripping the gushing wound.

Reece grabbed the thug's revolver. Sensed movement and turned; far too late, he knew. But the second gunman was falling through the bat storm. Tripped over Mira, it seemed.

He sprawled and Reece could almost touch the greaseball's forehead with the barrel of the revolver. Close enough.

The report was deafening.

Newman loomed on the other side of the sofa. The shotgun thundered, ripping bats apart. Reece pointed the pistol, but the hammer clicked empty.

Newman swung the barrel toward him. Actually took the time to smile as he shouldered the gun, the barrel filling Reece's vision.

Through the flitting maelstrom of bats, a figure hunched at the far end of the hall. A hand up to ward off the bats, a handgun. Kevin fired from the hip.

Bullets chewed the wall, the doorway, the gunman. The body sprawled, bare feet pointing to the ceiling.

He ignored the body as he advanced. Bats filled the lounge room. They were tangled in curtains, had hit the hanging chandelier of lights, making the light sway and flicker like some insane disco where the only beats were the myriad flaps of wings.

A man stood near the sofa, banging away with a shotgun. Bats fell and flapped and screeched. Timber tore and flared. Stuffing flew from a couch in great puffs. Furniture shattered.

The gunman took deliberate aim at something on the floor, presenting his profile to Kevin.

Kevin shot him.

Newman jerked like he'd been hit with an electric shock, and fell boneless, out of sight.

The bats cleared, almost as dramatically as they'd arrived, funnelling out the hall.

Reece crawled to Mira.

Blood trickled from her eyes. Not sorrow, he thought: pain. On her wrist, two bracelets of scarred flesh showed where two of her blood links had been recently severed. Either one would have been enough to knock her comatose. Fresh blood glistened on one hand. Curious.

His gut ached in the aftermath of the action, the wound feeling as if it might've reopened.

Windows were shattered; the walls were peppered with holes and splattered with gore. Newman and his thugs lay dead amid the carcasses of bats. Felicity lay on her back, her expression frozen in consternation, as though she were working out some pattern on the ceiling.

Which left Reece with a pain in his guts and an empty pistol in his hand, Matheson with a smoking machinegun and Mira prone on the floor.

Interesting.

SEVENTY-FIVE

Kevin couldn't see the other two gunmen. Couldn't see anyone. He sent the bats out, leaving the reek of shit and piss, blood and gunpowder.

A heavy silence cloaked the room, broken only by the flopping of a few injured bats, someone breathing heavily. Kevin raised his weapon and stepped forward.

'Hunter? Reece?'

'Here.'

Kevin stalked around the sofa, gun levelled.

Reece was on his knees beside Mira, a gun in his hand, the bodies of two GS soldiers nearby.

Vee sat in an armchair. He-she, had been hit hard. Kevin didn't think the vampire would be coming back. Not with that much neck missing. The corpse was already showing signs of decay as the body chewed itself up in an attempt to heal the mortal wound.

But this wasn't about Vee.

He pointed the gun at Mira. Finally.

Reece stood to face him over Mira's body. His shirt was soaked and clinging with blood, his trousers dark with the stuff. The woman stared straight up. Blood had splashed her, but

Kevin couldn't tell if it was hers. She wasn't staked, but she lay still, mouth slightly open, a dimple in her forehead suggesting all the noise had left her slightly perplexed as to the cause of the racket.

'So it's true? About the bedlam?'

'Maybe your mother was what tipped her over,' Hunter said.

'She was fine at the gorge,' Kevin said. 'That was after she'd killed Mum.'

'Holding on by her fingernails? Slowly being sucked under. And once you'd saved Danica–'

'Stop. Enough. Don't tell me that they somehow, I dunno, somehow cancelled each other out. It doesn't work that way.'

'Isn't that what this is all about, Kevin? An eye for an eye?'

'Enough, Hunter. Fucking enough!'

'Y'know, I've made a career out of telling people what they don't want to hear. It's whether they take any notice that's been the telling point.'

Kevin's finger tightened on the trigger. Hunter tensed. The man's revolver held little danger for Kevin. He was so much faster than the red-eye, his weapon already poised. He could take them both with one burst.

'What's it going to be?' Hunter asked.

Kevin remembered his mother, the image rocking him with its intensity: the hair pasted to her forehead, the skin paler than pale. Throat torn, arm torn, where Mira had drained her with teeth in flesh, lip on skin; had drained her of life and the life lived, left an empty shell of rotting corpse behind.

Mira stared up, sightless, locked inside her own mind.

If he drained her, if he could navigate the bedlam, sift the enormous flood of her life; if. His mother was in there, somewhere. No, not his mother. Her life. Her memories. But she – the woman – was no more inside Mira than inside the long-cold flesh he'd buried back out west. Mira had ended his mother's life. And, quite possibly, his mother had ended Mira's.

Would it be justice to kill Mira? Or mercy?

Mira blinked. Reece sighed and sank to the sofa, a hand to his stomach. Mira sat up, her gaze fixed on Kevin.

'Can you do it, grease monkey?'

'Thought you were in bedlam.'

'Would it make it easier if I was?'

'No.'

'Do you think this is what *she* wants you to do?'

He frowned. Had she seen inside his head? Did the blood link give away his doubts?

'Would you like me to tell you?'

'Don't.'

Hunter said, 'Mira…'

She ignored him.

'Do you remember her?'

'Of course.'

'Do you really want to know how she remembers you? What happened on her wedding night? All her secrets?'

'Why did you take her?'

'Because I needed a little snack. Because I wanted to know you, the better to find *my* mother. Looks like we both came away disappointed.'

'Danica is dead.'

'And so is your mother. My *Vater*, your father: both dead. You see, we aren't that different.'

'I am nothing like you.'

'And yet there is a little piece of me in you.' She looked at the gun, then back at him. 'Your call, grease monkey.'

Kevin's finger eased off the trigger as tears rolled down his cheeks.

His mother was gone. What remained was a scrapbook, a ghost. It was not outrage he felt at Mira, but simple jealousy, a sense of affront that she had taken what was rightfully his. Or perhaps no one's.

Taking something and keeping it were two different things, Taipan had told him. Not only had taking Kevin's mother helped tip Mira into bedlam, it had revealed something else as well: a mother's love for her child? Or simply a degree of belated understanding about what it's like to bury your own.

Kevin stepped away; numb, uncertain, so very tired he could barely hold the gun. A shape on the floor caught his attention.

A box, earbud wires snaking from it, near the dead suit in the hallway. On the back of the box, a piece of red tape. His initials: KM.

He picked up his lost MP3 player. Smiled grimly. Road music. That was something.

Mira watched.

Sirens approached.

'You'd better skedaddle,' Hunter said. He was stuffing a sheet under his shirt, the fabric soaking through with scarlet.

Kevin nodded, turning the player in his hand.

'You got somewhere to go?' Hunter asked.

A smile flickered on Kevin's lips, unbidden and sudden. 'There's a girl.'

'There's always a girl. Hey – leave me the keys?'

Kevin considered, listening to the sirens, fingering the music player. Hunter looked so grey in the face, his skin gleaming with sweat, hand pressing the bunched sheet against his guts.

Mira sat unmoving on the floor, as though waiting for him to change his mind.

'Sure. Your sword's in the boot.'

SEVENTY-SIX

Reece sat on the stairs, smoking despite the pain. He'd done all he could.

Mira sat beside him. 'He's gone.'

'You're not.'

'I – I'm fragile.' Her breath gusted hot and fetid against his ear, his cheek. 'Reece, you're bleeding.'

'It's not for you.' He forced the words out, clinging to them as his vision swam. Light headed. His cigarette tasted of dung and burning leaves, but he dragged it in. No point quitting now.

'I could heal–'

He shook his head, just once.

She put her arm around his shoulders. She was as cold as he felt.

'How long you been compos mentis?' he asked.

'A few hours. Tran gave me sips of his blood. Called it research; trying to use a blood link to understand bedlam. But I think he really just liked the idea of having his blood in me.'

She rubbed her face against Reece's cheek, breathed in deeply; her lips dry against the pulse in the side of his throat.

Her breast pressed against his arm. A fang threatened to pierce his flesh. He held his breath, waiting, but she leaned back, rubbed her face, forced her shoulders back, smiled a chilling grin.

'He was foolish to let me taste him. There's nothing quite like the news you're about to be made an example of to cut through the cacophony. I stole *Vater*'s idea, the same one he used on Melpomene, and gave Tran more research material than he could handle. It was quite cathartic.'

'You killed the others in the ward, I take it.'

'Bedlam builds a thirst, Reece.' She rubbed her wrist, where the blood tattoos had shrivelled into ugly welts. Only his and Matheson's remained, twin pulsing scars.

'Welcome back.'

'They killed Vater, you know. It was in Tran's blood. Campbell and the others, they tore him down like hyenas on a lame wildebeest. I think, at the end, he was glad.'

He blew smoke away from her, hearing himself wheeze with the effort of talking. 'The Needle. A coup.'

'Two in the one night. Do you know who won?'

'Find out... when those cars get here.'

The sirens were louder, now; the wind had risen, frigid air gusting against him, and clouds hanging low and lit by lightning, growling with drumrolls of thunder that shook the windows.

Would the sirens reach him in time? Would they care?

Mira pulled her knees up and hugged herself around them, as though feeling the chill. The death of her father – her vampiric father – would have rocked her, as well as the loss of her two blood-linked servants, Vee and Felicity. It was a wonder she could walk, let alone talk.

'Where do you think the grease monkey will go?' she asked.

'South, prob'ly. The Japanese... at the cemetery... on the

island... Rodan's. Prob'ly hopin' to get Melpo cured there somehow.'

He slumped, the words having taken it all out of him. Could barely hold his ciggie. It loomed large, a red sun flaring in the dark.

She squeezed his arm, the pressure coming at a great distance. 'He has an over-developed sense of loyalty, that boy. It's an admirable trait.'

They sat quietly then, Reece considering whether she'd just thanked him for saving her life. Surely she couldn't want to go after Matheson? The kid could've killed them. Put them both out of their misery. Maybe.

'Nice view of 'Bane from here,' she said, pointedly not looking at him.

He smiled at her nickname for the city. It had proven accurate. 'It is.'

'Nice, at night.'

'Better by daylight.'

She sounded, not so much disappointed, as resigned, when she said, 'But there's so much of it, Reece.'

'Depends on your perspective.' He coughed, wetly, tried to ignore the scarlet on his fingers, on his cigarette.

'I should leave before the police get here.'

'Shame you can't drive.' His fingers, numb, groped for the Monaro's keys but failed to find them. He'd never got to drive it, and that filled him with an incredible weight of regret.

'I'll wait till you've finished your cigarette,' she said, holding him upright. 'I've got time.'

And then the storm broke, rain crashing down hard and dark and cold like the end of the world.

EPILOGUE

Kevin drove south in one of Maximilian's SUVs, given to him by the Needle. In the centre console was pepper spray, a Taser and a Staker. Under the floor of the boot were firearms of various calibres. He wore a handgun in a shoulder holster and had another strapped to his ankle, a dagger sheathed on his left forearm. He hoped he wouldn't need any of it, but five months in post-revolution Brisbane had taught him you could never be too careful.

He pulled over to check the GPS. This was the place. He was early. He'd passed an imposing set of gates guarded by men in penguin suits; they were out of sight on the other side of a slight rise. He moved the car onto a wide section of gravel shoulder next to the property's iron fence from where he could see the manor through a thin line of scrub.

The manor was of stone, with a tower that spoke to Kevin of armed guards and attack dogs but was probably just a nice spot to take in the view.

And what a view it would be. The building sat, surrounded by bare grape vines, on the crest of a hill, lights blazing like a cruise liner against the dark backdrop of the Blue Mountains. Sydney lay sprawled across the eastern horizon, erasing the stars with its glow. The winter chill crept through the windshield, the cold having come down with the night.

Yoshi had told him to be here and here he was. Armed to the teeth. As nervous as hell.

Kevin had all but given up hope that Yoshi's mate could bring Melpomene out of bedlam. Everyone had been so sure that only Danica or Mira could do it. Danica was dead, and Mira, well, for all he knew, she and Hunter could be dead by now, too, although he suspected she wasn't – that was something he reckoned he'd feel, in the blood.

The sound of an approaching engine made him sit up, reach for the gun on the seat next to him. A glow of headlights suggested a car coming his way, but they dimmed on the other side of the rise, and an SUV beetled up the drive, eventually parking in an area of the lawn already crowded with cars.

Party time.

He waited, the clock ticking down toward the rendezvous time like the fuse on a bomb. Finally, a car left the house. It came over the rise. He flashed his lights. It pulled over. Kevin stepped out, pistol gripped under his coat.

The vague shapes of two people showed palely behind the windscreen.

Yoshi got out from behind the wheel, slick hair pulled back, and wearing a suit that jarred Kevin. He had never thought of the man as a corporate lackey.

'I didn't bring your bike,' Kevin told him, although that would've been evident.

'I've got another,' Yoshi said, dismissing the comment, and flashed a smile. 'And someone to see you.'

He went around to open the passenger door, but the passenger was already out.

Melpomene.

'Hi,' she said.

She wore a low-cut dress, clinging around the hips. She pecked Yoshi on the cheek and walked over to Kevin, stepping gingerly on the gravel road in her heels.

'All better then,' he said, Mr Obvious striking again.

She gave a catwalk twirl, hem rippling around her ankles. 'Clean bill of health, thanks to the Strigoi.'

'Mira?' He looked around, half expecting to see her lurking in the shadows.

'Long gone,' Yoshi told him. 'She said if anyone asked, to say she'd *gone walkabout*.'

'Weird, huh?' Mel drew sombre. 'Do you know what happened to Blake?'

'I hoped you might, him being your bludger and all.'

'I *feel* him, but there's no contact.'

He answered with a nod that he hoped conveyed sympathy.

'So, how are things back in 'Bane?' she asked.

''Bane?' He knew someone, or knew someone who knew someone, who called Brissie that. The thought made him frown, a half-remembered dream with a sense of lingering importance.

'Yeah, pal, what's been happening back in Brisbane since you helped bring the house down?' Yoshi asked.

He told them how the Needle had taken a lot of pleasure in showing him the tapes from the council meeting. How Treasurer Tony Campbell and his minions had come stomping in only to find the Needle sitting in the head chair, the meeting truly stacked. By the time the smoke had cleared, there'd been plenty of empty chairs for the filling.

The green-uniformed VSS had sided with the Needle, much to Campbell's fatal surprise. There was footage of the Needle sliding a folder across the table to the Marshall – she was the one who'd put Campbell down; rolling him onto his back so he could watch her put two rounds through his head.

'Running some casino now,' Kevin said.

'And what about you?' Mel asked.

He'd been waiting for a phone call; he'd hoped Kala, but it'd been Yoshi who'd rung. Not that he told them that; just stuck with the simple fact that he'd been doing odd jobs for the Needle as he'd set up his new regime.

'What kind of jobs?' Yoshi asked.

'Mechanic,' he mumbled.

'Mechanic? With cars or what?'

Kevin shrugged, then added, 'The Needle wants me to, um, find Blake.'

Mel nodded. 'Ah. So it's not just my good looks.'

'Your personality as well,' he said, and was rewarded with a lift of the lips.

'Well, I still appreciate you coming all this way. Is there a plan?'

'I can take you wherever you want to go. No rush.'

'Good. After being... preoccupied for so long, I really feel like painting the town red.'

He baulked as he tried to work out her meaning, that sense of a haunting dream hitting him again.

She took his hand. 'Metaphorically, Kevin. *Metaphorically.*'

He shrugged off a feeling of unease. For whatever reason, Mira had been here and healed Mel and then left.

A peace offering? Or another game? It didn't matter.

Mel was with him and she was fine. Together, they would make a good team.

ACKNOWLEDGEMENTS

The story of Kevin Matheson was always a road trip, extending from the Queensland outback to the coast and the capital city of Brisbane. That journey has changed significantly, spanning more than a decade and multiple iterations, culminating in the publishing of *Blood and Dust* in 2012 as a digital-only book. But that story began and ended in the outback: Kevin's journey was only half done.

So I am indebted to Clan Destine Press and publisher Lindy Cameron for backing this duology in both paperback and digital formats, and for giving me the opportunity to work with editor Dmetri Kakmi on *The Big Smoke*.

I'm also thankful to the staff of Xoum and my agent Selwa Anthony for their support of *Blood and Dust* and allowing CDP to slip into the driver's seat.

Along the way, the story that became the duology benefited from the feedback and guidance of numerous writing groups and writing buddies: these friends we make are the true milestones of the writing journey.

I also owe a debt to my dice-rolling mates from the Rockhampton days who provided creative sparks for the original story; those sparks flicker still within these pages.

Finally, I thank my wife and fellow writer Kirstyn McDermott for her enduring support and faith.

VAMPIRES

IN THE

SUNBURNT COUNTRY

VOLS 1 & 2

CLAN DESTINE PRESS

GENRE FICTION
SPECIALISTS

www.clandestinepress.com.au